"A wild, danger-f... cludes a perfect blend of ... , intriguing characters, a... ...ited and fast-paced, this book contains a satisfying arc of development for our heroine, culminating in two very different conflicts: one that threatens her life and one that threatens her soul."
— *Romantic Times*

"*Death's Rival*, the spectacular fifth installment in the superb Jane Yellowrock series, delivers on every level.... Each chapter in this engrossing and addictive series reveals another facet of Jane's character as the layers of her past get peeled back.... *Death's Rival* demonstrates once again Hunter's grasp of what makes urban fantasy special as a genre—the effective and tactile blending of elements, which she serves up in a smoothly flowing narrative style that never misses a beat." — Bitten by Books

"*Death's Rival* is a thrilling mystery with epic action scenes and a kick-ass heroine with claws and fangs."
— All Things Urban Fantasy

"Hunter has done it again, delivering a thrilling combination of mystery and romance that will delight her fans." — SF Site

Raven Cursed

"Faith Hunter has outdone herself in *Raven Cursed* ... rife with snarky dialogue, vivid descriptions, and enough hairpin turns to keep a fantastic driver busy.... A lot of series seek to emulate Hunter's work, but few come close to capturing the essence of urban fantasy: the perfect blend of intriguing heroine, suspense, [and] fantasy with just enough romance." — SF Site

"Hunter doesn't disappoint.... *Raven Cursed* is the natural result of the previous three volumes while still working well as a stand-alone book. Still, I say you can't get enough of one of my favorite kick-ass heroines, so if you are new to the series, give yourself the gift of books one through three. You won't regret it." — Fresh Fiction

"A super thriller.... Fast-paced, *Raven Cursed* is an exhilarating paranormal whodunit with several thriller spins."
— Genre Go Round Reviews

continued ...

Mercy Blade

"Fans of Faith Hunter's Jane Yellowrock novels will gobble down *Mercy Blade*, the third installment in this series, which has all the complexity, twists, and surprises readers have come to expect . . . a thrill ride from start to finish. . . . Hunter has an amazing talent for capturing mood."
— SF Site

"There was something about the Jane Yellowrock series that drew me in from the very beginning. That hunch was solidified with each book I read into a feeling of utter confidence in the author. . . . *Mercy Blade* is top-notch, a five-star book!"
— Night Owl Reviews

"I was delighted to have the opportunity to read another Jane Yellowrock adventure. I was not disappointed, but was somewhat overwhelmed by the obvious growth in Faith Hunter's writing skill."
— San Francisco Book Review

"A thrilling novel. . . . Fans of suspenseful tales filled with vampires, weres, and more will enjoy this book. Jane is a strong heroine who knows how to take charge of a situation, and kick butt if necessary."
— Romance Reviews Today

"Faith Hunter has created one of my favorite characters ever. Jane Yellowrock is full of contradictions. . . . As with the other books in the series, good and evil are far from clear-cut, with sympathetic villains and many fascinating characters with shades of gray. Highly recommended."
— Fresh Fiction

Blood Cross

"Mystery and action are at the forefront here, but the romance from the first book continues to build slowly. Readers eager for the next book in Patricia Briggs's Mercy Thompson series may want to give Faith Hunter a try."
— Library Journal

"In a genre flooded with strong, sexy females, Jane Yellowrock is unique. . . . Her bold first-person narrative shows that she's one tough cookie, but with a likable vulnerability . . . a pulse-pounding, page-turning adventure."
— Romantic Times

Skinwalker

"Seriously. Best urban fantasy I've read in years, possibly ever."
— C. E. Murphy, author of *Truthseeker*

"A fantastic start to the Jane Yellowrock series. Mixing fantasy with a strong mystery story line and a touch of romance, it ticks all the right urban fantasy boxes." —LoveVampires

"Stunning . . . plot and descriptions so vivid, they might as well be pictures or videos. Hunter captures the reader's attention from the first page and doesn't let go." —SF Site

"A fabulous tale with a heroine who clearly has the strength to stand on her own . . . a wonderfully detailed and fast-moving adventure that fills the pages with murder, mystery, and fascinating characters." —Darque Reviews

"A promising new series with a strong heroine. . . . Jane is smart, quick, witty, and I look forward to reading more about her as she discovers more about herself." —Fresh Fiction

More Praise for the Novels of Faith Hunter

"With fast-paced action and the possibility of more romance, this is an enjoyable read with an alluring magical touch." —Darque Reviews

"The world [Hunter] has created is unique and bleak . . . [an] exciting science fiction thriller." —*Midwest Book Review*

"Entertaining . . . outstanding supporting characters. . . . The strong cliff-hanger of an ending bodes well for future adventures." —*Publishers Weekly*

"Hunter's distinctive future vision offers a fresh though dark glimpse into a newly made postapocalyptic world. Bold and imaginative in approach, with appealing characters and a suspense-filled story, this belongs in most fantasy collections." —*Library Journal*

"It's a pleasure to read this engaging tale about characters connected by strong bonds of friendship and family. Mixes romance, high fantasy, apocalyptic and postapocalyptic adventure to good effect." —*Kirkus Reviews*

"Hunter's very professionally executed, tasty blend of dark fantasy, mystery, and romance should please fans of all three genres." —*Booklist*

BLOOD TRADE

A Jane Yellowrock Novel

Faith Hunter

A ROC BOOK

ROC
Published by the Penguin Group
Penguin Group (USA) Inc., 375 Hudson Street,
New York, New York 10014, USA

USA | Canada | UK | Ireland | Australia | New Zealand | India | South Africa | China

Penguin Books Ltd., Registered Offices: 80 Strand, London WC2R 0RL, England
For more information about the Penguin Group visit penguin.com.

Penguin Books Ltd., Registered Offices:
80 Strand, London WC2R 0RL, England

First published by Roc, an imprint of New American Library,
a division of Penguin Group (USA) Inc.

First Printing, April 2013
10 9 8 7 6 5 4 3 2 1

 REGISTERED TRADEMARK—MARCA REGISTRADA

ISBN 978-0-451-46506-1

Printed in the United States of America

PUBLISHER'S NOTE
This is a work of fiction. Names, characters, places, and incidents either are the
product of the author's imagination or are used fictitiously, and any resemblance
to actual persons, living or dead, business establishments, events, or locales is
entirely coincidental.
   The publisher does not have any control over and does not assume any responsibility for author or third-party Web sites or their content.

*To the Hubby, my Renaissance Man,
for all the everyday declarations of love. And for the new
shelves and cabinets in my writing room. Squeee!*

ACKNOWLEDGMENTS AND NOTE

I want to thank my fans. You have made this series a success. I adore each and every one of you! Next time you eat a piece of really good chocolate, think of me!

A huge thank-you to Lucienne Diver of the Knight Agency for her comments and suggestions. *Blood Trade* is much better because of her. And my fantasy career—well ... I wouldn't have one but for her.

A huge, HUGE thank-you to Jessica Wade, my editor at Roc. This book survived only because of her magical hand, amazing talents, and inexhaustible patience. I need to buy you a tiara.

And a special thanks to Mike Prater for helping me with weapons info. Fewer errors took place in this novel because of you. (And all errors are mine!)

Note to readers:

I often change places, things, and people in my books from the reality, and I am not just talking about making magic or skinwalkers real. Sometimes it's more subtle, like changing street names for my convenience or the layout of a police station to protect our men in blue. And sometimes I change history.

In *Blood Trade* I changed Under the Hill. If you go to Natchez today, Under the Hill looks nothing like the place I have imagined. It's Under the Hill as I want it to be, if the witches had been able to hold the earth secure during the huge earthquake of 1811–1812. But hey—it's fiction.

The church I described on Jefferson Street is wholly from my imagination.

Enjoy reading.

Faith

CHAPTER 1

Been There, Shot the Place Up

I threw my leg over Bitsa and slammed my weight down on the kick start. The engine fired up with the rumble only a Harley can boast. It should have made me feel better, that lovely roar, but it didn't. I was too ticked off. Or something. I wasn't big on introspection or self-analysis; I just knew I wasn't happy and hadn't been in weeks. It had started back at Christmas and New Year's, which I'd spent alone. Well, as alone as a girl can be living with two men.

Previously, my new roommates—the Younger brothers—and I had spent days training, learning how to work together, wisecracking, and picking on one another. More recently, they had proven themselves good about giving me space and letting me hide in my room. My black mood had started when the Kid, the younger Younger, demanded a Christmas tree and gift giving. I have no idea why. But I'd been impossible to live with for weeks and I knew it.

Stretching back, I locked the gate blocking the narrow drive of my freebie house in New Orleans and took off into the dawn. It was chilly and damp, gray and miserable. Winter, Deep South style, suited my mood. I'd never been the emotional type—no weepy Wilma, not whiny, teary-eyed, depressed . . .

My inner self stilled, the wind buffeting me as I leaned over Bitsa and gunned the engine, heading out of the French Quarter. Smelling the now-familiar scents of Cajun food and water-water-everywhere. Thinking about that word—*depressed*.

Crap. I'd never been depressed before, but I was now. Classic case of it. Lack of interest in much of anything, sleeping too much or unable to sleep at all. Not eating enough or binging on protein. Staying in my room with the door closed, lying on the bed, staring at the overhead fan. Not shifting into my Beast-form to hunt in months had to be contributing to it. Not dealing with Beast's *little problem*.

I'm a skinwalker, a shape-changer, sharing my physical form—and physical forms—with the soul of a mountain lion I'd accidently pulled into myself when I was five years old and fighting for my life. And Beast's current *little problem* was a good reason not to shift, though it left her feeling ticked off, and a ticked-off big-cat isn't a pretty thing.

The only thing I *had* been doing was riding my bike through bayou country all alone, sightseeing, trying to see how far away from New Orleans I could get before that Beastly problem made distance difficult. Or impossible. And I'd been working out, lifting weights. A lot of weights. I had put on twenty pounds of pure muscle. When I finally shifted into Beast again, she was going to have to accommodate the extra poundage. Somehow.

"I'm depressed," I murmured into the wind, trying the words on for size. Yeah. Depressed. I felt a shadow lift off me just admitting it to myself.

I knew why I was depressed. I'd screwed up so bad, so often, in the past year that I'd lost friends, lovers, and, well, that was enough. Wasn't it? Now that I knew what was wrong, I could do something about it. If I could figure out what to do. This moodiness was uncharted territory.

Letting that thought simmer on the back burner of my mind, I wended my way through the city, heading uptown, which meant upriver, as everything in New Orleans was about the Mississippi River—uptown was upstream; downtown was downstream (something new I'd learned about the city that was my temporary home). I needed to cross the river, and though I could have taken the newer Crescent City Connection, part of I-90, I took the older, narrow, dangerous, two-lane hell of the Huey P. Long Bridge. I liked the old bridge, maybe *because* it was so dangerous; it had character, like an old noir film, a bridge leading out of the Land of Shangri-la.

On the other side of the Mississippi, I headed through Westwego and then vaguely west, like the town's name suggested. Unsurprisingly, I found myself headed to Aggie One Feather's place, adjacent to the John Lafitte Preserve, a wilderness area where the Cherokee elder who was my personal shaman—and probably my personal counselor too, now that I knew my emotional state—lived. But I could tell that she was still out of town. No car in the drive, shades pulled, no smell on the still air of coffee or bacon cooking, and the sweathouse out back had no smoke seeping from the chimney.

I slowed to a stop and set my boot soles on the shell-based asphalt, thinking about going into the sweathouse by myself, but I'd had some difficult experiences going it alone in there and wasn't ready to try that again, even with the depression to motivate me. Even though I had some really heavy stuff to deal with. And so did my Beast.

I thought about the mountain lion soul who lived inside me, but she was still asleep, curled into a tight ball, her nose under her long, thick tail. She had been sleeping a lot lately, angry because I wasn't letting her out to hunt—because I was afraid she'd do something stupid, like track down the vampire Master of the City, roll over and show him her belly, and then lick his feet. My fear was caused by a silver chain that no one but Beast and I could see. It was in the place in my mind that Aggie One Feather called my soul home, and the chain was some kind of binding that curled from Beast's leg across the floor to a shadow in the corner of my mind, a shadow that was Leo Pellissier, the Master of the City of New Orleans and the entire Southeast USA, with the exception of Florida. Leo was the biggest, baddest fanghead I'd ever met. He was also my boss, for now, because I couldn't actually get away, or not for long, and Leo knew nothing about the magical binding that kept me in New Orleans, because it had been accidental. I was not about to let the MOC discover how deeply I was tied to him. The vamp was like the left hand of the devil and would use and abuse the binding to get his way in everything. *Ev-ery-thing*. Like me in his bed *and* as his dinner, and I'd stake him before I let that happen—and suffer the consequences. Heck,

I'd stake *myself* before I let that happen. Yeah. I had lots to be depressed about. Beast's *little problem* was at the top of my list.

My cell jangled out a reggae dance number and buzzed in my pocket, and I jerked my attention out of my own mind and back into reality. I unzipped my leather jacket to pull out the phone. It was snugged right next to my shoulder-holstered Walther PK380, loaded with standard rounds. The .380 had less stopping power than a nine millimeter, but it was perfect when collateral damage—hitting humans—was possible. That one single-action semiautomatic and the short-bladed knife strapped to my thigh were my only weapons, which was really stupid. I was a target to some of the blood-servants and blood-slaves in the area, and while vamps needed nighttime to roam free, their minions could attack me anywhere, anytime. Or maybe being depressed made you unknowingly lax about self-preservation. *Yeah. That.*

I flipped open the cell to see Reach's new icon—Darth Vader with a fanged happy face in place of his mask. I slid the cell up under the helmet to my ear. "You're up early," I said. "I'm not paying for this call."

"No. A vamp is. I have a gig for you, for a vamp with deep pockets. Remember the name Hieronymus? A Master of the City who was attacked by de Allyon?"

I grunted, "Vaguely." Lucas Vazquez de Allyon had been the Master of the City of Atlanta and greater Georgia until he developed delusions of grandeur and decided to take over Leo Pellissier's territory. It had been a pretty good plan until I sawed off his head. "What's Big H want and where is he?" I asked as I maneuvered the bike off the road near a ditch and cut the engine.

"He managed to hang on to the MOC status of Natchez, Mississippi." Reach would know. He was *the* best researcher in the United States, and if Reach didn't know something, it couldn't be found out.

"Natchez? Been there; shot the place up. Why should I go back?" The comment and question were rhetorical and maybe just a bit to yank Reach's chain. Anywhere outside of New Orleans suddenly suited me just fine, and Natchez was just inside of the outer limits of my Leo-binding. Perfect. The black cloud that crouched inside me grew a little lighter at the thought of leaving.

"Two reasons. One: because he needs your help. De Allyon left Naturaleza running around loose, and they're kidnapping and draining the populace. Local law enforcement can't get a handle on it. Over a hundred people are missing in Adams County and across the state line in Vidalia, and yet very few bodies have turned up drained, which, if you ever listened to the news, you would know. Two: Hieronymus pays better than most. Even better than Leo." My ears perked up at that one. Or they would have if they hadn't been smashed under the phone and helmet. "He also pays me a finder's fee if you take the job."

"Of course he does. I'm guessing that since you're now working to hire me away from Leo, the Master of the City can't listen in on this call?"

"I always did love a smart woman."

"You love info and money and would sell your mother into sexual slavery if the opportunity presented itself to make few thousand bucks."

"True, though Mom does make the best pies I've ever tasted, so it would have to be high six figures to give that up."

A smile ghosted on my lips. It felt odd there and I had a feeling that I hadn't smiled recently. Another sign of depression. "Details."

Reach filled me in. "According to the Natchez Police Department, the vamps are faster than anything they've ever seen, and they're disappearing street people, anyone caught out alone after dusk, and two entire street gangs. The loss of gangs has its benefits," he admitted, "but, frankly, cops versus Naturaleza are no contest. Cops lose. They have skills but no experience. Hieronymus knows he has to take care of it himself. Pronto. Which is where we come in for mucho dinero."

I focused on the most important part of his intel. *"A hundred people?"*

"Over the past four months."

I shut off the bike, put the cell on speaker, and took notes on the little spiral notepad I now carried with me. The pad wasn't high-tech, but it did allow me some privacy that electronic devices didn't. The Master of the City kept tabs on me through all the fancy gear he paid for.

"Talk to me."

"It started out with a decrease in street people. Shelters and churches who feed the homeless saw a sudden drop. Then the gangbangers started disappearing."

"How many Naturaleza are we talking about for them to have killed more than a hundred humans?"

"At least twenty." That was a lot of fangheads to take on, but since I wasn't working alone now, and since we were smart enough to split them up and not take them all on at once, it was doable.

I said, "Negotiation: tell Big H that I'll take the job if he pays for housing. I liked that place we stayed last time. Toss that in and he's got a deal."

"You left that place rather the worse for wear. You won't stay anywhere else?"

Rather the worse for wear didn't half cover it. We had been attacked by blood-servants and had shot the old, pre–Civil War mansion to heck and gone, but I liked the place and I knew for certain that the house, garage, and grounds had been repaired because I'd seen the work order at vamp HQ. I'd also learned that saying yes to a job offer without negotiation meant that my employers would never value me highly enough. "Nope," I said.

I heard keys clacking in the background and pulled off my helmet. Cold air bit my sweat-damp scalp. "There's the Hampton Inn and Suites in downtown," he said. "Natchez Inn and Suites looks nice."

I let my half smile grow as he worked, trying to talk me out of the house I wanted. This was negotiation for real, which meant that Reach had already checked on the house we'd damaged and knew it was out of the picture. "Nah. That house," I said.

"There's a Days Inn and several other three star B and Bs. And there's the Natchez Grand. I can book you a room that overlooks the Mississippi."

"Nope." I said, letting my amusement sound in my voice. I had missed this kind of verbal sparring. I'd been hiding in my room too much.

Reach sighed. "I'll get back to you. But if you can get the house, you'll take the job?"

"Housing and all costs above and beyond my fee, including the price of hiring a team, to be paid by Big H."

"You already have a team living with you," he growled.

"And I gotta pay the boys. Yes or no?"

"I'll have an answer for you by ten a.m. Oh, and by the way, the Naturaleza and some of Hieronymus' people have the vamp plague." The connection ended, and I stared at the cell. I hated it when convos ended up with the other guy having the last word. I helmeted up for the trip back across the river. That had been fun. Which was a clear indication that my life had been terribly boring for a long time.

I hadn't accomplished a dang thing on my ride, but I was feeling a whole lot better when I pulled into the side gate and parked my bike. I patted Bitsa fondly and left the helmet perched on the seat. Inside my house, Eli and the Kid were just sitting down to breakfast. My plate was in my usual place, and Eli slid six eggs and a rasher of bacon onto it as I entered. I dropped the leather jacket—which was a little tight across the shoulders now—and poured hot tea, smelling a good gunpowder green. This was the best part of having hired the boys. My meals were always cooked the way I liked them—high in protein, and no one griped about my needing grains, fruit, and veggies. I sat down and dug in. Eli, former Army Ranger and now my weapons specialist, was a great short-order cook.

Two eggs later, I realized that no one else was eating, and looked up. "What?"

"You're smiling," Eli said.

"So?"

"You've been a bitch for a month," the Kid said.

Eli slapped him up the back of the head, not hard and not as a sign of disagreement, but for the *B* word. Not allowed in my house. I stuffed a crisp piece of bacon in on top of my chuckle. It was maple bacon with lots of black pepper, just the way I liked it. "We may have a gig," I said through the food. "In Natchez, bringing in some Naturaleza vamps left over from de Allyon's brief visit." There were two kinds of vamps: Fame Vexatum vamps, or Mithrans, the kind who made the news, looking sleek and refined and beautiful, and the Naturaleza, the kind who treated humans like food to be hunted and killed. Lucas Vazquez de Allyon, also known as Death's Rival, was the latter kind. Naturaleza were faster and meaner and harder to kill, hence more money per head.

Eli's expression didn't change—the former military man's expression didn't change much at any time—but his scent smelled relieved. And the Kid blew out a satisfied breath. Their relief let me know how bad I'd been. I set down my fork, poured more tea, added sugar, and sipped. Eli leaned back in his chair, his T-shirt molded to the body of a soldier who believed in keeping fit—very, very fit—and exposed part of the newish scar that trailed down from jaw to chest. The scar was a lumpy mass over Eli's collarbone and his almond-mocha skin still pulled on it in odd ways when he moved.

Eli looked relaxed, but he watched me with an intensity that Beast wouldn't have liked, had she been awake. The Kid—my electronics specialist—with his shaggy, ungroomed hair and his body in the middle of a gangly growth spurt, looked back and forth between us with an eagerness I didn't understand.

"I'm sorry," I said into the silence. "I *have* been grouchy. I let . . . stuff"—I shrugged at the vague word, because they didn't know about the binding and I wasn't going to tell them—"get me down. I just realized that today. And while I still have to deal with that *stuff*, I'm better. A change of scenery will do me good."

Getting away from Leo Pellissier's binding would do me even better. Maybe when I got back from Natchez, my Beast and I could find a way to free Beast from the clutches of the MOC. Or maybe I'd just behead the fanghead and be done with it.

I chuckled softly at the thought and waved away the curiosity on the faces of the two guys. "Never mind. We should hear something this morning, but go ahead and pick up anything you need for your arsenal," I said to Eli, my tone wry. Eli believed that one never had enough guns. To the Kid, I added, "Generate a list of electronic gear we might need. Start with throwaway phones and some com units that can't be listened in on. Unlike most of the Deep South, Natchez has some underground areas, and since we'll likely be tracking down vamp lairs and taking them down by daylight, we'll need equipment that will either penetrate below-ground or allow us a work-around."

The two guys shared a look while I chewed on another piece of bacon. It was one of those guy looks that seems to suggest the little lady needs protecting or maybe is on the stupid side. "What?" I said, irritated.

"Natchez might be a problem," Eli said. "It's out of state."

I stopped chewing. "Well, crap." I hadn't thought about that. The Kid was a convicted felon, on probation, and though we had gotten permission *once* to take him across state lines, the resulting shoot-outs had not gone unnoticed. Things would likely be harder now. Before the Younger brothers came to work for me, Alex had hacked into the Pentagon, looking for his brother's war records, hunting for clues about the origin of the scar and the reason for Eli's early military retirement. And had gotten caught. Now Big Brother wanted to keep an eye on him. "Even if it's for legitimate work?" I asked.

"I know a judge," Eli said, grudgingly. "I'll see if I can get some help with the parole board in allowing him over the state line into Mississippi."

"Yeah. Okay." I sopped up the grease on my plate with a piece of bread and realized the guys were still looking at me. "What else?"

"Nothing," the Kid said, applying himself to his eggs.

"It's just good to have you back," Eli said blandly.

And then I got it. I swallowed, drank some tea, poured some more, and said carefully, "You guys were planning on leaving." I felt Beast wake up and listen in, ear tabs twitching.

The Kid blushed and concentrated on his plate. "We talked about it," Eli said easily. "We need a job. We figured we could pick up something farther north, but still in state. I have a few contacts."

I stuffed in another bite of egg and pushed in a triangle-shaped piece of toast after it, but watched them as I chewed. When I finished my plate of food I set my fork to the side and blotted my lips on the paper napkin. I was still wearing the shoulder holster, the Walther, and the vamp-killer. Unstrapping the blade, I lay it on the table, removed the Walther's rig, set it beside the knife, and leaned back in my chair, mimicking Eli's posture.

I took a slow breath and let a hint of Beast into my gaze. I said, "Were you thinking about leaving because I've been difficult and moody or were you thinking about taking my business away?" I'd made it an either-or half question, half accusation, but there were more things to consider. "Or maybe you have a thing against skinwalkers."

The Kid's eyes went wide because I hadn't spoken aloud about my most recent revelation when I shifted in front of nearly every person I knew in New Orleans, giving away my secret in a very public way. I had, in fact, refused to speak about that incident at all, and Eli and the Kid were still curious about it. Insanely curious.

"Or maybe," I went on, before either could respond, "Rick LaFleur offered you a gig that he would ordinarily have offered to me, but he's ticked off with me—okay, for good reasons—and is looking for ways to shut me out of his life. So he offered it to you instead."

Eli's eyes shifted away just a hair and back. The Kid's mouth dropped open and stayed there. *Bingo. Dang it.* "Rick," I said. There was a complete lack of emotion in my voice, but I might as well have cursed from the way the Kid flinched. Rick worked for PsyLED now, Homeland Security's Psychometry Law Enforcement Division, investigating supernatural crimes. He was my ex and I wasn't happy about the way we'd ended things—with me accusing him of attempted murder. Of me. Relationships aren't my strong suit.

I kept the pain off my face by some small miracle and pushed away from the table, standing, towering over them. I felt more than saw Eli tense and ready himself for movement, violent, physical movement. Alex watched us both, eyes darting back and forth. Neither brother moved overtly. Neither said anything. But Eli's pheromones changed, smelling and tasting bitter and full of adrenaline, a taste like pine tar and burned bread.

My index finger started tapping on the edge of my plate with a steady *tink*. Eli's lips came together in a slight purse and his stink lessened. He crossed his arms over his chest, as if he were holding in something. I wondered if he knew how much he was giving away. And I wondered how much I was giving away. I curled my fingers under, and the silence that settled between us was charged and prickly. I realized that I didn't want them to leave—I actually liked having them here, in my house, in my life, which was a huge, unexpected shock—but no way was I going to say any of that. Not if they were going to leave.

I sighed and gathered my gear. "You want to work for him, fine." I left the kitchen for my bedroom, my boots clomping on the hardwood floors.

"Yellowrock," Eli called. I stopped in the foyer, waited without answering, knowing he knew I could hear. "You get the gig, we'll find a way to take it. You don't get the gig, we'll find something else the three of us can do together."

I was glad my back was turned, because a smile busted out all over my face, showing me how much I had come to depend on the guys being in my life. They were like ... *Crap*. They were like family or something. Which was freaking *stupid*.

"And we don't give a rat's ass that you're a skinwalker," the Kid added. I heard the slap on the back of his head, and my smile went even wider. He'd braved a head slap to reassure me in that gutsy, bigmouthed way teenaged boys have. "As long as you don't shift and get hungry enough to think about us as dinner. 'Cause, like, that would, like, totally suck."

I laughed silently and said over my shoulder, "I promise not to have you or your brother for dinner or a snack. That good enough?"

"Yeah. Cool." I started for my room, and he added, "But I want to see you shift into the mountain lion." And I heard another head slap, as though the Kid had just crossed an additional line by asking, perhaps one his brother had ordered him not to cross.

The Kid seeing me shift would mean my being mostly naked in front of him. Not gonna happen. I said, "No," and closed my door. I had packing to do. My phone reggae'd again and I pulled it from my jacket pocket. "That was fast," I said to Reach as I pulled my vamp-fighting gear out of the closet.

"Your new boss agrees, but there's two more things you should know before you take the job. Hieronymus and Leo haven't kissed and made up. Leo Pellissier will not be happy if you go to work for a scion he's unhappy with."

"Icing on the cake as far as I'm concerned. Ticking off the MOC has become one of my favorite personal pastimes."

"Just make sure he doesn't get so pissed that he kills you for it."

"Awww. I'd think that was sweet concern for me if I didn't know you better. You'd miss out on the finder's fee if I were dead."

"Like I said. Smart women are hot."

"What's the second thing I need to know?"

"You have an appointment with a reporter-turned–book writer in Natchez at four this afternoon. She's writing a book about vamps."

I chuckled sourly and picked up my combat boots and a pair of green snakeskin Lucchese boots. I tossed them onto the bed. "No, I don't."

"Stop being contrary. You know this chick. You were good friends. BFFs. Her name is Camilla Hopkins. You were raised with her in that high-class joint the state stuck you in."

I hesitated, thinking through all the names of all the girls I'd roomed with in my years in the Christian children's home. There were a lot of them. Most of the girls were there only a short time before going home to distant family or entering the foster-care system. Or jail. Juvie was where the troublemakers went. I'd almost ended up there myself a time or two. But I didn't remember a Camilla.

As if reading my mind, Reach said, "Camilla is her professional on-air name at Torch News. In the home, she went by Misha."

The name clicked and my lips turned down in distaste. "She was never my pal. More like a neutral observer." Misha had never directly attacked me at school, but she never did anything to stop what the other girls did, either. Until I learned to fight, my life had been fairly awful, and no one had helped to make it better—not Misha, not anyone.

"A little verbal and physical abuse is good for the soul," Reach said.

"I'm not talking to the press. No matter who it is."

"She said to tell you she was bringing Bobby."

I went still. *Bobby*. I hadn't thought about him in years. Bobby Bates had been a special kid a couple years younger than me, with an IQ of 74—too smart to qualify for federal help. Like me, he'd fallen between the cracks and only the charity of Christians had given him a place to live. Bobby had been picked on at school, and I had protected him when I lived there. I had gone back a few times in the years before he turned eighteen, making sure he was left alone by the kids who might otherwise have made his life miserable. Then he'd gone to live with an aunt or his grandma or something and I never saw him again.

"Why does she have Bobby with her?"

"She didn't say. If you want to know, regular rates apply."

I shook my head and checked the time. "No, thanks. How did she know I'd be in Natchez?"

"She didn't. She called me for an intro to the Louisiana and Mississippi vamps for her research, and your name came up."

That made sense. Anyone doing research into vamps would contact Reach. And that same anyone would hear about me sooner or later.

"She could have e-mailed me for an intro to them," I said.

"She tried. No reply. Which is a sloppy way of doing business," he said.

His statement stung, but he had a point. I couldn't remember the last time I checked my business e-mail. Weeks probably.

"Camilla Hopkins is already in Natchez," he said, "staying at the Grand. I told her you'd be taking a gig there and she wants to renew old acquaintances."

I had no doubt Misha had paid him to arrange a meeting. Besides having compiled the largest vamp database, Reach was also a master planner and manipulator, merging multiple job opportunities and always managing to make money. "Where do I meet her?"

"I'll text you all the details. Oh, and check your frigging e-mail." The connection ended. In disgust, I tossed the phone on the mattress and started packing in earnest. If I was going vamp hunting, I'd need all my toys.

CHAPTER 2

You Might Have to Kill Something

I was standing outside when the blasted cell rang, and I knew who it was without even looking. Not by a ringtone, but because Beast started purring. Her hyperawareness of the MOC was one big reason why I hadn't let her out to hunt. I stared at the phone, considering not answering. It was daylight and that meant Leo was up past his bedtime and likely cranky.

I sighed and answered. "Yellowrock," I said.

"It is my understanding that you have accepted a job with Hieronymus." Leo's heated, silk-velvet voice caressed me, the voice vamps use when they want to seduce for sex or dinner. Or both. Once upon a time that compelling tone had very little effect on me. With Beast bound to him, I wanted to strip naked and hop on Bitsa for a quick roll in the Master's bed. Beast sent me an image of Leo and me on silk sheets, all hot and sweaty and bloody.

Not. Gonna. Happen. I took myself under firm control. *Not. Gonna.*

"Yep. I took the gig." I was pleased when I sounded normal—professional and calm, with just a hint of snark that always came out when I talked with Leo. "Big H pays even better than you do." I talked while securing my gear to the back of Bitsa. The guys were stowing weapons and our new underground com unit—UCU—in the SUV out front, so I had privacy to needle the MOC.

"You are on retainer, and you are my Enforcer. You may not leave the city without my direct order."

"Whoa. Not the way retainers work, Leo. Get one of your minions to bring you the paperwork. My retainer with you doesn't preclude my taking other jobs when you don't need me. If you fall under attack, you can send your helo and I'll be back to New Orleans in a little more than an hour, well inside the two-hour window required." Leo started to say something, so I interrupted and talked fast to keep him from getting a word in edgewise—as a matter of principle. "Besides, as your Enforcer, this gig fits under that umbrella. Big H has Naturaleza vamps running around loose, vamps with the vamp plague, likely infecting other vamps. It's *your* job as Blood Master of the Southeast USA to address that issue, *your* private lab in Texas that found a cure for the vamp plague, and therefore it falls under the umbrella of *your* responsibility to provide treatment." All it took was one dose of the medicine—like a vaccine. The syringes were packed up in my supplies; the doses were easy to administer to vamps in civilized surroundings, requiring a shot to the arm muscle; to treat vamps in the wild, I had a dart gun and one of the specially made darts used by vets for sedating wild game. Of course, I expected to stake any sick vamps I met in the wild, not cure them, but at least I had the option.

Stretching my desire to needle the MOC, I said, "As Hieronymus' blood-master, you should have gotten up off your blood-sucking butt and made sure your people were treated. Since you didn't, this is now a loose end that needs tying up in order to"—I took a breath and put on my best lawyer voice, quoting from the retainer contract—"protect the security of the territory, hunting grounds, and territorial borders claimed by Leo Pellissier." I let the legalese tone drop away. "Big H's problem is directly to your north border, he is still legally sworn to you, and therefore he is your problem—and mine." Which was absolutely the truth, and I felt all righteous having come up with it while I packed.

His voice took on a more demanding tone. "You will not speak to me in such a manner, my Enforcer. I require you to remain in New Orleans." The MOC wasn't used to people saying no to him.

"Hmmm," I said. While I decided how difficult I was going to be, I checked the straps on the gear. Nice and secure. And I *was* feeling difficult, so I decided to go with that flow. "Yes, I will, and no, I won't. The safe room at Katie's is finished. The safe room in your new clan home is standing in the middle of the construction like a vault. You have more than sufficient security twenty-four/seven at vamp HQ, plenty of privacy, and no problems securing ample blood supply. You do not need me, and I got nothing to do here until it's time to install the security in your new house, and that won't be for another month. I'll give Big H your regards."

"You will not," he hissed. I hit the END button, grinning happily. I did so love yanking his chain. I walked through the house one last time and picked up a boot box from my closet, the one that held my paltry jewelry collection and my neck protectors. Locking the house, I added the box to the stuff bungeed to the back of the bike, pushed Bitsa around front, and swung on. The guys were sitting in the oversized SUV, idling in front of the door, waiting. I lifted two fingers to Eli as I motored past and headed for Highway 61 and Natchez. The phone buzzed madly in my pocket and I laughed happily as I motored away from Leo.

The roads in Louisiana are on the far side of horrible. They had been constructed with expansion joints, a necessity because of the weather, but somehow when the road surface expanded into the open spaces of the joints, it all rose a little. Riding on Louisiana highways was a constant, unpleasant, thumpty-thump that dulled the mind and wore out the backside, and with the state's current financial crisis, none of the potholes had been repaired, further adding to my discomfort. It was a miserable trip made worse because I was in a hurry and wanted to get to Natchez as quickly as possible, so I didn't stop for anything. I didn't want to talk to Misha Hopkins, I didn't want to take that trip down memory lane, but all I could think was that Misha had Bobby with her, and Bobby was on my personal list of people to protect. Always had been.

Near two p.m., I pulled up at the mansion where we had stayed last time. Rich people wouldn't have called it a mansion, of course, maybe a cottage or something, but to me it was huge: three stories; set off the road; the grounds planted with live oaks, magnolias, pecan trees, and azaleas, with an eight-foot brick wall enclosing the large backyard. The house was maybe a little over ten thousand square feet, not counting the servants' quarters under the eaves on the third floor or the multicar garage out back, with rooms over that. The last time we were here, Eli had originally declared the house difficult to secure, but the walls were two feet thick, the windows were easily shuttered, and four shooters had held off an armed attack, which made it mighty nifty in my opinion.

I pulled Bitsa into the shade and studied the facade. The bullet holes had been repaired and the place looked good. The guys pulled in behind me and, just like last time we were here, I left them to unload while I took the three low steps to the door, which opened before I knocked. The owner stood there wearing a huge smile, a bizarre mixture of colors and fabrics, and her trademark string of pearls wound around her neck and resting across her little rounded belly. Esmee was a skinny, wrinkled woman with shocking red hair and no fashion sense. Today she was wearing purple velour elastic-waist pants and a frilly shrimp-toned blouse with full, pleated sleeves, bright red lipstick that had bled into the creases of her mouth, a stars-and-stripes scarf, and a pair of emerald green ballet slippers with feathers on the instep.

Hands clapping joyfully, she rushed through the door, saying, "You came back." She held her arms out to me for a hug.

Crap. I'm not a hugger. I don't like to be squashed up against a stranger. I'm not even real fond of back-slapping handshakes. I took a quick step back, but Esmee was fast for a tiny elderly woman, and she caught me. She was also stronger than expected. Her grasp on my elbow stopped me in my tracks and she wrapped her arms around me, her head stopping about midchest on me. She rocked me back and forth in a fast little shimmy. "My son said you'd never come back, but I'm so glad you did."

I managed a startled, "Huh?" *Son?*

She pulled away to look up at me. "I hadn't had so much fun in years as when you were here last. Not even when Ronald and his charming wife stayed here."

She was talking about President Reagan and his wife, Nancy. Esmee's home had been a B and B for years. "Um." Succinct. That's me. I added, "We got the place shot up."

"I know," she said, as if that was the best thing in the world. "I hadn't shot my gun in years till that day. Since then, I've been target shooting several times, and the sheriff and I even shot some skeet. I beat the pants off that girl. Come in! Come in!"

I looked back over my shoulder to see Eli watching, one corner of his mouth tilted up. I was reasonably sure he was laughing at me as I was pulled inside.

Esmee's grasp on my hand was like the talons of a hawk as she pulled me through the living room, past the dining room, butler's pantry, wine closet, and coffee bar. Off to the side were the wet bar, billiards room, music room, TV room, servants' toilet, powder room for guests, and a coat closet bigger than a small garage. The downstairs was exactly as I remembered it, sans holes in the ancient plaster. The place had copper-coffered twelve-foot ceilings and tricolored wood parquet floors covered with silk rugs. Her family had been rich for centuries and the place was full of antique wood furniture. It was decorated in generations of treasures, stuff you might see on *Antiques Roadshow* that was worth tens of thousands of dollars. Each.

A maid and the three-star chef lived upstairs, which meant we would have to do no cleaning and someone else would keep lots of food on hand, which always made me happy. Esmee stopped in the small nook off the kitchen, where there was a table and four cozy chairs, probably a breakfast room. A roast piglet—still steaming from the grill—lay on a cast-iron tray on top of a trivet, the kind that whirls around for ease of serving. My mouth started watering as if I hadn't eaten in days. To the side of the trivet were small bowls of condiments and a loaf of homemade bread with several slices already cut. There was also a bowl of fruit and a tray with cubes of different cheeses, each stuck with a toothpick.

"I asked Jameson to put together a small repast. Now let's see. You take tea—am I right? Sit, sit." She pushed me into a chair and I sat. It was that or fall over from her shove. The little woman was wiry and strong. "Jameson?" she called. "We have guests."

The nearly unflappable man appeared in the doorway, a white apron over his khakis and button-down white shirt, a white linen towel over one arm. In the other was a teapot, the spout steaming. He didn't look quite as happy as Esmee did to see me, which was not a surprise—the last time I was here he'd ended up under a table during the gun battle— but he didn't try to scald me with the tea or stab me with the knife beside the piglet, so I was okay with that.

"Good day to you, Miss Yellowrock." Turning to the side, he said, "And to you, Masters Younger. We have water for the elder Younger and cola for the younger Younger." Which made me grin, but the brothers had obviously heard it before, because they ignored it.

Esmee pointed to seats and took the one that Jameson pulled out for her. The brothers sat as Jameson poured tea and brought drinks and passed out plates before taking a big, two-pronged sterling silver fork to the piglet and pulling meat off the bones. The smell was heavenly, divine, fabulous—all the words that meant "good." Beast watched the fork pull on the succulent flesh and thought about catching a wild piglet in the forest.

Esmee said, "So, my dears. Who do we need to kill this time?"

My appetite went into hiatus.

Esmee clasped her hands before her like a little girl waiting on Santa. Jameson's brows rose so far that they nearly sandwiched into his hairline. The Kid snickered. Eli's lips twitched and he leaned back in his chair as if watching a show. I opened my mouth, closed it, opened it again, and realized I had no idea what to answer.

Eli snorted softly and said, "Miz Esmee, we're just here to reconnoiter and for Jane to do an interview. The press, you know."

Jameson gave a small nod of approval, but Esmee's face fell. "But . . ." She looked woebegone, as if we'd stolen her favorite doll and cut off its head, but then she smiled, showing off dazzling new white teeth. "Once you reconnoiter, *then* you might have to kill the vampires taking our people. Yes? And I get to help."

Carefully, Eli said, "If we find something to kill and have time to come get you, we will."

"What fun!" She clapped her hands, and Jameson looked

at her fondly, as if she were a dotty favorite aunt. "But the press was awful to the Reagans when they were here. The media is not allowed on the property. I hope you don't mind, dear," she said to me, "but you will simply have to meet with them elsewhere."

"I don't mind at all, Miss Esmee. That privacy—and your ability with firearms," I added quickly, "are the very reasons we wanted to stay here with you."

"Aren't you sweet?" She patted my hand and said, "Serve these charming young people, Jameson. They have reconnoitering to do."

To Eli I mouthed a silent thank-you. His lips quirked up on one side and he gave his attention to a piglet sandwich, heavy on the pork, light on the bread, with a plateful of fruit to the side that might have satisfied a troop of monkeys. Eli ate healthy, while his brother's sandwich was heavy on the sauce and bread, with an apple slice and three grapes to the side. Mine was more like a plateful of pork with no bread and no fruit at all. I groaned with delight at the burst of roast piglet flavor and said, "I may have to marry you, Jammie."

"I'd rather be married to a cobra, Miss Jane," he said gently in what might have been a Boston accent. "No offense."

Miss Esmee gasped and Eli chuckled. I sipped my tea to hide my smile and said, "No offense at all, Jammie." I pointed with my fork. "Good pig."

"Thank you, Miss Jane," he said, sounding serene.

After a meal fit for a carnivorous king, I took my personal gear upstairs and picked the tiny bedroom I'd napped in the last time I was here. The mattress was that memory-foam stuff and no way was I giving that up to one of the guys. The upstairs had eight bedroom suites and five baths and slept sixteen easily, more in a pinch. They could make do with whatever other room they wanted, and if it didn't have the memory foam, well, too bad.

Tossing my bag on the bed, I cleaned up in the attached bathroom, braided my hip-length black hair, and let it hang down my back. I put on fresh black jeans, ironed by one of the girls at Katie's Ladies, and a tailored dress shirt created for me by Leo's fashion designer—of *course* the MOC of the Southeastern states had a fashion designer on retainer.

It was a shirt that worked well with any of my jackets to hide my weapons—in this case, my Walther in a spine holster, a six-inch silver-plated blade, and four stakes. I tossed extra magazines for the .380 into a fanny pack and pulled on the green snakeskin boots. Western boots might be more ubiquitous in Texas than in Mississippi, but not by much. Everyone wore them in this part of the country when they weren't wearing Gucci, Ferragamo, or Prada stillies—or cheap knockoffs of same.

With time to spare, I dropped to the bed, because what else was I going to do for half an hour? And the mattress was so tempting, all fluffy with a down comforter to keep off the chill. Arms above my head, the backs of my hands against the inlaid headboard, my boots crossed at the ankles and dangling off the mattress, I was instantly besieged with memories, images that had been dredged up by my subconscious to ambush my mind the moment I stopped.

Misha as a thirteen-year-old girl, her long chestnut hair in a ponytail, the tip pulled around front and held between her lips. She had been delicate, shorter than me—though that wasn't odd, because even at twelve I'd been tall—and held herself, arms hugging, shoulders hunched, eyes wide. She had a habit of standing against the wall, where her back was safe. Like prey. She had watched and listened as the other girls in the group house tormented me. Not helping. Not defending. In my mind's memory I studied her, my eyes closed against the winter light pouring through the blinds. And with the hindsight of years, I realized that she had probably been an abused child, maybe for years. Scared. Scarred. Memories holding her down.

That abuse explained the cautious and nearly compulsive way Misha went about her life and studies, always working bent over her desk, always finished with a long-term assignment a week early. Her tiny room was always spotless and neat, with nothing at all on the bureau or desktop. *Compulsive*—that was the word for her. Watchful, worried, fearful, and compulsive. Needing control over her life.

On the nice soft bed, I blew out a breath, hearing the air whisper raggedly out. *Why hadn't I noticed her wounds back then?*

The other girls had ignored her as they had ignored me, as long as the housemother, Belinda Smith, had been in the room. I had liked Belinda. She had been the best of what an alpha woman should be; strong enough to keep us all in line, and gentle enough to teach us what we needed to survive when we left Bethel Nondenominational Christian Children's Home. I had even liked Misha a little, as well as I could like anyone back then, as I learned how to speak English and tried to catch up in school. I did catch up—eight years of learning in two years. And Misha had been there, on the sidelines, watching, silent, back-to-the-wall prey.

And then there was Bobby. My strongest memory of him was the day I left the children's home at age eighteen, a couple days after the birthday they had assigned to me when I was found wandering the mountain woods. Bobby Bates had come to tell me good-bye—and to try to talk me into staying. He had been prey too, his red hair bright in the afternoon sun, his freckles a cinnamon spatter. He was standing with his shoulders hunched, arms crossed, hands under his armpits, eyes staring at the asphalt. Afraid. He had always been afraid.

Prey, the insistent, soft voice had whispered in my mind. I hadn't known then that the voice was Beast, looking out at the white man's world through my eyes. I'd thought the voice meant that I was insane or maybe a psycho in training. With long practice, I had shoved the voice down deep, ignoring it. It had hacked with amusement but subsided, watching. Waiting.

Like me, Bobby wasn't like the other kids at Bethel. But while I was just different, he was a little slower than most, both physically and mentally. Bobby was seventeen going on ten. And, like me, he was lonely. Looking back, maybe we had all been lonely and I'd simply not been able to see it.

Bobby had been picked on mercilessly by the other kids, except when a group-home parent was nearby, of course, or a counselor was watching. When no one was looking, his life had been a constant torment until I'd taken him under my wing. It had been the middle of winter when I was ... fifteen?

I already had a rep as a fighter at the school, but despite how tough I was, from the first day he came to Bethel, something about Bobby called to me. He was like a day-old kitten mewling in fear. I fought for Bobby, protected him, made sure the other kids left him alone. My threats and fists had meant that no one picked on him even when I wasn't around. Once Bobby left Bethel, I'd never returned to the children's home.

And now the two prey were here, back-to-back in vamp territory. *Crazy.*

I must have napped, because I woke with a start when my doorknob squeaked. I moved Beast-fast, and when the door opened I had risen in bed, back curled like a half sit-up, with a Walther, round chambered, held in a two-hand grip, aimed at the door. The Kid backed up fast into the hallway, hands up in the universal peace gesture. Except on him it was more like the universal "I'm stupid" gesture. In one fast sequence, I pointed the weapon at the ceiling, released the magazine, unchambered the round and tucked it into a pocket, and set the weapon on the bed.

"You have lived with a soldier and with me for months now. You want to explain how you can still be such an idiot?" I demanded.

"Sorry. I was trying to see if you were awake and I didn't want to wake you if you were sleeping."

"And if I'd been standing here naked and screamed, what then?"

The Kid laughed. Seriously, he laughed. *Idiot.*

I rolled to my feet and stretched. The catnap had done me good physically, but had done nothing for my crabbiness. "I'd have shot you, and you'd have deserved it." That shut him up. "What time is it?"

"You have half an hour to get to your talk with the reporter. Eli said he needs to pick up a few things in town and he'll drive you." The Kid shut the door without waiting for a reply.

I wanted to yell, *What if I want to ride Bitsa?* But I kept it in. Irritable, I freshened up in the small bath and pulled a casual jacket out of the single piece of luggage I'd brought. It was wrinkled, but I slid into it anyway. With my new muscles, it was snug across the shoulders, but the fabric was stretchy.

When I turned off the lights, I peeked into the adjoining room just in case one of the guys had claimed it. The room looked untouched, but I locked the bathroom door on that side anyway. Despite the years in the children's home, where nothing was ever really private, I'm not good at sharing.

On the way into town, I studied the intel sent to me by Reach, mostly Natchez's Clan home, blood-masters, heirs, and primos—the basic building blocks of vamp society. Eli was content to let me read. I liked a man who didn't chatter and who didn't expect me to chatter. His eyes were taking in the scenery, charting roads, locations of businesses, alleys, and empty storefronts. Recon. Part of his training, and part of my nature. We made a good team. He slowed down as we passed by the three-story building where we'd had a firefight not that long ago. We'd killed a lot of vamps, like, fourteen vamps, which was a *lot* of vamps. The place looked deserted. Eli said nothing as he motored on past, and I stuck my nose back into the research.

Natchez, which is perched high upon a bluff above the Mississippi River, is the first major port north of New Orleans and had once been a key hub of trade and steamboat travel. Unlike most of the rest of the South, Union troops had decided not to burn it to the ground in the Civil War, using the port instead to move troops and gear and to secure the waterway. After the war, Natchez had been left with most of its charm: lots of fancy, prewar buildings, antebellum homes, churches, graveyards, and old live-oak trees swathed in moss—as well as its notorious past. Its location had allowed it to maintain its infrastructure and rebuild faster when most other towns around the South had suffered harder and longer.

During the Reconstruction, carpetbaggers brought in trade opportunities, work opportunities, and an influx of cash for the newly impoverished whites and the newly freed slaves, many of whom were trained as dockworkers or mule handlers or seamstresses or hat makers, as well as the freemen of color who had been educated doctors and poets and lawyers, many of them land owners who had owned slaves of their own. The town survived and thrived.

Eli dropped me off in front of the Natchez Grand Hotel, not coincidentally one of the hotels Reach had suggested I stay in. The place was redbrick and—arguably—had the best location of any hotel in town, boasting views of the historic old downtown on one side and the Mississippi River and the river walk on the other. I took the elevator up to the top floor, where Misha had a two-bedroom suite, and knocked. I sensed a person on the other side of the door, and felt myself studied for a moment through the peephole, Beast's instincts alerting me to surveillance. The door opened to Bobby's smile-wreathed face.

"Jane!" he shouted, and grabbed me in a bear hug that cracked my back.

I was prepared for this one; Bobby had always been a hugger. A silly smile on my face, I hugged him back, squeezing him hard. Bobby believed that the harder the hug, the more love was in it.

"I missed you, Jane." Bobby rocked me in his arms — discomfortingly similar to the way Miss Esmee had — and his red hair tickled my chin and cheek. He had changed, his body filling out, and he was taller than I remembered. But his scent was familiar: baby shampoo, foot powder, and Bobby. For some stupid reason, tears gathered in my eyes as I held him.

In the room, I scented cleansers, fabric fresheners, Misha, perfume, and herbal bath products; I also smelled another human, a child. But there was something else beneath the familiar scent of Bobby and the smell of a hotel room, something not quite right. I felt Beast stir and stare out at the world through my eyes. I drew in the air, uncertain of the strangeness in the weak scent. Something chemically astringent and harsh, and something else — something sickly. "I missed you too, Bobby boy."

Gently I pushed him back and blinked away the tears to study him with my eyes, rather than just my nose and hands, seeing the teenager he had been and the man he was now. Bobby would never grow up like other people did; he'd always have the mental capacity of a ten-year-old, always filled with the wonder, the joy, and the hopefulness of a child. But he *had* grown older. He had fine wrinkles at the corners of his eyes, and his freckles had grown closer together than when he was a teenager. The extra pounds I had felt in the hug were well distributed on his frame, and the weight looked good on him.

"You're different," he said, squeezing my shoulders. "All muscley."

"And you grew at least ten inches," I hyperbolized. "You grew up on me."

"Come on in and meet little Charly." Bobby took me by the hand and led me into the living room area of the suite. A little girl was curled up on the sofa, watching TV. "Charly, this is Jane." The little girl waved to me shyly. "Jane, this is Charly. She's Misha's little girl and my best friend." The child was maybe seven or eight, skinny and pale, with thin brown hair cut in a pageboy to her ears. She was bundled up in pink velour sweats that were sized to grow into, and a blanket covered her legs. She wore a pearl ring on her left hand, something that looked too adult for her but seemed to fit. I lifted my hand in greeting, and she pulled the blanket up to her chest as if uncomfortable with my gaze, so I looked away and took in the suite.

Misha had paid for a hospitality suite with adjoining rooms. Fancy digs for a reporter-turned–book writer. There were children's books and toys in a large wicker basket, a lavender hoodie jacket on a hanger on a hat rack instead of pitched over a chair back, a pair of women's running shoes placed precisely side by side below the jacket, a packet of folders lined up neatly at the corner of a table. From the way her shoes were lined up and her hoodie so carefully hung, I didn't think the control freak I remembered had changed all that much. A coat sized for Bobby was on a hanger on a doorknob to a room with two double beds. Across from it was a room with a king-sized bed. The place was decorated in beige and a soft rosy red, with dark wood furniture. A soothing palette.

Bobby said, "Misha is in the bathroom. We're watching Disney. Charly likes *The Lion King.*"

I nodded, scenting again that faint hint of sickness. I looked Bobby over and thought about his scent rising to me when we hugged; he was fine. I looked at Charly again, my nose tracking both the sickness and the scent of chemicals to her. Her paleness wasn't natural to her skin tone, but was the pale of anemia. Her hair lacked the sheen a child's usually had, and was dull and far too thin. On the sofa arm beside her was a small clump of hair. There was another clump on her shoulder. And a small bald patch on her crown.

Her hair was falling out.

Charly was getting chemo.

Kit, Beast thought at me, staring at Charly. *Sick kit.*

I stood rooted to the floor, horrified and totally out of anything that might have resembled a comfort zone. I was in a hotel room with Bobby Bates and a very sick child. Fortunately, before I had to react to my sudden new knowledge, I heard a noise from the open door.

CHAPTER 3

I'll Break Every Finger . . . One by One

A door opened in the room with the large bed and I turned in time to see a light switched off and shadows move. I had no idea what to do with my hands so I tucked them into my jeans pockets, but that felt posed so I gripped them behind my back, which felt even more posed, and I realized I was nervous.

Beast, who had been oddly silent, chuffed with amusement. *Jane is afraid of prey.*

Not afraid, I thought back. *Uncertain, maybe. And she isn't prey.*

Prey or hunter. Or plant. Or earth and rock. Or water and air, she added with a soft snort. *There is nothing else.*

I stifled a sigh just as Misha walked into the room. She had changed since the children's home. She was taller, her hair worn in a chic, tousled bob, and much blonder. The highlights made her blue eyes look bluer and accented her sharp cheekbones. She was wearing jeans and layered T-shirts in bright blues, shades of royal and indigo, fuzzy socks on her feet, and was color coordinated from top to toe. Her only jewelry was a large pearl wrapped in silver dangling on a silver chain. She moved with an unself-conscious poise. Misha had grown up. She stopped in the doorway and we stared at each other, silent. In the background, the volume went up on the TV as the kids got bored with watching us. I recognized strains from the animated Disney movie as I studied the woman in the doorway.

Beast was good at waiting games, but my nerves didn't let me wait it out. I lifted a shoulder in a tentative shrug. "Hi."

A slow grin spread across her face. She'd had her teeth fixed, and the effect was blinding white against her pale skin and all that blue. She looked gorgeous. "Hi back. Are we supposed to hug?"

I didn't know what my face showed, but whatever it was made her laugh softly. "Yeah. I'm not much of a hugger either. And it feels stupid to shake hands." When I didn't respond, she said, "You've met Charly?"

I nodded.

"I have coffee and tea on the way up."

"Tea, please," I said, with my best children's-home manners. Then, because I was getting more nervous, I added, "You look gorgeous."

"And you look dangerous." She flashed me a quick smile and I knew that she meant it as a compliment. "Just like you did back in the home, except with better-quality clothes." She tilted her head. "I never had a chance to thank you."

I just stared, not knowing what she was thanking me for, but obscurely pleased by the compliment.

"For what?" I finally said.

"Do you remember Ann Shelton?"

Instantly the vision of the bitter, angry girl flashed into my memory. Blond and blue-eyed, her mouth turned down in fury. She would have been cute except for the constant rage. Ann had picked fights anywhere she could, anytime she could, with any girl she could. Her forte was goading them into fighting and then ripping off the clothes of her victims, leaving them exposed, crying, and hurting. I had hated her, totally and without shame. "Yeah," I said. "I remember. But I haven't thought of her in years."

"She was taunting me one day in school, in the gym locker room after volleyball practice. Her buds were around her, laughing. I was crying. I knew what was coming. And she pushed me. I hit a wall at my back. All I remember is that suddenly she wasn't in front of me anymore. You were. And you said, 'The next time I see you picking on anyone—anyone—I'll make sure it's the last time you do. Ever.'

"And Ann got up in your face and said something stupid like, 'Yeah? Whatchya gonna do, bitch?' And you got this *look* on your face. This look. And your voice dropped to this slow growl, and you whispered, 'I'll break every finger in your hands. One by one. And then I'll break your nose so it will never heal right. And I'll blacken both your eyes. And then I'll break both your knees. You'll be disfigured and have to go through multiple surgeries. And you'll never be the same again. Ever. And if your little girlfriends try to stop me, I'll do the same to them. One by one. Got it?'"

As she spoke, I remembered that incident and said softly, "Ann said I'd go to juvie."

"And you said it would be worth it. And I never thanked you."

I shrugged and crossed my arms over my chest. "I didn't remember it was you. I just wanted to make sure she stopped picking on Bobby and kids like him." I looked over at the TV to find Bobby watching us, though I was pretty sure he couldn't hear a word we said over the Disney music.

"And none of us thanked you. None of the picked on kids thanked you back then. You risked a lot to make sure Ann Shelton stayed away. So. It's a long time coming, but thank you."

I opened my mouth. Closed it. I shrugged again. That's me. Just chock-full of social skills.

"I've been reading about you," Misha said. "According to Reach, 'Jane Yellowrock,'" she quoted, "'is arguably the best vampire hunter in the business.' And that was before the info was updated with all the kills in Natchez last year."

I had no idea what to say to that, so I said nothing, which was better than opening my mouth and inserting my foot, boot and all. Just when the silence—my silence— became uncomfortable, a knock came at the door. Misha crossed the suite and opened it. A bellman entered, pushing a cart into the room. It was laden with a small cheesecake and a plate of petit fours, a bowl of Chex mix, a plate of chocolates, two juice bottles, a carafe of coffee, a pot of hot water, mugs, clear glass teacups, and various tea bags. It was too much to hope for loose tea, even in a nice joint like this.

Misha tipped the bellman and then concentrated on making up a tray of treats for Bobby and Charly. I watched as she worked, trying to reconcile this self-assured woman with the Misha of memory. She glanced up and said, "Help yourself," with that new, quick, professional smile, as she carried the juice and plate into the TV area.

I moved to the far side of the fancy tea cart, where my back went to the wall, leaving the entrance, the windows, and Misha all in my visual range. I picked through the tea bags and upgraded my opinion of the tea selection. There was a white peony, a green chai, and a spring oolong, all imported from China. There was also one called East Beauty Blooming Tea—a ball of green tea leaves sewn together by hand with jasmine and chrysanthemum flowers. When dropped in hot water, the tea ball would open, appearing to flower and bloom.

I didn't usually care for flower-flavored teas, but I picked the blooming tea, which said something about both Misha and me, but I wasn't smart enough to figure out what. I opened the package and dropped the ball into a glass teacup, not sure if manners dictated that I wait until Misha served me. But the thought of her waiting on me was an uncomfortable one, so I poured the hot water into the cup, over the ball. Instantly the leaves started to open and flower as the hot water rehydrated and relaxed them. It was like watching high-speed photography of a flower blooming, and I could smell the jasmine. As the tea steeped, I unwrapped a chocolate, leaned against the wall, and popped the candy into my mouth. The taste of hazelnuts, mocha, and vanilla, perfectly balanced, melted on my tongue. I'm not normally a chocolate eater, but I nearly groaned, it was so good.

"I know," Misha said, walking back to me, a grin on her face. "Best chocolate *evah*."

"Yeah. It is," I said around the chocolate. "Um, why am I here?"

Misha pointed to the comfy upholstered chair set cater-cornered to the tea table, and I took my seat as she served herself chocolate and coffee. As she mixed her coffee, she said, "What did Reach tell you?"

"That you had a book deal. Book about vamps."

"Yes." She looked up under her brows, the grin still in place. "You don't have to look so ferocious about it."

"I'm not looking ferocious." *What does ferocious even look like?* "I look worried," I said. "Vamps are dangerous."

"Not the sane ones," she countered.

I sat back in the chair. "You're kidding, right?"

For a moment, Misha's face altered with some inexplicable emotion, but before I could identify it, the emotion vanished, replaced with the professional Misha. No, the professional Camilla Hopkins, reporter for Torch News.

"According to all my sources, the Mithrans who live by the Vampira Carta live by the rule of law, protecting blood-servants and blood-slaves, providing them legal rights and opportunities and the freedom to leave service anytime they want." It sounded like a promo quote from a vamp PR firm. Just what we needed, the media believing the vamp crap.

I picked up my tea and sipped, stalling, trying to figure out why Misha was here and why she wanted to talk to me. "The Vampira Carta also tells them how to divide up territory," I said distinctly, "and the cattle that live in it. Cattle are humans. They eat humans."

That odd look flashed across her face again and it left me feeling cornered somehow, as if I was way more involved with the project than I knew about. Shock raced down my spine, hot and then frigid. What was her book really about? Some kind of *exposé*?

"Mish, what's your book about?" I asked carefully, not letting my reaction show. "And don't fob me off."

Misha passed me a sheaf of papers, and I set the weak tea down to go through the typed pages. There were twenty, the content in outline form. The first pages had HISTORY, broken down into CREATION, MITHRANS, NATURALEZA, THE DIASPORA, EUROPEAN COUNCIL, NEW WORLD MITHRANS, and MISCELLANEOUS, with even more subcategories and suggestions and explanations beneath. The next section had POLITICAL HIERARCHY, with MASTERS OF THE CITY, HEIRS, SCIONS, PRIMOS, SECONDOS, BLOOD-SERVANTS, and BLOOD-SLAVES. "This is your outline for the book?" I clarified.

Misha nodded, sipping her coffee, hiding her lower face behind the cup. I remembered her doing that when we were kids, only back then it was orange juice or iced tea she hid behind. I flipped through the pages. There was one labeled HOW TO KILL MITHRANS—HUNTER METHODOLOGY. Another was labeled WHAT SCIENCE HOPES, and beneath that was a list of researchers' names and the higher-learning institutes that paid them to think. One read MITHRANS AND MAGIC, another was labeled MITHRAN BLOOD AND MODERN PRESERVA-

TION. There was MITHRANS AND WITCHES, and I flipped on through, not liking this. The vamps I knew were not going to like this, either. Leo was going to have kittens. And maybe kill me for being part of it in any way.

And then I found it. Near the back there was a section on VAMP HUNTERS. My name was at the top. The chill I'd been holding down shocked its way through me.

I had never hidden what I did for a living—killing vamps was my main source of financial income. I had a Web site dedicated to advertising my skills, with a headshot of me in vamp-hunting gear, a bio (mostly candid), and a list of kills. I hadn't updated it recently, but clients could reach me through the contact link. No, I didn't hide who I was or what I did, but I didn't put it out there for the whole world to see either, especially in what could become a best seller.

I closed the pages and set them on the table between us. The anger I had kept from my face vibrated through my voice when I said, "You're making me a target. And you want me to help you?" I stood and pivoted on my heel, heading for the door. Somehow Misha reached it before me.

"Not outing you," she stated. "Not going to say anything you don't want said."

I let a small smile pull up one side of my mouth. "Oh yeah? You gonna let me have the right to edit out anything I don't like?" Misha's face fell. "I figured not." I reached around her for the doorknob.

"Okay," she said. I stopped. "I'll let you read over anything I write about you, and if it's wrong or untruthful I'll take it out."

Which wasn't a huge help. The truth was bad enough, and I wanted to keep the few secrets I had left to myself. But if I left the hotel room, even the right to take out the lies would be off the table. I was smart enough to know that much. Reach would tell her anything she wanted if the price was right. If I stayed, I might be able to bargain for my privacy and secrets. My fists clenched and opened as I hesitated. "What do you want from me?"

"I need an intro to Hieronymus here in Natchez and to Leo Pellissier in New Orleans. I've tried but they won't talk to me. I need someone to give me that extra edge."

I stepped back and stared at her, waiting, giving Misha a chance to make her case.

"My book deal is structured so I get the biggest payout on delivery of the manuscript. I need the money."

"We all need something."

She ignored my derision. "So far, all I have is a contact with a primo blood-servant of a minor clan here in Natchez, a human I talked to ten days ago named Bryson Ryder." She was watching my face, and hers fell. "You've never heard of him?"

I shook my head. I didn't remember that name from my quick perusal of the Natchez files, and the first thing I had looked at was clan names, their blood-master's heirs, and primos to get a handle on Natchez's organizational structure. "Clan name?" I asked.

"Clan Petitpas."

I shook my head. There was no such clan, not among Natchez's established houses. Misha turned her head away, letting that blond hair cover her face for a moment before lifting her eyes. "Bobby said you would help. He said to tell you that I need you."

Bobby looked up at the sound of his name and I met his eyes across the room. The words *I need you* triggered a memory from our mutual pasts. Bobby Bates lying on a playground, beaten and bloody, the bullies having run off, one eye already blackening, his red hair mussed and filled with playground dirt. "I needed you, Jane," he had whimpered. "And you came."

Unlike when I had trailed Ann Shelton and her pals down to the gym, finding Bobby on the playground, being attacked by a small group of vicious boys, had been luck. If I hadn't . . .

Bobby looked from me to Misha and back. And smiled.

"Okay." I hadn't expected to speak—I certainly hadn't expected to agree to help Misha write a book—so I clarified, "I'll tell you what I can that isn't covered by the employee/employer relationship." I walked back to my chair and picked up my teacup. "You do know I work for Leo, right?" She nodded, and I sipped. The tea was light and flavorful, delicate like the "flower" that had bloomed in the cup. And from out of nowhere I got an idea. Go me. "I'll share, but I want it both ways. I'd like what info you already have on the local vamps."

"Quid pro quo," Misha said, her eyes dancing. "Fine. As long as you agree to not write a book on the subject."

"Write a— Yeah, sure. Fine. Done. I'll try to arrange intros. But if the vamps you want to talk to say no, then I have no control over that."

"No ambushing them in alleyways and making them talk by threatening to break their fingers one by one?" She smiled, her blue eyes sparkling.

"No. None of that. They'd break me in two with one hand tied behind their backs. I want all this in writing."

"I'll have my lawyer send you something to protect your interests and privacy and give you the right to read the book before it goes to the editor. So let's start there, with the Mithrans' physical strengths. My sources tell me that the Naturaleza are harder to kill than regular vampires. Yes or no? And Jane. Thank you again."

I didn't try to stifle my sigh this time, remembering the feel of Lucas Vazquez de Allyon's flesh trying to reknit and heal, even as my blade severed his head. "Yes." I drank my delicate, flowery tea, feeling like an idiot. I had been played. I knew that. I just wasn't sure how it had happened. "Definitely yes."

My appointment with Misha and my trip down memory lane concluded, I was back in the SUV cab with Eli, the Kid on speaker phone while I instructed him to research Bryson Ryder. If the human wasn't a primo of a known clan, then I wanted to know what he really was. It was dumb, but I felt responsible for Misha. "While you're at it," I suggested, "create us a listing of any properties owned by Big H's clans."

"Yeah, I'll just snap my fingers and they'll appear, collated in a file," the Kid said, his tone full of snark. "I'm not Superman. You have no idea how impossible that last request is, do you?"

"Nope," I said. "Don't know, don't care. But if it makes you feel better, I'll buy you a cape and matching tights." I hit END on the call.

Eli looked at me out of the corner of his eyes, a faint grin present in the crinkles of his eyes. "Cape and matching tights?"

"He'd be cute. We can call him Captain Nerdman."

Eli actually chuckled, an evil little sound.

Back at Esmee's, I changed into blue jeans and an old jacket over a T, weaponed up with nine mils, one in a spine sheath for left hand draw and its twin in a shoulder holster that put the weapon beside my left breast and under my left arm for right-hand draw, extra mags easy to hand, and blades in boot sheaths. I joined the boys in the breakfast room.

"Here's what I have on the name Misha mentioned," Alex said. "Bryson Ryder is human, married, a father of two, lives across the river in Vidalia, Louisiana, in a three-bedroom house. He works as a CPA and keeps a small office off Carter Street that advertises open hours in the daytime."

"Misha said he was a primo blood-servant," I said. They were usually well-off and lived on the vamp's premises, where they were handy to do laundry or clean the pool or, in this case, do the books. And be available for sex and dinner, of course.

The Kid said, "He's more likely a vamp's occasional snack, and Misha was using him for background info. And before you ask, no, there's no answer at his home or office."

"We've got the time, and nothing else to do until eight. Let's do a run-by," Eli said, studying the addresses on satellite maps. "If the office and the house are empty, we can check them out and be back in plenty of time. If there are people there and it looks okay, then we've had a nice drive."

By *check them out*, I knew Eli meant "break into and look around," which sounded fine to me, except for any getting-caught-and-slapped-in-jail part. Our eight p.m. meeting was with Hieronymus, a meet and greet to sign contracts. Eight was just after breakfast time for a vamp, and we wanted to be armed and dangerous and ready for anything.

"And about that other thing," the Kid continued. "Charly's leukemia? I verified that she's on chemo, on six different kinds of meds, including prophylactic antibiotics, some supplements to mitigate the effects of the round of chemo she finished last week, and one I can't pronounce or find online."

"Misha took her daughter away from home and on the road, on business, the day after she finished a round of chemo?" I asked, startled. "I am not happy with Mish. But I guess there's some reason for what looks like total stupidity. I mean, okay, she has a book deal going, but surely any publisher would delay a deadline for a sick child."

Eli said succinctly, "Deductible and twenty percent."

"Oh. Yeah." Insurance and medical bills were not things I had to worry about, not with my skinwalker metabolism and healing.

"She has her job as on-air personality at Torch News," the Kid said, "and full benefits. But according to her financial records, Charly's uncovered medical bills are already at twenty thousand dollars. I don't know what she got for her book deal, but that's a lot of dough."

"Okay, Misha has to bring in large amounts of cash and fast," I said. "But still. The day after a round of chemo?" I shook my head. "Something feels hinky."

Back in the SUV, Eli pulled out and headed west, over the Mississippi. Lately, my whole life seemed to be spent crossing the Old Miss.

We took 84, also known as John R. Junkin Drive, across the river and into Vidalia. Eli found the business, and we both noted the Closed sign and the dusty Christmas tree in the front window. I didn't need to look at Eli to know how strange that was. We drove around several blocks, looking for banks and ATMs, which had the best security cameras, and any other businesses that looked profitable enough to have cameras running. When we were satisfied that we had a line of entry that would be unobserved, we parked the truck near a trailer park and meandered back on foot, moving with enough purpose that we looked like we belonged, but not with so much intent that we looked like we were working ourselves up to rob someplace.

When a cop car motored toward us, Eli's entire gait changed into badass street thug, and he took my hand. I cozied up to his shoulder and giggled like some mindless girl in love. Beneath his jean jacket I felt a blade sheathed to his arm and muscles hard enough to crack a coconut. The cop glanced at us but didn't react otherwise.

When I figured he was gone, I glanced back and let go of Eli. "Not bad," he said.

"Not bad, yourself. Where did you pick up that swagger?"

He didn't reply and I didn't really expect him to. We were at the fence a block behind Bryson Ryder's office. We split up, and Eli took the direct route along the fence. I strolled down three more buildings and walked along a narrow path between two that had been visible on Google. What had I ever done without satellite mapping systems?

I turned at the corner and walked by the front entrance again, seeing no one nearby, and I texted to Eli quickly, *Go*. I heard a muted *thump* and a moment later I walked up the steps to the small house-turned-storefront, and Eli let me in. I was hit with the smell of mold, dust, and human. Fainter was the smell of vamp, mixed varieties, like the way an herb store might smell if all the canisters were emptied onto the floor and allowed to dry rot. A little chamomile, some red pepper, rose hips, lilies, and dandelion, and a hint of vanilla, but all old. Nothing fresh.

Eli was wearing black nitrile gloves and tossed a pair to me. I caught them out of the air, two-handed. Black gloves were way cooler than blue or green. I had even seen where they made purple, fuchsia, and neon yellow, but I was partial to the black.

"No active security," Eli said to me. "Looks like it was turned off and never turned back on. Backup battery is dead." Talking on a headset to his brother, he said, "Booting up." He started up the computer, murmuring quietly as the Kid walked him through the dull intricacies of breaking into an old PC. The Kid had wanted to come along, claiming it would make our job ten times faster. Eli had vetoed that. The little felon was in Mississippi by the good graces of a lenient judge, and no way was Eli going to let anything criminal come within ten feet of him. No. That was for us. *Lucky me.*

Gloved, I looked the place over. There was dust everywhere, even on the PC keyboard and the phone. There were spiderwebs in two ceiling corners. A roach motel behind the desk was full. That was one thing about the Gulf states: roaches were everywhere. They were the size of a wrestler's thumb, crunched like bubble wrap and squirted green goo when you stomped on them, and sometimes even busted up and leaking they'd still crawl away. I'd learned to hate roaches. They were fearless. Not that long ago I found one crawling under my toilet seat. I managed not to scream and inform the boys that I was truly a girl, but it was a near thing. And it wasn't the first time my privacy had been so rudely interrupted.

The answering machine—an old digital model—had a blinking light. I pulled a tiny recorder the Kid had given me and hit RECORD on the mini recorder, then PLAY, on the machine, half listening as it played. Bryson hadn't answered his messages in weeks. Maybe months. One of the last ones was Misha's voice, still listed under "new messages," as if it hadn't been played. Which was odd. The calendar on the wall was still on October of last year. There was a dead plant in the corner. Whoever Misha had talked to, it was beginning to look like it wasn't Bryson Ryder, unless he had gone into hiding for some reason that let him abandon his business and yet talk to a reporter. Which was not impossible, but was highly unlikely.

On one side of the back door that Eli had kicked in there was a miniature kitchen with a small steel sink, a cheap microwave, and a tiny brown fridge, like one a college student would have kept in his dorm. The fridge stank of rotten broccoli and mystery meat, but at least Bryson's body hadn't been carved up and forced inside. A bathroom was on the other side of the door, and the water in the toilet suggested that it hadn't been flushed in ages, an iron-brown ring showing where water had evaporated.

I pulled open a file cabinet. It wasn't locked. The files inside were hard copies of his customers' yearly taxes, three five-foot-long drawers' worth. Nothing personal had been kept in the drawers that I could see. But in the bottom one I noticed a name on a file: CONSTANCE PERRAULT. Next to it was COLEMAN PÉRODEAU. Both were vamps. According to Reach's preliminary research, both were lower-level scions of Hieronymus. I did a quick look for the clan Misha mentioned—Clan Petitpas. Just as I'd thought, there was no such listing.

One knee on the floor, I flipped through the files and recognized more vamp names, blood-servants, and commercial businesses owned by the same. "Eli. Got something." He looked up from the PC. "Misha was right about one thing. Bryson Ryder is the tax consultant to the fanged and their dinners." I pulled out a file from the *H*'s. "Including Hieronymus."

"I have something too. There's nothing new on his computer for the last six weeks. But before that, it looks like Bryson somehow got on Hieronymus' bad side. There is a file of e-mails for each of his vampire clients, and under Hieronymus' name is a series of thinly veiled threats written by the MOC's lawyer. Legal threats," Eli clarified. "Bryson was being threatened with a lawsuit."

I tucked the mini recorder into a pocket and made sure everything appeared undisturbed while Eli went for the SUV. Just a little B and E and electronics theft before my afternoon snack.

Bryson's home was a comfortable brick place, added on to since the Google street photos had been taken, with a big live oak shading the front yard and a mailbox full of mail at the curb, envelopes and flyers sticking out. "Not good," I said.

Eli said nothing as he parked behind a new-model car in the drive, but he checked his weapon and chambered a round as he got out, taking point as we moved to the front door. He carried the gun one-handed, pointed down beside his leg, where it couldn't be seen from the street. It seemed like a bit of overkill, but I unbuttoned my jacket so I could get at both of my weapons and walked facing the road, keeping an eye on the yard, street, and the neighbors' houses at our rear.

It was typical suburbia for this time of day: quiet, no traffic, no activity. Ryder's car had a lot of cat tracks up and down the hood and the front window. A children's tricycle was by the front tire, on its side, and a doll lay on the walkway to the door, looking as if it had been outside for a while. The smell hit me about ten feet from the door. Something was very wrong at the Ryder home. I stopped and put all sensory clues together. "Eli. We got bodies inside."

He stopped too, not asking how I knew, but his bearing went from vigilant to hyperalert. He held his gun now in a two-hand grip pointed at the ground in front of him. "Details."

"Old blood. A lot of it. Sickly sweet. It's been there a while."

"Let's go." He moved back to the SUV and got inside. I followed, buckling myself in as he drove away. All I could see was the doll and the tricycle. "A family is dead for weeks and somehow no one's noticed yet?"

"You smelled the time frame?" he asked as he pulled back onto 84, heading for the river.

"Part of it. Another part was cat tracks on a new car, the mail in the box, and toys left out in the weather." As we were crossing the river, I thought about calling Misha and telling her that her contact was dead, but I just burgled his office, so the less I told the press, the better, old friend or not.

Below us on the water, a barge loaded with train cars and two tugs were pushing slowly upstream, the wake turbulent behind and beside them. The barge was sitting low in the water, and it had to take a lot of power to fight a current so heavily laden. "Does it bother you that I can smell blood?" I asked Eli. Meaning: *does it bother you that I'm a skinwalker?* But not said.

Eli looked at me from the corner of his eye. "No. I'll make sure a report is called in to the police about Ryder and then I'll have Alex monitor the police bands and obtain copies of the reports. We'll know what the cops do without getting involved."

"The Kid can do that?"

"My brother can do almost anything," he muttered. He didn't sound very happy about it.

CHAPTER 4

Have Stakes, Will Travel. Amusing.

An hour later, cops were swarming all over the Ryder place, and the Kid kept us updated on what the cops found. Four bodies, two adults and two children, all in advanced stages of decomp. COD was officially undetermined, but from police chatter, it sounded like a vamp attack. If that was true, then Big H had decided to handle things himself instead of following through on the threatened lawsuit, or Ryder made some vamp mad, or . . . or . . . I didn't know what. Something was really hinky here and I wasn't a big believer in coincidence. No matter what was really going on, I should give a heads-up call to PsyLED. Which meant calling Rick.

Esmee was taking her nap, Eli was going through the stolen electronic files on the vamps, and the Kid was helping while illicitly listening to the Vidalia police channels. Jameson was clanking around in the kitchen, listening to opera, and the maid, his wife, who had nodded politely to me before scuttling away, mop in hand, was cleaning. I was in the middle of nothing and feeling antsy, so I took my cell and went for a walk on the grounds. The backyard was enclosed by an eight-foot-tall brick wall and boasted a multicar garage, a pool, and gardens that my friend Molly would have adored. I didn't see any of it as I walked, holding the cell phone in my hand, staring at the contacts list on the bright screen.

PsyLED had issued new rulings that went into effect in the New Year. Now when humans were injured or killed by possibly paranormal means, law enforcement and private citizens were required to call PsyLED so one of their investigators could take psychometric readings. Rick was the special agent in seven states in the Southeast, including Louisiana and Mississippi. The cops would call. Eventually. But jurisdictional conflicts meant it would be later rather than sooner, and valuable evidence might be lost. I had almost asked Eli to make the call, but that had smacked of cowardice and so here I was, in the winter-chilled garden, surrounded on all sides by dormant vegetation, my knees knocking and a thumb poised over the phone. I put a foot on a garden bench and spun around so that I was sitting on the bench's back, feet on the seat, the garden spread out around me. The live oaks and magnolias near me whispered to one another, birds twittered and squawked, and two gray squirrels raced around a tree trunk, chittering, tails snapping. I could smell rain on the breeze. I really didn't want to do this. I hit SEND.

I had a mental image of Rick pulling out his phone, staring at the screen, knowing it was me, and remembering the last time we spoke, when I accused him of trying to kill me. Stupid, stupid, *stupid*. I was so stupid. With my idiotic accusation, I had caused irreparable harm to a relationship that could have gone somewhere.

After four rings, I heard Rick say, "Jane."

That was it. Just my name. Not *hello*, not *missed you*, not a rampage, which might have meant feelings for me. Just my name. I sighed slowly. "Yeah." I wanted to say, *How are you? Do you forgive me for being stupid? I miss you.* Instead what came out was, "I think it's possible that vamps drained and killed a family of four in Vidalia, Louisiana. And there are Naturaleza vamps in the area."

"Business," he said.

I couldn't tell if he was disappointed or not. "Yeah. I guess."

After a moment he said, "Do the local LEOs know?"

"Local law got a tip. They don't know the COD yet. It's my understanding that the bodies were too far gone to make a determination without postmortems. But they've sent for the local medical examiner, so they'll know soon."

"Why are *you* informing me instead of the local law?"

Because I wanted to hear your voice. No way was I saying

that. "They'll get around to it. A national-media type claims to have spoken to him recently, but if the smell is anything to go by, he musta been doing that while dead. The timing is hinky. I thought you'd like a heads-up." *But I wanted to hear your voice.* Okay, I was being stupid and girly. But I wanted to hear his voice.

"Where are you and how did you find it?"

I filled him in on everything except the B and E, and when I was done, he said, "I'll make a call. I'm in Tennessee right now and don't know if I can get away, but someone will be coming. They'll take over."

Which meant that someone would discover that Ryder's office had been burgled. *Oh, goody.* I didn't respond, and after an uncomfortable silence, Rick disconnected. I closed the cell and sat in the weak winter sun, beating myself up.

When I stood, I noticed a large stone beneath the nearest maple tree. Pocketing the phone, I walked over to it and realized that it wasn't a stone from here or from anywhere around here. It was rounded and vaguely flat on top, maybe eighteen inches high, and, weirdly enough, it was pink. Pink, white-veined marble. I bent over it, and two feet away in the brush, I spotted a rusted steel pole about three feet tall with a verdigris metal lion on top. A mounting block and horse tie, remnants of a nonindustrial past, a slave past, if the age of the thing was any indication.

I sighed again and made my way back inside. I so did not fit in here. Not at all.

Back inside the house, I discovered that an hour had passed and that the Kid had made headway on our stolen e-records and on Mish. He had discovered how my old acquaintance had used her reporter's job contacts to get a nonfiction book deal on the nation's vampires and the people who feed them, love them, care for them, or hunt them. Harder to find was info about Charly, but the computer whiz had succeeded without even being asked. The little girl had been diagnosed with acute lymphoblastic leukemia, or ALL. Her doctors narrowed the diagnosis to a type called T-cell ALL, a form of the disease that had a less-than-rosy prognosis. Charly had started on something called induction therapy, chemo with a mix of drugs I couldn't pronounce. Then her white count dropped and the oncologist took her off chemo for ten days to allow her body to gain strength. He had given her permission to travel as long as she didn't overdo it.

Misha had ten days to do the research that would allow her to write a book that would help pay for her daughter's possible cure. She had been desperate when she called Reach to get him to help her make contacts in the vamp world, and already one of her contacts was dead. I thought about Misha doing anything she could to raise enough money to protect her daughter. And I remembered one of Beast's memories of a male big-cat invading her den and killing her young. Beast had tracked down the cat, ambushed him, and killed him. There was a common thread there, one that made me uncomfortable for reasons I didn't understand.

As dusk drew closer, I joined Eli in the breakfast room, where paperwork was scattered across the table. Eli glanced up at me and without preliminaries said, "Cops are doing their thing with Ryder. You maybe oughta call your gal pal now. Get that guilt off your soul."

"That obvious?" I asked. When he didn't answer, I punched in Misha's number and was shunted directly to voice mail. I said, "Your contact, Ryder, is dead. Call me." To be on the safe side, I texted her the same message.

With nothing better to do and a gut feeling that things were going to go very wrong very soon, I dove into the research sent to me by Reach and the scant intel collected by the Kid. There was something about this town. Every time I came here, things seemed to get so freaking complicated.

It was after dark when I got dressed for my interview with Big H. Going into the presence of unknown vamps was never safe, despite the PR that let the world think they were sexy and sparkly and only mildly dangerous fun. I wanted to go in to his presence armed to the teeth, but sometimes carrying a big stick could actually start a fight. For this howdy-doody interview there would be no leathers. I had brought dress pants in a winter-weight wool, and I pulled them on over stretch leggings, and stomped into my green snakeskin Lucchese boots. Into each boot went a sheathed knife, one with the hilt visible and one hidden deeper down. I wore a white silk shirt with billowy sleeves and a velvet vest with slits for the throwing knives and silver stakes, which I limited to three each. The loose-sleeved jacket was tight across my shoulders—all my clothes were, but I would put off a trip to Leo's designer as long as possible. The old woman terrified me. My hair I braided and twisted up in a high bun, and put more stakes in it, pushed down so I could ride in the SUV without stabbing myself.

From a shelf in the closet, I removed the box I used for my jewelry. It was a Lucchese boot box, old and starting to show the wear, but it did the trick, and though I had no intention of dressing up, the box also held some of my protective gear. I opened the flap, and sitting on top of the socks that protected my small collection of jewelry was a carved bone coyote earring. I had no idea how I'd gotten the earring, which was a mystery for another day. I'd woken up from a crazy dream and it was lying on the bed beside me. Just the one. And I didn't wear earrings. This one tingled of magics, as if it had been spelled once long ago, but something about it was still magically active, literally. The little sucker moved around. I kept the coyote in a sock. I had put the two magical pocket-watch amulets inside socks too, and now they cradled the coyote on either side. Weird. But then, my whole life was weird these days.

I dumped the pocket watches into a sock together again, and wiped my fingers on my pants. The amulets smelled like meat. Like thinned blood. Kinda gross. They were not something I wanted to keep, but since I had no idea what they did, I was loathe to toss them into a river or something. From beneath the socks, I removed a black velvet box. Inside was my chain-mail throat protector, which I latched on, the silver over titanium cold on my throat and chest. I put the boot box away.

At seven-thirty, Eli and I were driving through the dark, on our way to the meeting with Hieronymus, bristling with weapons and with Leo's vamp med kit resting on the back seat. Though silence was usual between us, this time Eli said, "So. How do you want to handle this?"

"Too many unknowns. When I do this kind of thing I just fly by the seat of my pants."

"And if the vamps go into a feeding frenzy for some reason and attack?"

"We were invited, so I don't expect trouble. That said, if something goes wrong we shoot, stake, and run."

Eli actually smiled. "I love my job."

I answered his grin with one of my own. "Yeah. Me too." I went back to studying the photos of the vamps I was to meet, photos the Kid had loaded up into an electronic pad that looked like something out of the future. Big H reminded me of a bust of some ancient Greek king, but bald. Like, the guy didn't even have eyelashes. And then there was his love and heir, Lotus, a lovely female vamp from somewhere in Asia. In one photo, she was standing next to Big H and she looked like a teenager, her black hair a veil of silk drawn to one side and hanging below her waist, wearing some kind of kimonolike robe and scarlet shoes. H's sons, Zoltar and Narkis, were next in the file. *Zoltar* meant "life," which the vamp no longer possessed, and *Narkis* meant "daffodil." I shook my head. Vamp names were weird. The boys were prettier than their father, but not by much. I also looked over the profiles of the local clans' blood-masters, primos, and secondos. There were photos of bars and warehouses and businesses in the file too, properties owned by vamps.

"We're in On Top of the Hill," Eli said of the old historical district. "Destination?" I gave him the address, turned off the tablet, and set it in the side pocket of the SUV.

Hieronymus didn't ask us to meet at his Clan home, which was an antebellum plantation home outside of town, but rather in an old warehouse in Natchez Under the Hill. Under the Hill had been changed drastically by the earthquake of 1811, an earthquake so violent that it altered the course of the Mississippi River. The eddies, floodwaters, violent swells, floating debris—including trees and fully laden, crewless boats carrying whiskey, furs, flour, hardwood lumber, and other items from the North—landslides, and avalanches had taken off over a hundred acres of the old streets. And when they were rebuilt, and then rebuilt again under General Ulysses Grant, they were much different from the original.

There were three Under the Hill streets, each over a half mile long, forming tiers or terraces, running parallel with the river. Each street cut into the slope, making sharp-angled hairpin loops on the ends that put Lombard Street in San Fran to shame, while innumerable little cross-street alleys zigzagged up and down the hill between houses and gardens and businesses. Earlier incarnations of Under the Hill had offered no attempt at beauty, but once vamps came out of the coffin, when Marilyn Monroe tried to turn the president in the Oval Office, it was discovered that vamps had made Under the Hill their home, digging into the earth of the hill, making dwellings and businesses in the half-cavern buildings. With Beast vision overlaying my own, like my version of 3-D glasses, I could see witch magic everywhere—reds, yellows, silvers, and greens all infused with black and silver and gold sparkles of power. It seemed concentrated in three places, one location on each street, the three forming the points of a triangle with the apex at the hilltop.

We were meeting at a warehouse on the middle street, Tin Alley, near the old McHenry's Gambling Establishment. The building was an old redbrick two-story and was situated on a corner, up against the sidewalk. The twelve-foot-tall wooden front doors were banded with rusted iron and open to the night air. Music, sounding like live stringed instruments, flooded through and into the street. The windows were narrow and covered with solid iron shutters, sealed tight. The place was a firetrap, with limited exits and gas lighting—I could smell it on the night air—and vamps were flammable. How stupid was all this? It had to be something to do with the history of the city and Big H's clan, something ritualistic. Vamps were big on history and ritual, having lived through most of the former, and the latter allowing the predatory hunter clans to live in proximity to one another without all-out war.

We drove around the block before parking, weaving between the fancy cars of the fanged and wealthy. Vehicles lined the streets, as there was no parking in front or at the side, only a tiny lot in the back that was packed with cars secured behind a twelve-foot-tall chain-link fence with razor wire on the top. Inside it were a dozen black Lexuses, three Caddys, and one old Bentley, its cream paint gleaming under the streetlight. At each car stood a human blood-servant—security types—armed and dangerous. Several smoked, and I lowered my window an inch to test the air. Floating over the herbal scent of vamp and the stink of gas lighting, I smelled cigars, cigarettes, chewing tobacco, and marijuana.

"Sloppy." Eli said.

"Yeah. And no limos, no armored cars; just ordinary cars right off the car lot. That's odd."

"Or you've been spoiled by Leo and his über-rich cronies."

Which wasn't something I wanted to consider, but was a possibility.

Along the side street, the building boasted three arched openings sized for horse-drawn carts and wagons, solid-looking wooden doors closed over them. An alley ran along the other side, a windowless brick expanse two stories tall, the upper story painted with an old ad for Brown & Williamson Tobacco. The back of the building had only one entrance on the ground floor and it was sealed shut, guards standing to either side, both wearing vests with small sub guns of a make I'd never seen, tucked under their arms.

Eli murmured a soft curse. "They're carrying German UMP .45s. Even people with military connections have a hard time getting those, and they cost a fortune. Now you know why there aren't any limos. They put their money into firepower."

I pulled on Beast's night vision to get a better look. I had seen pics of the UMP on the H&K website. It was a vicious little weapon. Not worth a dang at any distance, but it would chew a body in half at close range.

Fully automatic weapons were never covered in the constitution's ruling on citizen militia members owning and carrying guns. They were not used for hunting. They were used for killing sentient beings. Period. Which is why I didn't carry them, own them, or want them around, despite the number of such weapons Eli owned, and despite how handy they would be against vamps.

I looked over the guards' heads to see a second-story door open for fresh air. "I don't like the fact that there's only one door open on the ground floor."

"I'll stay by the entrance while you talk business."

"And shoot anybody who tries to lock us in."

"That's the idea." We were both packing silver shot rounds, so shooting a bad guy with fangs meant he'd likely stay down. Shooting a human with *anything* had the same effect, but I was not here to kill anyone. That was not in the plans.

Eli parked the SUV one block down, doing a fast parallel parking job but with one front tire on the sidewalk. When I looked my question at him, he said, "Saves us time if we get blocked in and have to jump the curb."

I studied the area and realized he had chosen a spot that would let us pull out over the sidewalk and down a side street. I was used to bikes and they were easy to get out of narrow spaces, so I didn't think about getaway routes as a matter of course. Eli made me think outside my own coffin-sized box. I got out to adjust the weapons on my person, and the smell of vamp hit me like a wrecking ball. I put a hand on the SUV to steady myself and sniffed. A vamp smorgasbord met my nose and I opened my mouth, drawing in air over my tongue. Beast reared up in my mind and sniffed with me, parsing the scents.

Good vampire smell, Beast thought.

I grimaced. Not that long ago, Beast had thought vamps smelled like things to hunt. Not so much now that she was chained to Leo—something I had to correct as soon as I figured out how. My new mantra: *Get free from Leo.*

I adjusted my weapons, chambering rounds but safety-ing everything. Popping Velcro loops, making sure the blades would slide free, and hearing Eli do the same on the other side of the vehicle. There would be a tug-of-war at the door, Hieronymus' goons trying to take weapons off me and me not letting them go. I had a statement to make and keeping my weapons was going to be part of that. I wasn't dressed in vamp-hunting armor, but I wasn't dressed like a little old lady for Sunday church either. I repositioned the ash and silver stakes in my bun, fanning them out like a deadly halo. I'd had to smash them into the hair on the ride because they kept hitting the top of the SUV.

This event should be a simple business meeting, but with vamps nothing is ever simple. They were always trying to see who was an alpha predator and who was prey. So this little conference was going to be a dance on a knife blade, poised and balanced, having to prove myself on one side but not going too far and getting myself sucked dry on the other. I was much better at getting myself in trouble than anything else, but no way was I coming across as prey.

Lastly, I pulled a dirty white handkerchief out of the glove box and tucked it into my décolletage. I saw Eli watching and I said, "Insurance."

It was a hanky with Leo's blood on it. The scent claimed me as his. Bruiser, Leo's primo, had marked me with it once to keep me safe. I'd been ticked off about it back then. Times had changed. Or maybe I had changed.

In theory, the MOCs of one city were supposed to respect the life and "property" of another MOC, but it didn't always work that way in real life. I had no idea if Leo had enemies in the crowd I was about to meet, enemies who would kill me to tick off the blood-sucking fiend I worked for. Come to think of it, Leo likely had enemies everywhere.

For safety reasons, I had to go in looking like the Enforcer I was, but, technically, I wasn't here in the capacity of Leo's Enforcer. I was here outside of that job description and the safeguards it provided, so a little scent reminder of the biggest bad among the Big Bad Vamps might be a good thing.

"Ready?" Eli asked. I nodded and headed toward the door; Eli fell into step a little behind me at my left. I could hear the roar of voices and the *plink* of music from inside and smell the vamp scent. It made my nose itch. Ahead of us, two male vamps walked arm in arm, heads together, either chatting or necking—which had a totally different meaning with vamps. The wind swirled and they both slowed, turning to look at us, catching our scents. I saw human-looking eyes widen before the vamps seemed to disappear. Even over the distance I could hear the pop of displaced air as the bloodsuckers achieved super vamp speed.

"Oops. Most vamps don't like my scent," I said as a warning to Eli. "They smell another predator."

We kept moving, and three steps later two armed blood-servants rushed out the front door, weapons at the ready. I took a slow breath and felt Eli do the same, though neither of us missed a step or seemed to tense visibly. The humans pointed small submachine guns at us, but we just kept walking. Along the street, the security types moved in, forming a loose half circle near the door. The music from inside went silent. So did the voices.

"Looks like our cozy couple spread the word that something dangerous is approaching." Eli said.

"Afraid so. And here I thought being an invited guest

would make it easier." I could think of four ways to handle this: stop and chat and get strong-armed, shoot them all and likely die in the ensuing firefight, run like my pants were on fire and lose total face, or take them before a fight could even start.

I drew on Beast and felt her pawing, milking my mind, her claws bringing on a headache. Strength flooded my system with a burst of Beast-adrenaline. My pace didn't alter, but I smiled—a Beast-type smile, all teeth. I felt her looking out at the world and knew my eyes were doing that weird glow thing they do when she's close to the surface.

We reached the door. I acted like the thugs weren't there and put one foot on the single step. The two guys from inside moved quickly in front of me, close enough to make a wall of their chests and guns. I didn't slow. I hit out fast, striking one in the side of the neck with my right fist. Pivoted hard. Kicked the other in the left knee. It was so fast and balanced, it worked like a single move. I heard a gag, a pop, and an agonized scream as I pushed between them and they started to fall. I walked into the warehouse-turned-party-room as if I owned it, trusting Eli to make sure I really did. Behind me, the sounds indicated that Eli further incapacitated the men I had taken down, and then started in on the rest of the security. Good thing vamp blood heals their servants' injuries so well. My booted feet rang on the old wooden floors in the silent room as I left my backup behind.

I took in the place and the occupants. One big room on the lower level; lots of small tables and chairs. The seating was from various time periods and cultures: long couches in the Roman style; pillows, rugs, and hookahs in the Persian style; some odd seating that must have been African or maybe South American, the chairs low to the ground and carved from dark wood, dished like dough bowls. Weird.

Vamps in black tie and evening gowns were everywhere. Humans half-frozen in position looked to their masters for orders. From the loft overhead I smelled humans and blood. They had set the blood bar upstairs, with matching spiral wrought-iron staircases on either side and exotic, scantily dressed human blood-slaves at the bottom, like advertisements. The place reeked of vamps and blood and sex and sickness, but the sick stench was elusive, so I figured only a few vamps here had it. The vamps themselves couldn't smell the disease, which was how it raced through them with such speed. Vamps shared a sick blood meal, and the partakers all became infected.

As the security detail tried to rush through the front doors and Eli reacted, I spotted Hieronymus against a wall on the lower level, sitting in a big peacock-style chair made of wood inlaid with green and blue mother-of-pearl and paua shells, delicate and beautiful.

I turned on Beast-speed and darted to him. Stopped fast, my boots sliding for the last few inches on the wood. "I'm Jane." I flicked a business card into his lap. Behind me were grunts and thumps as thugs and their weapons hit the floor.

Big H stared at me with eyes that were bleeding slowly vampy. "You profane my presence with weapons and attacks upon my people?"

"You block the door and meet guests with guns?"

Hieronymus looked past me at the doorway while I studied him. He was paler than most vamps I'd met, and though his face was unlined, he had probably been older when he was turned than most—maybe forty human years. He wasn't classically pretty, which was rare in a vamp, and, like in his photographs, his head was totally bald. The only hair I could see was a thin fringe of eyelashes, which hadn't been present in the pictures I'd studied. He wore a tux, tie, cummerbund, and shirt all in black, and had an ancient copper chain around his neck, over the fancy clothes. Dangling from it, in the middle of his chest, was a sliver of corroded metal shaped vaguely like a toothpick, wrapped with copper wire. It was a peculiar fashion accessory—butt-ugly. It hadn't been around his neck in any of the photos I'd seen of him.

The front door slammed shut and I heard something heavy fall. Keeping my host in sight, I risked a glance in that direction and saw Eli standing with his back to the closed and barricaded door, nunchacku in one fist, brass knuckles on the other, and blood on his face and thigh. "Any trouble?" I asked him, letting the words drawl.

"Negative." He slammed his weapons into their hidey-holes and drew two handguns, holding them at his sides. He wasn't even breathing hard. And only because I knew him fairly well could I tell he was having fun. Uncle Sam trained its killers well.

At his feet, five humans lay, all out cold, and I chuckled

at the sight. Their weapons were in a pile in one corner. I shifted my attention back to Hieronymus. Big H sniffed the air once, taking in my scent. He cocked his head as if processing the signature and stared at me for a time that I could measure in my own heartbeats and that lasted way too long. He was doing that dead-as-a-marble-statue thing they do, where they don't blink or breathe and you just know that in a fractured second they can be on you and drinking dinner. My chest started getting tight, my breath wanting to come too fast. Tension spread into the room like a wave of polluted water. I did not want to have to fight all the vamps in this building, but I could feel their bodies aligning toward me and their eyes boring into me as if picking which pulse points would be the most tasty.

I didn't see his heir, Lotus, in the crowd behind him, but it looked like enough of his people had shown up that they could drain and kill us before I could fire off a single shot. Tension skittered up and down my spine like an army of fire ants, and I broke into a hot sweat that the vamps had to be able to smell. I worked at keeping my breathing slow and measured, but much more of this and my knees would be knocking. I decided to go with bravado. "Let's start over. I'm—"

"Jane Yellowrock," he said, reading my card as if he had never heard of me. "Have Stakes, Will Travel. Amusing. This is your motto?" He had an elusive European accent, the kind that likely started a thousand years ago and had undergone dozens of changes as languages transformed and evolved through the following centuries.

"My mission statement and company slogan. The weapons and the motto are for rogue vamps, Naturaleza vamps, and vamps targeted by the local ruling council as dangerous to their way of life and continued undead health. I'm not a vigilante. Much. I'm a licensed hunter. And as for the little display at the door, why hire me and my team if a few poorly trained human security toughs could take our weapons away? You want to hire the best? You've met us."

Big H breathed out and leaned back, letting his body lounge against the pretty chair. I remembered to inhale. "You are impertinent," he said. It wasn't a question, and it was the truth, so I didn't reply. I'd been called worse. "You are here with Leonard Pellissier's acquiescence?"

"Not exactly. I work on retainer, under contract, like we're proposing to do."

"His Enforcer works on retainer?" It wasn't exactly a question, more like a stunned recap.

"The Blood Master of New Orleans, Sedona, Boston, and Seattle, and all of the Southeast except Florida, needs more than one Enforcer. I'm his . . . part-timer."

"It is not possible to bind more than one Enforcer," he said.

Which was news to me. So I just raised my eyebrows, stared him down, let one corner of my mouth relax in what might charitably be called amusement, and waited. Never admit you're wrong when silence lies that you're right. Not that long ago, I'd have felt guilty about letting a falsehood persist. Now I just let it hang. And let my partner beat up humans. And didn't even think about it. I was so going to hell.

"Leo released you to work for me."

I let my smile rise. "Not only that. His laboratory in Texas came up with a cure for the vamp plague, so you won't have to keep drinking down humans carrying the antibodies." Big H sat up slowly, his hands resting on the inlaid chair arms. "I brought a supply with me," I continued, "and will be giving out the cure to anyone who needs it. If we can come to an accommodation." Which didn't exactly say that I had permission to cure someone Leo was ticked off with, but I was going to hell already, so in for a penny, in for a gallon of blood.

Hieronymus' eyes bled back to fully human. He lifted his fingers to his neck and stopped, then dropped the hand. As he did, I caught a whiff of the sick scent of the vamp plague. Big H had the disease. "You have this cure with you?"

"Not on my person, but it's available to me. Leo is powerful enough to be . . ." I searched for a word and settled on "magnanimous." Which didn't actually make him magnanimous, but I didn't say that. Skirting the truth with a vamp was scary business, because they could often smell a lie and they could always smell nervousness.

"I will validate our proposed contract, including the changes your legal advisor, Alex Younger, has suggested."

I nearly dropped my jaw at the thought of the Kid as a legal advisor. And he had done *what* with my contract? "Ummm," I said.

"You will destroy the Naturaleza who run rampant and wild through my countryside, and I will pay you the agreed-upon price—"

"Couple questions," I interrupted. Big H frowned. Master vamps don't get interrupted often. "How many are there, what steps have you taken to correct the problem, and where do you think they're hiding?"

"My Enforcer was killed trying to track them down. Witnesses said he was attacked on all sides by the Naturaleza and torn to shreds. He is mourned and will not be forgotten. My primo, Clark, has all other details." He waved a negligent hand at a nondescript human man to his left. Clark was a medium guy. Brown and brown, maybe five feet seven, slender, wearing—yes—brown.

Clark stepped forward, bowed slightly, and handed me a leather folder. "Estimates on numbers are imprecise," he said. "Originally we thought less than twenty, but before he was killed, our Enforcer staked four who were later seen on the streets."

"Naturaleza are hard to kill," I said. "Locations?"

"They have been spotted all over the county and in Vidalia as well. We do not know where they lair." Lairs were jealously guarded daytime resting places for vamps, so I wasn't surprised, but it did make my job a lot harder. "If we knew where they were, they would be dead now," he said, sounding just a bit snippy.

Big H was clearly done with question time. "I will accept the largesse of my sworn master," he said, "and the cure he can provide my people. If you also negotiate a parley that repairs the rift between my master and me, I will provide you a generous bonus. The business details you may discuss with Clark at a later time. You will attend me before dawn with this cure."

Before I could reply to that order, Big H stood, lifted his arms, and raised his voice. "My people. We have a guest. Meet and speak with Jane Yellowrock, the Enforcer of Leo Pellissier. She brings good tidings from my master and a cure for the plague that infects some few of us. Rejoice and enjoy the festivities." Some of his people applauded and a number of others moved forward with unseemly haste. *Scuttled like bugs* was more like it, but I was feeling generous. I figured they were sick vamps needing the cure.

Hieronymus extended his hand, palm out, holding them back, and passed me a business card. "This is Clark's contact information. Whatever you need, all assistance we can provide, is yours. And"—he gave me a fangy smile—"we are very generous."

"Good to know." I pocketed the card, in case my electronic genius didn't have all the contact info already.

He handed me a microdrive shaped like a shark's tooth, which was way snazzy. "The dossiers of the Mithrans you have permission to deliver true death to, and descriptions of the ones who were never mine and who are unknown to us, the ones brought by Lucas Vazquez de Allyon, may his soul rot in hell." Big H dropped his hand, I pocketed the shark's tooth microdrive, and was surrounded by vamps. Sick vamps. Desperate vamps.

I do not like being surrounded by vamps, especially plague-ridden ones who wanted to shake my hand, kiss me on both cheeks like some Old World mafia family, and tell me all their symptoms. I didn't know if they were trying to thank me or infect me. But I survived the glad-handing and, promising to bring the cure to the MOC's Clan home before dawn, slid out the front door as fast as I could. Eli covered my rear.

There was no security committee waiting on us this time, and though I didn't race back to the SUV, I didn't saunter either. Eli gunned the engine and had us two blocks over before my heart stopped stuttering and the rhythm evened out. "Crap," I said as we curved up the hill and into the old downtown.

Eli gave a twitch of his lips, which could have been indigestion, but I chose to interpret it as mirth. I called Alex. When he answered, I said, "*What* did you do with our contract? Without telling me. Are you insane?"

"No way. I showed it to Eli. He agreed."

I narrowed my eyes at my driver, who was chuckling, and wondered if I could take over the driving and shove him out into the street. And then maybe run over him a few times. "Nobody screws with my contracts."

"We just added two tiny clauses," Eli said. "One that lets us take the head of any vamp who attacks us unprovoked, and one that lets us take the head of any vamp not on the list who has gone over to the Naturaleza."

I thought about that for a while as the tires sang on the pavement. I wanted to find fault with the clauses but they were good ones, ones I should have included myself, and would have to add to my standard boilerplate. "Let's say I decide not to kill you both for changing my contract. And you both agree to discuss stuff like this with me and let me handle it."

Eli scratched his chin and said, "We're supposed to be partners of a sort. How about we buy in to Yellowrock Security. Alex and I have a little money from our parents' estate." He named a figure that made me blink. And then mouth it, trying to blend that six-figure number into my lifestyle. You coulda picked me up with a spatula. I had no idea what to say, so I said nothing. Taking my silence as a positive response, Eli went on. "If you agree, we could actually organize this company legally instead of flying by the seat of our pants, Jane style. Get tax stuff and insurance stuff handled, Liability insurance."

Which I had never thought to need, but if I was going to have partners and hire humans to work with me, I guess I needed it. All of it. *Crap.* I never intended to be a part of big business.

So I thought about that a while too. About not being in charge, not making all the decisions, not having my way all the time. And about having backup all the time. And having the boys stick around.

"I'm not saying yes." But my mouth went on as if part of my brain had been thinking about this for a long time. "But if I was, I'd be thinking that I get sixty percent," I said. "You two split forty. I handle all legal matters, with your input. Salaries to be decided, commensurate with company earnings, and expenses to be discussed at a later date. And you can stay with me as long as you like."

"Done," Eli said, as if the division of the company that had recently been mine alone was exactly what he had been considering before he made his offer. A glow moved out from my torso, making me feel light and kinda weird. I realized I was happy. Content. For all intents and purposes, I had just sold forty percent of my company. And my life. And I was *happy* about it. A small smile started and I let it take over my mouth all by itself.

We made it halfway back to Esmee's before Eli said, "So.

All of your meetings go like that? The one with Hieronymus, not the one with me."

"Pretty much."

"How much of that was bullsh . . . malarkey?"

I laughed under my breath. "Not all of it."

"Good. Because that means it isn't a hidden lie that has
us being tailed."

"Crap." I looked over my shoulder and saw three cars in
the distance. "Which one?"

"All of them."

CHAPTER 5

Four Dead Vamps Under His Tree

I started pulling and checking weapons, and wished I had been paranoid enough to bring the M4. I didn't place the guns on the seat, but reholstered them. If Eli had to do any fancy driving, I didn't want them slinging around the interior. "What do you have with you?" I asked.

"A dozen flashbangs, which are essentially useless in open space. Six frags, and in the back enough nine mil and .380 ammo to kill off a small tribe of werewolves or vamps."

"Silver, then."

"Yeah. If we're being followed by humans, that changes things. You want to call it in?"

"If we call in the cops and the people behind us are drunken rednecks out for a little fun at the vamp hunter's expense, we'll look stupid. Looking stupid is dangerous in a town full of vamps. It makes us look like prey." I repositioned all my spare magazines into my pockets and crawled over the seat back. There was a midsized tote bag full of boxes. Heavy boxes. *Ammo*. I stuck extra mags into my pockets and waistband, but I didn't take any boxes of bullets. Chances were, if we needed to reload the magazines we had on us, we'd already be drained.

"And if it's Naturaleza vamps out for a little blood at the vamp hunter's expense," Eli said after a moment's thought, "we'll look *dead*."

"True. You want me to call it in?" I asked.

"No. There's an open field a mile ahead with a shed full

of hay. If we can make that, we can make a stand from the woods or the shed. Decide later how serious our tail is."

"Works for me." I said. I remembered the location he was talking about. The shed was at the back of the field, about a hundred yards off the road, near a stand of trees. A shed full of hay was moderately good at stopping bullets. So were trees. Options are nice to have.

My foot hit something on the floorboard. I bent and lifted it into the faint light. "Did you know there's a shotgun back here?"

"Huh. I wondered where that thing had got to."

"Yeah. Mine runs and hides too. What's it loaded with?"

"Your rounds. More in the ammo bag."

My rounds meant the weapon was loaded for vamp with silver fléchette rounds. Vamp killers. Expensive vamp killers I hadn't known I had paid for, but under the circumstances, I wasn't about to protest.

"Hang on," he said. I gripped the leather handhold over the door as Eli whipped the wheel. The SUV crossed the shoulder of the road before leaving the paved surface, tilting down and back up. I felt the steel frame give, heard the suspension twang and the tires spit dirt and gravel. My head slammed against the SUV roof, grinding my hair-stick stakes into my skull. And then we were up and over and bouncing across the grassy field. I grabbed handholds and seat backs and glanced through the back window to see three trucks following, bouncing over the low ditch. Headlights passed through truck windows, and I counted three or four heads in each. That meant more than nine, though less than twelve, opponents, which were not good odds. If they were all Naturaleza vamps, we might be screwed.

"Hang on!" Eli shouted again. The brakes slid and caught with an antiskid shudder. I slipped across the seat, tightening my grip on the overhead handhold at the last second, seeing the shed whip by. And then I was out the door, into the woods, Eli on my heels. He had left the engine running to cover the sound of our movement, the exhaust to hide our scent, and the SUV's bright lights on to damage the pursuers' eyes.

Beast was close in my mind, her claws a steady pain on my brain, her strength and speed flooding me. I raced into the night, her vision brightening the dark, turning the black into silvers and grays and shimmering greens. Where the moonlight filtered between the leafless trees it lit up the ground like daylight. Eli was slower than I was but fell into place behind me, trusting me to see in the dark until he got his low-light vision eyewear over his head. He moved to my side when he could see.

Behind us I heard engines and doors slamming and then silence as all the vehicles were turned off, including ours. There were no voices, no sound of running feet, no flashlights. Vamps have excellent night vision; they didn't need flashlights. *Crap*.

The night was hushed, no bird sounds, no nearby car sounds. The air was still and cold, as if waiting for something to happen. Ahead I could smell standing water, stagnant with rotted vegetation, and a mixed bag of strong chemicals. Fertilizers. Herbicides. Bug spray. Over it all was the stench of drying cow manure. A stand of young live oaks, maybe fifty years old, stood in even lines, the only trees in sight that still had their leaves. We were in the back of a plantation home, in an area used as a nursery.

I stopped at the second tree and grabbed Eli, pulling him close, my mouth at his ear. "Get up in the tree. I'll take a tree a row over and down a few. Let them get between us, then shoot down on them. Pincer style."

He looked up and shook his head. I understood what he was thinking. He didn't have time to climb that high before they were on us, but he'd forgotten about my skinwalker strength, now augmented by all my new muscle. I laced my fingers and made a cradle of my hands. He put a booted foot into them and I tossed him up into the tree, holding my place until he was situated, his face just a little stunned. Then I raced across and down, choosing a tree about thirty feet away on the diagonal. I bent into a crouch and leaped, grabbing the lowest branch and hoisting myself up. All the months of exercise paid off as I muscled myself halfway up the tree and straddled a branch. On the rising breeze, I smelled vamp and sickness and a beery stench. And human blood. A lot of blood. These were Naturaleza. And they were *here*.

They poured into the wide space between trees. Three in front; two behind. Others farther back in the trees were closing fast. The three in front dropped forward, feet and hands to the ground, and raced into the clearing between the rows of trees, noses low, sniffing. The hair along my body rose in alarm. The vamps moved like a cross between reptiles and spiders, with a soupçon of wild hog. Their spines seemed to be jointed at the waist and nape, allowing them to bend in strange places, their legs folding oddly. They were *fast*.

I tucked Eli's shotgun into my armpit, knowing that the recoil would tear at my shoulder joint, but there was no other way to fire downward without the recoil knocking me to the ground. I aimed at the base of the tree, aware that Eli had done the same with his handgun. There were five vamps in the clearing now, all racing around, all acting peculiar, and for vamps that was saying a lot. These were acting notvampy. More like something else, though I couldn't say what, but the sight of them scampering through the moon shadows of the trees gave me a case of the willies. They were something not meant to be on this world. Something *wrong*.

The hair on my arms tightened painfully. One of the vamps paused at the base of my tree, nose to the ground. I could hear the sniffing breaths as she took in my scent. She lifted her head straight up, at an impossible angle, as if her neck were made of rubber.

I fired. Into her face. It disappeared. So did her head. The rest of her fell like a rock to the ground. The blast ripped the night sounds away. My armpit took the recoil; I'd have a bruise and stretched tendons. Thoughts for later.

I shifted the weapon up against my shoulder and fired again, taking a vamp midback. He fell, his upper body writhing on the ground, his lower body unmoving, his mouth open.

I slammed the shotgun into a fork of trunk and branch and pulled a nine mil. I wouldn't have the luxury of the spread pattern now. I'd have to aim and hit—which meant waiting until they were still. A vamp paused in the center of the space between rows of trees. Moonlight danced across his unnatural body. I squeezed off three rounds just before he took a step. He went down with a load of silver to the thigh and lower belly.

One leaped into the tree, landing beside me. I fired at point-blank range into his groin. He fell, and even with the concussive damage to my eardrums, I could hear his scream. I adjusted my aim in a modified two-handed grip and fired straight down, directly into a face. A female fell, her eyes fully vamped out, two-inch fangs white in the night. Something caught my eye. My last round hit a vamp in midair. He looked like he was flying. Right at me.

And then I saw something that shouldn't—couldn't—be. The vamp I'd hit in the middle of the back with the silver fléchettes pushed himself to his feet. I'd severed his spine. I *knew* I had. And yet he had healed even with silver in his system.

Not possible.

I aimed carefully and triple-tapped him, two chest shots midcenter and one slightly to the left. He staggered. And then he turned and stumbled away, into the trees, back the way he had come. The female I'd shot followed him, holding her face. But walking. Full of silver that should have burned them with mind-shattering pain until it poisoned them true-dead. Dead vamps walking. A moment later, only the one I'd hit first, the one with the head shot, was left.

I studied her from the tree. She was dead, true-dead, though somehow, she had regenerated slightly, fresh pinkish skin and smooth bones showing where only fragments and blood and mush should have been. I looked around the rows of trees. They were all gone. Why had they just left? If they can regenerate like that, even full of silver, they should have stuck around until we made a mistake, and then eaten us for dinner.

Across the way, Eli slid out of the tree and landed loose-kneed on the ground, his weapon in a Weaver stance as he studied the area. At some point there had been four dead vamps under his tree and four or five beneath mine. Now we had one DB. No way should so many have survived. Something was hinky here. Very, very hinky. I'd be chatting up Clark *very* soon, and not just about business.

I reloaded and handed down the shotgun, changed out magazines, and chambered a round. One-handed, I gripped the limb I was squatting on and swung, dropping bent kneed to the ground.

There wasn't enough of the vamp's head left to take it for a trophy, and a filthy turtleneck top covered her chest and arms. Her jeans were dirty too, like something a street person would wear, not a top-of-the-line predator. I lifted her hands, which still displayed the two-inch-long claws. They were jagged and torn, unlike the usual manicured talons vamps displayed. I pulled my phone and took several shots of her. I'd need proof to try to collect the bounty—*try* being the operative word. Without fangs in a head to display, no vamp MOC had to pay me anything. Still, I sent the pics to Big H's Clan home, and to Bruiser, Leo's right-hand blood meal, with a text about vamps who were resistant to silver. It seemed like something that the MOC of the entire Southeast USA should know.

Eli jutted his chin back the way we had come, and this time I followed him. When we got to the SUV, it was sitting there in the small space between the hay shed and the tree line, four doors open, engine off, keys in the ignition. Eli had disabled the interior lights long ago, so the interior was dark. Eli crawled underneath—I guess to look for bombs—while I checked under the hood and sniffed for anything odd, but, really, neither of us expected to find anything. Our expectations satisfied, we climbed inside and closed the doors, and Eli handed me the shotgun. Tonight had given the old saying "riding shotgun," new meaning. I lowered the windows and pointed the muzzle out at the night. Eli started the engine and drove us home. We didn't say a word on the remainder of the trip. Not one.

He swung the SUV into the guest-parking space and cut the engine. We sat there, listening to the engine cool down, hearing night birds hoot and sing. Watching through the windows of Esmee's house as the Kid walked through the rooms, his head bent over an electronic tablet, hair hanging down in scraggly curls, his face illuminated by bluish light. "My brother has absolutely no sense of self-preservation or survival instinct," Eli said. "He has no idea we're out here. We could be silver-eating, flesh-regenerating, vampire zombies, and when we busted through the door to eat his brilliant brain, he'd look up and say, 'Huh?'" When I didn't respond, he said, "What *were* those things?"

"I don't know. They didn't talk that I heard. You?" I asked. Eli shook his head. "They didn't make the popping sounds that vamps make when they move fast. They just flowed, like water." Eli tilted his head in agreement. "And I never ever saw a vamp move like it was half spider, half lizard, half wild hog," I said, knowing my math was totally wrong—but was also totally right. "And I think I saw one actually flying."

"Jumping. He jumped into the tree beside you and jumped between the branches right at you. Good shot, by the way."

"You're sure the shotgun was loaded with vamp rounds?" I said, not doubting, but needing to be certain.

"I stole them from you. So yes."

I made a *humph* sound. Broke open the shotgun and removed the fresh rounds. In the feeble light, I determined that they were indeed my rounds, hand-loaded with silver fléchettes by a gun nut pal in North Carolina. I dumped them into the bag with the others.

We could have gone inside. We should have gone in. But we sat in the SUV, night air moving through, chilled and damp. I started to speak, but Eli beat me to it.

"We need to find a way to kill silver-eating, flesh-regenerating vampire zombies." His brow crinkled. "They weren't zombies. Were they?"

"No. They were vamps. But they were a different kind of vamp. I informed Bruiser. Maybe he'll know something."

"Maybe." He opened his door, and I followed Eli Younger into the bed-and-breakfast, to discover that our problems of the night were only just beginning.

Jameson met us in the foyer, hands on his hips and a frown on his face. "Where is she?" he demanded.

"Who?" we both said.

"Esmee." His eyes widened and he dropped his arms. "She didn't meet you?" I could smell his alarm over the stink of gunfire that clung to us. At our puzzled expressions, he fished a key out of his shirt pocket and opened the door of an inlaid cabinet to reveal a gun safe. Four empty spaces showed where weapons had once hung. He scrubbed his face with one hand. "Beau is going to kill me."

"She took guns?" I said. And then I understood, putting together all of Esmee's earlier comments about killing things. "She's gone to hunt vamps."

"Most likely with two of her less-than-civilized, less-than-refined, uneducated neighbors. She left just after you did, claiming that you had asked her to introduce you to the mayor as part of your research and that you were sending a car for her. But I would bet a month's pay that Buddy and Bubba picked her up, and I doubt that those two even know that we have a mayor."

"Buddy and Bubba?" Eli said with a half-lifted brow. Everything the man did was low energy, the barest minimum of motion and muscle needed to accomplish the deed or indicate the emotion.

"Twins. They share a defective brain between them, and they have been taking Esmee for target practice on the back forty." He stood, and it was the first time I had ever seen Jameson without his apron. He was awfully buff for a hash slinger. Middle-aged, but in good shape.

"You double as security for Esmee," I stated.

"Yes. Her sons, Beau and Gordon, hired us. My wife is a licensed practical nurse. We take care of Esmee. She said you sent a car for her, or I'd have driven her into town."

"Does she have a cell phone? We can trace it. Maybe use it to track her."

"Already did," the Kid said from the next room. "Sending coordinates to your cells, with an overlay of nearby streets. Her position is constantly changing, and right now she's off road."

"The twins have off-road vehicles. Those small four-wheel-drive things," Jameson said.

"ATVs," Eli supplied.

"We'll bring her back," I said, racing up the stairs. "I have to change." I needed armor and my M4. It was a far better weapon in a firefight than Eli's shotgun or my semiautomatics.

Eli was tight on my heels, our feet loud on the old wooden stairs. "I have something that might make a difference with the silver-resistant vampires," he said at my shoulder.

"Rocket launcher?" I asked, remembering the head of the only vamp I had killed tonight.

"Something like that."

Sighing, I entered my room to discover that someone had unpacked my things. My few clothes and armor were hanging in the closet, and my toiletries were on the bath cabinet. I wasn't used to life with servants.

I changed into vamp-hunting clothes: combat boots, and motorcycle-style armored leather pants and jacket over

fleece to keep me warm. I double-checked the placement of
the removable, padded-armor pieces and made sure my
weapons were in snug and the M4 was loaded with seven
silver vamp-killing rounds. Way better than Eli's two-load.
I slid the weapon in and out of its harness several times. I
didn't want it hanging up when it was needed; that kind of
thing was the difference between life and death. I added
another handgun to the three I already carried and slid a
small derringer into a boot. Lastly, I rearranged the hair-
stick stakes in my bun and grimaced at the pain. I had
banged my head on the roof of the SUV and stabbed myself. Dumb. I could smell my own blood, which I hadn't noticed until now. I didn't have time to shift into Beast and
heal, and there was no way to bind the scratches. I was going to be a calling card to every vamp in town, but there was
no help for it. I didn't bother to check myself out in the
mirror. I wasn't going to a fashion show.

Four minutes after I entered my room, I was back at the
front door. Eli was waiting and his hands were empty, but
he had a huge grin on his face, or as much of a grin as he
ever had, meaning that the flesh around his eyes was faintly
crinkled. "Where's your toy?" I asked.

He lifted the corner of his jacket. In a small holster at his
side was a tiny folding weapon. "A Magpul FMG-9."

"Specifics," I requested, holding out a hand. Almost rev-
erently, Eli removed the small gun and passed it to me. "A
buddy got it for me. It's a 2008 prototype for a new genera-
tion of folding submachine gun."

It was made from a lightweight polymer material, not
metal, making it very light and easy to carry. It was well balanced for a sub gun, and small enough to fit in the back
pocket of most dress pants. Only a passionate gun lover
would think it was pretty, but I could see the purpose and
function. It was a gun made to kill people. Like the folding
machine guns carried by Big H's security goons, it was perfect for concealed carry and could be disguised in a small
bag or package. I removed the magazine and looked my
question at Eli.

"It was developed for the Secret Service for personal-
protection details," Eli said, "but it's not in mass production
yet. It uses the semiautomatic firing mechanism from a
nine-mil Glock 17 pistol, but mine is modified to use a

Glock 18 machine-pistol mechanism. It is practically jam free, and—"

"Meaning it's a nine-mil, fully automatic weapon," I said. "And totally illegal."

He handed me a headset with a mic. "Let's go."

From the breakfast room the Kid said, "They're on the move. Keep your com units on and I'll update you. Right now it looks like they're heading back into town. Ten bucks says it isn't to meet you at the mayor's." He looked up from his laptop screen at his brother and took us both in as we rushed by. "I guess it's too much to ask you to take me."

Eli reached out and ruffled his brother's hair. "You guess right, kid. Later."

"I'm not a kid," he muttered, sounding disgusted.

CHAPTER 6

And Me Holding Only Ash

"I've lost them. She turned off her phone," the Kid said, his voice crisp and clear over the headset. We were on Broadway Street, coming up on Cock of the Walk, and Eli slowed.

"Show me her last coordinates," I said. When they popped up on my cell, I said, "They went Under the Hill. Send us maps of the place."

Esmee had disappeared on the lowest street, a narrow lane unimaginatively called Water Street. It was bounded on the west by the Mississippi River and on the east by the towering bluff on which Natchez sat. Warehouses, wharves, and main shops on Water Street stood on pilings, some jutting far out over the murky, lapping Mississippi. As in earlier days, many of the Under the Hill businesses were legitimate: a saloon called the Silver Street, Ltd., the River Boat Gift Shop, the Cock of the Walk, and the Natchez Landing. But others had very different reputations—places where vamps trolled for fresh dinner when they were feeling frisky and adventurous, or where newly freed vamps looked for their first blood-servants. In some back rooms were trapdoors, presumably leading to storage, though rumors had persisted for decades that they had other, more sinister uses, such as for holding pens for kidnap victims or ways to dispose of bodies. Reports claimed that these were locales where beautiful women or boys were drugged and dumped through trapdoors until they were disappeared into the lucrative sex trade, or were turned over to less-than-savory vamp masters. Or were dumped after being drained.

We eased our way down the hill, looking for anything that might clue us in to Esmee and her redneck hunting buddies.

"Esmee's cell-phone locator vanished at Silandre's Saloon," the Kid said over the com gear.

"Details," Eli said. We could hear keys tapping in the background.

"SS has been open for nearly a hundred years, in one guise or another," the Kid said. "And now that it's no secret Silandre's a vamp, it's clear that she owned the place since its original opening, just after the earthquake."

"She's not on our kill list. Is she?" I asked.

"Nope. Uh, negative," the Kid said, and Eli's lips twitched at his brother's attempt to sound military. "This totally sucks," he added. "Silandre is known to have a hot temper and to not take kindly to strangers." He paused as he pulled up more research. "Aaaaaand she's a special friend of Hieronymus."

"Well, that complicates matters," I said. "Betcha big money H won't give me permission to go in after Esmee, blades slinging." Eli watched me out of the corner of his eye. I blew out a ticked-off breath. "Therefore, I need to go over his head." At which Eli smiled, that annoying twitch of his lips.

"Kid," I said into the headset, "send your brother pics of Silandre and her scions and blood-servants."

"Copy," the Kid said. "On the way. Now."

Reluctantly, I dialed Bruiser, Leo Pellissier's *real* Enforcer and right-hand meal. And the blood-servant who had betrayed me. Holding that thought firmly in mind, I ignored that my heart did a little backflip when he answered, "Jane."

Deep inside, Beast leaped to her feet and stared out at the world. It was just my name, but the way he said it sent tremors through her, and therefore through me, that settled into my belly with a liquid heat. Beast started to purr with delight. Which was all so very, very unfair. Because of her, my body was a traitor to the man who had handed me over for the violation of forced feeding and binding. I needed to hate him with a white-hot passion, but Beast's binding to

Leo also made her want Bruiser even more. My life was so horribly messed up.

"How are you?" he asked.

I shoved down on Beast's autonomous reaction and managed to sound businesslike. "Bruiser. I'm good." *No thanks to you,* I thought.

"I certainly expect so."

I ignored that. "I need help." He took a slow breath and I shook my head, saying flatly, "Not that kind of help."

"Reading my mind, little sweetheart?" Bruiser was one of few men who could reasonably call me little; he was six-four to my six feet even.

"Not psychic, Bruiser. And it's business, not personal."

"If the help is for Hieronymus, Leo has forbid me to help you unless you give me excellent reasons. Do you wish to barter for my services?" He sounded so British at times like this, when he was flirting, or when he was angry.

"No." I knew what Bruiser would barter for, and my bedroom services were not going to be used as payment, no matter how much fun Beast thought that might be. "I have a missing octogenarian human female, last see near Silandre's Saloon. She's vampire hunting."

"Silandre . . . Silandre. Oh. Yes," he said as the name found its place in his memory and the relationships, political and romantic, sorted themselves out in his brain. "Hmmm." His tone changed, sounding uneasy. I let him think about it all for a moment as Eli studied the streets, keeping watch. "If this grandmother has staked Silandre," he said, "there will be political repercussions. But if the grandmother is disappeared or drained," he said, "that would reflect badly on Hieronymus and therefore eventually on Leo. So as the MOC's primo, it behooves me to assist, even against his express command. You are tricky, Little Janie."

"I'm learning."

"I will make a call and see if I can provide you with access."

"Thanks. And while you're at it, Big H and about twenty of his scions have the vamp plague. I'm going to give them treatment."

The light-and-playful tone disappeared. "Leo will not be pleased."

"He pays me to protect him from dangers, and the way I

see it, part of that includes danger to his reputation and his public image. An image that will suffer if vamps in his territories start spreading the plague. So tell him I said to get off his blood-sucking ass and negotiate a parley with Hieronymus." I started to hang up, but stopped midthumb and said, "We'll be at Silandre's Saloon in ten minutes." Then I disconnected the call, and heard Eli's quiet laughter.

"When are you going to give the guy a break," he asked, and spoiled it by adding, "and jump in the sack with him?"

The Kid sniggered into the headset.

Men. I didn't answer, and Eli handed me his cell with pics of our prey displayed, as he eased back into traffic and down the hill.

The bluff on which Natchez sat was huge, and the road zigged and zagged and curled and twisted and dropped—like something Dr. Seuss might have imagined in a book titled *The Cat in the Hat Drinks Blood.* It was definitely interesting. While atop the bluff everything was high-class, the preserved remnants of plantation owners' slave-labor past, while along the drop to the Mississippi it was something else entirely. Not that it wasn't old—a lot of it was really old—but it was a mishmash of styles and colors and building materials, many unrestored, unpainted, and unrefinished, dives that hadn't seen a hammer or nail or paintbrush in a hundred years sat right next to cute, well-maintained cottages, some with dream catchers hanging in windows or pentagrams and witch circles in backyards, and even stained-glass windows rather than clear glass. Bare dirt yards and sullen, chained dogs were separated from tiny lush gardens by picket fences, gardens that should have been winter gray but were brilliant with winter flowers, demonstrating the hand of an earth witch with her classical green thumb. Saloons were five feet from old-fashioned banks. A white-painted chapel with a tall, slender steeple was across the street from what looked like a yurt with a hand-painted sign advertising PALM READING and YOUR FUTURE READ BY A DIVINER, with a note to bring your own chicken or goat, presumably for sacrifice. My house mother would have had apoplexy. Beast was having a ball with the scents, and I stuck my head out the window to give her better access.

Blood and vamp—lots of vamp scents—and witch and

human and water, water everywhere. Meat cooking and the smell of milk, goats, dogs, and house cats, mold and flowers and growing things.

Eli pulled past a white-painted, narrow, shotgun-style house and idled the SUV while we studied the facade through the back window. "You're kidding, right?" I asked. Even in the uncertain light, the building was not what I'd have thought a vamp saloon would look like. The house had dark fuchsia shutters and elaborate fuchsia gingerbread at every eave and all over the tiny front porch. A pink front door, with a brass doorknob and knocker, was centered on the porch, and a pink wreath with pink bows hung in the middle of it. The yard was planted with pink-flowering sasanqua bushes. And, honest to God, there were a dozen plastic pink flamingos in the minuscule patch of grass.

"This is supposed to be a saloon, and the vamp is supposed to be a badass?" Eli deadpanned.

"The pink is camouflage?"

We both snorted. The bright and innocent color scheme could also mean that Silandre's mental state had shifted, a polite way of suggesting that she was no longer completely sane. But there were two ATVs pulled to the side of the narrow road, and in one was a leather Gucci bag, metal buckles reflecting the moonlight. The sight made my mouth tighten in worry.

The building was three times as deep as it was wide, maybe more, with a back corner hanging high over the water, propped on stilts that looked new, as if the Mississippi had taken out the building's foundation in some flood and it had been replaced. It didn't look very reliable, more like a stiff breeze or a good rain could take it down.

"Typical Jane Yellowrock entrance?" Eli said. At my questioning glance he said, "Seat of our pants, weapons ready, shoot anything fanged that moves?"

"If he gives us a go-ahead, yeah. That." My phone vibrated, and it was Bruiser. I opened it and said, "Jane."

"You are difficult," Leo said, using the captivating tone they employ when they go after free-roaming prey. "Most cats are."

Beast sat up and stared out through my eyes at the cell.

I pulled my gaze back to the house as a light came on inside. "I do try," I said.

"My George has explained what you are doing and why, and though you deserve punishment for going beyond my wishes, I will allow you the latitude to pursue this in your own way. For now. I approve your desire to approach Silandre and deal with whatever events may be transpiring—and their ramifications. My George will call Hieronymus' primo and inform him of my decision."

"Thanks," I closed the cell and put it in a pocket, "for letting me take the heat."

"Problems in blood-drinking paradise?" Eli asked.

"Always. We have access to Silandre," I said. "Let's go before the fanged monster changes his mind and gives her a call with orders to kill us instead."

"You like to yank *his* chain too," Eli said, holding up his cell phone so I could see the photos. "One redheaded beauty coming up." Silandre was a classically beautiful woman with scarlet hair, according to the photo on her driver's license, sent by Alex. Which was just too weird— vamps with driver's licenses.

Together we exited the SUV and moved quickly to the front door of Silandre's. Eli had his little deadly toy in the crook of one arm, but since this was ostensibly a visit by Leo's Enforcer, I left my weapons holstered, going for rep, street cred, and moxie over bullets. I didn't bother to use the knocker; just turned the knob and entered. It wasn't locked.

Knickknacks met my eyes everywhere I looked, kitsch down the ages, salt and pepper shakers, boats in bottles, and hundreds of dolls, most of them the collector's porcelain type about eighteen inches tall, wearing hoop skirts or evening gowns, with real hair and perfect painted faces. And fangs. Collector's dolls with fangs. I just shook my head.

There were Tiffany lamps, tassels, rocking chairs, piles of silk pillows, fanged stuffed animals, and everything had price tags hanging on them. Silandre's Saloon had been converted into Silandre's Shoppe. The smells were nearly overwhelming: scented candles, dried herbs, potpourri, popcorn, vodka, and blood. The dried herbs were mixed vamp; the blood was human. I tensed, hearing a gurgle from ahead in the depths of the shop. No one was screaming, no one was fighting; whatever was happening was obscured and muted by all the stuff in the building.

The room was maybe eighteen feet wide—the width of the house—with narrow windows down each side in rows like in a church. From what I could see, which wasn't much, the building was at least sixty feet long. Shotgun style for real. From somewhere ahead, a phone rang with an old-fashioned, tinny sound. The gurgling got louder and took on a gasping rasp.

I pulled two ash stakes and moved down the aisles between all the stuff. I could immobilize with ash, keeping the vamp alive for questioning. Or whatever. Or I used to be able to do that, before vamps changed into the things we'd fought in the trees. And me holding only ash. Rethinking, I replaced the stakes with vamp-killers. With Eli covering my back, I stepped into the second room. This room was painted in the same garish pink as the trim on the house and it was full of handmade quilts hanging everywhere, in every kind of fabric: silks, satins, wools, even flannel, many in what were probably traditional patterns, others in modern scenic patterns—whales and dolphins cavorted next to angels and trees of life and pentagrams. This room was short, with an old-fashioned fridge and stove in one corner and a closed door in the other marked RESTROOM, in hot pink, of course.

The gurgler just ahead started to moan, a rhythmic, pained sound, and the scent of human fear added to the stench riding over the perfumed air. My cell buzzed. I ignored it and sped ahead, into the last room. I took in the details fast.

It was lit with candles on every surface and was decorated in white and pink, with a Victorian four-poster in the middle of the floor space. The linens were thrown back and mussed, as if it had been used recently, but the bed was empty. There were silk and tasseled ottomans and dainty chairs and more dolls on shelves. The windows were covered with modern, sunlight-blocking shutters, but the back door was open, letting in the night and the sound of the Mississippi skirling past. Against the back wall of the feminine bedroom, beside the propped door, two humans stood, each with black bags over their heads, hands behind their backs, as if they were lined up for a firing squad. Judging by the clothes and stature, the one on the left was Esmee.

Four vamps stood at parade rest, two on either side of the humans, all male, wearing powdered wigs and those weird clothes they wore way back when, with stockings and big buckles on platform shoes, and padded shorts. Vamped out, with blacker-than-black eyes and fangs just a bit over an inch long, which identified them as young vamps, easy to kill.

The details merged into a deadly whole. I was already moving as I took in the final particulars and bloody minutiae.

On a chaise longue lay a female vamp wearing a scarlet dress the exact shade of her hair and of the blood that smeared her red lips. In her lap was a human, blood drunk, his head lolling, his camo fatigues open to the waist, exposing his hairy belly and unshaven neck and face. Blood poured in a steady stream from his neck, which had to be deliberate. Vamp saliva was both healing and a constrictor, causing blood vessels to close and skin to tighten, stopping bleeding almost as soon as a vamp withdrew her fangs. The human was breathing, but his pulse, visible from the way his head and neck were extended, was too rapid, and he was pale. She had taken too much, too fast. The vamp's head snapped up and she met my gaze.

As my arm swung back, the blade catching the candle-light, I recognized Silandre from her photo, her hair the color of a sunset before a storm, eyes the blue of hyacinths. In her photograph, her skin had been the white of a corpse, blue veins visible beneath its pale surface, but was now pink and flushed. She had been drinking her fill. Whatever she had been before and whether she was on Hieronymus' list or not, Silandre was now a Naturaleza. She hissed at me like a cat, and I realized she was also totally nutso. *Crap*. The crazy ones were always the worst.

I slashed forward.

In one of those faster-than-possible moves, Silandre tossed the body at me. Into the path of my blade. I spun, dodging the flying human. Silandre rose to her feet, eyes vamped out, her lips curling in a snarl, revealing bloody, two-inch fangs. Her bodyguards attacked. Knowing I would be too slow, I continued my spin, blades out to my sides. As we all moved, Eli shot, the clatter of his weapon ripping into the air. Time slowed and shifted, and I saw the bodies of the guards to my left fall. The ones on my right reached me, slipping past my knives. Instinct made me leap to the side and down, rolling, scissoring my legs. I cut behind the knees of both bodyguards and rolled again. The gun clattered. Herbal-scented blood splattered me. Both vamps fell. Heads mostly gone from the automatic fire, hamstrings severed. I pivoted to my feet.

A flash of scarlet caught my eye at the open door. Silandre fleeing. Eli followed her while I bent over the human on the floor. He was still breathing. I raced to the back wall, pulled the black bag off Esmee's head, and ran a short blade through her bonds. Her arms fell limply to her sides and she dropped to her knees. Just as the vamps on the floor started to struggle.

"Stay put!" I shouted to Esmee, my own voice lost beneath the roar in my ears. I dropped my bloody knives on the bed and pulled an eighteen-inch blade, effectively a short sword. Picking the vamp who seemed the most lively, I shoved him flat on the floor with my booted foot. Raised the vamp-killer over my head and brought it down. Hard. It's a lot more difficult to behead someone with a sword than most people think. Sometimes it's more like chopping wood with a dull steak knife. It was a lucky strike, because his head rolled cleanly away, gallons of fresh blood gouting from the stump, a lot more than usual in vamp kills.

Rogue vamps, Naturaleza vamps, uncured vamps still in the devoveo, and crazy vamps murder humans. I get paid to kill them for it. So I've become somewhat of an expert at head lopping.

I stepped across his body to the next one, prepared to repeat the measure. The vamp struggled on the floor and got one arm beneath him, pushing to rise. On the vamp's chest were a line of holes; the stink of silver and vamp blood reached me. Eli had used silver rounds and, just like the vamps in the woods earlier, the silver hadn't stopped the vamps any better than lead.

My partner stepped back inside and shouted, "She's gone. Down the scaffolding to the water." Which was not what I wanted to hear.

I beheaded the second vamp and moved to the others as

vamp blood gushed across the floor in spreading pools, staining the white rugs. The third vamp didn't want to die, and despite the silver in his blood, he grabbed the handle of the sword as I brought it down. I didn't have to be able to hear to know he was growling. His fangs slashed at my ankle, and I kicked forward, breaking a fang with a snap that reverberated up my leg, into my spine. Fangs were hard. When his head snapped back, I struck down and again. And again. Until he was in two parts. The fourth vamp was fully awake by then and I realized I had made a crucial mistake. He came at me.

CHAPTER 7

Sheet Creases on His Left Cheek

I raised the bloody, silvered vamp-killer. Before I could bring it down, Eli emptied his gun into the vamp's chest. Which disintegrated like a watermelon at a shooting demonstration. It was easy work thereafter to pin him to the floor with my blade. I stood over the vamp corpse, breathing heavily. He wasn't moving and he might even be true-dead, but I wasn't betting on it.

Eli touched my shoulder to get my attention and motioned to the vamp, then tapped his own neck with the edge of his hand, asking me why I hadn't beheaded him. We were still deaf from the weapon fire and I mouthed, *Prisoner. To question.* Eli frowned as if he didn't think that was such a good idea and started checking over the injured humans, freeing the last one. Actually, I didn't think it was a good idea either, but I needed info on the Naturaleza, and one of Silandre's goons might give it to me.

While Eli made sure Esmee was okay and led her to the doorway of the room, I texted Big H's primo for three things: a silver vamp cage, and to send a cleanup crew to the house and another one to the woods where we had left the other body. Vamps didn't want medical professionals to have access to vamp bodies, blood, or genetic material. Until recently, even Homeland Security hadn't gotten hold of a true-dead vamp corpse, but on my last visit to Natchez, we had left so many lying around that I figured at least one vamp had gone missing and into their clutches. Rick had been on scene so it stood to reason that some giddy government forensic anthropologists and pathologists had carved one up. Not that I had mentioned that to Leo yet. I was getting smarter. I also texted the Kid to tell him we had Esmee and that she was unhurt.

Esmee tapped my arm and I jumped. I had gotten so busy texting that I'd forgotten to keep aware of my surroundings. Not smart. I was getting too dependent on Eli for backup. I put my phone away and led the tiny older woman outside. It was testament to the political power of the vamps Under the Hill—or to Bruiser and Leo's helpful interference—that no sirens had sounded despite the gunfire. I put her in the backseat of the SUV, where she sat, silent, staring down at her wrists. Though my ears were still ringing and hers had to be even worse, I tapped her wrist above where it had been abraded by the rope that had bound her.

Esmee shook her head and lifted it, meeting my eyes. I half read her lips when she said, "I nearly got those boys killed."

I knew about guilt. I knew about guilt that was richly deserved and guilt that was misplaced, and this guilt fell into both categories. "Miss Esmee, what you three did was utterly crazy. You three, Eli, and I could have died tonight because of your ill-conceived and ill-thought-out vamp-hunting plan. But unless you held a gun to their heads and forced them to dress in camouflage, loaded their guns against their wills, and then drove them here under threat of death, you are not ultimately responsible for the actions or the current state of health of two grown men."

"I should have known better." She stroked her wrist and flinched at a tender place. "I never saw a vampire move so fast. I didn't know they could do that. I thought we'd just bust in and shoot 'em and rescue some of the missing humans. Case closed. But there weren't any humans there. The men vampires reached out and took our guns like we were babies. Just plucked them away." She shook her head, her eyes swimming with tears. "We were tied up so fast. And we could hear Bubba crying." She blotted her cheek. "Is he going to die?"

I looked at Eli coming through the door, Bubba's arm around his shoulders, the anemic man being half carried. I got out and watched as Buddy and Eli helped the injured man into the backseat. "I think he'll live," I said, closing the door. "He probably needs a transfusion."

"I ain't gonna take no blood," Bubba said, his lips blue and his head lolling. "I might get some gay man's blood and turn into an abominable and go to hell."

Eli's brows went up and I turned so no one could see my grin. "I think he means an abomination, and I also think he thinks being gay is contagious."

"Our preacher says it can be spread just like any other disease," Buddy said.

"Your preacher a doctor?" Eli asked, and started the engine, leaving it running with the heater on full. "No. Your preacher's an idiot."

"No blood," Bubba said.

"And you're an idiot too. But have it your way." Eli went around to the back of the SUV and tossed me a bag. I caught it, surprised at the weight. "Silver restraints for your captive."

I grinned and went through the house to the bloody bedroom in back. I might be becoming too dependent on him, but it was great to have a partner who could read my mind. The room was splattered with vamp blood, the once-white carpet saturated, as were the walls, the bedspread, and the kitsch for sale.

My vamp captive was unmoving. He should be true-dead. He didn't have much left where his chest used to be, and silver to a vamp's heart should have killed him. Even if his maker had been a thousand-year-old master and poured his powerful blood into the vamp's mouth the instant he fell, the silver should have killed him. That much silver and that much blood and tissue loss should have killed any vamp of any age, and the only way he should have survived was if he was buried with the commingled blood of all the nearby clans. Or just buried, and maybe—not likely, but maybe—he might rise three days later as a revenant. I'd never had to kill a revenant, but it was reputed to be messy, bloody work. Revenants and young, uncured vamps were where the myth of zombies came from. I remembered the way the vamps had moved in the dark, under the trees. Though the vamp should be dead, as I stood over him I could actually see the tissue of his chest grow out, healing.

Even revenants didn't heal like that. I was getting a bad feeling about all this.

I dumped Eli's bag of supplies onto the bed and discovered silver handcuffs with silver spikes on the inside and outside. Ankle cuffs made the same way. A neck cuff was included, and maybe it was being surrounded by the remembrances of slavery in this lovely little town, but the collar reminded me of the collars slaves used to wear. This one was silver and spiked, and a metal handle came out of the side to better control the captive.

Shoving away my disgust, I clapped the restraints on the vamp, wrapping Eli's silver chain through the ankles and wrists, and then pulled tight so the vamp was curled up and fastened in the fetal position. Last, in spite of my revulsion, I applied the handled neck collar, because if he came to on the ride home, that could be deadly. I removed my vamp-killer from his shoulder, cleaned all three blades on the bed-spread, and sheathed them.

In the bathroom, I ripped down the shower curtain—pink, of course—and lay it in the doorway. Then I used the collar handle to roll the vamp in the plastic. With the mess and gore contained, I dragged him across the room, through the house and outside, where Eli and I manhandled him (*vamp-handled him?* I wondered grimly) into the back of the SUV, and got in the front seat. Eli swung the SUV into a five-point turn and gunned the vehicle back up the bluff as we started home.

"Hey. What about our ATV?" Buddy asked.

"I'll see you get home. You can get your ATV when you can both walk under your own power." Eli added, "Make sure your brother drinks a lot of fluids, and none of it beer or shine or wine or malt liquor or regular liquor. Get him some Gatorade. Feed him liver for the next three months or so."

One of the men gagged but no one replied, and the ride to the boys' single-wide trailer was made in silence except for monosyllabic directions. We were met by four pit bulls chained to trees in the bare-dirt front yard. A rusted red pickup truck was up on blocks near the front door, a dis-used chicken coop was to the left of the trailer, and a patch of what looked suspiciously like marijuana and turnip greens growing together was to the right. Everything was lit like the noonday sun by two security lights, bright enough to see that the front door was open and the trailer was missing several windows, the holes blocked by grocery bags and duct tape. Eli helped the men inside, and Esmee and I waited in the safety of the SUV.

When Eli got back in, he said, "Those two boys are one match away from a bonfire or an explosion. They're living on borrowed time."

"How so?" Esmee asked.

But Eli just shook his head and spun the wheel into the night. I caught a whiff of something like ether and I swiveled my head back to the trailer. Ether was often used to make methamphetamines. *Great.* Esmee was friends with idiots who aspired to be drug lords.

"Where do you want to keep our fanghead guest?" Eli asked.

"Big H should be sending a silver vamp cage to Esmee's." Even as I said the words, a car pulled up beside us and a vamp rolled down the passenger's window, flashing us some fang and waving before easing in behind us to follow us back to the B and B. Eli laughed, a breathy sound, part amazement, part disbelief, and shook his head.

We were met back at the house by a stranger standing on the front porch. "Oh, dear," Esmee breathed when she caught sight of him in the headlights.

"Your son?" I asked.

"Yes. That tattletale Jameson must have called him." Her tone didn't portend good things for the chef-cum-bodyguard.

She opened the door and slid to the ground the instant the SUV rocked to a halt. I figured she would slink up to him and take a tongue lashing. Instead she squared her shoulders and stormed up to the man. "Gordon. You will mind your manners. If you open your mouth for so much as *one word* of condemnation or one of your legal-based tongue lashings, I will rewrite my will and leave everything to Jane Yellowrock." She stormed past him and inside, slamming the door.

"Oh, crap," I said. Eli burst out laughing. I followed Esmee to the front door and the steely-eyed man there. Before he could open his mouth and take out his ire on me, I said, "I don't want her money. I don't want your money. I am not responsible for her chasing out after the vamps. She went with—"

"Her vulgar druggie friends."

"Yes. And they won't be taking her anywhere anytime soon."

Gordon, a fair-haired, blue-eyed man wearing a dress shirt and dress pants under a tailored wool jacket, lifted his chin. "And why might that be?"

"Because by his symptoms," Eli said, coming up behind me, "one lost about half his blood supply, and he won't feel up to hunting anytime soon. Their transportation is still parked Under the Hill. And we have the boys' weapons." Instead of going to the hatch, which would have exposed the bloody pink shower curtain to the world, he opened the back passenger's door and reached behind the seat to lift three shotguns, broken open so they wouldn't fire, and four handguns, all of their magazines missing. "From the quality, I assume that these are your mother's?" He handed over a shotgun, a rifle, and two handguns to Esmee's son.

"Good lord. She's gone bonkers."

"No," I said. "She's just bored. When's the last time *you* took her shooting or fishing or shopping?" I made it more of an accusation than a question, and followed it up with a left hook. "Big, fancy lawyer hands off his mother to the help and then wonders why she acts out? Spend some time with her other than holidays, and maybe she'll stop." I grabbed the vamp med kit that had somehow survived the hellish night and set it inside the house door.

"I'm not a practicing lawyer," Gordon said. "I'm a judge."

"*That's* what you heard out of what I just said?"

Behind me, I could hear Eli's soft laughter. "Still," he said. "The lady has a point."

"Humph," I said, and thought, *Lady? Me?* I went back outside and met the vamps just getting out of the car that had followed us. I waved them back into their older-model Caddy, saying, "In back, in the garage. Eli, will you bring the car around?" Gordon stood on the front porch, looking nonplussed. I had the feeling he wasn't used to being ignored in his mother's home. I also had the feeling that he would have a lot to say about a vamp being kept caged in the garage, so I wasn't going to tell him.

In minutes we were in the garage, the delivery vamps

standing back, watching, as we worked to assemble the silver cage, which was bigger than the ones I'd seen in Leo's city, bigger and woven with silver-tipped barbed wire. Ingenious and horrific, and the pointy bits had traces of dried blood on them that I could smell. I removed the silver chains in which I'd bound the injured vamp, and Eli tossed him inside. I locked the cage shut.

"He true-dead, he is," one vamp said, sounding very Cajun. He was wearing a searing-bright lime green shirt, bright enough to reflect the moon. Big H's vamps were nothing like Leo's, style-wise. "Why you cage him?"

"No one wit'stand dat much silver," the other one said, tucking his long blond hair back behind both ears. "Him come back rev'nat, two, tree day from now, you don' take his head."

"That's the usual way," I agreed. "But this fanghe—vamp is coming back alive. Or undead. Whatever. He's healing." I pointed to the fresh flesh on his ribs. "Half an hour ago, he didn't have ribs. Now he has skin over a rib cage and organs inside it."

The vamps leaned in and studied the prisoner. "Him smell wrong, he do," Blondie said.

"Stink, he do," Limey said. "Like smell of poison and rot in ground and blood magic. Like dem new vamps brought by dat de Allyon, what come and try to take over Hieronymus' territory."

"Different kind vamps, dey was," Blondie said.

"Yeah," I said. "About those different kinds of vamp. Did de Allyon actually come to Natchez himself, or did he send an intermediary?"

"Hem come," Limey said, sounding disgusted.

Blondie snorted. "Hieronymus be sick wit dat vamp plague, or de Allyon not take over."

"Hem and he humans go first to Hieronymus, invade his sleeping lair, place what should be secret but he know it," Limey said, making sure I understood that it had been an inside job. "De Allyon come out in charge, big man, act like king wit he queens on he arms."

"Den dey tell us Fame Vexatum is ended and humans is prey again, to take and drain and kill. Our priest say no, and de Allyon kill him."

My ears perked up. *Priest?* But before I could ask, they

went on, and because they were so chatty, I didn't want to derail them with my curiosity.

"We call Leo Pellissier in New Orleans for help, we did," Limey said. "And we wait."

I opened my mouth and closed it fast. *More hinky.* Either the disloyal vamps in Leo's camp hid the call for help or . . . or Leo refused it.

"De Allyon, hem bring twenty Naturaleza wit him," Blondie said. "Twenty is like forty of us. Maybe sixty. Dey kill . . . Dey kill seventeen of us dat first day, true-dead."

"And when Leo not answer, we go into hiding." Limey spat to the side to show his disgust. It landed on the garage floor with a soft *splat* of loathing. "Politics is what dat was. Hem put politics before us."

"How soon after de Allyon got here did you start noticing the difference in vamps?"

Blondie made a little chuffing sound, much like Beast might make, part laughter, part loathing. "Dem Naturaleza is faster, stronger than us. But they start to crawling like bugs, only later, after *she* join him."

"She?"

Limey elbowed him. "Enough. I hear when Hieronymus tell her to call Clark. He tell her what she need to know."

"Mmmm. You ask Clark," Blondie said to me, "about dese vamps what scuttle like bugs and stink of dead earth."

I had gotten a lot more from the vamps than I had expected, so I didn't protest. Bumping the silvered cage with a toe, I said, "Smell or not, I'm hoping he'll tell me what I need to know." I frowned grimly and gestured the vamps out of Esmee's garage. As they drove off, Eli and I headed to the kitchen, following the smell of steak. I wanted to sink my teeth into a thick juicy, bloody, rare one. I spotted Jameson in the back entry and heard him murmur as I passed, "Thank you, Miss Jane, for bringing her back."

"Welcome, Jammie. Do I smell steak?"

"I have just now removed it from the grill, rare and cold in the center. And I promise not to spoil it with sautéed mushrooms or salad."

"You're a good man."

Jameson held out robes, one to Eli, one to me, thick

white, soft ones. "If you'll give me your bloody leathers, I'll see to it that they are properly cleaned."

My brows went up. "Yeah? Cool." I could get used to this. "No chemicals," I warned, sliding out of the crusty jacket. "Not even mink oil. Vamps can smell it. I usually just rinse it off and wipe it down. The blood residue confuses future vamps and gives me an edge." Eli looked at me curiously. "What?" I said.

He shook his head, dropped his jacket, and pulled down his pants zipper. I quickly faced away and pulled the robe over my shoulders before dropping my own leather pants. "The things you say," Eli said, "and the things you think about. That's all."

I had no idea what he was talking about, but I didn't really care either. I smelled steak and my stomach rumbled. Beast purred. *Food.*

After I finished a hunk of beef worthy of a king, I showered off, pulled on warm clothes, and dialed Clark. He answered with a "Miss Yellowrock?"

"Got it in one. Is it true that you called Leo when de Allyon got here and he didn't come?" The silence was long and chilled, and I realized it must have sounded like a verbal ambush with a damned-if-you-do and damned-if-you-don't reply option, so I added, "Because if you called Leo, I'll be looking into that for you."

Clark expelled a breath. "Thank you. It would be—" He stopped and rephrased. "*I* would be happier if I knew that my master was safe and not still in great danger from *politics*." He said the last word as if it was something vile, and it wasn't like I could argue.

And then it hit me. "You're wondering if I'm here to help or to harm Big H. Aren't you?" His silence was my answer and was almost enough to make me cuss. I echoed his tone and said, "I *hate politics*. You understand, Clark? I'm here to fulfill my contract with your master. And keep him alive. And restore peace to this territory. That is all. On my honor."

He breathed out again and said, softly, "Thank you."

"You're welcome." We said polite good-byes and hung up, which left me staring at the walls. What the heck had I gotten myself into? And how long before the local cops paid me a nasty visit and threatened to lock me up? Knowing I needed to get a handle on this investigation, I took Big H's kill list to bed with me.

A little after two a.m. the doorbell rang and I jerked up in bed, shoved the paperwork I'd fallen asleep reading to the floor, and yanked on clothes, seeing flashing lights in the front yard. At least three official cars and no one trying to hide who they were, which could mean a lot of things, none of them good. So much for my question about when I'd receive a visit from the local law. Downstairs, I threw my hair over my shoulder, deactivated the security system, and opened the front door to see a very unhappy member of county law enforcement. "Sheriff Turpin," I said, stopping myself from saying more when she glared at me from my bare feet to the top of my head.

Sylvia Turpin, whose family had a generations-long tradition of law enforcement in Adams County, took her job very seriously, and despite the fact that Leo had contributed a hefty sum to her election campaign, she didn't like me. I sorta understood her feelings, because the last time I was in her town, I kept her people and the city cops awfully busy at various crime scenes. "Yellowrock. I should have known." She didn't ask to come inside, but pushed past me, which I thought was against the law unless she had a warrant or probable cause. But, then, in her mind, I was likely probable cause. "Where's Gordon?"

"I'm here, Sylvia."

I looked down the hallway and saw Esmee's son, his robe floating behind him, his slippers making small *shuss*ing sounds on the wood and carpets. His hair was mussed and he had sheet creases on his left cheek. The one on his face. He was wearing jammies, so I didn't know about sheet creases on any other cheeks.

"I thought I'd be notified if she came back to town."

"I wasn't notified myself until this evening." He paused and blinked, as if still waking up. "This past evening, now. She didn't go through the agency. She called Mother directly." He slanted his eyes at me. Like he was blaming me.

"Don't look at me. I didn't call anyone. I have"—I chuffed at what I was about to say—"people for that."

Eli stepped in through the front door. He wasn't carrying his toys, but he'd been on watch. I needed to get him some backup or he'd never sleep. "Everything okay here, Miz Yellowrock?"

"Eli, meet the sheriff. Not sure you had the chance last time we were in town."

He glanced down at the petite, pretty, redheaded woman, and his eyes widened slightly. A more-than-half smile drew his lips up on both sides and exposed his teeth, an expression I was sure I'd never seen. It transformed his face. "Ma'am."

Honest to god, the lady sheriff blushed. She squared her shoulders as if she could feel the heat on her face. "I remember you. You work for Yellowrock."

"With," I said. "My company has expanded, Sheriff Turpin. He works *with* me."

"Partners of a sort," Eli clarified, his eyes holding to the sheriff's with near-predatory intensity. "Though we're still working out the kinks. And I only saw you from a distance when we were here before, ma'am." He stepped closer, his black camo muted in the dull light. "At the time I wasn't worthy of being introduced, being the hired help." He smiled down at her, his face developing a look I could only call weird. Or stupid. Or maybe insipid. Yeah. That was a good word for it.

Turpin's breath caught and heart faltered before catching a harder, faster rhythm, the kind of thing I can hear when Beast is paying close attention. She raised a hand and pushed her hair back behind an ear, the gesture out of place and puzzling. "I see. I hope you manage to keep her from causing too much trouble in my county this time."

"It's a hard job, ma'am, but someone has to do it. You have any suggestions on how I can . . . do it better?"

And then the pheromones hit it. Mating pheromones. They liked each other. A lot. That hair thing had been all girly and coy. And Eli was making goo-goo eyes back at her. Beast panted with amusement in the back of my mind, and I rolled my eyes. "Good grief," I muttered. Louder, I said, "Leo Pellissier sanctioned my presence in the county, ma'am. I should have had his primo or the Natchez MOC's primo, Clark, send a notice of my arrival. I apologize for any inconvenience I've caused."

She glanced at me, and I noted her eyes were an amazing shade of blue, brilliant against her fair skin and dark red hair, and her pupils were dilated with desire as much as with the dim light. "Have him send me notification. I understand there were some problems tonight Under the Hill. I guess you didn't think to inform local law enforcement," the sheriff said, more a statement of irritation than a question.

"Oops," I said. "Um. My bad. Sorry."

"I also got a call from Homeland Security about problems across the state line, and word that an agent is on the way. I am not happy, folks."

My heart did a fast three-beat trip before it fell. Homeland Security meant PsyLED. Which could mean Rick. Or not.

"I'll need to start the necessary paperwork for PsyLED, so who wants to give me a report about the DBs in my county?"

As part of the new ruling affecting vamp hunters— unless the courts tossed it out on appeal—paperwork was required wherever there was a hunt for rogues or Naturaleza. Because it was an expense most money-strapped states could ill afford, few places had instituted it yet, but it seemed that Mississippi and Turpin had. It made my job harder, but, then, government always made things harder.

"I'll drive into town and give a report later on today, ma'am," Eli said.

"And I'll inform the PsyLED agent we've checked in, belatedly," I said, "and get the local MOC to send you notification. Thank you, ma'am."

Grudgingly, Sylvia said to the pajamaed man who had been listening as we jockeyed for position, "While I hate to say anything nice about a bounty hunter in my county, we've received reports that Yellowrock saved your mother and two other citizens from a vampire attack. We might both want to think about that, Gordon."

To me she said, "I'd appreciate it if you warned my people when you go hunting. We have a small number of good ol' boys who think killing vampires is a nifty way to make some extra cash, and not all of them understand the difference between sane and legal vamps and the new, crazy kind. Add in a little illegal substance before they start shooting, and it's been a problem. I have four locals in lockup now with charges pending for attacking Hieronymus' people instead of the crazy ones he's licensed for bounty. Hopefully that's all of the dumb-asses, but you never know, so that warning, and open lines of communication, are paramount."

"Yes, ma'am. Hunting vamps for bounties is dangerous," I agreed. I mean, what else could I say? And the bounty was mine. I'd won the contract, so the good ol' boys needed to take a backseat. I couldn't figure out a way to say that so I kept my mouth shut. Go me.

"We've just instituted a mandatory curfew to keep the citizens safe, from sundown to dawn, but I'll add you to the list of exceptions, along with law enforcement, fire, and hospital employees. We have enough problems in this county with missing-persons reports without adding in outsiders and hunting parties."

"How many missing people?" Eli asked.

"If I count the homeless and transients, which I do, I'm looking at a little less than one-hundred twenty missing people. Missing *humans*."

I had been hoping the numbers were skewed, but Turpin was right in line with Clark. Not good. Somewhere there was an unofficial graveyard full of dead people, and maybe some devoveo and revenants who might rise. More not good. Worse, somewhere else there were likely kidnapped, penned, and tortured humans who were being drained.

"We'll call you with everything we learn, ma'am," Eli said.

Turning to him, Turpin said, "Pleasure to meet you," and handed Eli her card before she stepped down toward her car. Eli tucked it into his pocket with that odd look still on his face. The closest I could come to describing it was wonderment. *Crap*. Eli and the sheriff. And he liked her in a very carnal way, if the smells wafting from his pores were an indication. That could possibly help things, but I was betting that it would only complicate matters. We all stood staring out the front door until the three sheriff's deputy cars pulled away.

Gordon and Eli both turned to me, Gordon getting in the first words. "I apologize. I assumed you had made an end run around me and the system I set up to protect my mother. And, had you not been here tonight, Mother would have likely gone out with the brainless duo anyway and might have . . ." He stopped as the realization hit him.

"No *might*. She would have died," I stated. "You're welcome. And if someone sends an anonymous report to the sheriff, that duo could end up in jail on multiple charges for drug possession. I hate to send them to the county lockup, but that might protect your mother."

"And keep them from blowing up half the county," Eli added.

"I'll call Sylvia tomorrow," Gordon said. "Thank you again. But please take this in the spirit I intend it. When this job is finished, you aren't welcome back here."

"Got it," I said. Gordon *shush*ed into the dark. I looked at Eli, who was again holding Turpin's card like he'd won the lottery. "She's pretty," I said.

He gave me the usual quirky half smile instead of the bigger one he'd given her. "Yeah. And she likes guns. She was carrying three, an H and K nine mil under one arm, a small semi in her spine holster, and something on her ankle, under her pants."

"A match made in heaven," I said.

"Or on the shooting range. Hope she likes coffee."

"She does. Black." At his questioning look, I gave a hand shrug and said, "I smelled it on her. She's been mainlining the crappy stuff they keep in cop shops for hours." Eli grinned happily, real emotion on his dark-skinned face. The last time I'd seen that much mobility on his features, I'd just kicked his butt in the dojo. "I'll hire some backup to keep watch so you can get some sleep."

"No need. I'm good," he said. But I was sure he only half heard me. He was thinking about Sylvia again, in a most erotic way. I shook my head and went back upstairs to my bed. I had about two hours before I had to get dressed for my next meeting with Big H, and I wasn't feeling all fresh and daisyfied. I needed to be at my best when I made my next call to Leo and also when I set up the med clinic to treat the sick vamps.

I texted Clark about the legal paperwork and to ask about the unnamed *she* our Cajun fanghead had mentioned, stripped off my pants, and was climbing into bed when a knock sounded. I was marginally presentable and I covered my bare legs. "Come in."

The Kid opened the door, the hallway dark behind him, his face and white T-shirt lit with the bluish light from the laptop he was cradling. He was wearing flannel SpongeBob

SquarePants pajama bottoms, and I held in my grin. "I
found something I think you need to see," he said. He
walked into my room uninvited, flipped on the switch at the
door, which turned on the bedside light, and handed me the
laptop. An Internet file was open. "If you tell my brother,
I'll be in trouble, but I drilled into Camilla Hopkins' publisher's Web site and found this on her editor's PC."

"Drilled?" I asked. He shrugged. "Hacked is soooo yesterday," I said. He shrugged again, not making eye contact,
and pointed to the laptop.

It was a book proposal created by Misha, and it was very
different from the one I'd seen in her hotel room. Under the
section title about research on vamp blood was a new listing
of research papers, all papers written by human researchers
on vampire blood for medical research.

I skimmed down until the word jumped out at me. *Leukemia.*

The Kid said, "Several docs are proposing that vamp
blood might cure leukemia," he said.

Recently, I'd met a Cajun preacher man who claimed
that vamp blood had cured his cancer, though it had taken
a long time and a lot of blood, a debt he was still paying off
years later. I thought of Charly, her body thin and her hair
already falling out. I wasn't sure, but I thought hair didn't
fall out until later rounds of chemo. The stuff Charly was
on was pure poison, and it had only a slight chance of curing
her. But maybe mixed with vamp blood . . .

Because of her research, Misha had known vamps could
maybe offer a cure. Misha was a single mother with a
daughter who meant everything to her. Misha was desperate.

"I have a feeling that Misha's not just planning to interview vamps for her book," the Kid said, sounding worried.
"She's also trying to find a vamp who will give Charly
blood."

Which, if I'd had half a brain, I would have realized from
the moment I saw the child. I am such a dweeb about humans. Asking a vamp for blood was offensive, and humans
who were so importunate or stupid as to ask had been
known to vanish without a trace. Mish hadn't replied to my
voice mail or text about her dead contact, Ryder. I frowned
and checked my cell. Nothing.

"Another thing," the Kid said, sounding uneasy. "It might be nothing." I gave a little finger curl to continue. "Misha has a concealed-carry permit for the state. And I found a receipt on her bank card for a load of silver shot. So maybe if the vamp she was going to interview wasn't willing—"

"She might be planning to shoot him, kidnap him—or her—and force him to feed Charly," I said. "Crap." I scrubbed my hand across my head, mussing my braid. "I'll go see her after dawn. Talk her back down from this stupid plan."

"That might be a good idea. Assuming we're reading it right. But maybe we're not. Bright side and all that." The Kid picked up his laptop and backtracked through the room, turning off the lamp. "Get some sleep," he murmured, and closed my door. Like that was gonna happen.

CHAPTER 8

Makes It Easier to Stomp 'Em to Death

But I did, somehow, get two hours of catnap before my phone alarm sounded just after four a.m. I dressed in jeans and weaponed up, the movements so automatic I seldom even thought about the process anymore, and slung the medical kit with Leo's vamp-plague cure across my shoulders. I met Eli in the hallway, catching a whiff of aftershave and man.

"You think our captive is alive again?" he asked as we quietly descended to the main floor. "And sane?"

"We should check," I said, yawning.

"He'll be hungry."

I chuckled. "Kinda counting on that."

"Anyone ever tell you that you have a cruel streak?"

My step faltered, a slight hitch that I caught, hopefully before Eli noticed it.

"Not that I think that's a bad thing," he added. "Too many people are fu— freaking bleeding hearts without the guts to survive when the sh— uh, malodorous refuse hits the fan."

Cruel? Me? Beast purred, happy, while I felt . . . what? Not much of anything. Not even guilt, which was odder than I wanted to admit. I lifted a shoulder and turned through the house to the kitchen, where I opened the fridge and lifted out a raw, chilled steak. Watery blood was pooled in the corner of the zip-lock plastic, and so I grabbed a roll of paper towels and some hand sanitizer on the way out back.

Cruel. I didn't have time to deal with the accusation, and filed it away in my hind brain for later consideration. Hopefully, I had a starved Naturaleza vamp to interrogate. I could deal with the truth later. I said, "Thank you for not cursing in front of me."

"I can kill in front of you, but not curse?" He sounded amused.

I shrugged again. "We all have boundaries."

Eli pulled his shotgun around front, from where it rested like a sling on his back, opened the door to the garage, turned on the light, and stepped through, the motion gallant, the big man willing to take the hit for the little lady. Gallant but kinda stupid. I could heal from most anything with my skinwalker metabolism. Eli was human. He couldn't. Still, I appreciated the gesture.

Inside, the vamp shielded his eyes with an arm and moved through the small space where he was trapped, his body flowing weirdly, like one of those vamps in the woods. And the vision of what he looked like was suddenly there, blinking on my eyelids. He moved like one of those feathery centipedes, all long legs and bizarre body mechanics and aggression. He hissed. It was a primal sound, and Beast rose in my mind and stared out through my eyes.

I gave her control and dropped the plastic baggie to the floor. Squatting in front of the vamp's silver cage, I chuffed softly and pulled my vamp-killer. I twirled it in my hand so the silvered blade caught the light. I smelled the peculiar scent of silver-poisoned vamp, his blood on the spikes of the cage. It was sickly and slightly burned, like the studio scent of a metalworker, pickling solution and fire and heated silver, topped off by the old blood like a rancid top note on a really bad perfume. Ugly, but fascinating to Beast. She growled low in my throat, a sound no human can make.

I smiled when the vamp's eyes widened. He was Caucasian with the pale, pinkish skin of the Irish, dark hair and green eyes, handsome, as most vamps are. He was also vamped out, sclera bloodred, pupils so dilated his eyes were black, and I could smell the hunger on him. Dangerous. I widened my smile, showing blunt, human teeth and a predator's confidence.

"You should know," I said, conversationally, "that the Master of the City, Hieronymus, has put a bounty on your head. I make around forty thousand dollars if I take it to him. Separated from your body, of course." The vamp snarled. It was really effective with the fangs and all, but Beast's fangs were longer. I didn't flinch; I smiled wider, twirling the vamp-killer. The blade was fourteen inches long, the flat plated with polished sterling silver, the steel edge so sharp it could cut flesh before the human eye could even see it.

"I am hungry," he said, his fangs making it hard to understand. His ability to speak meant that he had at least one lung functioning in the hollow of his chest.

"Tough. But we can make a deal. Dinner for answers. I have questions."

He hissed at me. I shrugged. And opened the raw steak. His eyes darted to the baggie and stuck there like a fly on flypaper. "Give," he demanded, thrusting his open hand at me. "Feed me."

"Nope."

His eyes flashed back to mine, compelling. "I'm hungry, little nonhuman." It was a Southern accent, a well-bred one, with a hint of old in it.

"Don't care, little fanghead. If you want to drink anything, or even suck on the juices of this steak, you have to tell me what I want to know."

"Animal blood and meat will not nourish me."

"It's better than nothing, fanghead."

His eyes went back to the steak and his fangs clicked shut on the little hinges in his mouth. "And what is it you wish to know?"

"For starters, your name."

"Francis Adrundel, at your service."

Yep. Only one of the old ones would say *at your service*. And poor Francis was on the bounty list, good for nothing but a good beheading. He'd been eating humans, a Naturaleza, transported in by the now-true-dead vamp who had started this whole mess, Lucas Vazquez de Allyon. But at least I had Francis talking, which, as everyone in the interrogation business knows, is a necessary first step to getting your subject to tell you anything. "Age?"

"I was born in the seventh month, on the twelfth day, in the year 1820."

He was older than I expected, by nearly a hundred years.

Interesting. "How did you get here to Natchez? Did de Allyon fly you in?"

He closed his eyes and took a slow breath through his nose, scenting, smelling the blood in the bag. And maybe my blood. I'd forgotten that my scalp had taken a scratch or two. And Eli, who had shaved very recently and likely drawn blood to the surface of his skin even if he hadn't nicked himself. It was like a vamp buffet in the garage. "Answer the question," I said.

"Yes. Flight," he said, with his eyes still closed. "And the lovely place in town. And all the slaves and servants I could drink. I liked being sworn to Lucas. I like being Naturaleza here, in this town, where the humans are such easy prey." His eyes popped open and he vamped out, fastfastfast. Eyes bled wide, sclera went pale pink, and fangs dropped down on their hinges again, with a *snick* of sound. "The Naturaleza here have much power, all the power that Lucas ever dreamed of having, and more. Here we are finally free. Feed me," he commanded, his compulsion wrapping around me like a silken veil.

Beast pressed claws into my brain and flopped down in the forefront of my mind, her thick tail tip twitching slightly. She gave me the control I needed to withstand the coercion in his eyes. "Nope."

Francis rushed the bars, vamp fast, appearing inches from me, growling, but without the pop of sound that most vamps make crossing a larger distance. I didn't drop away, but it was a near thing. I felt Eli tense. "Feed me, woman," Francis demanded.

"Tell me who's in charge of the Naturaleza now that de Allyon is true-dead. Tell me where the monsters sleep. And tell me where the humans they're feeding from are being kept. Be a good boy, and you might earn yourself a pint of human blood." I let a smile start, showing my blunt human teeth.

"Give me a human to drink and I will tell you what I know," he bargained.

I tossed the steak on top of the cage and the vamp followed its transfer with his entire body, a near backflip of motion that ended with two fingers pinching a corner of the baggie and letting the watery blood drain into his cupped palm. He slurped it while his other palm caught more. He made a face like it was nasty, and Beast agreed. *Nasty water-blood of old dead cow, cold and tasteless. Vampire will hunt us and kill us for this.*

"Maybe," I said aloud, not caring that no one knew what I was talking about. "Talk."

"I know nothing about humans except the ones I owned, and they are drained husks."

I kept my anger off my face and forced down the spike of fury that followed his statement. Behind me, Eli had no such skills, and his anger swirled into the air. This undead dude was a true-dead man, just as soon as I could arrange it. Too angry to allow him any respite, I reached to take away the steak, but he grabbed the baggie through the silvered bars and yanked it, tearing it and releasing the blood in a wide splatter.

The caged vamp sucked on the tip of the steak and said, "I was going to gather more cattle, but you arrived, and now everything is changed."

Go me, I thought. Nothing made my day like screwing up vamps' plans. But I didn't say it.

"But I know other things," he said, his fingers getting a grip on the steak and squeezing it, forcing out the watery blood. He was hungry enough that he didn't even care that the silver was touching his back where he lounged and blistering his skin through his tattered shirt. The metallic stink of poison and scorched meat filled the garage and made me want to sneeze. He bit off an edge of the steak and sucked, which was what I'd expected but was still icky.

"How about your master's cattle? Ones still alive? Are they penned?" I asked.

"My mistress keeps her humans beneath the ground, in basements and darkness." He looked at me slyly. "She owns many properties, and her cattle will be in one of them. She detests them, except those she has for dinner." He sucked the gob of raw meat until it was dry and spat the husk to the floor before biting off another. Which was just *ewww*.

"Is her name Silandre?"

"No. But I know her. She is growing into a Naturaleza power to be reckoned with. You will give me a human to drink?" he asked.

"For that info? No," I growled. "Starve."

Beast stared out through my eyes, and the caged vamp

paused, his mouth on the dried out gob of meat. "I have heard one other thing," he said. "You should search for full circles. The great one is once more complete."

Which made no sense to me, but the vamp smelled of truth, beneath the stink of whatever he was becoming. So maybe it was important and fitted into the picture somewhere, somehow.

Keeping my reaction off my face, I stood and left the garage, turning off the light as I went, Eli on my heels. "*Food?*" Francis shrieked. I shut the door as my answer.

"If our friend Francis gets free, he'll come looking for you," Eli said casually.

"Yeah. He will. He's on the list, though, so it won't be a loss."

Eli snorted through his nose, a near-silent laugh.

"Have your brother do a search for circles. Crop circles, witch circles, even tribal circles. Maybe some local tribe had one in the past that's been reactivated or something."

"And maybe he can get a handle on this new female master he mentioned," Eli said. "Could there be a new, secondary master of the city here? Maybe two different masters claiming one city? Hieronymus and de Allyon's heir?" I shrugged, and Eli finished with, "I'll get Alex to start a search on her too. We need a name."

"Good. While he's at it, get him to see if there's any record about what happened here in Natchez while de Allyon was in charge. That info would go a long way toward helping us see what's happening now. And see if he's turned up anything on why these vamps are moving like insects. It creeps me out."

"Just makes it easier to stomp 'em to death," Eli said, "emotionally, and morally."

He had a point.

We left the property, hearing only the soft purr of Eli's SUV, and arrived at the Clan home of the Natchez MOC a little after five a.m. The house was an amazing structure, three stories of brick and sandstone. The windows were full of light that spilled out into the night, windows even in the roof, showing that under the eaves was more living space. Rounded towers were on either side at the front, topped by peaked roofs like parapets with flags flying from them. The house was surrounded by live oak trees with sinuous twisting limbs so heavy that they had lowered toward the ground and now seemed to dance across the grass like massive, frozen snakes. Moss hanging from the higher limbs moved in the night breeze. Cars were everywhere, parked on the grass and along the drive, a few vehicles I recognized from the first meeting in the converted warehouse.

Pulling on Beast's night vision, I spotted humans in the dark, keeping watch, noting that security was better there than in town. Or perhaps the fact that Eli and I had taken the humans down so quickly had warped up the human servants' awareness.

Eli pulled directly to the front door and stopped, the tires grinding on the white shells. Not asphalt made with white shells, which was common in the South, but loose white shells used like gravel. When we got out and walked to the front steps, the sound of the shells beneath my boots was like the sound of crunching brittle bones. We walked up the seven steps and stopped in front of the door. To the three well-armed humans standing there, I said in my best vampire fancy talk, "Jane Yellowrock and company, here to provide surcease from illness and pain for the Master of the City of Natchez and his scions." Which I thought sounded spiffy.

One of the humans opened the door and two stepped aside. I walked in, knowing that Eli had come through the doorway on my heels, moving fast, and faced back at the opening until the door closed softly. Then he moved out to my left into the formal foyer, checking it out while I stood in the center of the magnificent circular space and took it all in. The scents hit me first: vamps, candle wax, smoke, leather, roses, and the faint smell of human blood that pervades every vamp dwelling.

I had been in Leo's Clan home, and Grégoire's, and Rosanne's in Sedona, and others', and they were all like something out of a magazine titled *Cribs of the Disgustingly Rich and Fanged*, but, frankly, I'd never seen or imagined anything like Big H's house. The foyer was thirty feet wide, round, and three stories tall, with a three-tiered, humongous chandelier hanging down from forty feet overhead. A stairway curved around and around the walls, rising the full three stories, its handrail painted gold and shimmering in the light.

There was gold-veined white marble everywhere, on floors, pillars, walls, and statues, gilt work on the ceiling moldings and floorboards, and gold candles burning in white and gold candle holders, the flames flickering. On the ground floor, there was a large round table to my right— white, of course—centered with a scarlet vase three feet tall and filled with white, gold, and scarlet roses. A sitting area was across from it, the furniture upholstered in white leather and tone-on-tone cloth, set with scarlet pillows and resting on a scarlet rug. White silk draperies cascaded along the windows, tied back with scarlet tassels. A scarlet and gold family crest—a lion and something geometric—on white silk took up one wall.

There were arched openings in the marble walls, and through one was a dining room with an ebony table and chairs that could easily seat forty. The table was covered with a white linen cloth and set with white-and-gold place settings. Through another was a traditional living room, all the furniture upholstered in white leather. Another room sported a full-sized white concert grand piano. Through a fourth opening came the aroma of old books, and I wondered if they had all been re-covered in white bindings or wrapped in white paper, and a small smile lifted my lips. It was overdone and tasteless, and the blood-splattered-on-drained-flesh image of the color scheme could not have been by accident.

"You like my home?"

I lifted my head, saw Big H standing one floor above me, and said, "It's awesome." But my mind was thinking, *Awesomely gaudy.* I didn't say it, of course. He was wearing a red silk dressing gown that matched the scarlet of the décor, with white silk jammies beneath. On his feet were white calf-skin slippers that I could see when he leaned over the balustrade, hands on the banister, his ugly necklace dangling away from his chest, the chain swinging negligently.

"You brought the antidote to the *Sanguine pestis*?"

My mind stalled out and then I put it together. "The cure for the vamp plague. Yes." I patted my go-bag. "All I need are the vamp . . . ires." I added the second syllable as an afterthought, out of politeness. I mean, I was in his home. No need to be insulting without cause. "And a table and chair."

From the doorways on the second level, vamps poured

out and down the stairs, gathering behind H, all looking eager and smelling sickly, all dressed in casual evening wear and not jammies, thank goodness. Big H walked down the stairs, leading the way into the dining room, and I counted twenty-two vamps. Their sickly sweet stench overpowered the scent of roses and leather. I glanced at Eli, but he was otherwise engaged, keeping an eye on everything else. It was good to know my back was covered.

I entered the dining room and saw that every vamp was sitting at the table, with H at the far end. The chair there was shaped like his peacock chair at the warehouse, but made of black wood, probably something that was now extinct, and he had one elbow on the chair arm and the other on the table top, his sleeve rolled up.

None of the others was sitting in that position, so I strode down the table to him and set my medical kit on the surface. When I opened it, I could feel most of the vamps straining to see, so I laid everything out on the pristine white tablecloth. "I have sterile needles and syringes, several bottles of the antibodies, gauze pads, and alcohol pads." When the kit was empty I placed the container on the floor and said, "This is really easy. I just roll up your sleeve, draw up the antibody fluid in the syringe, and give you a shot into your arm muscle. Because your hearts beat so seldom and your blood flows so slowly, it will take a day or two to totally flow through your tissues. But because you don't have human kidneys and digestive functions and processes, you need only one dose. Your bodies don't filter out the drug, so it stays at a high concentration for long enough to kill the disease. The only side effect is a total lack of energy, requiring most vampires to stay in their lairs for a while with their blood-servants, where they feel safe. Oh. And everyone complained of a bitter taste in their mouths."

"All who feel the need to rest may do so," H said, making it a proclamation to his people. "We will not convene here again until all are well." The vamps all nodded once, as if taking an order. "How long for this bitter taste?" Big H asked me. "It has been many years since I tasted bitter."

"According to Leo's people, the shortest time for the energy loss and taste was four days, for the young ones. The longest time for the oldest-lived was sixteen days."

"Proceed," Big H said.

I cleaned the bottle top, opened and inserted a sterile needle, drew up one dose of the drug into a three-millimeter syringe, and changed needles, leaving one needle in the bottle and putting a fresh one on the syringe. I hoped I was doing this right. I'd seen it done in my emergency medical class, but I'd never actually given a shot. To refresh my memory, I'd watched a video online to get the basics down, but I had no idea if the videographer knew what she was doing. I cleaned Big H's upper arm and popped the needle into the muscle. Carefully, I pressed the plunger down and let the clear liquid enter Big H's arm. Then I pressed a piece of gauze on it and said, "If it doesn't stop bleeding, have a healthy vampire scion spit on it to close it."

Big H's brow crinkled in surprise, and his eyebrows would have risen had he possessed any.

"Yeah. I know. Gross, right?" I said. Then I smiled brightly down the table. "Next?"

By five fifty a.m., the vamps were all dosed up and had departed or headed to the MOC's guest sleeping quarters, leaving me with Eli and Big H. The MOC still occupied the flared-out chair and lounged back in it, one foot up on his chair seat, one elbow resting on his knee, and a glass of red wine before him, which he turned around and around on the linen cloth. His other hand swung the ugly necklace in the air, mesmerizing as a hypnotist. He hadn't moved from that position since I started dosing his scions. Something about his posture reminded me of a young Hugh Hefner. It had to be the silk jammies and the décor.

A silence settled on the room as I packed up my waste paper from all the sterile needles and syringes, and if Eli hadn't been there, still watching my back, I'd have been nervous with the vamp's intense gaze. It was almost as if he were trying out his compulsion on me or something, and it gave me the heebie-jeebies. I snapped closed the lid to the medical go-bag, slung the strap over my back, and opened my mouth to say good-bye. The MOC beat me to it.

"You do scent of Leo, but only vaguely, as if you have not drunk from him in a long time. Longer than most Enforcers."

"It's been a while," I hedged. "I'm the part-timer, remember."

"Mmmm. How many of my enemies and my people have you dispatched since your arrival?"

The topic switch took a moment to follow, but Bruiser had called Clark about Silandre, so this must be my come-uppance. "Four. A woman who followed us from your meeting and attacked us in the woods. Silandre had gone over to the dark side and was drinking humans to death. We killed three of her scions. Silandre and the others got away or healed from silver shot and scuttled off like insects. I sent pictures to your scion with a request for payment."

"I did not authorize Silandre or her scions."

"Yeah. About that. Leo approved her beheading, and I expect to be paid as per our revised contract," I said, thanking my lucky stars that the Younger brothers had amended my boilerplate. "Got it?" I let a bit of Beast shine through my eyes, just in case he was thinking about paying me only for vamps listed.

Big H made no alterations in his body posture or movements. The wineglass kept turning, the wine inside moving slightly up and down with each turn. "You will be paid according to our agreement." He looked up at me under his hairless eyebrow ridges. "Lucas de Allyon was evil. He took being a Naturaleza to new and lower depths. He wanted for my kind greater power over humans. He desired a return to the sun. All that he set in place—" Big H stopped as if his words had been cut off. He sat up in his chair and pushed his wineglass away, still holding his copper necklace like a talisman, his fingers shaking. "All that Lucas did was of the dark," he finished, his voice a croak.

I wasn't sure why Hieronymus was acting so weird, but I knew about de Allyon's background. He had been around for longer even than Leo and had enslaved and murdered thousands of tribal Americans, drinking them down with abandon, Cherokee, Mississippians, Natchez, and Choctaw, just for starters. The old vamp had killed so many of my own people, the skinwalkers of the Cherokee, that we never recovered our numbers. He was the first European to import and own slaves from Africa. He was brutal and amoral pure evil, and killing him had been one moment of violence I would never regret. "Any idea how the new Naturaleza manage to heal from mortal wounds and silver?" I finally asked.

Big H didn't answer for a long time, long enough for the room to brighten through the windows as the sun worked its way toward the horizon and dawn. "Perhaps it is magic."

"Yeah." I frowned at his flippancy. "Have your scion deposit my money in the account or I'll leave you to deal with the magic insectoid bloodsuckers all on your lonesome." I slung the kit around my shoulders and left the room, trusting Eli to shoot Big H if the vamp tried to chase me down.

As I opened the front doors, the window shades—which must have been on timers or sensors—started to close with a rattling whir. The door closed behind me and Eli and I drove off at a sedate pace.

"Magic?" he asked.

"Vamps are magic of a sort. He was probably yanking our chains," I said. "But to be on the safe side, see what the Kid has on our circle info. And see how many of our missing humans are witch-born. Something about that conversation has my gut in a twist."

"Good thinking," Eli said.

"Did you get the whole Hugh Hefner vibe?"

"I kept looking around for bunnies in corsets."

"In your dreams."

"True dat. Eeeevery night."

I let another smile take over my face. There was something satisfying about banter with Eli Younger, something I had missed while I was depressed and chained in New Orleans. That family feeling, I was guessing. Maybe now that business partner feeling. I realized how much better I was feeling since I got to Natchez. "Huh," I said. When Eli glanced my way, I waved his curiosity off as unimportant.

"You know there's an IHOP on Highland Boulevard, don't you?" he said.

I sat up in my seat. "Nope. But I can always eat."

"So I noticed. International House of Pancakes coming up."

Bellies so full it hurt to move, we were back at the B and B as the sky grew noticeably gray. We opened the door, and my pocket buzzed, the number unfamiliar. I picked up. "Yellowrock."

"Jane, it's Bobby." He was whispering and I smiled, remembering the young Bobby telling me secrets one day as

I walked him from the school bus to his group home. I started to reply when he said, "Misha's gone."

I checked the time. Too late to be a vamp interview/kidnapping. "Gone where?"

"I don't know," he whispered. "She went out last night to see somebody and she didn't come back. Charly's still asleep, but when she wakes up, she's gonna be scared."

I could hear Bobby's own fear, a prickly tension in his voice. "I'll be right there," I said.

CHAPTER 9

"You Here to Even the Score, Dog Boy?"

I stroked Bobby's red hair, holding him gently in the hug he needed. "Who did Misha go to meet, Bobby?"

Without letting me go, he pulled me to the table and picked up a manila envelope. "She left you a letter."

Which did not sound good at all. I accepted the envelope. It wasn't sealed. I opened the flap and removed a stack of pages, the back part of it printed tourist-trap stuff about local restaurants and plantation houses and sights to be seen in Natchez Under the Hill. The upper part was what looked like printed legal papers, and the very top sheet was a single handwritten letter, signed by Misha.

Hey, girl.
    I should be back by morning, but if you are here and have this letter, then things didn't go like I planned. I have a meeting with a human named Wynonna, a primo blood-servant of a vampire named Charles Scarletti. I am hoping that Wynonna will take me to meet her boss. Wynonna has agreed to be interviewed for the book, and I had to go quickly or risk her changing her mind. If I'm not back by sunrise, and if I don't answer my cell, would you look after Charly for a few days? And if I'm not back in a couple of days, well, that means the shit hit the fan. (I know, right? Our housemothers would beat us black and blue for cussing.) So anyway, if I'm not back, will you

find Charly's biological father and see that she gets to him? I haven't seen Randy in years, and, frankly, he doesn't even know about Charly, but he's a good guy and my estate and insurance will pay for her continued treatment. Just in case, there are two thousand dollars in this envelope to cover expenses, and the numbers to access my checking account and savings.

Everything you need is in this folder.

And yeah, I know how awful this is of me, but if I don't come back, I want to make sure Charly doesn't end up in the system, and I know you will help her. Strange, isn't it? Of all the people I'd leave my baby with, the one I chose first is the most violent person I know. But also the most honest, ethical, and—in your own way—the most loving. I know we weren't friends. But I always felt safer with you there. Still do, I guess.

I'd end with "Hugs," but I know how you feel about them.

Mish

P.S. FYI: Bobby is a sort of a dowsing rod. He gets a salary for it and everything.

"Son of a . . ." The swearwords disappeared into a whisper. I stood holding the letter, my mind full of the white noise of shock. Beast pressed down on my brain with her claws and I took a fast breath, shocked by the pain, but it started me thinking like a security expert again. I opened my phone and checked the time. Misha was way overdue from an appointment with a vamp's dinner. And that vamp was on my kill list.

I'd been trained as a security expert when I was fresh out of high school, before I started staking rogue vamps for cash. I knew about keeping calm and imposing order on unmanageable situations, but the current situation didn't feel like an emergency, not with *The Princess and the Frog* soundtrack playing.

I walked to the TV, where Bobby and Charly were curled up again, Charly under blankets and cuddled up in pillows. Muting and pausing the film, I said, "Bobby, Charly, I need you to think. Did your mommy say where she was going for her meeting?"

"Noooo," Charly said. "She said you would ask, and she said to tell you that everything you need is in the packet." Bobby shook his head, agreeing that Misha had said nothing to them.

None of this made any sense. Why leave me a letter telling me what to do if she died? Because that was surely what she had left me. No mother in her right mind would go off and leave her sick child with a mentally challenged man and a crazy biker chick/vampire hunter. Which made Misha mentally unbalanced or with a hidden agenda or in deep trouble. I was betting on a combo, starting with Misha looking for vamp blood to heal her daughter.

I texted the names Wynonna and Charles Scarletti to the Kid with orders to research STAT, then I reread the letter and dumped the packet out on the table. The first thing I saw was the legal paper Misha had drafted and signed to allow me the right to see her book before it was finished. The second thing was a last will and testament. "Crap in a bucket," I said under my breath. "Crap, crap, crap, crap."

I realized that they had heard me when Charly giggled and Bobby shook his head. "You still say that, even after you got in trouble for it."

"Sorry," I said, feeling embarrassed for no good reason. *Crap* was not a bad word. It was the shortened name of the marketing genius of the best known flush toilet, John Crapper. Really. It was. But not everyone saw it that way, including a short-term housemother when I was growing up. She hadn't been with us long enough to make any major changes in our lives, but she had put the kibosh on any "bad words," including crap. Thanks to my mouth and fighting, I'd practically lived in house detention, with toilet duty—crapper duty—for the three months she lived with us. She was one housemother I had been glad to see go.

I dialed Misha's cell number and was shunted directly to voice mail. I left a short message and closed my phone. The kids were watching me. Okay, Bobby wasn't a child, but still. What was I supposed to do? How long was I supposed to wait before assuming that Mish was in trouble and track down Randy, Charly's bio dad? I looked at the time again and said, "Charly, does your mom have a laptop?"

"My mama has everything," she said, rolling her eyes. She pointed to a satchel near the neatly aligned running shoes, and I pulled it out and booted it up. While it was working, I called my personal, five-star hacker. He answered, and I asked, "We have a missing mother. Misha had a meeting with Charles Scarletti. He's on our kill list. Is there a way for me to send you every file off a laptop so you can get started working on it?"

"Yeah, sure. What kind of laptop?" I gave him the name and model of the laptop, and he asked, "Can you get online with it? If you can get online, you can e-mail me everything or just anything that looks interesting. It'll take a while either way."

I checked the laptop and said, "Yes. And . . ." I clicked through to discover that no files were password protected, and her e-mail passwords were remembered by her system. "I see several things in her most recent files. I'll zip them up and send them to you."

"Good. And bring the laptop and anything else electronic when you come. And don't think I'll be doing babysitting duty. Not gonna happen." He disconnected. Crap. That was exactly what I'd been thinking.

I ordered breakfast on Misha's room service and while we waited for it to arrive, I asked more questions and called Eli to fill him in on the situation. When he asked what I intended to do with Bobby and Charly, I said, "I'm bringing them back to the house."

"Jameson is gonna poison your piglet."

"Yeah. I know." I raised the volume on the TV and walked away before I went on. "I can't leave them alone here. My alternative is to call in social services, or whatever they call them in Mississippi. I have a signed piece of paper that says Charly is in my care with permission of her legal guardian. And I think Bobby is emancipated, or as emancipated as he can get. He tells me his grandmother passed on last year and he's been working for Misha since then, though he isn't real clear in what capacity. Misha hired him as a dowsing rod. That make any sense to you?"

"Not a lick," Eli said. "I'll be out front of the hotel in fifteen. We can load your bike up in back."

"Yeah. Okay." I hung up and started gathering clothes and toiletries for my new charges, my brain feeling like it was stuffed with steel wool, all snarled and useless. Beast was clearheaded and happy. She had a kit to mother. Sometimes my life made no sense at all.

Back at Esmee's, I looked over at my new charges sitting at the breakfast-room table, eating leftover piglet sandwiches. "Bobby? Can you take care of Charly while we're gone?"

"I'm her babysitter. I always take care of her," he said.

"Ah. Good." One problem solved.

"She takes her nap at three," he said, "and she gets her next medicine at five."

Charly looked up at me from the plush chair, with a foam-backed blanket over her legs and snugged to her armpits. Her hair was dull and lifeless, and Beast peeked out from my eyes, seeing the sick child. At her feet, Bobby turned on the TV, starting *Beauty and the Beast*, which seemed oddly apropos. Charly pulled the blanket higher, up under her chin. "Are you really my mama's friend?"

I felt itchy under her stare. Thinking about Misha. And the friends we might have been had I ever had the slightest notion of how to make one.

"Uhhh. Yes. Yes, I am," I halfway lied.

"Are you gonna find my mama and bring her back?"

Beast slammed down on my mind, her claws shooting through me with an instant headache. "Yes," Beast answered, my voice low and gravelly. "Will find her."

"You do know how stupid that promise was," Eli said to me later as I sat at the breakfast-room table with the cell phone in my hand, staring at the blue screen. Papers and laptops and e-tablets and phones were scattered across the table top, along with coffee cups and mugs and small plates and scraps of food.

Before he left and went back to Jackson, where he lived and worked, Gordon had suggested that we might be more comfortable in the larger dining room, but the breakfast room was closer to the kitchen, the coffeemaker, the teapots, and the food. All pluses.

I closed the phone with a snap. Since we got back with Bobby and Charly (and Esmee had gone bonkers over Charly, putting her in the princess room, and Bobby across the hall from her, and all that rigmarole), Alex had been working on locating the blood-servant and vamp Misha had

purportedly gone to visit—Wynonna and Charles Scarletti.
The Kid had four computers and laptops going at once. It
was something to see. I had tried to contact blood-servants
in Natchez, to ask about missing humans and vamp properties with basements. I was figuring that Misha had ticked off
a vamp and was stuck in with the food supply. Maybe it's
cliché, but basements and vamps have always gone together,
maybe because the rooms are underground and keep out
the light, or because of the old saying that vamps keep their
young chained in the basement for ten years until they cure.
But whatever the reason, vamps always seem to have basements. Or safe rooms. Or both. Basements were rare in the
Deep South, because of hurricane storm surges and high
water tables, so I assumed this had to be fairly easy to narrow
down. I had been wrong. The online site for the property-tax
division of the Mississippi Department of Revenue wasn't
particularly helpful or user friendly. It was taking time we
likely didn't have.

Nothing was happening. The sun had risen and the sick
vamp in the silver cage in the garage was asleep. Leo and
Bruiser weren't taking my calls, and I was loathe to phone
my own witch contacts, Molly and Big Evan. I guess killing
a family member makes people stop being your friends.

Misha's book research had now impacted my own investigation. I needed to concentrate on the vamp angle, as in
tracking them down and killing them, per my contract with
Big H, but now any action I took might conceivably endan-
ger Misha. Big H had said something about magic when I
talked to him, so maybe I should call a local witch—but
witches didn't advertise their covens. Whatever was going
on in Natchez sounded like a story that a reporter/book
writer would jump on in a skinny. But my reporter/book
writer was missing. Wouldn't you know it?

"Did you hear me?" Eli asked, irritation in his voice.

"Yeah, I heard. I kinda figured it was a stupid promise
even before I said it. But"—I shrugged—"I said it and I
meant it. I'll find that child's mother or die trying." Eli
shook his head, an unreadable expression on his face and
no telltale change in his pheromones. He was easy to read
only when his scent pattern changed, which I hadn't told
him. A girl needs an edge sometimes.

As I sat, phone in hand, it buzzed and rang and Reach's

icon appeared on my screen. Darth Vader's fanged happy
face was silly, but, like earlier, I had a feeling between my
shoulder blades that things were going downhill fast. I
pressed the SEND button and said, "Reach."

"Company's coming," he said, sounding amused and
gleeful and just a bit evil. He hung up. And the doorbell
rang.

"I just know I'm gonna hate this, whatever it is," I mumbled under my breath. I sat there, Eli's and the Kid's eyes
on me as Jameson moved through the house to the front
door. I caught the smell of cat and tightened up all over as
Rick LaFleur's scent blew into the room.

I had known on some level that Rick would show up in
Natchez, in person—he was PsyLED's hand of the law, after
all—but it never occurred to me that he would come *here*,
to *this house*. Stupid me. Worse, I didn't know if he was here
personally because of the case, the gig, and the missing humans, or because he still had feelings for me, or to arrest me
for something. I let my mind range back over my kills for
the last week. They seemed righteous to me, but . . . maybe
not to a cop, with all the rules and regs and courts and all
that.

"She's right this way, sir," Jameson said. I couldn't help
myself. I swiveled in my chair and looked as he stepped silently into the room. And I caught my breath.

Rick had changed from the pretty boy/bad boy I had met
on my first day in New Orleans. He had been dressed then
in jeans and Frye boots, looking carefree, a little bit dangerous, and human. A lot had happened between then and now.
Now he was dressed in cop casual: charcoal slacks, black
shirt, black jacket, and gray tie. He was clean-shaven, and
with his Frenchy black eyes and hair, he looked good enough
to eat. I smiled when that thought popped into my mind,
but the smile slid away when I recognized his expression—
closed, hard, unfeeling. I had accused him of trying to kill
me when we last met. I sucked at relationships.

Behind him was Soul, one of his partners, a supernat of
unknown origins, a tiny thing with silver hair, curves in all
the right places, and eyes like the sky at night. She wore her
traditional garb of flowing skirts and robe, today made of
blue, heavyweight, watered silk in honor of the season. I
hadn't liked Soul the first time I saw her. It had been a stu-

pid, instinctive, competitive reaction. This time, I nodded to her, determined not to be an idiot. Padding behind her was the white werewolf, stuck in wolf form, the neon green grindylow clinging to his back. The grindy looked like a green-dyed kitten, too cute to be dangerous, but her species' mission in life was to act as a deterrent to the spread of the were taint. If Rick or his wolf tried to pass it along, she would attack and kill them without hesitation.

My eyes flowed back to Rick as Eli stood and shook Rick's hand, then Soul's. I stayed in my chair, watching them all, perhaps a little too intently. The wolf growled, and I said to him, "I carry silver shot." The words were mild, but the growl stopped. The grindy chittered in what sounded like amusement, but I hadn't learned to translate the language of the species, so what did I know?

Soul moved around the room and held her hand out to me in a pointed gesture. I met her eyes and slowly stood, taking her hand. She bowed over mine and I hesitated only a moment before bowing back, slightly to the side so I wouldn't bonk her head coming up. But Beast pushed down on my mind and I followed her unspoken command, letting my bow drop lower than Soul's. Beast was better at interpreting alpha gestures and relationships than I was. When I rose, I was being regarded with an emotion that was foreign to me—calm and centered and serenely Zen. I felt that calmness flow up my arm and into me. "Jane Yellowrock. We should talk, you and I."

"I'd like that," I said.

Soul released my hand, but the calmness stayed with me. I had no idea what her power was, but I liked what I had seen. Until she turned and touched Rick's arm. The touch was almost intimate, and the calm she had lent to me cracked like a hot stone dropped into icy water. Deep inside, Beast hissed, and my eyes flared with gold. I dropped my lids fast. I had no idea what my face suddenly showed, but I knew I couldn't stay in the room with all the people. My cat was too angry; I might hurt someone. Most likely me. I whirled on one toe and left the room.

In the mudroom, I slid into my boots and went out back into the cold. Bobby and Charly were in the yard, tossing a ball back and forth, Charly sitting on the bench, Bobby doing all the running. I hadn't bothered with a coat, and the cold bit through my clothing with spiked teeth. I'd been living on catnaps and stress for several days now, and when I shivered, I told myself that cold and stress were the cause, not the look in Rick's eyes or the touch between the partners. Not that I believed myself. I was such a liar.

I headed toward the kids, and when he saw me Bobby tossed me the ball. It was high and to the left, but I jumped, caught it, and underhanded it back to him. The ball hit his chest. He tossed it, far more lightly, to Charly. We three played toss the ball for several minutes until Charly visibly tired, at which point Bobby pulled me to the bench, pushed me to sit, and picked up the little girl. With a small smile, he placed her in my lap and sat beside us. The day was clear and chilled and silent, no birds twittering or chirping, no sound of traffic. It was peaceful, and I felt Soul's calm try to rise up my arm again. I shoved against it, and Beast added her power to the intent; the spell of false calm fled.

"We need to talk," Bobby said, staring at the ground between his feet. The adult-sounding words nearly mirrored Soul's, but his lips were pushed out in something like an obstinate pout.

"Yeah? 'Bout what?" I asked.

"About my dreams. Misha is in trouble."

I didn't understand what one had to do with the other, but I asked, "You dream?"

Bobby nodded, eyes on the dirt at my feet. "I dream about stuff that's gonna happen. And stuff that's happening now. It started when I was fifteen. People made fun of me, so I stopped telling them."

I shivered again, this time not even a bit from the cold. "Oh," I said. Unspoken between us was the fact that I'd left Bethel when he was fifteen. "Ummm. Prophetic dreams? Is that why Misha called you a dowsing rod?"

Bobby shrugged and scuffed his toe in the dirt.

I cocked my head, thinking about the dowsing rod label. I had no evidence, but if Bobby's dreams were prophetic and if he was dreaming about Misha being in trouble, then at least she was still alive. Though it might have been better if he'd dreamed an address, or, even better, a dream that would have kept Misha from leaving in the first place. Not voicing any of that, I asked, "What do your dreams tell you about her?"

He nodded, then shook his head. "Not much. She's in the dark. She's . . . kinda like drunk."

Drugged, maybe. Since she went to see a vamp, she was likely blood drunk in a vamp's lair, drained dangerously low of blood and filled with endorphins that gave a false sense of safety, pleasure, and ease to the victim.

"She's sitting up and she's trying to fight, but she can't."

I didn't know if he'd understand the word, but I asked, "Is she under compulsion? Is someone trying to get inside her brain to make her do things?"

Bobby shrugged. He'd given me all he knew. "Thanks, Bobby. You did good." He was beaming when he lifted his head, his mouth pulling his freckled cheeks into apples. I remembered that same happiness from the children's home, anytime someone gave him praise. It didn't happen often. "If you think of something else or dream something else, let me know," I added, and he bobbed his head with determination. "You did good too, little girl," I said to Charly.

The little girl went still, like, nearly vamp still, for a dozen heartbeats. Then she swiveled in her seat and wound her arms around my neck. I inhaled slowly as she said softly against my collarbone, the breath of her words warm, "Well. I did well."

I chuckled, remembering English and grammar lessons that were always ongoing in the group home. Obviously, Misha had continued them with her daughter. "Yeah. You did well." I felt her smile against my throat. And I heard Bobby's breath hitch just before the smell hit me. Werewolf. Grindylow. And no Rick or Soul with them.

All in one motion I rose and set Charly on Bobby's lap. Turned and faced the door to the house. The wolf and his rider stood on the stoop, the wolf's hackles raised, his head and ears low. "Stay put. Keep Charly here. Don't move," I said.

It wasn't smart to challenge a ticked-off werewolf, but it was certain from his body language that he wasn't gonna back off, and the wolf and I needed to get a few things straight. I stepped away from my charges, meeting and holding his gaze in challenge. The wolf had crystalline eyes that sometimes looked blue and sometimes looked gray, but always looked threatening. Or had since I coldcocked him and broke his jaw the first time I laid eyes on him in human form. I let a taunting grin spread over my face. "You here to even the score, Dog Boy?" I asked.

He growled and rushed me. Beast rose in me and took over.

Everything happened in a single breath. I inhaled and ground the balls of my feet into the grass. As the chilled air flowed into me, the two-hundred-plus pound wolf roared and leaped. Cold air flowed through his white hair, rippling. His mouth opened, lips drawing back to expose killing teeth. I braced, fisted, punched, all my body weight torqueing into the blow.

My fist hit the wolf's snout in midair. The roar turned to a squealing yelp as I spun to the side and the wolf shot past me to crash into a tree. He fell and lay at the base of the old live oak, leaving the leaves shivering. I exhaled and shook out my fist.

The grindy held on through the leap and the hard stop and turned to me, chittering. I could have sworn it sounded like gratitude. Mighta been. The grindy seemed partial to the wolf, and if he'd bitten me, the grindy would have had no choice but to kill him for transferring the were taint. And then maybe kill me too if I didn't get to a mercy blade in time for healing. I cocked my head in acknowledgment. All that occurred in a matter of two seconds as the tree still quivered.

Then the pain hit. I shook out my fist and said, "Awww-weeee. That hurt," like I'd punched a brick wall, not a snout. From the house, I heard laughter.

I looked up and met Rick's eyes. His laughter died away, but his smile stayed put. "You have no idea how many times I've wanted to do that."

"Yeah?"

"Yeah. Once, he got pissed at me and peed on my laptop."

"Ick." I looked at the unconscious wolf. "I don't guess this makes us even?"

The smile slid away. "It . . . could be a start."

I nodded once, a short jut of my chin. "Let me know who else to sock."

The smile curled back up a bit, and Rick went into the house. The door closing sounded less judgmental than it might have.

"Are you gonna kiss him?" Charly asked.

My mouth opened wide before I closed it in shock. Bobby answered. "They already did. I can tell."

"How?" Charly asked.

"By the magic that bounces off them."

Slowly I turned, careful to keep my reactions—all of them—off my face. "You can see emotion, Bobby?"

"Nope. Just magic." When I looked perplexed, his face scrunched up and he said, "Love is magic. It looks just the same."

"Well, I'll be a monkey's uncle," I breathed. This explained . . . This explained *everything*.

I lifted Charly from Bobby's lap and we followed Rick back into the house. At the door to the breakfast room, everyone stopped talking, leading me to believe that they had been talking about me, but I no longer cared. "Bobby, come here," I said. "Tell me what Rick looks like."

Bobby slid into the room, his back against the wall, and studied Rick. "He looks mad at you."

"Yeah, yeah, yeah. I know. I mean, tell me about his magic." I rocked my body and Charly back and forth, holding her close. She felt cold to me as her arms tightened around my neck.

"He's all blue with red sparkles," Bobby said.

I started to smile. Even I couldn't see much of Rick's magic except when the full moon pulled at him. "How about Soul? The pretty woman?" I pointed with my chin.

"She's all black and silver and kinda sparkly."

"And me?" I asked.

"You're all yellow and silver and sparkly black."

"And the humans?" I asked.

Bobby shrugged, lifting his shoulders up to his ears, then dropping them. "They look like me. Normal. No magic."

My grin spread wide. "Once you see a person's magic, can you always see it? Can you tell where it is?"

"No," he said, shaking his head. My spirits plummeted. "Not always. But sometimes."

"Dowsing rod," I said, my smile drawing back up. Bobby could help us with this case. I pulled him to a chair. "Bobby. It's a gift. Some people are just too stupid to see gifts like this."

"Stupider than me?"

"You are not stupid," I said. "You are gifted."

He looked at me. "That's what Misha called it. My gift. She said it made me special in good ways, not bad, retarded ways."

"That's a bad word," Charly whispered into the crook of my neck.

"Yes, it is," I said.

Soul asked Bobby, "Did your friend Misha have you searching for something? Something magical?"

Bobby's face scrunched up, his *thinking face*, remembered from childhood, and I felt my expression soften. "She had me looking for all sorts of things. She said she was training me to use my gift."

"I'm tired," Charly breathed against me.

I could smell her exhaustion, feel it in the droop and weight of her limbs. "I'm taking Charly upstairs to rest."

"It's time for her pain medicine," Bobby said. "I'll get it."

I went up the stairs, Charly drooping into sleep and barely able to keep her eyes open long enough to take her medicine and eat the saltine crackers Bobby brought with the drugs.

When he felt she was deeply asleep, Bobby went to his room to watch cartoons, and I covered her up with the blanket, pressing it close like swaddling, before I returned to the grown-ups. The men were gone, and Soul was alone in the breakfast room. I didn't really want to be in the same room with her, but I figured she had heard me coming down the stairs, so I stepped inside and took my usual chair. Soul was studying a series of the Kid's printouts, while a video ran, over and over, on a laptop screen. It was turned away from my chair, but I could see enough to tell it was a low-light video of vamps running in a group, and they were all like the ones in the woods—insectoid and utterly alien. The creatures were green on a dark background, and they raced like centipedes across the ground, feathery limbs and oddly jointed bodies. I wanted to kill them all.

CHAPTER 10

I Want You to Chill, Babe

Without looking up at me, Soul spoke, and I jumped a little. "Thank you for breaking the wolf's nose. He'll heal, but he will surely remember his lesson."

"You're welcome. I think."

Soul smiled, still without looking up. I didn't want to like her, but she had a really sweet smile, one I didn't think could be faked. "I'm not sleeping with Rick," she said, and shifted papers to uncover a buried pile.

"Yeah." I said shortly. When she didn't say more I added, "That's a good way to go furry."

"We also are not romantically involved."

"Oh." Okay. Stupid, but a happy flush coursed through me. "Are you two—you four—staying in Natchez?"

"Yes. Ms. Esmee has provided us rooms. If that makes you uncomfortable, we can, of course, take rooms elsewhere."

I opened my mouth to ask *Why are you staying here? Whose idea was it? Does Rick like me? Check here for yes and here for no.* So juvenile. I wanted to ask but didn't have the social skills to peel away the layers without sounding like a lovesick teenager. I was an idiot for even thinking it. I closed my mouth, the questions unasked, but no way was it coincidence that they were staying here. So I blew out a breath and shrugged instead. Which was even more juvenile. "Um. Stay. That's fine by me. And all." I wanted to kick myself.

Soul didn't react except to say, "PsyLED acquired a few police reports from the local sheriff and the chief of police. Interestingly enough, your young man had already discovered the same information quite independently, and quite a bit sooner than law enforcement."

My young man had to be Alex, and if he acquired info on his own it was by illegally drilling into information centers, like police networks. So I said nothing. Nada.

Soul passed me a sheet of paper with Alex's info and handwritten notations on it. "Among Natchez's missing are twelve witches, gone in the last four months. I understand that you asked Alex to hunt for this information specifically?"

I sat up straight. *Twelve out of 114?* "Yeah. Something someone said made me curious. Those percentages seem off." I said. "Witches might make up one percent of the population. Not nearly ten percent."

"Twelve is a perfect number for a mass working," Soul said. "One more or less would leave a working unbalanced."

Another word for a mass working was a circle. For which we were searching and had been since Francis—still caged in the garage—had mentioned one. "Holy moly on a broomstick," I breathed. "What kind of mass working needs twelve witches?"

She handed me a sheaf of papers. "The kind used for moving hurricanes or shifting weather patterns. The New Orleans coven didn't have enough members still in town to move Katrina, which is why they could only bring the storm down from a category five to a cat three. If they'd had enough witches working together, they could have moved it—which is much harder—*and* decreased the storm's power." I took the pages and started scanning them. Soul kept talking. "A group of twelve can also make armies sick or affect the impact of political advertising on the masses. Many historians believe that Hitler had several covens of twelve in the early years of his political and military life, which contributed to his success in warfare. Attila the Hun and Genghis Khan each traveled with a coven of twelve. Alexander, Cyrus the Great, Julius Caesar are believed to have had witches at their command. And, of course, Napoleon Bonaparte had a very loyal coven. Such large covens are dangerous. Do you like history?"

It was obvious, even to me, that she was trying to put me at ease by chatting and not meeting my eyes, something my Beast would have appreciated. And it was working. I huffed a breath and forced my shoulders to drop, making myself relax. "It's okay," I said. "It was interesting in school, but it was also like eating only the icing instead of the whole cake, you know? No depth. Anyway. Okay. Covens of twelve are powerful. How about making vamps move like insects and heal from silver?"

Soul met my eyes. "I have never heard of such a thing until now."

I pulled my phone and showed her the photos. "This vamp is dead, but it took way more weaponry than it should have. A bunch more got away, one after being spine shot with silver."

"Oh, my." Soul leaned forward in her chair, studying the shots. "Did they move like the ones in this video that Alex sent me?" She spun the small laptop so I could see it full-on.

"Yes. Exactly. Creepy insectoid-snakey-octopuslike."

Soul asked, "Did you look at their hands and feet? Did you examine them thoroughly? Had there been any physiological changes, like extra digits or formation of carapace? Scales? Anything that might suggest a genetic-level mutation?"

"No, no, and nothing that I saw." There was a strange look on her face, as if she had seen something recently that prompted the questions, but I didn't ask and she didn't offer the answers. "If witches are involved and magic is letting them heal against silver, then maybe the full circle is involved too?" I asked. *And maybe Big H, with his mention of magic, knows about it all and has from the beginning,* I thought. *Except why bring me here and then only toss out clues about it?*

"Whoever is directing the circle would need a focus, something to gather and concentrate the spell and the energy of the coven, like a large amulet—a statue, a live oak, anything big enough to hold the power. Something potent that could be driven by the twelve missing witches. Something that has been working for quite some time. Perhaps since Lucas Vazquez de Allyon arrived in Natchez."

"How about an ugly, corroded metal-and-copper necklace?" I asked, thinking about Big H's jewelry.

A necklace would be too small," she said definitively.

I thought about the blood diamond I had put in the safety-deposit box and the amulets in my boot box. The diamond was well protected; the others didn't feel or smell powerful enough for the changes I'd seen in the vamps. But what did I know? I'd gotten them from de Allyon's Naturaleza followers before I killed him, so I knew where they'd come from, just not what they did. "Wait here." I raced up the stairs and brought back one of the pocket-watch amulets for Soul to inspect. "This is the only amulet I've seen that has something to do with Lucas Vazquez de Allyon."

The nonhuman woman held it in both hands and closed her eyes. At one point she cocked her head, a puzzled expression on her face. She opened her eyes and looked at it with surprise. "It smells like old blood and warm, raw meat. But it does not feel like a blood-magic amulet. Perhaps a low-level communication charm? A way for two vampires to speak to each other?"

I huffed. So much for that idea.

She held the pocket watch out to me and, reluctantly, I took it, tossing it to the table, where it slid under a sheaf of papers. I wiped my hand on my jeans and noticed Soul doing the same thing on her skirt. I'd smelled something like the scent recently, but I couldn't place it. "You want some tea?" I asked. When Soul's eyes lit up with interest, I said, "Jameson has some gunpowder green, a nice little oolong, some jasmine that he says is tasty, and a good strong black, a GFOP golden monkey." The initials stood for Golden Flowery Orange Pekoe, a top grade of tea, and golden monkey was my favorite tea lately. "It's really good iced, and not bad hot."

"The golden monkey sounds wonderful. Hot, please."

"Anticipating your need," Jameson said, pushing open the door to the coffee and tea bar, "I have brewed a pot for you." The smell of hot tea wafted through the room, caught on the currents from the house's air system.

"You are most kind, Jameson," Soul said.

"He's a wizard with anything in the kitchen."

"Miss Jane speaks figuratively," he said. "I have no magic at all."

I grinned and accepted a mug of black tea with cream and sugar. Soul took hers black. And I figured we were bonding. Either that or she was casting some sort of spell over me again.

"So," she said, when Jameson had withdrawn, "someone has possibly forced a coven of twelve, possibly composed of witches who had not previously worked together, so far as we know. An acceptable deduction would be that the resulting magic would be spotty, sketchy, difficult to control."

"And a reporter comes along asking questions," I said, "and someone makes her disappear. Misha's disappearance might be related to our insectoid vamps, or maybe she stumbled on the witch connection, or maybe . . ." I closed my eyes, trying to see clear outlines in the mishmash of information. "Maybe nothing is connected anywhere."

"And we have this." Soul handed me an envelope. "Your young man, Alex, gave it to me on his way out. I believe you call him the Kid?"

I opened the envelope and pulled out three pages of printed material. The page on top was taken from Misha's e-mail account, a series of e-mails and texts to Wynonna about the vamp Charles Scarletti. It was a list of questions she wanted answers to, including one about the history and whereabouts of a vamp named Esther McTavish. Esther was also a vamp in the files given to us by Big H, one on his kill list, one of de Allyon's Naturaleza. Maybe this was Francis' master? The puzzle pieces weren't starting to make sense, but they were forming a vague pattern, one I couldn't quite see but could almost feel.

"Yeah," I said, opening her file on my tablet. "There's not much in her file. So where is Esther McTavish? There's no address on the MOC's list of BBUs." At Soul's raised brow, I said, "Big Bad Uglies. Or BBVs—Big Bad Vamps."

Soul grinned, and she had a dimple. It was . . . cute. And I hated it. As if she had read my mind—and maybe she had. Who knew?—Soul laughed, and then waved the laugh away as if it were unimportant or inappropriate.

Aloud, I summarized as I read, "Esther was turned one-hundred twenty-three years ago, and she once served under Hieronymus. But she left Big H's clan in 1947 and swore to de Allyon in Atlanta." My heart rate sped. This was our first tie between Big H and de Allyon. I grinned at Soul. "Our little vamp was sworn to the Fame Vexatum as outlined in the Vampira Carta, but she went to the dark side and Naturaleza. And that means she knew the political situation in Natchez, at least as far back as the forties, and she knew vamps and people in H's clans. I think we found ourselves a spy. Go, Kid!" Though not one who would have known where Big H's sleeping lair was located.

I scanned through, back to the beginning. "I get the whole Naturaleza thing, hunting, drinking down, and killing any human a predator wants, but the Fame Vexatum. Is that what I think it is? Starvation?"

"Yes," Soul said. "The Holy Roman Church forced it upon the Mithrans living in Rome at the same time the drinkers of blood were forced to write the laws of the Vampira Carta. For the Mithrans of the time, it was be destroyed or adapt to the humans and their world. They adapted to living within human law by developing their intellect instead of the instinct of the hunter. They adapted by acquiring many blood-servants and slaves to feed from, rather than killing to survive. They adapted by developing their compulsion skills to make humans love them and want them. They adapted by never, ever drinking enough to satisfy or satiate. The Fame Vexatum stole much of their raw power from them, but left them with mental gifts no one had expected."

I grunted in agreement. "Which is why they're all so slender. They're starving to death. Or undeath. Whatever. And the Naturaleza don't starve, so they get beefier and a lot harder to kill. But the silver resistance is new. So is the buggy thing." Flipping to the next page, I made a soft snorting sound. "The Kid thinks the abundance of blood did something different to Esther. That it made her more powerful than the other Naturaleza." I flipped to the last page to check the Kid's documentation on Esther and said, "He got this stuff by joining a social media site for Natchez blood-slaves? Un-freaking-believable what people put on the Web and think it'll be kept secret." I put down the pages. "So if magic is involved, then maybe a BBV kidnapped the witches and created the coven, and . . ." my mind raced, putting possibilities together to see if any of the puzzle pieces fit.

At my side, Soul inhaled sharply, the breath a faint whistle of surprise, and started tapping away madly on her laptop. She didn't enlighten me about her little gasp.

I said, "Maybe the coven is tied to a focus, an amulet that lets the leader—maybe Esther, maybe someone else—do some new magical thing and not react to silver." I stared up at the copper-coffered ceiling, thinking. "Maybe the whole walks-like-an-insect is a side effect? Or a mistake? Something some vamp is trying to make go away so she can be supervamp?"

"Possibilities. Not evidence," Soul said, sounding distracted. "If your theory is correct, then Esther McTavish is likely also sick with the vampire plague," Soul said, "but isn't succumbing to the disease."

I folded the pages and creased them back into thirds, thinking, and reached for the amulet I had tossed aside. "Yeah. I see that." Feeling the cheap metal under my thumb, I stroked the amulet, the oily, greasy sensation on my fingertips and the odd stink of blood rising to my nose. "Maybe she's made a full circle and is using an amulet and magic from the kidnapped witches to keep healthy. Maybe the silver resistance was a lucky side effect? Maybe now she's trying something new with the spell, and the vamps are going all buggy?"

"Again, we have too much information and not enough evidence," Soul said, which summed it up nicely. But Misha was still missing and we were no closer to finding her. "You should consider applying to work for PsyLED," she added. My eyebrows would have bounced off the ceiling if they hadn't been stuck to my face. Soul chuckled and waved away her words. "It wasn't a job offer. It's just... you have an interesting way of thinking. Of putting things together that don't seem to match at first. Like with your friend Camilla and her interest—"

As if conjured, my cell rang, interrupting Soul. It was the number assigned to Camilla Hopkins. *Misha.* I answered, "Yellowrock. Misha?"

"Jane." The voice was hoarse, the way people sound when they've been screaming for hours or when they haven't had water for two days. Or both. My body flushed, then locked down hard. I stood, gripping the phone. Soul stood, staring at me. "Take care of Charly. Okay? And Bobby." The line went dead.

I immediately called Mish back. I was sent to voice mail. "Misha. Call me back. Misha!" Not that she could pick up midcall. I closed the phone and my eyes, instantly seeing the memory of Misha, standing with her back to a wall, arms holding her middle, eyes wide, watching me being teased, as two older girls tossed my sneakers back and forth. Before I learned to fight and made a place for myself in the home—which Misha never did. I blinked back tears and strode from the room, pulling a throwaway cell and dialing the Kid. If anyone could find Misha's location from a fifteen-second cell phone call, it was him. But to back him up, I also called Reach and put him on the job. I got them to track and triangulate, if possible, any incoming calls to my official line or from the number Misha used to call me. It was a testament to my emotional state that neither guy told me it was impossible.

Needing to do something—anything—I left the house and headed to the garage and the prisoner caged there. The steel side door closed behind me, leaving me in the dim light that passed through the windows of the garage doors, windows that someone had covered with black paper secured with packing tape. I clomped across the concrete and flipped on the overhead fluorescents. The lights were blinding, and my well-aimed kick slammed into the silvered cage so hard, it scraped across the floor and bumped into the far wall. "Wake up, Francis!" I shouted. Adrundel rolled over and stared up at me, his eyes totally vamped and his fangs showing. He hissed. And lunged at me, talons reaching through the cage, the stink of burning rotten meat filling the garage.

"Sometimes when the poop hits the fan, we should block it and run," I told him. "Sometimes we should haul off and knock it for a loop, back at the spinning blades. Wisdom is knowing two things. One is which time is which. The other is that no matter what you do, you're gonna get crap on your hand." I kicked the cage again, harder. The vamp inside lunged at me. And I laughed.

"Who is your blood-master? Is it Esther McTavish?" When Francis laughed at me, I kicked the cage again, and this time Adrundel was flung loose to bounce against the barbs of the cage. His blood stank of metal and rot and sickness, some of the scents almost buried beneath the stronger smell of fresh vamp blood. "Where does Esther lair? Give me a place, or you have no value to me alive."

He growled at me and shivered, sticking his hands into the pockets of his ragged pants—the only article of clothing that was left to him. He looked cold and miserable in the unheated garage. His chest had healed, skin over concave ribcage, and I could see each breath he took and the irregular beating of a heart pulsing in the notch where the ribs came together. There was no carapace and no indication of new limbs. I'd have to remember to tell Soul when I got over my mad. I kicked the cage less violently, more to make my point. And I pulled a vamp-killer from a spine sheath. Francis Adrundel got a totally different look on his face.

"I wasn't joking earlier about your head being worth forty K to me. Alive, you're worthless."

"Esther had a place she kept in town. One of those historical-society houses."

Vivid joy shot through me, hot and vicious. I kicked the cage again and spun the knife so the reflective silver caught the light. "Healing from silver poisoning is a nifty talent, but it doesn't help much when your head is disconnected from your body."

"You are one crazy bitch."

"I've been told that by better people than you," I growled. "Address."

"I don't know. I didn't care at the time." I reared back and he quickly added, "But it was off of Orleans Street. I know that much. It had a tower on the front corner."

I sheathed the knife and pivoted on my heel.

"I need blood. Human blood. I'm starving!"

I paused, thinking. "I'll have more questions. When I ask them, if you answer sufficiently well, I'll see about getting a blood-slave in here to feed you. Fame Vexatum."

"I am a Naturaleza," he said, nearly spitting the words.

"And that makes you a dead fanghead. Forty K, remember? Think about it." I closed the door to the garage after me and went to Bitsa. Someone was sitting in a deck chair, positioned in front of my bike, holding a pocket knife, whittling. *Whittling*? I couldn't remember seeing anyone whittle, not ever, except on TV reruns of Mayberry and in Western movies.

I cocked a hip. "Whadda you want?" I demanded.

Without looking up, Eli smiled, that tiny quirk of expression almost impossible to catch unless I was watching for it, and sliced a long, sharp sliver from the wood. It tumbled off his hands to the ground, joining dozens of others there. "I want you to chill, babe."

"I am not your babe. And I'm plenty chilled."

"You're raging mad, worried about your old school friend, who you feel that you somehow failed way back when. You're even more worried about the child upstairs, who may be dying of cancer. You're upset because your boyfriend-who-isn't is here and acting like an ass. You're upset because a beautiful woman has a relationship with him when you don't. And you haven't been laid in ages."

Laughter bubbled up in me at the final comment, and he glanced at me under lowered brows before returning to his work. Some of the tension eased out of me with my laughter, and when it had run its course, I said, "That is such a guy comment."

"Yeah. It is. But it's true. You've been depressed, impossible to live with for weeks. Now you're here, finally doing something, and nothing is going right. And then Rick shows up. And his Soul. And you get punchy mad. By the way, is our prisoner still alive?" Another curl of wood hit the ground.

"Marginally. If undead is actually considered alive."

He gave me that twitchy smile. "So. You need to hit someone? Spar a bit?"

I blew out the rest of my irritation. "Thanks. Yeah. Maybe later. Right now, I need to check out an address our prisoner gave me. "You want to ride shotgun?"

"Thought you'd never ask." He closed the knife and rose to his feet in a single fluid motion and looked me over. "That all you're wearing?"

I knew he was talking about my lack of firepower, and I grimaced. "No. Guess not."

"Pissed off is not the same as well armed," he agreed, leading the way into the house.

"I'll remember that."

Minutes later we were pulling into town in the SUV, and shortly after that we were on Orleans Street, looking down cross streets. It took a while, like, maybe half an hour, before we had narrowed the houses down to the most likely. Natchez had several houses with what might have been classed as towers on them. We parked on the street and made our way to the door.

I smelled vamp and blood and put a hand on Eli's arm to stop him. I opened my mouth and drew in air over my tongue as Beast might have done, smelling, identifying, and classifying the various scents. Eli watched me and the street and the house all at once, a gun in each hand, but hidden out of sight behind his leg and behind my back. "Blood-servants, too many to count, have been in and out of this house. Vamps too. But mostly we have something dead inside. I think several somethings."

"Recently dead? Human dead? How many?"

"Yeah. More than one. We need to call your girlfriend."

I drew a weapon as Eli holstered one of his and hit a single number. He had Sylvia Turpin on speed dial. Wasn't that sweet? I didn't say it, but it must have showed on my face, because Eli said, "Shut up."

I laughed softly as he said, "Syl. We have a house in town with multiple DBs in it. I'd rather not call it in to the city LEOs, but we need to see it. We also have PsyLED in town, and we have not notified them. How do you want to handle it?"

I heard her say over the phone, "It's never too soon to start campaigning. I'll meet you there and call it in myself, if you don't mind. I'll call your PsyLED pals too. Address?" He gave it to her, and the sheriff signed off with the words, "I'm close. I'll be there in twenty. Meanwhile, stay out of my crime scene."

We sat parked in front of the old house until the sheriff's car pulled in to the drive. Sylvia got out of her unit, looking trim and fit and—if Eli's scent signature was anything to go by—incredibly sexy.

I got out, and we three met at the steps to the front door. "Eli. Yellowrock," she said. "So how do you know we have DBs inside?"

"I can smell them," I said.

"Dead dog? Dead cat?"

"Nope."

I could see her thinking about calling the city cops for backup, but she decided not to.

She shrugged at her own conclusion, saying, "If you're wrong, if it *is* a dead dog, we'll be wasting their time." *And looking stupid,* which she left unsaid. She went to the front door. It was unlocked, and even Sylvia backed away when the smell gusted out. She cursed under her breath and ended it with a head shake and the word, "Okay." She drew her weapon, off-safety'ed, and chambered a round. She looked at Eli, and the sexual tension between them was like little sparks of static against my skin. "I'm guessing you two will follow me no matter what. Wipe your feet, stay behind me, put your feet where I put mine, avoid stepping in anything. When I say back out, do it." She pushed open the door, and I steadied my nine mil.

Sylvia Turpin might not have had paramilitary training, but she knew her moves and stepped past the door fast, her back to the wall. The foyer was clean, but the living room was a mess. Someone had drained and killed four humans, including a teenager, and someone else had staked a vamp to the floor with a four-foot ash spike and then chopped off her head. It hadn't been an easy task. From the amount of blood, she had been drinking freely, which meant speedy healing.

The vamp was Esther McTavish. The one potential lead we'd just found was already dead. Whoever had killed her hadn't been working alone. From the bruises and talon cuts on her limbs, it had taken several very strong vamps to hold her down and take her head.

The scents on the still, chill air told me that the place had no living inhabitants, so while the gun nuts searched the house as a weird form of courtship, I pulled my phone and snapped shots of the entire room and close-ups of the vamp. I then followed my nose to a hidden door in the kitchen and opened it. The charnel-house effluvia that burst from it was enough to gag a hippo, and I left the kitchen in a hurry. When I met the happy couple in the hallway, I said, "I left the concealed basement door in the kitchen open. I didn't go down the stairs and I don't *want* to go down them."

I stopped, knowing that one reason I didn't want to go down the steps was because one of the bodies might be Misha. I managed a hoarse breath and said, "And I recommend whoever does the brave deed wears a full biohazard suit. It smells like dead vamps—sick from the vamp plague and killed and left unburied. Those kinds of dead vamps.

And enough of your missing and now-dead humans to fill a graveyard."

Sylvia cussed once, succinctly.

Eli wrinkled his nose and swore, saying, "I smell it from here."

CHAPTER 11

So Let's Get It on, Baby

It was well after noon when I got back to the B and B, and instead of going inside I went straight to the garage and kicked open the door. This time, I left it open, allowing the thin winter light to brighten the place. Instantly I smelled scorched skin and was delighted that at least something hurt the vamp captive. He was asleep, whimpering, both hands tight around his middle, like a hungry child.

It had worked well last time, so I slammed my booted foot into the cage. He groaned and covered his eyes with skeletal hands. There were ragged talons at the tips of his fingers and his beard was growing, a tangled scruff. I wasn't sure I had ever seen a vamp with a scruffy face. "I am hungry," he said from behind his hands.

"Stop this," a soft voice said from the shadows. I turned to find Soul standing at the door, which she closed with a tolerant, quiet sound. "You will not hurt this vampire again."

"Yeah?" I gave her my back and slammed my foot into the silver chain again. "How many humans in that house just off of Orleans Street did you drink down and kill? Huh?" I felt Soul at my back, but I kicked the cage again, shouting, "How many?"

The vamp on the floor of the cage started laughing, and if it started out as a pathetic gallows laughter, it ended up the goading taunt of the unrepentant killer. He dropped his hands and opened his eyes in the dark, staring at me through the gloom. "I lost count of the adults. But the children," his laughter grew in power and resonance, seeming to bounce off the garage walls, "I remember them, each and every one. I drank down their terror and their whimpers. I sucked down their fear and panic like the elixir of life it was."

I felt Soul step back. I smelled her reaction and so did our captive. With that fluttery, feathery motion, he crossed the small space to me and reached out, gripping the silver supports of the cage with one hand, his palm and fingers not smoking where they touched the metal. He pulled himself to his feet and crouched, his hair a scant inch from the cage top. His bare body was covered in scars and welts and fresh skin from the accelerated healing. Even starving, he was healing.

"Come here, nonhuman woman," he said. This time he was speaking to Soul. "I will show you what I do to women. I will show you how I drink them down." He closed his eyes at the remembered experience and swallowed, his dry throat making a noise like rubber tires on muddy earth, a squelch that lasted far too long. It left me with a sensation of how much he had enjoyed drinking the helpless to death.

Soul turned and left the garage, closing the door with an entirely different sound. I didn't know how she could direct emotion into the sound of steel on steel, but I felt it. Soul would not try again to interfere with my treatment of the prisoner. She wanted him dead too.

Francis laughed, the sound low and vicious. "She should have stayed. I would have told her how my cattle died, with the women and their children weeping and begging."

My foot slashed out and hit the cage so hard it slid across the small space into the back wall. Francis' laughter died. He gripped the cage, stinking of ammonia and death, his body whipping with the force of my kick.

"Which vamp is in charge of the Naturaleza of this city now that Esther McTavish is true-dead?" I asked.

His face changed, his eyes bleeding back to near-human, his fangs *snick*ing back into his mouth. He dropped to his knees on the floor of the cage. "She is dead?"

"Yeah. Headless, in the living room. And the basement was full of dozens of dead humans and several other vamps, all staked with silver." Francis' eyes lost focus at the thought, and when he didn't reply, I said, "It looked like there had been a fight. A Blood Challenge, maybe?"

"Naturaleza do not challenge. They die by blood feud. They die by war. And each war is different from the others. How did my mistress die?"

I smiled this time, and his eyes widened at the expression. "She was staked through the abdomen and her head sawed off. Not hacked off. Sawed." I chuckled slightly. "It's the way I killed Lucas de Allyon, and it takes determination, a lot a free time, and a really sharp blade."

His face changed again, and this time I couldn't follow the emotional voyage. "You are the creature who killed my master?"

"Yes. In mortal combat, mano a mano, so to speak. So. Who might have killed your mistress and her scions? And who is in charge now?"

"There are three possibilities." Francis sank back onto the cage floor and wrapped his arms around his legs. "I'll give you one possibility for each Naturaleza blood meal you provide."

I was willing to dicker, because I knew that nothing acquired—or given up—easily is truly valuable, so I thought about his offer and who I could hit up for blood meals while I let the silence build. "All three names," I said finally, "today, for one drink, Fame Vexatum style."

The vamp frowned, but I could tell he was going to bargain. That was one thing the older vamps understood—the art of bargaining. They had lived preretail, when humans often traded goods for goods in a marketplace. "One *possibility*," he corrected me, "per drink, full meal, Fame Vexatum," he said.

"All today—three drinks, for three *names*, within the hour. And if you drink and don't tell, I'll treat you like I did de Allyon."

"To give you the *names* is to foreswear my allegiance. But the words I say will guide you."

"And if they don't?"

Francis seemed to ponder that a moment. "I will give you the possibilities first. Then, if you are satisfied, you will feed me."

"Done."

"You have my former mistress, Esther McTavish." At my

lifted brow, he waved that away. "But of course she doesn't count, due to the pesky circumstance of her unfortunate demise. Charles Scarletti is Esther's favorite scion." I must have given something away when he said the name, because Francis gave a chuckle, low and hollow, like something from a *Friday the 13th* remake. "Yes, Scarletti joined us quickly after we arrived from Atlanta, eager to taste the wonders of the Naturaleza."

"One." I made a little give-it-to-me gesture with one hand.

He gave me a sly look. "And then there are the ones closest to Hieronymus' heart."

I drew in a slow breath. "Zoltar and Narkis?"

"I am not foresworn," he reminded.

"Yeah. Whatever," I whispered. "Big H's sons. I am so stupid."

I left the garage, dialing the number Big H had given me for his primo, Clark. When the call was answered, I said, "Jane Yellowrock here. I need three full meals for a hungry vamp prisoner. How quickly can you get them to my base?"

"I take it that you have bargained with food?"

"Yeah. Something like that."

"Half an hour. If the vampire hurts one of my master's blood-servants, I'll kill him," Clark said, his tone conversational.

I felt a real smile cross my face. "I'll hold him down for you."

Clark laughed, and it was strangely carefree for a guy who had just threatened death on a vamp. "One thing. Is the vampire in question ill with the *Sanguine pestis*?"

Crap. I'd forgotten that. Drinking from an uninfected human might infect the human. "Yeah. Send me someone who's had the vamp plague and has gotten better. And thanks for thinking about that."

"You're welcome, Miss Yellowrock. All in a day's work. Shall I send someone to supervise the feeding?"

I thought about what he might mean and said, "To keep the vamp from taking too much or hurting the . . . um . . . donor?"

"Exactly."

Both, then. "Well, you need to know that silver isn't going to hurt him and can't be used as a deterrent."

"Yes. I understand. But sunlight is still effective. And it's daylight."

I chuckled again, squinting up at the sun. "Yes, it is. Sure. Send along a bodyguard or two. And feel free to hurt the little vamp if needed, but don't burn him to a crisp. He's essential to my investigation for a while longer."

"Understood. Half an hour, Miss Yellowrock."

I hung up without telling him that his master's sons were plotting against him, and went into the house. I came back out with the dart gun and medical kit, loaded the weapon with a one-dose dart, walked into the garage, and, without asking his permission, shot the vamp. He wasn't expecting it, and the dart hit him midcenter of his body, just above his navel, where a mass of fading, puckered scars showed. Francis yelped and flung the dart away, cursing. It landed at my feet and I picked it up, turned on my heel and left the garage. Just before I closed the door behind me, I said, "You're cured. You're welcome, suckhead."

Back inside, I was putting away the weapons when my phone rang. I could hear a car and the sound of tires on roadway in the background. I was on speakerphone. "Yeah."

Eli said, "Two things. One: no way to track Misha's location from her cell. It's a dead end. Two: one of our staked vamps was Charles Scarletti," he said, "his human servant, Wynonna, dead in the crook of his arm."

"Well, crap. My sources in the Natchez vamp community are dying off faster than I can locate them for a tête-à-tête. According to Francis, Narkis and Zoltar have been plotting against their dad."

"He *did* name his boys Narkis and Zoltar."

"Good point. I'd have shot him too. Okay. I'll get the Kid to see what he can dig up." Pun intended. Before Eli could groan, I hung up. Staring at my cell, I considered my next call. I now had names given to me by a caged prisoner, yet I needed more data. I dialed Bruiser.

"Jane," he said, and my insides twisted. "How are things there with the boyfriend?"

I sighed, but kept the sound away from the phone. How was I supposed to answer that when Bruiser and I had ... issues? Beast's wanting-to-fool-around issues, and my the-man-betrayed-me-and-should-die-for-it issues. I decided to ignore it all. "Just ducky. What effect would vamp blood have on a child with acute lymphoblastic leukemia? The worst kind of all."

"One moment." I heard clicking and realized he was typing. Looking something up in a database I knew nothing about? I wanted access, but was in no position to ask for it. Dang it.

"The news is neither good nor bad," he said. "Sometimes it helps. Sometimes it does not. Are you talking about the little girl? Misha's daughter?"

"And you know about Charly how?"

I could almost hear his smile when he said, "Reach, of course."

"Humph." This call was on an official cell, so I figured that Reach was listening in. I said, "Hey, you big-eared rat. Telling tales works both ways."

There was a moment of silence, and then Bruiser said softly, "Thank you. Jane, if you decide to try to feed the child, I'll ask a Clan blood-master to attend you. Reach. I suggest that you call me. *Now*."

"Thanks, Bruiser."

I hit END and waited as I walked back out of the house, the cell in hand. The door closed behind me, leaving me standing in the chill air. Seconds later, my official cell rang. "What the hell was that about?" Reach demanded, heat in his voice.

There were lots of reasons why I'd given Reach away, the most important among them that Bruiser would have figured it out soon anyway and asked me why I let it continue. Being on retainer to the MOC meant I had to play politics, protect myself, protect the chief fanghead, and protect his interests. No way was it in Leo's best interests to have Reach listening in on the calls. And it sure wasn't in my best interests, not anymore. Now that I had the Kid, it was time to take Reach down a peg or two. I shook my head. "You figure it out, hotshot." And I hung up.

"You're just getting all your jollies today. Aren't you?"

Without turning around, I said, "You do know that sneaking up on a skinwalker is dangerous, right?"

Eli laughed. "I like you. I might be certifiable for it, but I like you."

It made little sense—except that somehow Eli had become family—but I smiled and ducked my head around to find him leaning against Jameson's car. He still smelled of charnel-house effluvia. "Yeah. I like you too," I said.

"So, why are you so jumpy today? Leftover depression working itself out of your system?"

I started to deny having been depressed, but it would have been a waste of time and a lie. "Probably." I felt better having said it aloud again. And I *was* jumpy. I frowned. "Want to spar?"

"Been hoping you'd ask. I found a gym over the garage." He jerked his head at the building and I followed him, our boots loud in the thin winter air. "So," he said as we climbed a set of outside stairs to the garage's second floor. "Are we ever going to end up in the sack together?"

I was startled and then amused. "Ewww. It would be like sleeping with my brother."

Eli burst out laughing, looked back over his shoulder, and teased, "So let's get it on, baby."

I shook my head. "Idiot."

"Bitch."

"Wrong species."

We were still laughing when we reached the room over the three-car garage and I stood in the doorway, taking in the gym. "Swuuueeet." It had everything: free weights, a ballet barre, a total-workout machine that targeted different muscle groups, ski machine, stationary bikes, two treadmills, a hot tub in the corner, a large open space with thick rubberized flooring suitable for yoga or sparring, and a shower and dressing area. I pulled off my boots, tossed them in the corner, and removed my weapons. In the opposite corner, Eli was doing the same, our reflections casting back to us from a wall of mirrors.

"When we last sparred, how much were you holding back?" he asked.

"You walked out of there." When he looked confused, I added, "I left your joints intact, didn't break your spine, and didn't hit you in the xiphoid process, piercing your diaphragm or liver. For starters."

Eli nodded. "Let's keep the same rules, then. You hold back. I'll try to kill you with my bare hands." I was still laughing when he attacked.

Beast slammed to the surface and spun me to the side, my left hand sweeping into a claw that had to hurt as my nails grazed his ribs through his shirt. He retaliated with a leg sweep and a series of fast punches, all below the belt, followed by a chest strike intended to bruise a breast. Two of the punches and the chest blow landed. I *oof*ed out a pained breath and hit in him square in the jaw, twisting into the motion with all my new, more muscular body weight. A lesser man would have been lights-out. Even Eli might have hit the floor, except that he landed on a weight bench and rolled over it, giving him the seconds needed to shake his head and come back at me.

"Your eyes are doing a funky gold-glow thing," he said, trying to distract me as he did a punch-kick-sweep-of-legs combo I hadn't seen before.

I dodged, blocked, and leaped over the leg sweep. "My Beast likes this," I said, hearing the lower, coarser grate of my voice, a Beast growl.

"Yeah? Screw your Beast." He caught my hand and flipped me in some kind of throw I'd never seen before, and didn't really see this time. I went flying. I landed on my back, hard. The breath *whoof*ed out of me and I didn't get back up. I lay flat, blinking up at the fluorescent lights swirling overhead. When Eli interposed his head between the ceiling and me, he was upside down and at an angle. I closed my eyes and waited for the ability to inhale. It was a long time coming, and when my lungs did finally expand, I thought I'd maybe broken something, it hurt so bad. It sounded horrible too.

Beast receded with a soft purr. She'd had fun and was now leaving me with the pain.

"What was that?" I said. Actually I whispered it, so I cleared my voice, took two slow sets of breaths, and tried again. "What was that?" It came out slightly better, but not by much.

"That was your tax dollars at work—MAC, better known as Modern Army Combatives."

"That was cool. Teach me. You know. When I can stand again. Breathe again without pain."

Eli lowered his hand and pulled me to my feet. He still had my hand when the gym door opened and Rick LaFleur stepped inside, his eyes glowing that green glow of his black panther. He gave a low growl, and before I could disengage my hand, he leaped. Landed on Eli.

The Ranger rolled with the impact, my hand jerking free. And suddenly the two men were yards apart, a spitting mad, neon green ball of fur and claws on Rick's throat. The smell of blood filled the air, blood not quite human, not quite were.

Rick screamed, a coarse, barking shriek of pain, all cat. The grindylow leaped away and landed on the nearest weight bench, her fur standing out all over, as if static electricity had filled her coat. Her jump left the raw, scored, bloody mess of Rick's throat visible.

He managed a wet-sounding breath, his hands reaching for his wound as his eyes blurred back to black. He was bleeding, but not the pumping of carotid blood, which would likely have been fatal because he couldn't shift. This time, he'd live.

Shock washed through me, an adrenaline wave that rocked against my nerves and rolled away. The attacks had both taken maybe three seconds.

"You idiot," I said to Rick, bending over Eli to see if the were-cat had punctured his flesh anywhere. "Did the idiot bite or claw you?" I asked the Ranger.

Eli rolled slowly to his feet, inspecting himself in the mirrors without taking his eyes from Rick. "No. I'm okay."

The juvenile grindy chittered and mewled and spat strange sounds at Rick, and we didn't have to speak Grindylowish to know she was giving her partner a tongue lashing. It was her ordained purpose in life to prevent him from spreading the were taint. "Yeah, yeah, yeah. I know," Rick whispered to the grindy. I watched as the bleeding slowed to a stop and the flesh of his throat seemed to grow back together. "It's close to the full moon, Pea. My cat got away, and I left my music in the room. It was stupid." To me he said, "Sorry, Jane. My cat seems to think we're mated. He didn't like the way Eli was touching you." To Eli, he said, "Sorry, man. Really sorry. It won't happen again." Rick turned and left the gym, and I stood there, still hearing the words, *My cat seems to think we're mated*.

I took a breath and smelled the scent of big-cat and blood. Beast rose in me, fast. I opened my mouth and scented the air across my tongue with a soft *screeee* of sound. Because even bleeding and shamed, Rick was still the prettiest man I had ever seen. We had been at odds for so long, yet at least part of him still wanted me. I blew out the breath.

In the mirror, Eli shook his head. "You two have the strangest mating rituals I've ever seen."

I ignored that. "I feel all better now," I said. "Thanks for the dance."

Eli snorted and led the way back outside and down the stairs. "Dance. Only woman I know who thinks combat is dancing."

I kicked him in the butt and looked at him from the side. "If you dance with me, you take your life in your hands."

"God, woman. I didn't know you could flirt."

"I can't."

"You might wanna rethink that." Eli almost looked like he was blushing, which was ridiculous.

But ridiculous or not, I did rethink it and decided he was being stupid or making a joke I couldn't follow. "I have a thought," I said. "It's convoluted, but hear me out. I think if we concentrate our research on the vamps who disappeared the witches we might find Misha. If she stumbled into the Naturaleza as part of her research, and the Naturaleza are the ones holding the witches, then she became a part of the food chain for them and she'd end up close by in a closet or the attic or—"

"Buried out back."

I stopped on the last step and grabbed Ranger Boy by the neck, digging in my fingers. "She is not dead." I shook him. "You hear me?"

"I hear you." He swept his arm up and around, knocking my grip loose. "Do that again and I'll hurt you for real."

"You got the drop on me once. Don't think it'll happen again."

"You gonna put on your big-girl panties and fight with the boys, now?" He looked over his shoulder as if he expected me to blush or something.

"Who says I wear panties?"

I was certain that he flushed red this time. Laughing, I left him shaking his head and went on inside to find the Kid. We had work to do.

Charly looked even paler when I checked on her, and Beast pressed down on my brain, holding me still, looking the child over, scenting her illness. *Sick kit. Smells like death soon to come. Protect from predators. Needs milk and mother's body heat. Warmth of den and litter mates.*

Yeah. But her mom is missing, I thought back.

Find mother. Soon.

Which was really good advice. But until then, I pulled my file of official papers and called Charly's medical doctor. It took a bit of work and one out-and-out lie before he would talk to me. On the advice of the Kid, I claimed that I was Misha's sister. Which worked. When the oncologist did call me back, he didn't bother with pleasantries. "How is Charly?"

Relieved, I described Charly's condition, and he said Misha and I should bring Charly to the Natchez Regional Medical Center for tests, that he'd pave the way with the Emergency Department doctor. I checked my watch, agreed, and hung up, shouting for the Kid to get me directions to the hospital, and Eli to drive.

The rest of the day was spent with me pretending to be Charly's mom; signing papers in her name; taking care of Charly, who needed tests; consultation between emergency doctors, medical doctors, and her oncologist; and a transfusion of blood and some meds to make her own body create blood cells faster than normal. Bobby stayed with Charly every single moment, as dedicated to her as he might have been to a baby sister, and as long as he held her hand, Charly was calm and relaxed and willing to be stuck with multiple needles. Far as I was concerned, Bobby was a saint. And I was a liar, but in a good cause. I wondered if that was any less of a sin.

It was night when we drove out of the hospital parking lot, and we were all exhausted. One might have thought that we had wasted the day as far as our primary goals—finding Misha and killing Naturaleza vamps—but the Kid made a lot of progress on three fronts in the ED. The most surprising one was when he located Charly's bio dad. Misha had good taste, I had to admit, finding a man who was rich, now a senator, and vaguely Kennedy-esque in looks. I took the info but held off on contacting the man for now. I intended to find Misha. She could do her own meet-and-greet later if she wanted.

The Kid got the rest of his new info when a *World of*

Warcraft buddy met him in the waiting room. He was a local who knew everything about Natchez's vamps and witches, and, best of all, Bodat was for hire. The Kid and Bodat—which had to be a nickname, though he didn't offer more—sat in the back of the SUV on the way home to Esmee's, comparing notes and updating our database with lots of local facts. Bodat smelled like teenage boy and garlic and onions, with a strong underscent of sausage—pizza, the go-to meal of teenagers everywhere. He and the Kid were taking the data and creating a plan of action, which made Eli smile, that twitch of lips that meant he thought his baby brother was cute and clueless. Probably true.

Bodat did offer one bit of information that I knew had to fit in somewhere, somehow. "Yo, Indian chick," he said to me. "You do know that Esther McTavish was tight with Silandre. Right?"

"Tight how?" I asked.

"Like, they were singing partners back in the day, that opera stuff. And even then, they were doing it like rabbits. Lesbo rabbits," he added, elbowing the Kid, who laughed with him.

"Children present here," I said, rolling my eyes, as Bodat snickered and whispered something to the Kid, who dissolved in laughter. Teenage boys and their humor. *Not.*

"Can you find out if they hung out with Narkis and Zoltar?"

"Give us an hour," Bodat said. Did I have a good team or what?

When we got back to Esmee's, I left the guys talking about our next move and carried Charly up the stairs to her room, Bobby on my heels. The little girl was exhausted and never woke up when I tucked her in. Bobby and I sat on the edge of her bed, staring at her in the dim light. I saw clumps of Charly's•hair on my shoulder and gathered them up, clenching them in my hand. She was so fragile. Yet her doctors thought that she was well enough not to admit her as an inpatient.

Sick kit. May die, Beast murmured inside me, sorrow lacing her internal voice.

"She's going to get well," Bobby said firmly, and I looked at him hard, wondering if he'd heard my internal monologue, and decided not. He was staring at Charly, his fists clenched at his sides, fear engraved on his face like grooves on a tombstone.

Bobby had a five o'clock shadow, I noticed suddenly. Bobby had a beard he had to shave. Bobby was all grown up. I felt the surprise flutter through me. "Misha—" he stopped, as if putting together Misha's being missing with also being fallible. His tone wavering, he finished, "Misha said so."

"Yes," I said. "Misha said so."

"But Misha's missing," he whispered.

"Yes. But we're Misha's friends and we'll do everything in our power to find Misha and keep Charly going until Misha is back and safe. Right?"

"Right." But I could hear the fear in the single, dejected word.

"Perhaps I can help?"

I turned to see Soul in the hallway, silhouetted in the light, all curves and all woman. I'd never have her shape or her sex appeal. Rick's cat might want me, but Rick would surely want Soul. "How?" I asked, my tone giving away nothing of my inner thoughts.

"If you have some of Misha's things, I might be able to use them to locate her general whereabouts," Soul said. "Nothing specific, mind you. Nothing like a GPS or an address, but some general direction?" She ended with an uncertainty, the last words rising in question.

"And you wait until now to offer?"

"It . . . It is not an easy thing for me to do." She pressed her fingers into her upper thighs, as if worried. Or afraid. I didn't know if it was true fear or something she wanted me to think of her—some game with a purpose I couldn't follow, but at this point I'd take anything. I stood and went to the closet where I'd stuffed Misha's things, the valuables I'd taken from the hotel suite that was still in her name, in case she came back there.

Thinking that Soul might need something biological to focus on, I handed her Misha's hairbrush. Soul pulled three hairs from the brush, inspecting to make certain that she had root as well as shaft. "This is good. We need a quiet place."

Bobby said, "There's a little room with a table and liquor downstairs." He looked at Charly as if to make sure she was breathing. "I'll go take a bath and put on my pj's. Then I'll make sure Charly is still okay. Okay?"

"Okay," Soul and I said together. We stood in the hall as Bobby went to his room and closed the door. Within seconds we could hear water gurgling through the old pipes in the even older house. Without discussion, we went to the wet bar on the lower level, as if Bobby's word had made it so.

The bar was more walk-through than actual room, with doors on all four walls to the dining room, butler's pantry, wine closet, and billiards room. The walls were antique wood with a patinated copper bar, soft lighting, modern fridge, blender, ice maker, and bottles, bottles everywhere, and not a drop to drink, as far as I was concerned. For me, liquor was no flavor and all burn, and since the alcohol did nothing for me intoxication-wise, it had no value at all.

Soul closed the doors and lit a candle on a small round table tucked in a corner between two doorways, and sat in a chair. I slid a hip on a bar stool and poured a large glass of water, drinking it down fast. I had no idea when I'd last drunk anything, but it had been before we left for the hospital. I poured another glass as Soul settled herself and turned off the lights, leaving only the single flame as illumination. I went still as she closed her eyes, not wanting to distract her.

I focused in with Beast-sight, and though they were weak, I saw her magics. They were a soft, mutating glow hovering almost out of sight, as if contained beneath her skin, and leaking only the barest minimum to the surface. They were more an iridescence than the intense hues of Molly's magic. Whatever she was, Soul wasn't a witch. Her magics were more like the magics of the outclan priestess, Bethany Salazar y Medina. Bethany was a black-skinned shaman from Africa, and was an accomplished healer for humans and blood-servants and vampires, and I'd take Misha to her before I'd let the child die, no matter what Bruiser's data on ALL had said about the healing power of vamp blood on leukemia. Bethany was nutso, but she was powerful.

The candle wavered in the small room, moving with Soul's breathing, in and out, back and forth. The shadows seemed to thicken in the corners of the room, and the glow seemed to thin and lift from Soul's flesh. Her lips were moving, but no sound emerged, and she kept her eyes closed as she raised both hands to the candle flame. "Where?" she breathed, and she dropped in a hair. The flame raced up from root to tip with a sizzle of sound, a flare of brightness, and an awful stench. "Where?" she said again, and repeated the action, adding to the reek in the room. "Where?" She burned the final hair.

Her magics rose from her skin to coalesce into a single thread, twining up with the stinking smoke, straight for the ceiling twelve feet overhead. But three feet from the copper-coffered ceiling, the smoke angled hard right and shot out of the room.

"Your friend is alive," Soul said without opening her eyes. Pointing, she said, "That bearing. Within ten miles."

It was crappy directions, but it was better than we had before. I spotted a pencil under the bar and marked the spot on the wall where the smoke disappeared. "All we need now is a compass," I muttered.

And maybe for me to transform into a bloodhound again. *Ugly dog. Good nose,* Beast thought instantly. *Good nose for finding mother of sick kit.* Which was high praise from Beast for any other animal. She hated it when I shifted into other creatures.

From upstairs at the back of the house I heard a thin wail start, the scream of a terrified child. "Nononononononon-onono!" It was Bobby, not Charly. I snapped open a door, hearing it ram into the wall, and raced to the second floor.

CHAPTER 12

The Idea of You Shackled and Bound Is Appealing

Bobby was standing in the middle of his bedroom, dressed in superhero red, white, and blue pajamas. His eyes were open but unfocused, and his wail rose and fell like a metronome, not sounding even remotely human. He was reaching toward the window, the fingers of both hands pointing into the dark. I raced there, but when I looked out, there was nothing except the ground below and the twisting limbs of an old live oak. The night had clouded over and rain had started to fall, a melodious patter on the winter-hard ground and in the stiff green tree leaves.

In the night-dark window I saw Soul reflected, her silk clothing the blue of the ocean, her silver hair like storm clouds. "What did your friend say about Bobby?" Her voice cut through the wails as I turned to her. "That he was a divining rod?"

"Dowsing rod," I said, over Bobby's unbreaking scream. He didn't pause in the awful sound, not even to breathe, but continued the wail with each inhalation as well as the exhalations. I reached for Bobby but paused before I touched him. I didn't know what to do. His doorway filled with the others, Eli and his brother, Bodat, Esmee in her nightgown, and, in the shadows, Rick, wearing all black, like the cat he was.

I turned to Soul. "What do I do?"

She shook her head, but said firmly, "Whatever feels right."

I completed my reach and took Bobby's hands in both of mine. A shock detonated through me, intense magical energies throwing me to the floor. Beast batted my mind with a paw, claws extended, catching the magic that coursed through me and tossing it away. The breath I took ached as if I had breathed fire. My eyesight cleared and I realized I was on my knees, Bobby's hands still in mine. He was watching me, his gaze full of trust. "Thank you, Jane," he said. "It hurts when it happens."

"What," I croaked, coughed, and tried again. "What happened? What was that?"

"It was magic calling. It wakes me up sometimes."

"Of course," Soul breathed. "Dowsing rod. He pivots toward magic; he followed my spell. I am betting that we will discover that the finding flame I used and Bobby's hands both point to the exact direction. The direction of Misha."

I forced myself to my feet and hugged Bobby. "Get in bed, little man. You have babysitting duty tomorrow."

"While you rescue Misha?" he asked, hope pulling his face up in childlike joy.

"I hope so. That's the plan as it stands now." I pointed to the tall bed in the corner, the sheets and linens folded back like at a fancy hotel.

Bobby ducked his head in understanding and crawled in, closing his eyes. "Night, Jane."

"Night, Bobby," I said.

None of us had slept, and there would be no rest tonight either. We needed to follow up on the few clues we had—and I needed an update on it all.

I entered the dining room, where an impromptu meeting was in progress, my favorite kind of meeting, one with mounds of food. There was thinly sliced rare beef; some kind of fowl carcass with a smaller mound of bird meat that had been pulled from the naked bones; a plate of pale, smoked, thinly sliced cheese; interwoven avocado and tomato slices; varieties of lettuce, pickles, and assorted green sandwich fixings. Even hot peppers and two kinds of onions, which, by the smell in the room, were huge favorites of the Kid and Bodat. Suddenly I craved all the green stuff, a decidedly weird feeling until I remembered that I hadn't shifted into my Beast in ages. My human body required a more green-based diet than my animal one did. I smeared mayo onto rye bread and stacked the avocado and tomato, pickles, lettuces, and the bird meat, which turned out to be smoked goose. I constructed and listened as the Kid recapped what we had so far. I even put fruit on my plate.

I also ignored Rick and Soul, concentrating on my own people, or tried to. But Rick was dressed in black jeans and a long-sleeved tee, sitting in a corner chair, one leg drawn up and his bare foot hanging off the chair seat. Bare feet. I loved a man's bare feet. They held such promise. I leaned against the wall, sandwich in both hands, and bit into it. I moaned softly, closing my eyes, seeing Rick on the dark of my lids, spread out on my bed, his abs clinching as he laughed at something I'd said. He—and the sandwich— were both totally delicious.

I was in so much trouble.

"We have a general direction for Misha and indications that she's alive," Eli said, bringing me back to the room. I focused on his words and chewed, paying no attention to Soul's intense scrutiny. "As the distance from this house increases, the directional arc of error increases, but close in, it isn't too bad." He laid a paper Natchez city map on the table; it was marked with a red triangle, the apex at Esmee's house. The triangle widened to include most of the old uptown, the riverfront, and, oddly enough, most of the city across the river: Vidalia, Louisiana. I looked up at Eli and he inclined his head, agreeing that it was a coincidence worth investigating if my clues in Natchez continued to be staked.

"Yeah. My bro, the ace Ranger, has a direction based on Soul's spell and Bobby's dowsing. Bodat has contacts in county records that point us in the direction of properties that were owned by Silandre and her cohorts in the past, under different names, and then were inherited"—he made little bunny-ear quotations in the air around the word— "prior to the sixties, when the vamps came out of the closet. We'll narrow them down to locations within the arc that Bobby and Soul established in their direction hunts."

Eli took over. "The properties were passed on through the inheritance laws to Silandre herself, of course, but under different names to protect the vampire identity. The different names opened up an entirely new set of research opportunities, and the boys have been compiling and cross-referencing the names."

"Which," the Kid hesitated and glanced up at his brother, revising whatever he'd been about to say. "Which revealed past—" He stopped again, and finished with, "Past *relationships* between Silandre and that Esther vamp." I figured he'd been about to say something crass about them in bed together. Again.

Bodat said, "Yeah, she went both ways, dude—AC/DC. Girls and guys." I wanted to slap the back of his head, but Eli beat me to it. "Bodat reared back in his chair. "Dude, what was that for? Whadid I say?"

"Stop with the comments. *Dude*," Eli said. "Ladies present."

Bodat looked at me and shook his head in confusion, clearly not putting the word *lady* into the same column as me. And then he looked at Esmee and said, "Oh. Like, sorry, uh, ma'am. Sorry." He looked over his shoulder at Eli and said, "You coulda just said, dude."

I hadn't really paid attention to Bodat except for registering his pizza scent, and I wasn't surprised that he was pudgy around the middle, with soft arms and droopy flesh, old before his time through lack of exercise and improper diet. On the other hand, the Kid was toned and fit, his arms showing muscles through the T-shirt material—the result of being forced into an exercise plan and better diet by his Ranger brother and his depressed housemate (me) for several months. "Anyway," Bodat said, "we also looked into them hanging with Zoltar and Narkis, and we got nada. No such luck. Other stuff is more interesting, like a relationship between Silandre and Leo Pellissier."

"Silandre and Leo?" I asked around my sandwich, trying to cover my mouth.

"Yeah," the Kid said. "Silandre and Leo had a . . . a *thing* before the Civil War, and she ran a . . . a brothel"—he smiled his delight in finding a word other than *whorehouse*—"here in Natchez for his uncle Amaury. When Leo took over as his uncle's heir, he gave her the house."

"Our city was rife with prostitution back in the day," Esmee said, sounding almost proud, crossing her ankles and lacing her fingers around her belly. "By some counts there were over a hundred catering to the plantation owners, the dockworkers and bargemen from the north, and visiting Yankees. Quite the moneymakers, they were. My great-great-grandfather owned such an institution in Under the Hill. I should look this up in the family histories to be sure of the address. I do believe it might still be standing."

Eli's brows went up at the pride in her voice.

Esmee added, "Oh yes. Early travelers described our fair town variously as 'a gambler's paradise, a sinkhole of iniquity, and a resort of the damned.' That is a quote, though I don't recall who said it, precisely." She preened. "My children are horrified at the histories. But the young tend to be such ninnies. Don't you agree?"

Smothering a grin, I chewed, thought, and decided not to reply to the question. "Hmmm. Vamp squabbles and wars and romances can go back for dozens of human generations, practically lost in time. But for them it's all like yesterday and they still get mighty unhappy about past slights and fights and betrayals. Okay. Soooo. Leo may know stuff about Silandre."

"I am quite certain that my master knows much about many of his sworn Mithrans."

The scent hit me. I whirled to the doorway, in the middle of swallowing, and nearly choked. I had to put down my sandwich or drop it. *Bruiser.*

Speak of betrayal. Speak of the devil.

The memory rammed through me. Bruiser holding me down, letting Leo drink from me. My heart thudded painfully. I forced myself to inhale slowly. His scent filled my nostrils. It was . . . not the same, not *quite* the same, as I remembered. And I didn't know why.

The energies and pheromones in the room stuttered and realigned yet again. Rick dropped his leg to the floor. He was professionally interested in the MOC's primo. He was personally interested in my reaction to the primo. Soul sat forward. The boys dropped their heads and shoulders and as if looking at tablet screens, studied the rest of us beneath lowered brows. Eli was watching my reactions, amused. Which ticked me off.

The teens were whispering, "Dude, isn't that MOC's top human blood meal?"

And, "Be polite, man. He's like, *right here*."

Soul swept her hair back. She was interested in Bruiser in both professional and very personal ways. Her nostrils fluttered. She liked the way he *smelled*. Beast rose in me and I felt my eyes do that glow thing, which meant she was looking out at the world through me. *Mates,* she thought at me, struggling for control of my mind. *Will fight for mates.*

Crap, crap, crap on toast. My breath came fast as I wrestled Beast down; she snarled at me, showing killing teeth. I'd rather fight a score of rogue vamps than face a difficult social situation—and this was going to be bad. I just knew it.

In the shadows behind him I spotted the sheriff. *Of course. Why not one more?* Murphy's Law was working overtime tonight. The sheriff hadn't been involved in the cleanup of vamp bodies the last time I was here, so she might be a new player to them. She pushed past and into the dining room, going straight to Eli, who sat up and sucked in his already rock-hard stomach. Wry amusement pulled my mouth to the side. I shifted my attention back to the doorway. Back to George Dumas.

Eyes on Bruiser, I took a breath to force some sort of equanimity, lifted my sandwich, and bit in. Bruiser looked like a million dollars, spiffy in suit pants and polished loafers with tassels. His white dress shirt was rolled up to his elbows, his tie loose, and his suit coat was slung over his shoulder by one finger.

Bruiser shifted his eyes from Rick to me and smiled. Beast's reaction started at my toes and curled up my body. Purring. *He betrayed us,* I thought at her. *He was disloyal.* Beast didn't care.

Sylvia, who had eyes only for Eli, said, "We have more preliminary data on the dead found in Esther's old lair. Nine vamps and forty-seven humans, twelve of them children." The room went still and shocked. "The chief of police and I got a call from the governor offering any and all help. And then, on my way over, I got a report on more missing witches."

The pheromones altered again, fast this time, to surprise and worry as we all turned to her. "Until today we weren't sure, as the Acheé family wasn't out of the closet, but it's always been a good guess—a family of all women and few surviving males is indicative of a possible witch connection. And their neighbors claimed the women could grow vegetables year round."

"How many?" Rick asked, standing and pulling a brand new, top-of-the-line cell phone out of his pocket to take notes.

"Four," Sylvia said. "Three adults and a thirteen-year-old who hasn't reached puberty."

Puberty was when most witches come into their gifts. "But the kidnappers might not know that," I said.

"Precisely. We have Crime Scene on the way there now. It isn't a pretty sight."

"Details," Rick said.

"Introductions," the sheriff said. If she had fangs, she would have been showing them. I chuckled softly and Rick sent me a glare that was all cat. Quickly, he returned his attention to the lady sheriff and smiled his million-dollar smile—which the sheriff totally ignored. He offered his intros, and Sheriff Turpin said, "You're part of the help the governor promised us. Law enforcement of Adams County is *always* happy to work with PsyLED." But her tone was dry and tight. Proper protocol would have been for Rick and Soul to report in to Sylvia before coming here, and she wanted them to know she didn't appreciate the misstep.

I watched as Rick made nice-nice with Sylvia Turpin, LEO to LEO. They seemed to be okay, and I tuned them out, watching other players in the room.

Soul and Bruiser were looking each other over, a small smile on Bruiser's face. They had met not that long ago, here in Natchez after the shootout. I had left the scene with Rick, and the glance they were exchanging suggested that the primo and Rick's Soul had spent time together. And liked it. *Crap.* Inside, my Beast hissed.

Yeah, I thought at her. *Me too.*

"NPD is handling the lair. The Acheé place falls under my jurisdiction. We're getting stretched thin, trying to keep citizens safe and run the crime scenes. First glance at blood spatter," Sylvia said, bringing me back to the present, "indicates they fought back. Our local expert says it's both Naturaleza vamp blood and witch. And the witches had silver-shot ammo on hand. It didn't slow the vamps down."

"Local expert?" Bruiser asked, his eyes still on Soul.

"Local vamp. Helps us out sometimes. And no. I won't tell you the name."

As the law enforcement and vamp-dinner types chatted and metaphorically scented one another's butts, I slipped upstairs for gear, and then out the back door and into the night. I needed to get out of there. There were too many relationships in the house and none of them going where my cat wanted. The Acheé house gave me an excuse, and though I knew it was running away and totally cowardly, I headed straight to Bitsa.

The air was cold and sharp and a dispirited rain drizzled down, some sleet mixed in. It fell in irregular patterns, as if unsure whether to quit and go dry or give in and have a thunder temper tantrum and mini flood.

"Let's take my vehicle."

I started at the sound of Rick's voice in the dark, from several cars parked in a neat row. His scent reached me, man and cat and sultry jungle nights. "What? Where?"

I heard keys jingle and amusement in his voice. "The Acheé family place. To take in the scents. That *is* where you were going. Right?"

I shouldn't go with Rick. I really shouldn't. Things are too messed up between us. I spun on a booted heel and said, "Sure. Let's go." So much for taking a stand.

Rick led the way through the small gate in the eight-foot-tall fence and around front. Silent, we got into his SUV, and I was buckling up when I realized Rick was standing outside with the back door open. The vehicle rocked when the wolf, Brute, leaped onto the bench seat and lay down, panting, his head turned away, the neon-green Pea clinging to his back. "Great," I muttered.

Rick, if he heard me, chose to ignore me. He got in, closed out the night, and drove into the dark, his electronic tablet glowing on the console between us with our path all plotted out. I noticed that the house we were going to was in the opposite part of town from the red triangle Eli had prepared for us to search for Misha, and wondered if that meant anything at all.

We wove through the city and out into the country, trees crowding against the sides of the road and the smell of water on the night breeze. We crossed over a mostly dried-up, winding bayou three times before pulling on to a drive and winding our way in the deeper dark. The live oaks branched over the narrow driveway, interlacing like fingers to keep out the moonlight. The Acheé house was a traditional tidewater, up on pilings with a front porch that ran the length of the house, a tin roof, and chimneys at both ends. When we got out, the smell of the city was gone and the smell of water and living plants was strong. To the side of the house was a circular open area marked with stones, a perfect witch circle disguised as a sitting area with a gazebo in the center.

I meandered over while Rick went to talk to the LEO guarding the crime scene until the techs could get there. In the open space, no trees were in the way to spoil the moon's glow, which suggested that a moon witch lived or practiced here. At the gazebo, I bent and spotted the cleverly disguised wheels used to push the structure out of the way when the family's womenfolk needed some moon time. The stones around the edges were all white quartz, and winter herbs were planted around the outside edge. The scent of rosemary and sage permeated the air here, contained by the chill. I walked around the gazebo, staring up at the moon. The silvery orb was nearly full, and Beast pulled at me to shift and hunt, not demanding, not yet, but making her needs known.

Have not hunted in many moon times, she thought. *Jane is selfish.*

Yeah, and you're chained to Leo.

Leo is not here. Leo is far away.

But his primo is here. That gonna make you get all hot and bothered?

Bruiser is good for mate. Will take Bruiser.

"Not gonna happen," I murmured.

Beast huffed and disappeared, and Rick said, "What's not gonna happen?"

"No witch circle this full moon unless we get the family back," I lied. Not so very long ago, I couldn't lie worth a dang. Now it came easily.

"We have entrée," Rick said. "Shall we?"

I wanted to say, "When and where?" but managed to keep it inside. I nodded mutely and tucked my hands into my pockets to keep from shaping them over his butt as I followed him up the wooden steps to the doorway. The scent of blood was like a barbed fist to the jaw as Rick opened the door.

The blood was vamp by the smell, and I stood transfixed in the opening, lips parted, sucking in air over the roof of my mouth. Over the biological scent of drying blood I smelled gun propellant, the stench of burned nitrocellulose. And then I smelled the scent of child, witch child, her blood spilled. My fingers curled and my Beast claws tried to press through my fingertips, a piercing pain. I hissed softly.

"Jane?"

I growled and whirled to see Rick holding out a pair of cloth booties and gloves and something white in a plastic baggie.

"Jane?" Rick looked away, turning his head but keeping me in his peripheral vision. A strange dullness tugged at his mouth, catlike, uninterested, while at the same time actively involved in an exchange. It was big-cat body language for *Not stepping on your toes. Your territory, your meat.* Big-cat manners, intended to defuse an angry mate.

I huffed and felt Beast slide out of my eyes. "Sorry."

"It's okay. But we need to preserve the crime scene. We need to dress out."

I took the pile of paper and nitrile and dressed in the white—white booties, white nitrile gloves, white hair cap that shaped itself like a soft mound of bread-dough when I put it on, and white paper robe that tied in back. It was hot and stuffy and I hated it, but I understood the necessity. I didn't want to leave my own stray hairs in the blood or ruin my clothes. It took me longer than it did Rick, and I followed him inside, placing my feet between blood splotches.

The wolf and his rider waited at the door, and I could feel more than hear the wolf's low growl deep in his throat. His lips rose to reveal the points of his fangs, and I kept my gaze to the side. Too many species in one spot; the language of body movements was not precise, but a direct gaze was a challenge among all animals, except sometimes humans. Brute didn't like the smells any more than I did, which made me feel better toward the wolf than I wanted to.

I concentrated on the room, walking around the perimeter first and then through the middle. Amid the visual positioning of the blood and the easily differentiated scent signatures, I put the story together quickly. I went to an opening and along the hall. Here the scents diminished, but they got stronger again when I backtracked and entered the kitchen.

There was blood spatter here. A lot of it. I studied the cheery room with its granite countertops and antique cabinets, tile, and vintage table and chairs. The family spent a lot of time here, cooking together, eating at the casual table.

Carefully, I drew on Beast's vision to see the magics that swirled. There had been wards in this room, wards of deep green and blue, woven out of love and cooking and family, but something had broken through them and attacked. I centered myself and sought out the patterns. Three adult witches lived here now. Generations before this, maybe as many as eight witches had practiced here, weaving wards of protection. And in the middle of them all, a hole had been torn, the edges waving in the air, blackened and burned. Now that I knew they were here, I could smell them, scorched energies like the stink of lightning and grave earth.

I turned and saw the same thing at the front door: a bigger hole, a hole that had taken the ward off the entire front of the house. It had taken some massive energies to do that. Rick stood at the door, a psy-meter in one hand, held above his head, alternately measuring the magical energies and taking notes on his tablet.

He was also talking to the wolf, giving him instructions. I shook my head in disbelief at the thought of Rick partnering with one of the werewolves who had tortured him for days. The huge wolf took the orders, though admittedly orders posed as suggestions and conversation. I shut them out and returned my attention to the kitchen, following the lines of attack.

Much later, I heard Rick enter behind me. "What do you think?" he asked.

"The vamps came in the front door, four of them, and attacked one witch in the front room. She was armed and fired off several rounds. I counted"—I tilted my head, bringing back the images of the living room—"five casings, so at least that many. Nine mil, silver shot, hand packed most likely. Look for a hand loader set in the husband's shop."

"Why do you think that?" Rick asked.

I shrugged. "Can't say. Something about the round casings

on the floor." I tilted my head the other way, eyes still closed. "Look for tiny pressure points like a vise might make."

"Okay." Rick's tone was halfway between impressed and doubtful.

I went on with my analysis. "She stopped firing. Maybe the gun jammed? And pulled a silver knife. Cut a vamp. But it rode her down, fangs at her throat. Draining her. Another took down the child standing in the hallway. Not so much blood from her, but she drank—" I stopped and sniffed again, turning my head back to the hallway to make sure. "Yeah. Female vamp. And her pals entered the kitchen. Two witches here. The vamps had a charm or something. They went right through the wards on the front of the house and in here and attacked. They were messy, but they were careful too. They didn't kill anyone, not here. Everyone was alive when they were hauled off. Alive and unconscious, still stinking of fear."

I opened my eyes and met Rick's. He was standing close, watching me, our gazes on a level. I smiled at him and knew it was mostly teeth and threat. "Hope you don't plan on taking any vamps in alive—or undead—on this one. 'Cause I'm gonna take their heads and you better not try to stop me."

Rick's lips softened, his stare dropping to my mouth. "How much are you getting per head?"

"Forty K."

Rick chuckled and shook his head. "And here I am working for Uncle Sam for the price of two heads a year."

"When you get tired of being cheap labor whose hands are tied by stupid rules, let me know."

Rick's Frenchy eyes followed the curve of my jaw like a tender hand. I shivered under the not-touch and felt something hard and cold start to melt deep inside. I had wounded his, but he had forgiven me, I realized, and the coldness melted even faster, running out of me.

"You'll take me in?" he asked, his voice a purr of sound. "Like a lost kitten?"

"We'd make a good team," I managed, my voice matching his, purr for purr.

"Yeah. We would. And George? You take him in too?"

All the happy-happy-joy-joy feelings froze solid. "That was low."

His eyes hardened. "You saying you aren't interested in the MOC's sex-and-blood meal?"

"You bringing your Soul in?" I countered. "How about your crazy wolf and the grindy who'd kill us in a heartbeat if we tried to have sex?"

Something flashed between us, something icy and flaming, velvety and thorny, like fear and need, anger and joy, all commingled together. I wanted to reach out and touch him, to break that cold/hot wall between us, but before I could lift my hand, Rick turned to the front of the house, his paper clothing crinkling. The door was still hanging open to the night. "We have company," he said, his voice displaying none of the emotion I smelled on the air. Vehicle lights sliced through the dark, a van and a car. Crime Scene techs were here, and they'd be ticked that we had entered.

"Good," I said, on the knot of anger rising in my throat. "Things were getting sticky in here."

"I like them hot and sweaty better," Rick said. But he'd turned and was at the door, stripping off his paper and nitrile. Not quite sure what had happened, I followed, picking up a few things I thought we might need on the way. I left my crime scene clothing in a pile with his, remembering a time when I'd had to separate our clothes, which had been tossed onto the floor, so we could dress. I'd lost so much by my own stupidity. My life sucked.

I waited in the SUV for him and when he got in, Brute again rocking the SUV's suspension, Rick slammed the door and looked at the stuff in my lap. "You took evidence from a crime scene?"

"Yeah. Arrest me."

"While the idea of you shackled and bound is appealing, no." I gave him a hesitant smile and he said, "What do you have?"

"Amulets. At least one witch was a moon witch." I showed him a moonstone paperweight. "One an earth witch, if you go by the garden. And one was an air witch." I held up the dried leaves I'd stolen from a bowl on a lamp stand. "There are bowls of dried leaves and twigs and pine needles everywhere, but nothing is scented, like for potpourri. And I can feel the magic on them." I crunched the leaves slightly and smelled only oak and pine rising from them. "The bowls of windblown leaves are probably set equidistant on the points of a pentacle."

"Not bad." Rick started the engine, pulling slowly into the night along the narrow drive, the oak trees sheltering us from the moon until we pulled onto the secondary road. Rick tensed.

"Full-moon problems?" I asked, keeping my tone calm.

"Yeah. Mind if I play my music?" Without waiting for my reply, he hit PLAY on the SUV's sound system and flute music skirled out. It was a spell, created by my once friend Big Evan to control Rick's need to turn furry for the three days of the full moon. His tattoos, magic woven into his skin, prevented his turning, and he had nearly gone insane with the pain until Evan had found this treatment.

I looked out the window, knowing I had been cut off. Yet knowing that Rick was as aware of me as I was of him. Knowing that Bruiser and Soul and our past together stood between us, as real as if they fought, swords drawn and blades clashing.

Under my T-shirt was another theft, an old photo of an American Indian woman wearing a homespun dress, soft-looking boots, and a feather woven into her braided hair. Not Cherokee. Maybe Choctaw. She had been staring at me as if begging me to steal her photo. And for reasons I didn't understand, I had.

CHAPTER 13

Make Ceremony with Me

Sitting on the edge of the bed in Esmee's house, I took out the old black-and-white photo and studied it. The woman was young, midtwenties, standing with shoulders back, wearing a Western cowboy hat, a gun belt around her hips, Annie Oakley style. Her dress was short for the era, stopping midcalf, revealing the boots that looked like deer hide, embroidered with porcupine quills and beads. The picture frame was wood, carved with tiny grooves that looked exactly like bird footprints, down to the talons at the end of the toes, the wood stained with some greenish-bluish tint that had penetrated the pattern carved into the wood, making the bird feet stand out sharply. The term came to me from high school art history class: *counter-relief*, or *intaglio*. Weird to remember that. I had sucked at art.

Misha had been in that class. She had taken to art like a bird to the air, freed by all the media, all the things she could shape and change and bring to beauty. All the things she could control. Unlike the rest of her life, which was out of her control. Like me, Misha had gone to regular counseling. I had gone for the experts to keep tabs on me and try to poke holes in the curtain of memory loss. I wondered why Misha had gone. I had no idea. I also had no idea why I had taken the photo. It had nothing to do with beauty or art. It had everything to do with the woman in the print calling out to me.

I sighed and set the picture facedown on the bed, reach-

ing for the phone. It hadn't rung, and I held it, waiting. Leo
wanted to chat and my bound Beast knew it. It was childish,
but I let it chime twice before I punched SEND. "Hi, Leo."
Beast started to purr and rolled over on her side. I could
feel the power of her breath rumbling through me.

"What have you done to my heir's house?" he spat.

I could tell his three-inch fangs had dropped down and
he was talking through and around them. "Good to speak
with you too," I said, not because it was true, but to yank his
chain. "Hope you are well and chipper and all that. How's
business?" Leo was raised in a more proper time, and when
he forgot or ignored the niceties it gave me an opening for
insult and snark. He didn't give me many.

"What. Have. *You*. Done. With my heir's house?"

"Ahhh." I relaxed onto the bed, understanding. I had
modified the house I was using in New Orleans and I hadn't
exactly asked permission. Part of the modifications were to
take over Leo's secret lair and make it into a combo safe
room and weapons room. "I take it you paid me a visit?"

"There is silver everywhere."

"Guns too. And ammo. And things that go bang."

"Silver in my lair," he grated.

"Yeah. Sorry 'bout that," I lied, and made sure he could
hear that I wasn't sorry at all.

Leo growled low in his throat; Beast rolled, pulling her
paws beneath her, ready to pounce or flee. "My house, Leo,"
I said, "for the duration of my stay in New Orleans, as per
my contract. No one said I couldn't redecorate."

The silence was too long, that potent silence the really
old vamps can do, because they don't breathe or have a
heartbeat. "We have much to discuss, my Enforcer."

"Yeah. I guess we do. I'll see you when I get back to New
Orleans. Meantime, stay out of my house." I hit END and
smiled slightly. *Bet that ticked off the MOC.*

Beast yawned deep inside and rolled back over. I
frowned at her. *Beast? You didn't go nuts at the sound of
Leo's voice. What gives?*

Beast is not chaser of squirrels.

It took a moment to realize that she was responding to
my *go nuts* phrasing.

Fast chase, small bite, crunch and gone, she thought. *And
Beast is still hungry.*

But you didn't get . . . I let the thought trail off. For the first time since Beast was accidently bound to Leo, she wasn't all *Pet me, mate me, rub my tummy* with Leo. In fact, she'd been calm. She had gotten good at batting away the magics used against her.

Fierce joy shuddered through me like an earthquake. The urge to shift slammed through like an aftershock. I hadn't shifted in *so* long, afraid of what Beast would do, afraid of losing myself to her binding to the Master of the City. I *needed* to shift. I needed the healing and the strength that shifting could offer, the renewal. I had denied my nature longer than at any time since I rediscovered my shifting ability when I was eighteen. And I had shoved that need so far down, so deep, that it exploded upward now, as if under pressure, desperate.

I stood, gathered my go-bag, and made my way out of the house, out into the last hours of the night. There were no stones here, not the kind I needed. And then I remembered the pink marble mounting block and made my way to it. It was well hidden beneath the overgrowth of shrubs and the low branches of the tree overhead, and when I climbed deep into the brush, I was hidden from the house. On my knees, I stripped, dropping my clothes in a heap, and strapped the go-bag around my neck with my gold nugget necklace and the mountain lion tooth I had wired to the gold chain. Naked, chill bumps rising on my skin, I bent to the stone and rubbed the nugget over the marble, depositing a small scrape of gold, a homing beacon if I got lost in this unfamiliar place.

I sat on the cold marble, the stone burning its frozen way into my skin, and grabbed the tooth like the talisman it was. I'd been afraid to shift for months. Now, suddenly, all I wanted was to shift and run and hunt and kill something. I blew out a breath and closed my eyes. And thought of the snake that rests at the center of every cell of every animal. The snake that is the RNA of creation. I sought the snake of form that was my Beast. The mountain lion. The *Puma concolor*.

I dropped front paws down to ground, back paws still on stone, and stretched hard, feeling new muscles and weight. Jane had lifted metal things and grunted like dog, sweated like horse; she had made me bigger big-cat. I looked over muscular shoulders at body and twitched long, thick tail. I was strong. I was big! Jane was good.

I looked at house and saw human-shaped form on back porch. Watching Beast. It was Bruiser. Bruiser had watched Jane shift into Beast. Bruiser knew all of Jane's secrets now. I chuffed my displeasure and caught his scent on night air. Bruiser had changed. His scent was no longer Leo's scent. Bruiser smelled of power and youth and many things that were good. But Bruiser was no longer bound to Leo as he had been. Bruiser was not blood-servant now. Bruiser was other. And full of power.

And now Beast was bound to Leo. I chuffed with amusement. We had changed places.

I turned and leaped into the limbs of tree with winter leaves. Walked along limb. Leaped to top of brick fence and over, into dark. I lifted snout into wind and smelled big water, river, name twisting like snake. It was too far to walk, but close to ride. Beast needed truck heading to sunset. I trotted along road, watching for truck, feeling new weight and power and mass in body and limbs. Jane did good. Jane did very good.

Trucks were few and I walked long before I saw/heard truck in distance, growling like Leo, eyes bright like twin stars, going toward river. I jumped into tree and crouched. Thinking. *Beast will have to land lightly, or new mass will rock truck, like throwing prey to its knees*. I crouched, and when truck was beneath I leaped forward, in direction of truck and landed lightly, scrabbling with paw and claws on truck top until balance was found. Then I settled, snout to the air, smelling, mouth open, lips stretched back to show killing teeth to world. *Beast is big! Beware of Beast!*

Truck stopped before reaching river, roaring heart gone silent. I landed in shadows at tail of truck. But truck had no tail. Not even boar tail or bison tail. No tail at all. Truck had no blood and had bones of metal. Was alive and not alive. Still did not understand. I wandered off into night, following wind that called to me of fish and water and river birds asleep on banks.

World fell away before and below. River with snaky name was down cliffs, farfarfar. Much farther across river was land—city of Vidalia—and man lights, to steal vision. But here night was greens and silvers and grays; water was rich and powerful, rising with mist on chilled air. I liked twisty big water. Scented water birds on air and alligator and fish and human smells of gas and oil and stinky breath of trucks and boats. One long boat floated below, calling lonesome into dark. Boat was barge. Remembered barge from hunger times. Sick and dying humans on board as it floated by. I snorted at remembered stink of putrid flesh.

Opened mouth to cleanse away stink memory, pulling in river air over roof of mouth with soft *scree* of sound. Flehmen behavior, Jane called scenting. Upstream, smelled human town of Natchez. Below, smelled/saw/tasted water. Had not rushed down cliff in many moon times, and this cliff had no rock to secure landing. But did have trees and roots and places to land/leap.

I spotted a limb far down cliff face and gathered body close, paws together beneath belly. Leaped. Extending front legs and front claws. Landed and pushed again, jumping to small root, too small for Beast mass, landed and pushed again, hearing old root crack and break. Body flying like bird, fastfastfast, downdowndown, hit log buried in up-and-down mud with front paws and shoved, twisting body, whirling tail for balance. Go-bag slid and bumped neck. Body went to side and small ledge of sand. Hit and pushed, hit and pushed, down and down and side and side, bag and nugget bouncing. Swiveled body, changed direction, landed, pushed. Heard falling stones and mud and man waste of plastic bottles and cups falling, slower than Beast.

I slammed into small tree, its roots clinging for life into mud and dirt. Roots held and Beast stopped. Fast. Hit hard on chest and belly. Chuffed with delight. Water was close, whispering like low growl of big-cat and vampires and like thump of many running prey through ground.

Vibrations, Jane thought at me, waking up from sleep of shift into Beast. *The vibrations of the water grinding on the earth, like a snake grinds on the ground to— Hey. How'd we get . . . ? No way. You did not jump. Crap. You are insane.*

I chuffed with laughter. *Was good leap. Ground is close.*

No! Ground is, like, thirty feet below us.

Not far. I leaped and bounded from small limb, letting it

bend with our greater weight and mass. Landed on mud at bottom. Jane said words in mind, words that she did not like. I chuffed again. Jane was frightened of short jump. Jane was silly like kit. I looked up cliff to sky, hidden by rising earth. Jane went silent in shock, as if shot by man gun. I chuffed again with laughter.

I hungered after shift and trotted upstream. Found sleeping place of water birds, all silent, white feathers bright under pregnant moon. I leaped and caught birds in claws of each front paw. Feathers flew into the dark. Birds made no sound of fear or death, but all other birds screamed and flew into night. Both birds in claws died. I ate, crunching bones and swallowing feathers and webbed feet and spitting out long bones and curved beak. Egrets were much good taste but not enough meat for new Beast shape and size. Wanted deer. Looked across snaky river to see deer on far side, safe from Beast. Snorted. Sneaky deer, to live on other side of river.

I smelled herbed smoke on wind. Stopped, snout high, sniffing. I remembered this scent.

Herbed wood smoke, Jane whispered. *Dried sweetgrass and sage. A tribal Indian scent.*

I sniffed into wind and trotted from bloody sleeping-place of birds. In distance, I saw flickering light. *Fire.* I slowed and curved from water toward fire. Scents grew stronger. Fire was burning plants used in Jane-ceremonies. I dropped to belly and crept closer, paws pulling-pushing me to light. When fire was close, the I/we of Beast slowed, stopping beneath leaves of winter plant, hidden.

Sitting across fire was tribal Indian woman, like Jane, but also different. Jane had strong nose and chin and golden skin. Woman across fire had knobbed nose and chin and darker skin, like metal coin humans used, left long in sun.

Old copper, Jane whispered to mind, seeing skin. Sniffing odor of fire she thought, *Rosemary, sage, sweetgrass, and marijuana. Weird.*

Old Indian woman smiled across fire, looking at Beast hidden in shadows. She had gray hair worn in a single braid over shoulder, and she wore a dress made from grain sacks, maybe blue with yellow flowers. Hard to tell in Beast night vision. On her feet were boots made from the skin of deer decorated with dyed porcupine quills. *This is the woman from the photograph,* Jane whispered to me, *but old. Really old.* I dropped head to paws, jaw heavy, ears curled forward. Nostrils wide and fluttering, I scented.

"Come, skinwalker," the old woman said softly. "Sister of my people. Conqueror of my people. Come make ceremony with me."

I brought paws beneath me, tight, ready for killing attack or running away, shoulders high.

Listen, Jane said to me. *Listen to her!*

"Come," the old woman repeated. "Sit with me." Smoke billowed before the wind. *"Nuwhtohiyada gotlvdi,"* she whispered. They were old words, *Make peace with me,* in Cherokee dialect. The words the white man spoke to the Cherokee before he stole the Cherokee land and forced the tribe west. Beast remembered, remembered the lie. Humans lied. Humans always lied.

But this is an Indian woman, Jane thought. *Not the white man, not the speaker of lies.*

"You will come to the church on the cliff at dawn," the old woman said. "It is an old church, white painted. A tiny chapel with a very tall narrow steeple. It smells of humans and witches and much time. Its roof is stone, like overlapping leaves in the sun, dark gray in the moon. And it is no more." She gave me an address on Jefferson Street. "You will come in human form. And you will know what you wish to know."

The old woman leaned forward and tossed branches on the fire. The scent of burning rosemary filled the air, intense, hurting my nostrils. I backed away on slow paws, leaving tracks in sand from river. Smoke from the fire billowed up and burned my eyes, and I backed faster. When the smoke cleared, the flames were gone. I pawed forward. The old woman was gone too. I crawled to the fire, smelling an ancient flame wet from many rains, cold for many more than five days.

She was never here, Jane murmured. *But . . . I've seen that church. I've seen it in a . . . a photo somewhere. Back at Esmee's. And if I remember right, it burned down in the sixties. We need to get back up the cliff.*

I tilted neck up. And up. Long climb. *Better if Jane walks than Beast.* I thought of Jane snake. And entered place of change.

No!

But it was too late. Beast was gone. Jane remained.

"You sneaky dang cat!" I dressed in the lightweight clothes in the go-bag: thin pants, flip-flops, long-sleeved tee, and a cheap hoodie. Somehow I'd forgotten to fold in panties, so I went without. Dressed, I looked up the cliff, which was a lot smaller here than where Beast had made her descent, and spotted a narrow path, something suited to a mountain goat, but it would have to do. Luckily, someone human used the path often enough to have left handholds of knotted ropes tied to roots and trees, and deep depressions where feet might go. I lost my flip-flops on the way up and arrived barefoot, sweating in the icy air and chilled to the bone, muscles quivering with fatigue and hunger, which was the body's way of asking, *What are you doing, idiot?*

Once at the top, I saw the lights of Natchez in the distance and thought about calling a taxi. Instead I called Eli, who answered on the first ring. "'Sup?"

"I need a ride and some clothes. I'm about a mile upstream of Natchez. I can see the city lights in the distance. And I see a car running parallel to the river, maybe a thousand feet from the river."

"Clothes? You want me to bring you *clothes*?"

"I'm not naked; I'm just underdressed for the weather. And bring boots and weapons. I have a place we need to check out. And stop and get some burgers. Maybe six."

To his credit, Eli didn't waste time with inanities like "Why?," "How?," or "Are you insane?" He said, "Google says Cemetery Road parallels the river. Get to the road. I'm not coming in the woods to find you."

"And socks," I added, but he had hung up. I started for the road in the distance and learned real quick about the burr grasses that grew offshore. The round, spiked seeds hurt like a son of a gun, and stuck fast to bare skin or clothes until pulled out. I said some more words I'd not repeat to a housemother, but I made it to the road in under an hour, which felt like good time, except that I could see an SUV parked on the verge in the grasses. He saw me waving and limping and was sporting nearly a full-sized grin by the time I got in and slammed the door.

There were no overhead lights, and so I demanded,

"Flashlight." Eli passed the oversized torch into my hand with a *splat*, like a tech with a surgical instrument. I used the bright beam to examine my sore feet. They were bloody, and several long slender thorns were deeply embedded. "If you make fun, I'll hurt you," I snarled.

"Me?" It was said with an attempt at innocence and a stifled snicker.

I slanted my eyes at him with a look that promised pain, and picked out the splintered thorns as Eli made a three-point turn. I remembered the street name of the church we were going to, though not the number, and I gave Eli directions before climbing into the backseat and changing clothes. I was relatively sure he didn't watch, but I smelled his amusement and practically felt his stifled desire to mock. We were back in town, stopped at a traffic light, when he said, oh, so casually, "So, you shifted and went hunting?"

I thought about not answering, but the cat was out of the bag, literally, and there was no point not sharing. I climbed back into the front seat, pulled on my old, scratched, worn, Lucchese boots. I started braiding my hair and said, "Yeah."

A weight fell off me, so heavy it moved like a landslide, thick and full of dangerous debris, a rumbling that I felt from scalp to toes. I took a breath and it felt just the opposite, weightless and softly lit, as if by candlelight. I blinked into the night, seeing but not seeing old houses and businesses as we motored past. All I'd said was *Yeah*, but it was like I found something that had been buried for eons. A smile formed on my face, all unwittingly, and to hide my reaction, which felt deeply private and personal and stupid too, I said, "So. Burgers? I smell 'em."

Eli handed me a paper bag with golden arches on it and I chowed down, putting away three of them in less than a minute, describing the church remembered from the photo between swallows of half-chewed bites of burger.

"Your mama nev—" He stopped abruptly, and I breathed out my laughter through my nose.

"I'm sure my mama taught me to chew my food. Right after I brought it down and ripped out its throat."

Eli laughed with me, a chortling snicker, soft but explosive. "Yeah. Okay." He pointed. "That the church?"

"Yeah." Eli pulled over and I got out, smoothing my palms on my jeans. I wasn't nervous. Not really. Or not totally. But my palms were sweating. Eli appeared beside me and I jumped. I hadn't heard him get out or walk to me. Okay, so I was nervous. "You mind waiting outside?" I asked.

"You mind taking a weapon?" He extended two of my own semiautomatics snapped into their leather holsters: the matching Walther PK380s. The handguns were lightweight and ambidextrous, with bloodred polymer grips loaded with standard rounds, in the event of a human or blood-servant attack. Normally, one went under my arm, its twin at the small of my back. "That is why you had me bring them, right?"

"No. Not right now." I wiped my palms again, this time feeling the damp of sweat through to my skin, chilled by the night air. "That's for later, if we need them. I can't take weapons into the church."

Eli shrugged and locked the guns in the case in the back of the SUV. As he came back toward me, I said, "Eli? The church may not really be there. Okay?" To his credit, Eli merely wrinkled his forehead. I headed up the white walk. It started to rain, soft, heavy splats that fell straight down and left marks on the white concrete shaped like the burrs I'd pulled from my flesh. It seemed significant somehow, that the bloody burrs and the raindrops left similar imprints. I reached the church doors, narrow and twelve feet tall, painted the color of old blood. Lightning flashed and hit with a sizzling crack that brightened the world, and the door turned color for a moment to teal green. I pushed both doors open and they felt oily and damp beneath my hand, the dark of the church ahead, the dark of night behind. They stayed canted open as I entered, the night breeze and scent of rain following me inside.

The interior of the church had oiled wooden floors composed of boards twelve inches wide, walls painted white, and benches stained a dark brown. Lightning flashed again, and the sound of raindrops began on the roof overhead, a muted water on stone. I heard a scratching sound and a light appeared ahead under the cross at the front of the church, a lantern lit by a woman's hand with a paper taper, her body oddly obscured by shadows. I walked forward, my boots echoing off the walls.

The old woman from the river appeared out of the

gloom, lit by the tiny flame, still wearing the blue-and-yellow-flowered dress. I sniffed and smelled polishing wax, wilting lilies, the smoke from the match, and another person — a witch — but the scents were faint, as if left over from a long time in the past, and there weren't enough of them. Even if the church wasn't still used for worship, there should have been the scents of human tourists, paint, mold . . . but there wasn't.

The light grew as I approached, and I looked back at the sound of a ringing thud. My shadow reached out behind me, darkening and lengthening as I kept walking forward. The doors had closed behind me, shutting off my escape. Little fear critters latched onto my spine, clinging to the fine hairs there. My breathing went deep as my heart sped. I turned back to the light and to the old woman from the riverbank.

She was American Indian, but I was less certain of her tribe as I got closer, and I didn't know how to approach, exactly, except as a petitioner. That was why I'd left my weapons behind. She was sitting on the small podium, her feet dangling off the edge, soft-soled boots barely scraping the floor.

"You came," she said, her accent not quite what I had remembered; less Louisianan or Mississippian, more Texan, maybe.

"I came," I said. "My father was *ani gilogi*, Panther Clan of the Tsalagi. My mother was *ani sahoni*, Blue Holly Clan." She nodded for me to continue, and I said, "I am called Jane Yellowrock, or Yellow-Eyes Gold, *Dalonige i Digadoli*, in the tongue of The People."

"Yellow-Eyes Yellowrock. A strange name for a child. But the people of my mother were always a little pretentious, a little bit touched in the head. Not right since the *nunna dual tsuny*, the time of the Trail of Tears." She must have noticed some small reaction at the insult because she laughed, not unkindly, and waved the words away, saying, "Don't take offense. It's just the words of an old woman who has lived too long and forgotten how to be careful of her tongue. No offense was meant."

One did not take offense at the capriciousness of the very old. I tilted my head in acceptance, waiting.

She pursed her mouth as if thinking. "I am half-Cherokee, part Choctaw, a small part Natchez, and some white man, but we all have that." When I didn't reply, she went on, "Call me Kathyayini. It means 'Goddess of Power' in Cherokee. Like I said, a pretentious people. You know why I called you here. Yes?"

I shook my head. "Not entirely, no."

"My son married an Acheé woman. He does not know his wife is a witch or that his mother is a spirit walker." When I looked puzzled, she said, "A wise woman with the power to walk in dreams."

Kathyayini rocked back and forth as if she were in a rocking chair, giving me time to absorb her words. The smell of the candle was filling the chapel, a sharp herbal scent like rosemary and lime. *The power to walk in dreams.* Like Aggie One Feather, back in New Orleans? I remembered the dreams I'd had in the sweathouse, and the forms Aggie had taken in them. Could she walk in dreams too? "Okay," I said.

"Okay," she repeated. "This old woman wants her secrets, and the secrets of the women, kept secrets," Kathyayini said. "The men, they are no good with secrets. They freak out."

I breathed out my laughter at the modern word on the old woman's lips, and Kathyayini laughed with me. "I think it's a bit late about the witches and Acheé men. They know. I'm sure the cops told them."

"Stupid cops." She shook her head. "No good comes of men knowing secrets. They do best when protected.

"I can see your soul, you know," she went on. "Old soul. Older than me. Skinwalker soul. I only ever see one like it, and she was even older than you. Long time ago, in another place," she said before I could ask. "You also coated with magics: magic of skinwalker, magic of a mountain lion, magic of blood-charms. Dark magic, blood-magic charms. You should throw them away. They no good for you." I remembered the charms in the boot box back at Esmee's and on the table with our files, and the blood diamond, hidden in a safe-deposit box.

"You also carry the shadow magics of *one who should not walk the face of the earth*," she said, emphasizing the phrase with nods of her head, "drinker of blood. All that is bad. All of it. But the shadow magics of the blood drinker, that is the worst."

Her talk sounded a lot like Aggie One Feather's mother's chatter, half incomprehensible. "Okay," I said, not meaning that I understood, but an acknowledgment that she had spoken and that I was listening.

"Blood drinkers are like *U'tlun'ta,*" She pronounced it differently from *hut luna* of the Eastern Cherokee. "Stone finger," she clarified, in case I had missed it. "Skinwalkers like you, but old. All stone fingers go crazy sooner or later. Then they should die true death. So should vampires, like the shadow one in your soul house."

And then I understood. She could see Leo in my soul house. If she could see him, maybe she could get him out of me. My heart thumped hard.

CHAPTER 14

Try Not to Poison Me

Before I could ask, Kathyayini continued, "I don't got so much time, so listen. Long years past was cold iron, blood, three cursed trees, and lightning. Red iron will set you free." Which made no freaking sense. She rocked some more, her blue dress emerging from and falling into shadows, the crevices of her face deepening and softening, like the way the moon shadows show the folded hills and valleys of the Smoky Mountains—the Appalachians. Kathyayini added, "All that is for later, not for today. Today is for this: shadow and blood are a dark light buried beneath the ground." Neither riddle made sense, but I had learned that they weren't meant to. They were simply meant to light a path into a possible future.

"The one you seek," Kathyayini said, "she is bound to the earth. She didn't mean to be bound, but she cannot get away now."

"Uh huh. Okay." My phone buzzed like a hornet in my pocket, but when I reached for it, it wasn't there. Yet I still felt the buzzing in my pocket, against my thigh.

Something was very, very wrong. I had told Eli that the church might not really be here in our reality, but I hadn't considered what that might mean about where I'd be if I went inside. "Kathyayini, where am I?"

She waved her hand as if waving away my question. "Neither here nor there. Nor any place in between."

"How do I get back?"

"You done asking questions of me?"

Not really, but I didn't want to stay wherever I was. "For now. Thank you."

Kathyayini tossed me something and I identified it as I caught it. A coin, larger than a penny, heavier than a quarter. The metal felt cold, the engraving smooth and ancient. "You want me again, you come here at night and put that coin on the ground. I'll come." She waved the back of her hand at me, like shooing a fly. "Go now. We talk later, if you need."

Behind me, the church doors opened, allowing in a strong breeze that swept through, making the candle flame flicker and sputter. I backed slowly toward the old church doors, my eyes on Kathyayini. When the door appeared in my peripheral vision, I turned and went out into the night and down the steps. And remembered to breathe. A fog had roiled up outside, moving on the breeze in fitful gusts of shadow and white, and I couldn't see anything except the old trees just to my sides, which I was sure hadn't been there before.

The church doors slammed shut, making me jump and turn. Behind me, the church was gone. "Crap. Crap, crap, *crap*," I whispered.

"Jane?" a voice called, sounding muffled and distant, directionless in the heavy air.

"I'm here," I shouted.

"Where? Say again!" Eli appeared in the mist, both hands clutching weapons, a nine mil in his right hand, his shooting hand, and a vamp-killer in his left. He brought up the gun, centering it on my chest, finger resting gently on the trigger. I had no doubt the gun was ready to fire.

I raised my hands. "Easy there, Eli."

"Prove to me you are who you look like."

That was a weird request, but no weirder than anything else had been lately. "I want a steak, still mooing, hold the salad."

"And?"

Weirder and weirder. "And your brother, the computer geek criminal, wants ravioli. What about you?"

"I eat the steak *and* the salad. With beer."

"I'm guessing these were identifiers. What's going on?"

Eli approached slowly, growing firmer out of the fog. "Open your mouth."

I frowned but opened my mouth and stuck out my tongue. "You want me to say *ah* too?"

"Nope." He sheathed the knife and ejected the round from the chamber before he holstered the weapon. "Just looking for fangs."

I tucked my chin uncertainly. "Say what?"

"You are the third Jane Yellowrock I've seen in the past two hours, and the others had fangs. I staked them both and took their heads, but when I did, they vanished, body and head. Illusions, but with tactile stimuli."

"You staked me and killed me." My tone went flat.

"Yeah. It sucked killing you too. Especially the first time. It was easier the second time."

I wanted to laugh, but I knew he was serious. The fog rolled in thicker, as if trying to separate us, and Eli stepped closer, until his sleeve brushed mine. "Stick close. This way out. By the way, where are we?"

"An old Indian woman I saw said 'neither here nor there.'"

"Yeah. That's what I thought."

Which seemed a little strange, but fit the evening so far. Around us, the fog thinned and the wind that caused the white to roll and billow fell still. And suddenly we stepped to the curb and into the street. I looked back and saw only an empty lot, narrow and filled with saplings. No fog.

"I want to go back to Miss Esmee's," I said.

"Yeah. And have a good, stiff drink."

I said nothing to that as we got in the SUV and drove sedately away. I looked back once and saw a hint of white fog, but that was all. Then I faced front and said nothing, studying the coin by the streetlights we passed. It was blackened, but I could make out the head of a dragon on one side, a dragon with huge spiked teeth. I turned the old coin over and over in my fingers as the sun rose, ending the strange night with a wash of pale pink, shrimp, and soft persimmon clouds against a golden sky.

Back at Esmee's, I knocked on the Kid's door. When he opened it, he was wearing a sheet and the stink of garlic and sweat; he needed a shower. Badly. I handed him the coin. "Shower and get logged on. Tell me about this—everything you can find. What it is, where it came from."

"Breakfast," he croaked.

"Shower. I'll whip up some eggs."

"Try not to poison me." The door closed.

"Funny guy," I murmured. In my room, I toed off my boots, tossed my clothes on the bed and pulled on a stretchy tee and soft sweater, with clean jeans and fuzzy socks with half boots against the cold floors. Louisiana might not have what I think of as cold winters, but the house was chilly. Downstairs, I didn't have to worry about poisoning the Kid, because my brother was already frying eggs and bacon, making toast, and percolating coffee. He even had tea steeping under a padded tea doily. "You're not worried about taking over Jameson's kitchen?" I asked as I poured a mug of strong black tea and added a slice of fresh lemon.

"I asked permission. He wasn't thrilled," Eli said as he slid a pile of scrambled eggs onto a plate, "but I promised to keep Esmee away from the battlefield, and we reached an accord."

"Ah. So. What's today's schedule?"

"Sleep. At least eight hours. Then I say we chase some Naturaleza vamps and take a few heads."

I hid my smile behind my cup and sipped. "You got any idea where we should look?"

"Yeah. Alex collated the addresses of properties owned by the fangheads on Hieronymus' kill list and compared them to properties owned by Silandre and Esther. They're on my bed, listed in order from most likely to least likely. I say we pick one, go in a few hours before sunset, and clean house." He dished up a rasher of bacon and put my plate in front of me before filling two more. Knowing I should wait for the rest of the expected diners, I dug in. Good manners were never my strong suit. I was better at killing things.

The Kid joined us at the table shortly, his wet hair straggling down his neck, sticking to his dark skin, dribbling onto his vintage Grateful Dead tee. He was wearing sweatpants and smelled a lot better, like strawberry shampoo. He set his laptop and the coin on the breakfast-room table and shoveled in bites while he logged in and started a search. Silent and comfortable with that silence, we ate. When we ran out of bacon and eggs, Eli got up and slid more onto our plates, having left the food cooking on the stove and timed it just right.

By the time I cleaned my plate with a triangle of toast and poured myself a second cup of tea, the Kid was done. Still wordless, he spun the tiny laptop around and pushed it to me. On the screen was an exact replica of my coin, a dragon head on one side, and what looked like a wagon wheel inside a square frame on the other. Of course, my coin was blacked with tarnish and filth. "Head of Ketos. Greek silver coin," the Kid said as he poured another cup of coffee, starting to wake up. "Ketos was a sea serpent. Latin was Cetus. There's a constellation by that name. Probably worth something on today's market as a collectable and just for the silver."

Sea serpent, not dragon. Somehow that made me feel better. "Huh." I studied the coin. "Wonder how an old Choctaw woman got one." When no one answered, I tucked it in a pocket and sipped my tea. Eli read a newspaper, a real paper newspaper, the *New York Times*, and the crinkle of paper and stink of ink took me back to my earliest days in the children's home. Usually there were eight children in one house, and a married couple, sometimes with children of their own, living there with them, in an attempt to give the children the American ideal of a two-parent, two-gender family. The housefather had read the newspaper every morning, absorbed just like Eli, the smell and sound so distinctive. His name was Carlton. Or maybe Kevin. Something like that.

Eli said, "Media is reporting the number of deaths due to vamps. Locals are having meetings about it."

"Yeah?" I said. "Maybe they can bore the fangheads to death with their meetings."

Eli snorted. "*Civilians*." It wasn't a compliment.

Silent as a cat, Rick entered the room and peered into the empty frying pans. "Bro, that's evil to fill the house with bacon smells and not leave a man any."

Eli offered one of his microsmiles and said, "Feel free to cook anything you want. Or you can wait on Jameson. He'll feed you after eight."

"I'll cook," a soft voice said from behind. It was Soul, and I realized that she had been nearby for quite a while, her scent on the air. Today she smelled blue with touches of rain, which was weird, but that was what Beast thought. Soul handed Rick a cell. "You talk. It's Monica." Rick's skin went a faint pink, and his breathing changed. His pheromones shifted from hunger into pleasure.

Rick has another woman in his life.

He wandered out of the room and toward the back door, his voice sounding far too interested, nearly cooing. Beast hissed with displeasure. I sipped tea, feeling a sense of space open up inside me, wide and empty. I wasn't sure what I was feeling, but it wasn't happy. It was empty and lonely and . . . betrayed. Yeah. How stupid was that? Feeling betrayed because my boyfriend-who-wasn't was chatting up some girl named Monica. *Monica.* Bet she had blond hair and big boobs and humongous green eyes. Or blue eyes. Yeah. Wonder how she'd look after tangling with Beast. A wry frown drew my mouth.

Eli got up and left. Alex picked up his tiny computer and wandered away, engrossed.

The sound of sizzling bacon rose from the hot frying pan. I sipped, but the tea had gone cold. After a few minutes, my lack of sleep caught up with me and my eyes started to close of their own volition. Rick still hadn't come back in. I stood and said, "Night." Soul didn't reply, so I headed up the stairs, except that my feet went the other way, to the back door where Rick had gone, and outside.

I smelled him in the distance, his voice a murmur. And then he laughed. Heat shot through me, the heat of anger, the heat of jealousy, spiked and scorching. I wanted to go to him and break the phone into little pieces. And then break him into little pieces.

Instead I slipped silently to the garage and inside. I stood in the darkness, letting my eyes adjust, letting my nose tell me the state of the caged vamp's health. I heard him breathing, scenting me as well. He was awake. And he no longer smelled sick. He smelled dry and dusty, like old ashes, dead roaches, and shed snakeskins. And he also smelled vaguely meaty, like a raw steak left out at room temp too long. Disgust made my shoulders cringe and made me want to look behind me for ambush, but there was nothing there. I knew that.

I moved through the dark to his cage, whispering. "Hey there, you blood-sucking piece of crap. Is it time for you to die, Francis?"

He didn't answer. Something slithered across metal and I drew on Beast's vision to see in the dark. Everything went sharply silver and green, the silver bars of the vamp cage looking like something out of a Disney movie, the thing inside like something out of a Wes Craven or Gregg Hoffman horror film. I leaned against the limo nearby, my weight on my left elbow—and was glad when an alarm didn't go off—and studied the thing. It was vaguely humanoid, but its eyes were multifaceted, like a fly's, black and sparkling. His chest was covered by a carapace, gleaming and dark, maybe brown. His hands were trying to transform into pincers, like a crab's claws, and they were a shimmery dark shade, maybe blue. The transformation had been fast. He was still wearing pants, which was a blessing. His feet were unchanged, except for the toenails, which had grown out curved and thick, like a really bad case of toenail fungus. I let my mouth curl at the thought, knowing from the swivel of his eyes that he could still see in the dark better than I could. Vamp vision was better than Beast's.

My big-cat growled deep inside and padded close. In Beast's vision, with the lights off, I could see the faint shimmer of magics on the vamp's transforming body. And now, standing still and close, I could smell the magics, oddly familiar beneath the ammoniac stench, but the memory wouldn't come. I let it slide away for now.

"The Cajun vamps. They got you some food?"

"Not enough," the vamp said, the consonants sounding mushy, as if his mouth didn't work right anymore. "Hungry."

"Fame Vexatum," I said. "Get used to it. If you live, it'll be the only way you will survive."

"I would rather die," Francis said after a long silence.

"That won't be a problem, actually. In fact, you've become a liability. The longer you stay here, the more you heal and transform, the greater chance that you'll cause me problems."

"Yes. You speak the truth. You smell of anger."

"Yep. I'm pretty unhappy. So you give me something right now, something I can use to find my friend, Misha. Something I can use to locate Narkis and Zoltar. Something that will take me to the leader of the Naturaleza. Something. Or I'll kill you. That's simple enough."

He tilted his head, and I realized that his neck had grown thicker and was jointed. Ick. "Our leader, if we had one, would need to communicate with us, mind to mind."

"Yeah. So?"

"That is my gift. If you are wise, you might determine what it means."

My whole face scrunched up. "Say what?" The vamp in the cage turned his head away. I shrugged and said, "No more food until you talk, Francis. Not one drop." I left the garage.

Without looking into the shadows that might be hiding Rick, I entered the B and B, climbed the stairs, and found my bed. Or I'm moderately sure I did, because I woke up lying on my stomach, face mostly buried in pillow, fully clothed, hours later. The sun was still up, light slanting through the blinds. I no longer felt empty inside. Rick had moved on to Monica. I could accept that. I had hurt him so badly when I accused him of killing me that, of course he moved on. Who wouldn't?

I blinked, lashes hitting the sheets. I didn't like that Rick had a girlfriend. But I didn't have to like it. I just had to live with it. I sighed, feeling the mattress move under me.

"I don't need a guy," I mumbled into the linen. "I love this bed, and it's better than any guy." The memory foam was even better than the mattress back at the freebie house in New Orleans, and that was saying a lot. I rolled over and stretched, pulling muscles that felt a lot better than they had recently. Shifting had been good for me, and when I'd shifted back, I had kept all the hard-earned muscles. I hadn't been sure I would.

I made my way to the bath, stripped, and stumbled into the tub and beneath a scalding hot spray of water. I stayed that way for a long, long time, breathing in the steam, before I soaped and shampooed and shaved off all the body hair that had grown back with the shift. Feeling better, I shut off the water and wrapped one towel around my head and my body in another; this one was huge, bigger than a beach towel and ten times fluffier. I shoved the shower curtain.

I froze, steam swirling around me. Bruiser leaned against the counter, his arms crossed, his head tilted slightly to the side, an intense look on his face.

He was shirtless, his arms to his sides, lightly gripping the marble countertop at his back, his dress pants hanging low on his hips and resting over his bare arches. A coiling tension stirred within me—Beast rising.

Scattered on the counter behind Bruiser was an electric razor with three large circulating heads, an old-fashioned shaving brush and modern razor, a green deodorant bottle, toothpaste tube and toothbrush, what looked like bottles and jars of cosmetics, and a man's black leather zippered toiletries bag. There was also a man's shirt on a hanger, a tie draped around the neck, and a pair of men's socks on the floor. I'd been too sleepy when I entered to see any of that stuff.

Crap. Bruiser had taken the room next to mine.

Bruiser, who had betrayed me.

Icy heat flushed through me from the soles of my feet to the top of my scalp. I had to stop and swallow down the acidic fury. The memory of being held down as Leo and his heir— My breath stopped in my throat as the remembered pain flashed through me again, the feel of fangs tearing through my throat, ripping, cutting; none of the painkilling, laving tenderness of a true feeding, but the torment of a forced feeding. Tears filled my eyes and one hand lifted to my throat to rest there, my pulse pumping hard beneath my fingers. "You let him force a feeding from me."

Bruiser's eyes were hard and hot with some emotion I couldn't name, some strange combination of anger and self-loathing and unknown purpose. But he didn't say anything; he just stood there, leaning against the counter, his gaze penetrating.

"I know we've talked about this," I said. "I know I should just be able to forgive and forget. But I still remember. Every time I see you, I remember."

He didn't move. He scarcely breathed. Waiting for something I didn't understand.

"I know," I said, my throat growing tight and painful with unshed tears, "that you were blood-drunk. I realize that you were dead and the priestess brought you back to life and that assuming command of your own mind after something like that must be nearly impossible. I truly understand that you had no control. But still . . . you let it happen. You were there. Letting them . . ." I took a breath that ached all the way into my lungs, "letting them hurt me."

Stupid tears rolled out of my eyes and slid down my cheeks. Burning. I caught them on the back of my hand and wiped them on the towel. My fingers were shaking and colder than they should have been on my hot face. I opened my mouth, taking in a breath, scenting the man before me, a tangy scent, prickly and warm, the color of sunlight on sand in Beast's mind. My big-cat was staring at Bruiser through my eyes, watching him like prey. Silent, she nudged me, and I said, "You have to say something now. I'm done."

His jaw bunched and relaxed, bunched and relaxed. A soft plop of water hit the drain from the showerhead. Bruiser opened his mouth. "I would—" He stopped and took a slow breath. His hands tightened on the marble, fingers whitening before he relaxed. "I would give," he said, his voice rough, "everything I am to keep you from being hurt. And that includes my freedom." I didn't reply, and another drop fell, measuring the silences between us.

"Freedom?" I asked. *How does a blood-servant get freedom?* Bruiser shrugged, his steam-damp shoulder moving stiffly. He went on more softly, "I remember, in my nightmares, the feel of your body." I took a sharp breath, loud in the silence. "My hands holding you still. I remember the fear and the shock of being unable to move. Being frozen. I couldn't stop them." He shifted on the counter, putting one hand back flat against the marble. "I couldn't stop myself. I was totally, completely under compulsion. For that I deserve for you to hate me. But I—"

He stopped again and raked his fingers through his hair, making it stand up straight and spiked, damp from the steam. "But it seems no matter what I do, I'm treading on your pain. As now. I am here because Leo sent me."

I didn't gasp or drop my towel, but whatever crossed my face made his mouth wrench to the side. He looked at the floor, his hair curling in the steam. Speaking to the tiles, he said, "I'll never keep anything from you, Jane. Even when it may be uncomfortable. Painful." Seconds went by. The shower dripped, loud in the silence.

I shuddered out a breath, feeling my throat relax just a hair, just a hint. A tear fell across my cheek, but this one felt different. No longer hot and burning. "Why did Leo send you?"

"He hired you in New Orleans for a job none of us could do. And you did that job, even when it meant killing his son. In his own way, he respects that. Before he sent me here,

Leo said, 'Jane Yellowrock has a propensity for luck.'" The words were stilted, a perfect mimic of Leo. He went on, imitating the MOC. "'She looks for the truth, no matter how unappetizing, and uncovers it, much like a muckraker or a gravedigger, but one who carries a stake and knows how to use it.'" Bruiser chuckled, but there was no humor in the sound.

"When he heard that Mithrans were changing shape in Natchez, Leo arranged to get you involved. Some of his people told Hieronymus about you."

Silently, everything began to click into place. *Some of his people . . . Like Reach. Son of a gun.* "He couldn't just up and send me himself. That would imply that he forgave Hieronymus, which isn't the fanghead way, not without a lot of bowing and scraping and pleading on Big H's part, but he could make sure things were okay in his territory."

Bruiser nodded. "Politics."

"I hate politics. And vamp politics more than most." I stared at the primo until his eyes lifted from the floor to me. "Can I ask questions?" I asked.

"I presume that you mean something more along the line of an interrogation."

"Pretty much. But I need to get dressed."

"I like you the way you are."

The last of the pain seemed to ease away at his amused tone, and I said, "Tough. Give a girl some privacy. "

Bruiser shrugged and left the bathroom, letting in colder air before he shut the door. I shivered hard and clutched the damp towel. I went to my own room and was dressed in thirty seconds, my T-shirt sticking to my damp skin. I was braiding my hair when the primo entered my room from the bath. He was wearing a dress shirt with a subtle pattern in the weave and the dress pants, wrinkled from the steam. He stopped in the doorway and stood there, watching, as my fingers twisted and tugged my wet hair, saying nothing, his face as impassive as a vamp's. For reasons I didn't understand and didn't want to explore, I didn't ask what he was thinking.

"Twenty questions," he reminded me.

"Tell me what you mean about having freedom."

"What else do you want to know?" he murmured. He shoved the covers out of the way and sat on my bed. The action was odd, as if it was summertime and the comforter was hot.

"Months ago, we were fighting vamps here in Natchez. I finished off mine, and you finished off yours, and I said something. I don't remember what. But you whirled on me, swords out. And you didn't recognize me. At all."

"What else?" he asked, his face taking on an intrigued attentiveness. "What else do you want to know?"

"Why has your scent changed?" I swallowed at the shift in his eyes as something feral stared back at me. "What are you?" I finished, whispering. Knowing that was the question he had been waiting for.

CHAPTER 15

You're a Gun Whore

He did that brow-tilt thing, only one brow going up, quizzically. It was something I had tried in the mirror, but it seemed the ability to lift a single brow was innate, not learned. "All of your questions have a single answer. Have you heard the term *Onorio*?" he asked.

I shook my head and slid into the chair by the bed. We were close enough that our knees brushed before I drew my legs into the chair and pulled the discarded comforter over me. He said, "It means 'honored one' or 'honored freeman.'" When I still said nothing, Bruiser said, "An Onorio is a revered and honored status among blood-servants, but few who attempt the position survive. Most end up dead or turned and chained. I was one of the lucky few, and only because I was mostly dead through it all."

I remembered when he had died, his skin so pale and gray. And when the priestess lay across his body, naked and drinking. "The priestess drank. And then she fed you."

"Yes. To keep me alive. That amount of ancient blood fed to a blood-servant begins a transformation, but doesn't necessarily finish it. In my case, it stopped just before I was turned. Onorio status means I have many of the skills and gifts of the Mithran, but few of the drawbacks. I'll be younger for much longer. I'll be faster. I can see in the dark nearly as well as a vampire."

Understanding beat its way into me. "Onorio. You mean like a Renfield?"

He laughed, the sound not particularly lighthearted. "Sometimes fiction writers get it right. Sometimes not. And sometimes only nearly so. Yes, we've been called Renfields, the special servants of the undead. And I will live a long, long time. Perhaps as much as three more centuries."

"You're hot, in an old, cold house. Even with my skin-walker metabolism, I'm chilled." I knew two other blood-servants who had higher-than-human body temperatures. "Grégoire's B twins, his primos, are they Renfields? Because they're the longest-lived servants I know of."

Bruiser tilted his head to me, the gesture oddly and uncomfortably like Leo's. "Yes. Brandon and Brian went through the process over a hundred years ago and both survived. They are the only other Onorios whom I know. If I tell you that Renfield is a derogatory word, will that only make you use it more often?"

"Probably. Once, a long time ago, you said something about there being a way for you not to drink. For you not to be bound." He had also said it was a way for us to be together, but I didn't repeat that part. "Was it this Renfield thing?"

"Yes. I had thought many times about trying for Onorio status." He shifted on the bed, leaning forward and taking my hand. His skin was feverishly hot. "I can share my thoughts and will and power with someone I bond with, much like a master vampire does with a primo blood-servant, but without the actual servitude. And, best, I have to drink only once or twice a year to maintain my status, and then from any Mithran. I am free of Leo. If I wish to be."

"Sooo, why didn't you do it sooner?"

"All blood-servants think about it at some time or another. It is a powerful position among the Mithrans. And we think about requesting that we be turned. But there is danger in either process."

"Yeah. Ten years of insanity, chained in the basement," I teased.

"The devoveo is a rite of passage," he said, amused.

"The devoveo is a time when the vamp disease makes humans go insane, reworks a human's body and brain into something new—" I stopped, remembering the insectoid movement of the Naturaleza that Eli and I had tried to kill.

"Son of a gun," I said, thinking, trying to put it together. "The Naturaleza here have been twice transformed. They got turned the first time; then they started drinking their fill, which made them stronger and faster and harder to kill, better at healing. Then they got the vamp plague." I narrowed my eyes, trying to bring it all into focus. It was here. The answer of what had happened to the supervamps was here. "And then someone started including magic powered by a full witch circle, and that did something more, probably something unexpected, and now they're transforming into something else. It's all connected somehow." It felt right. But there were still puzzle pieces missing, important stuff I needed to know, stuff that might help me kill supervamps and find Misha. Flying by the seat of my pants usually endangered only me. This time other people were in danger and I didn't like the feeling of responsibility.

A knock sounded at the door, two soft taps. "Up and at 'em, Legs," Eli said. "We got vamps to behead."

"I'm up," I called out. "I'll be ready shortly."

"Yeah, well, don't get all gussied up. It'll be a bloody night." He moved on down the hall.

"Jane?" Bruiser rolled off the mattress and to his feet, once again watching me with that intensity, unexpected and unnerving. "I can't join you hunting." He placed a chaste kiss on the back of my hand. "I have other duties. Be safe."

With no other words, he disappeared back through the bath into his room. Leo-type duties, I assumed. He might not be bound to the MOC, but he was still employed by the chief fanghead.

Alone in my room, I pulled my braided hair into a fighting queue and dressed in vamp-fighting gear. I've worn lots of different things when fighting vamps, from nightclothes and flip-flops—total accident—to full-on, high-impact, plastic motorcycle armor secured into my leathers. With the new vamps, I'd need all the good stuff.

I started from the skin out with the silver-over-titanium chain-mail collar Leo Pellissier had given me to replace the one lost in his service. It clasped in place over the gold nugget and mountain lion tooth on the doubled gold chain. I'd bought the chain before the price of gold soared so high. I couldn't have afforded it at today's prices. I unrolled and donned the silk-knit long johns that were perfect for hot, sweat-generating sports in cold weather, and laid out the now-tight leathers.

I inserted the flexible plastic into the specially made slits at elbows, knees, and my own customized areas: inner elbow, back of knee, and groin—places vamps wanted to drink from. The plastic on the inside joints had to be very pliable, and so, while it wasn't very thick, it was filled with silver foil set into the plastic when it was poured. I pulled on the skintight leather pants and a fleece top before lacing on my combat boots. I zipped up my pants and stomped the boots hard before starting the arduous procedure of weaponing up.

I carried thirteen crosses, all silver, all tucked away into pouches or under my jacket so the silver glow that alerted me that a vamp was near didn't alert them that *I* was near. Crosses worked on vamps when other forms of religious icons didn't, because vamps had been created with the wood of the three crosses of Calvary. It had been an act of black magic that went wrong. And didn't it always?

Three throwing knives were in sheaths specially made into the jacket front. Thirteen ash stakes and thirteen silver ones, each about fourteen inches long went into various loops and sheathes, ready at hand no matter how my body might be positioned, the sharpened tips either pointing away from my body or into the plastic protection of the body armor. Five fighting blades came next: the newest vamp-killer I strapped to my left hip for a cross-draw that resembled a sword draw in many ways; a blade into each boot sheath, one into my holster harness, and one in a spine sheath in the back seam of my jacket—a last resort draw that meant I was in major trouble.

The weapons harness was custom, and not the easiest thing in the world to put on, so I laid the harness out on the bed beside the jacket with the weapons: four semiautomatics—two nine millimeters, two .380s with red polymer grips—each with its holster, in the proper spot on the straps. Each weapon got a thorough look-see; I pulled back on the slide and removed the round from the chamber, ejected the magazine, and inspected the weapon for any visible problems. I saw none, at which point I reinserted the magazine and chambered a round. To make sure I had maximum firepower, I ejected the magazine again, reloaded the ejected round, snapped the mag home, and put the safety on. It was just dumb to run around with a chambered round and the safety off. I'd done it before, of course. But it was dumb. Each weapon got the same treatment. All four weapons were perfect, though all of them would be due for disassembly and cleaning soon. Like in the morning, after a night spent firing them. I holstered the semiautomatic pistols with regular ammo on the right, and the weapons with silver-based ammo on the left.

The Benelli M4 Super 90 slid into the spine sheath for an overhand draw. The M4 wasn't beautiful to anyone but a gun lover. Its steel components had a matte black, phosphate-treated, corrosion-resistant finish that reduced the weapon's visibility during night operations, like tonight. I didn't know how well the new vamps saw in the dark, but it had been impressive last time. I'd have to think of a new term for them—not supervamps, which made them sound like a good thing, but more like vamp squared, or snake vamps, or maybe spidey vamps. "Yeah," I muttered. "Spidey vamps tweak my spidey senses."

The shotgun was nearly idiot-proof, requiring little or no maintenance, and operated in all climates and weather conditions. It can fire twenty-five thousand rounds of 2.75- and 3-inch shells of differing power levels without any operator adjustments and in any combination, using standard ammunition or well-made, hand-packed rounds, without replacing any major parts. The smoothbore, magazine-fed, semiauto shotgun had been a big investment, and I had studied long and hard before putting my money down. It was a modern weapon, utilizing the autoregulating gas-operated—ARGO—firing system, with dual gas cylinders, gas pistons, and action rods for increased reliability. It can fire *and* can be adjusted or fieldstripped totally without tools. It's perfect for close-in fighting in low-light operations. Even after all these months, I thought it was a totally cool weapon. Mostly, though, I just liked the fact that it was idiot-proof.

The M4 was loaded for vamp with hand-packed silver fléchette rounds made by a pal in the mountains. Fléchettes were like tiny knives that when fired spread out in a widening, circular pattern, entering the target with macerating, deadly force. The fact that each fléchette was composed of sterling silver decreased their penetrating power but made them poisonous to vamps, even without a direct hit. There was no way a vamp could cut all of them out of his body before he bled out or the silver spread through his system. Well, until now, when they seemed to heal despite the silver in them. I opened the cock, inspected each round with eye and nose. Closed it and murmured, "Lock and load."

I slid it into the sheath and opened my door. Eli was leaning against the far wall, spine and one foot on the wall, arms hanging loose and ready. He was dressed for vamp fighting in gear that resembled mine, no matter that he'd refused not that long ago to wear leather. It looked good stretched across his shoulders, his scar rising from the high collar and snaking up his jaw. "Took you long enough," he said. "Painting your toenails?"

"You waited three minutes, give or take, while I did a weapons check," I said.

He answered with a lazy not-smile, pushed off the wall, and said, "You smelled me?"

"I heard you. Your combat boots make an awful noise on the carpet. The clomping stopped outside my door. You got the addresses?"

He nodded and tilted his head to the harness on the bed. "Need help?"

"Yeah. It gets harder and harder to get dressed by myself."

"Well, I'm better at undressing women, but I'll give it a shot."

"You're a gun whore." It was the standard chatter between us, comfortable and easy.

"Turn around. None of this would be so hard if you hadn't gotten so fat."

"I put on muscle. You helped." I slid into the jacket, the weight settling on my shoulders. The jacket was heavy, with a thin layer of silver-plated links between the leather and the lining. A small surprise for any vamp who wanted dinner. Eli helped me into the harness and started on the buckles and tabs, making sure the weapons were all easy at hand.

"All the weapons secured. Release straps secured," he said. "Extra mags?"

I opened the weapons bag and took out four magazines, inspected them each, and tucked them into the special pockets: two on the right for the nines, two on the left for the .380s, all loaded with standard ammo. Everything about my gear was special and it had cost a fortune. Some women spent money on shoes and mani-pedis. Not me. My next weapons purchase would be to acquire two new nine mils. The .380s had their uses, but in a firefight it was handy to use interchangeable ammo. "You got some of those sleepy-time bombs we used the last time we were here?" I asked.

Eli yanked the harness to position it midline with my body, so the M4 was straight up and down my spine. I had to raise my arm up high to pull the weapon, but it was out of the way until needed. There was another way of wearing the weapon on the harness that allowed it to hang free, within easy reach, but secured beneath my arm. "Yeah," he said. "But I can't get any more, so we have to be thrifty. Okay," he said, giving my clothes one last jerk. "Good to go." And he slapped me on my butt.

The growl from the doorway froze us both. Then Eli *moved*, and was holding a nine millimeter in a two-handed grip, pointed at the door, his feet positioned, legs braced for firing. He had a bead on Rick.

"You move, you're gonna bleed," Eli said. "You already jumped me once. Not gonna happen again."

"He's not going to jump you," I said, my voice without inflection. "He's going to jump me."

Eli's eyes flicked from Rick to me to the bed, and back to Rick as something seemed to rearrange itself in his head. "Same difference, were-cat. She's on my team, my pack. Back off or bleed."

Before any of us could decide to react, a green ball of fur slammed into Rick's side and knocked him off his feet. Again. I chuckled and walked from the room, stepping over the cop on the floor and the kitten-sized predator at his throat. "Some people never learn. Do they, Pea?" I patted her head and practically skipped down the stairs. "Hey, Rick. I like your pet!" I called over my shoulder.

Out in the SUV, Eli buckled himself in and pulled into the street. The sun was about two hours from setting, and that gave us plenty of time. I waited, knowing the Ranger was biding his time to say something about the contretemps in the hall. But he said nothing, and as we turned in to town, I caved. "Okay. *What*?"

Eli's mouth did that nonsmile thing and he said, "Your business."

I felt myself flush, and the stupid guilt I've lived with all my life rose like a whirlwind, even though I had done nothing—nothing—wrong. My own physical responses made me mad, and I shoved down hard on the useless guilt. "Yeah. *Mine*. My business."

CHAPTER 16

Maggots. I Hate *Maggots.*

Under the Hill wasn't deserted, but neither was it bustling; few people were out and about, with the reports of missing citizens keeping most indoors. In the sunlight, Under the Hill looked odd; it was a place for the shadows, the dark of a new-moon night, hard rains, and stifling summers. By day, the gardens of the earth witches were brilliant with flowers and winter vegetables, and the buildings that were painted were done so in vibrant color—blues, greens, barn red, and one old house that was lilac with pale lavender trim. It looked like something out of a Grimms' fairy tale, and probably was. It was attractive on the surface, but likely dark and bloody underneath. Cars were parked here and there, but not well-waxed vamp mobiles. These ran from well-kept older models to rusted-out hulks, SUVs and vans, some with conspicuous baby seats, others painted with advertisements for dog grooming, pet walking, personal gardeners, bakers, rune casters, artists of every stripe and kind. The typical witch wagons. Like Molly drove. I shook the thought away. You can't force someone to forgive you, not even a once-best friend.

When we parked, I searched for Silandre's Saloon but couldn't see it. It was downhill, closer to the water, and faced south. The buildings where we were parked faced north. The warehouse where we met Big H for intros was in the middle somewhere. Except for age, their history as saloons, and association with vamps, the structures had noth-

ing in common. We left the SUV unlocked and walked back
to an address the Kid had given us.

It was empty, containing only the stink of age, river rats,
and roaches. The next address was equally empty and dis-
used. But the third one set my Beast senses tingling. The
structure was a former warehouse and loading dock, converted into a saloon back in the day when Under the Hill
was notorious for the kidnapping of women and young
boys and their sale into sexual slavery. It was two stories,
the bright sunshine showing a brick exterior and rusted
antique iron shutters on both floors, the corrosion gathered
in the corners and across the center support bar. The trim
was unpainted and mostly rotten, with only traces of green
paint showing here and there. The porch was better made,
though, rust-stained concrete with terra-cotta pieces set in,
like something constructed in the nineteen sixties, but getting to it meant a huge leap where the steps had rotted
away. The porch roof was rusted tin, and the rust running
down from the constant rains had tinted the rotten wood a
deep brown.

I could smell the dead from ten feet away and wrinkled
my nose, making a spitting sound a big-cat might make before I could stop myself. "What?" Eli demanded, sotto voce.

"Unwashed humans inside," I said, as softly as he. "And
like the last house, DBs. Don't know how many, but dead
bodies."

"Reconnoiter," he said, and motioned me to move coun-
terclockwise around the house while he went clockwise. I
wasn't a witch and I didn't feel any witch energies, so widdershins was fine by me, but it would be different if spells
were being cast here. Witch houses had to be approached
very differently. I pulled a .380 and stepped off the sidewalk.

The surrounding shrubbery, all overgrown and spindly,
hadn't felt the sharp edge of pruning or lopping shears in
years. The foundation was cracked and broken in several
places, the crawl space narrow and currently unused but
smelling of the recent occupation of chickens—wet feathers and chicken poop. The windows at the side, like the
front, were covered with iron, but they hadn't been sealed
for as long as the front ones. Air still moved through some
of the cracks, smelling of blood and rot, and the sickly

sweet, beery, herbal scent of Naturaleza. The mingled stench made my skin crawl. I wasn't gonna like what we found inside.

From the building to the side, I smelled onions cooking, overlying the stink of turpentine and glue—the telltales of a live-in artist's studio. From somewhere upwind I caught the odor of blood magics in practice, harsh and fetid, but the unpredictable winds that always ran along the Mississippi River carried it away, leaving the nearer rot of the warehouse/bar at my right.

The back of the warehouse had been added onto, hiding the old carriage and wagon bays behind more modern but moldy siding. The new windows were shielded by shutters—the new steel ones designed in Asheville by an entrepreneurial vamp, with electric motors to open and close them. There were two cars parked at the back stoop, shiny and glossy with very darkly tinted windows, the way vamp cars are supposed to be.

We met at the cars, and Eli's eyes asked me if I found anything. I touched my nose and drew a finger across my throat, which made him snort, a breath of sound. Apparently, tough army dudes don't draw a finger across a throat to suggest a dead body. Still keeping his weapon low but at the ready, he pointed me back the way he had come and he took my path. I shrugged and continued my widdershins way, still trying to work it all out. It was like a video-game puzzle in the back of my mind, the blinking lights and neon obscuring more than revealing what was missing.

At the curb, Eli gestured to the front door and leaped to the porch. I put away my weapon and followed, stating what was bothering me. "I don't understand it. I never have. Why kill and dump the humans?"

"Naturaleza like to kill." For Eli, that was enough.

"I get that. When they first start out, there's the high of a predator stalking and bringing down prey. But at some point there's got to be a problem with diminishing returns, and someone in a vamp hierarchy has to consider the food supply. Once that's dead, they can't recuperate and make a new blood supply."

Eli tried the door, and though it was locked, it was also made of rotten wood. Studying the door, its hinges, its construction, he said, "You bring this up *now*?"

"We're getting ready to go kill sleeping vamps. We'll be busy." I pushed away my worries. "Are you shooting our way in?"

"Nah," Eli said. He reared back and kicked, his heel hitting squarely an inch beside the old lock. The wood splintered, leaving a hole and a crack that traveled up from the kick site to the top of the door and down toward the floor. I heard screams from inside and figured humans were escaping out the back, into the sunlight, leaving behind their employers and masters. Good. They needed to get away. But their screams sounded into the street. Loud enough to wake the undead, let alone the neighbors.

"Witnesses?" I looked around, but no one was in sight and no one ran out of nearby buildings to look.

Eli had surely made certain no one was around before the kick, though I hadn't seen him scan the area. He pulled a sleepy-time bomb—that wasn't what the military officially called them, but the name worked fine by me—and tore off the grenade's safety strip, snapped down on the handle, and tossed it inside. Then he taped over the hole he'd made in the door with duct tape, which he carried with him everywhere, looked at his watch, and sat on the porch with his feet hanging down, his body at an angle to see the door and the street out front. Basic security. "We got time to chat," he said. "Too bad there's no coffeehouse nearby." His brow crinkled faintly. "You're assuming a traditional vamp hierarchy with the killing-prey thing. Assuming someone is in charge to keep the rogues in line. Maybe they don't have one now that de Allyon's dead."

"Anarchy?" I tried that puzzle piece in the map in my head. It fit, but it wasn't a firm, solid *thunk* of info. "But why behead their own leader? Nothing makes sense."

I dropped slowly to the porch, my angle allowing me to see down beside the house, where I got a glimpse of someone rushing away. Both cars started in back and peeled out. Thinking, I looked up at the sky. Sundown was in less than two hours. "Three days." At his puzzled look, I explained. "Most vamps can be killed true-dead with a stake through the heart. But a small percentage will rise the third night as revenants, which is why I always behead my kills. These aren't normal vamps, so what if the percentages of revenants rising are significantly higher?"

"Wait. Not all the vamps at the last place were beheaded. Only the one in the front room."

"The cops didn't behead them?" I asked.

"I got no idea, but I'll text Sylvia to take the heads." He pulled his phone, thumbs working, mumbling, "I don't even know if the law allows LEOs to desecrate bodies. Here's a new one for the politicians.

"You ever seen a revenant?" he asked, changing the subject, his eyes on the phone. When I shook my head, Eli said, "Well, let's kill these, behead them, take pics so we get paid, and get to the county morgue. And you better call your jealous boy toy and tell him to contact PsyLED. They took a few of the bodies in Esther's basement off with them."

Until recently, Uncle Sam had never obtained the body of a vamp for a forensic autopsy. Vamps had policed their own and cleaned up their own messes. But then Lucas Vazquez de Allyon had challenged the status quo of the masters of the cities in this country and the numbers of dead vamps had risen substantially, clearly allowing some into the government's clutches. A small part of me thought it would be cool to be the proverbial fly on the wall in PsyLED's morgue when a revenant rose, but the rest of me knew better. Revenants would kill and eat humans.

"Yeah, no. No calls." I had no intention of calling Rick. Actual discussions were not something I wanted right now. *Big surprise.* "I'll *text* Rick about the potential problem and see if Big Brother had any difficulties with the last batch of true-dead. You text Sylvia. Let's see that we avoid a real-life remake of *Night of the Living Dead*." I pulled out my cell. Which was *so not* classic-hero motif. Once I texted Rick, I found a text from the Kid giving us more addresses. I copied them down on the little spiral notebook I carried. If I had to ditch the phone, I wouldn't lose the info. Inside the house, where the sleepy-time bomb was spreading its knockout fog, I heard thumps, muted and soft, as if several large things fell to the floor.

"What if — " I stopped and put things together about the new vamps. "What if they're *all* revenants? Francis too. What if the magic circle is powering them all to come back? And come back better and more powerful."

Eli paused too, in the act of checking his messages, let-

ting that thought percolate through his brain. "Huh," he
said, which pretty much summed it up. He went back to his
replies, bent over his phone, thumbs working, texting like a
college student—if that college student wore leather and
guns. He finished and stood, stretching, drawing a vamp-
killer. "We gonna do this?" he asked, and checked his watch.
"'Cause we need to get it done before dusk and the vamps
get energetic."

I put away my cell and rolled my shoulders and my head
on my neck as I drew my M4 and checked it, removed the
safety, and unfolded the stock before sliding the strap over
my head. I loosened the vamp-killer on my left thigh and
shoved it back on the straps for a left-hand draw. "Got
nothing better to do." Which was the truth, sadly.

Silent, Eli drew in his right leg, pivoted on his left foot,
and kicked out. His foot hit beside the taped hole and the
door snapped in pieces. The top half fell inward, landing
with two distinct *clumps*. The bottom was in a V, leaning
inside. Eli ripped away the rest of the door, letting in light
and fresh air, letting out the stink of rot. I could hear raspy
breathing inside.

The scent of sleepy-time was still strong beneath the rot,
and because Eli didn't have the gas masks we had used in
the past, we stood guard at the door and waited for the gas
to clear, which seemed to take forever. When Eli gave the
word, I rushed inside and slammed my back against the
wall, with Eli on the other side of the door opening.

Instantly I moved left, the M4 in both hands, held close.
The room took up the entire front half of the structure and
was lit by low-wattage bulbs in wall sconces. It had once
been a tavern, and a tarnished copper bar ran nearly the
length of the back wall, with a blackened mirror over it.
Someone had graffitied unimaginative erotica on it, mostly
oversized sex organs and fangs. It looked like something I
might see in a redneck vamp-biker bar.

The sunlight revealed abused hardwood floors; dark-
painted walls, maybe navy; and broken furniture. There was
a three-legged pool table propped up on a trash can, a sagging couch, a door laid out on sawhorses as a table, and a
few chairs. And humans lay everywhere, some looking as if
they'd fallen just now, others as if they'd been there quite a
while. There were body fluids puddled under some of them

and quivering movement over their flesh. *Maggots. I* hate *maggots.* I could hear the buzz of flies depositing more eggs, and as I crossed the room, they flew up, disturbed. *Yuck.*

I counted eight humans in the old bar, all dead except one, and she was nearly so. Eli pointed to the narrow hallway in back. It ran along the outside of the building, and the iron-covered windows had been boarded over, then painted a hideous shade of violet over the chair rail and an even more hideous shade of mustard below. I took point. Two doors opened into the hallway, and Eli positioned himself to cover me. If a sleeping vamp was using it as a lair, I'd be toast. If humans were hiding there, they probably wouldn't have inhaled enough sleepy-time to be out.

I opened the door. The room on the other side had once been the men's toilet, but the plumbing had stopped working recently and no one had bothered to fix it. I made a face at the stink and the mess and closed the door. Quickly. Shuffling silently, I slid my back down to the next. It was the women's toilet. And it was where the vamps kept their snacks.

Three naked women were handcuffed to the exposed pipes, and all showed crusted wounds at every major pulse point, blackened eyes, and bodies covered in pustules, evidence of the vamp plague. One cradled a broken arm. Her eyelids fluttered open and she started to whimper, stinking of pain sweat and fear pheromones. I wanted to curse, but I placed a finger over my lips to silence her. Her eyes went wide and she started to cry, realizing that help had arrived. *Five minutes,* I mouthed to her, showing her my open fingers.

She nodded hard and fast, and mouthed back, *Don't leave us.*

I nodded and closed the door. Like I'd ever leave someone prisoner. I held up three fingers to Eli so he knew what I'd seen, and moved on down the hallway. The door at the end hung crazily by one hinge. I ducked my head out and back fast, letting my brain make sense of what I'd seen. Another large room, part storeroom, part kitchen, with a large walk-in refrigerator taking up one corner. Debris and busted furniture covered the floor, but no bodies. Eli joined me at the doorway, still covering our backs, and I moved into the room, checking to make sure I'd missed nothing, no hiding places for a blood-slave with a weapon, no vamp lying in wait for fresh food. I approached the refrigerator. Its door was open and it was empty except for a large white circle painted on the floor. I'd seen one once before and closed the door, making sure it wouldn't open from the inside. Eli looked curious, but said nothing.

I pointed to the side of the fridge and waggled two crooked fingers, miming climbing stairs, before I stepped over parts of a chair and put my back against the wall. Air flow was moving slowly along the steps, with cooler air moving downstairs near the floor and warmer air near the ceiling rising to the second story, mixing and commingling right where I was breathing. I dropped to one knee and opened my mouth, drawing in air from above over my tongue and the roof of my mouth.

There was the usual herbal smell—sage, grass, and a faint undertang of pine—and there was the fermented smell, slightly beery, I'd come to associate with Naturaleza. But beneath it, like the odd bottom note of a really weird cologne, was a dry, musty, limy scent, like cement dust and roaches. I tried to remember if I'd smelled this particular stink when the vamps attacked Eli and me in the woods, but I hadn't noticed it. The air had been open and moving there. Here the vamp reek was concentrated, and it smelled dry and scaly, like Francis in Esmee's garage.

I stayed where I was, kneeling, parsing the scents until I was certain. Upstairs were at least two, maybe three vamps. I held up two fingers, made a waffling motion with my hand, and held up three fingers. Eli bent and looked up the stairs quickly, pulled back, and nodded. He pointed to the flashbangs on his belt. I hesitated and then shook my head. I couldn't explain it, but the place felt open and large. Flashbangs worked best in enclosed spaces and small rooms.

He shrugged and gave me a thumbs-up. I rose, readied my shotgun, and peeked up the stairs into the pitch-dark. Eli didn't have his low-light equipment with him. He would be blind. I pulled on Beast's night vision and speed, taking the steps two at a time, not bothering with stealth, my boots pounding on the treads. My vision expanded into sharp focus, blues and greens and silvers. The upstairs was one large room, exposed rafters, wood floor, low furniture, the ceiling held up with columns. The first vamp charged as I cleared the stairs. I swiveled the M4, squeezed the trigger, and took off his head. He fell as the boom reverberated, and I lost hearing. I raced inside and felt the vamp more than saw her as she leaped at me. From across the room.

I missed the head shot, my round taking her in the shoulder, spinning her off course enough for me to drop the shotgun on its sling as I drew the vamp-killer. She landed with a bounce on her injured side, and screamed the high-pitched squeal of the dying or severely injured vamp. It was loud enough to hurt even above the shotgun-induced deafness. I raised the blade and brought it down with my weight behind it, grunting hard.

The strike cut through the side of her neck and buried the blade in the floor. She stopped moving on one side, so I'd done some spinal damage, but she clawed at me with her other hand. I glanced around, making sure I wasn't under attack by the remaining vamp, and put a foot on her chest, yanking to free the blade. The fast healing of the Naturaleza half-sealed the cut. She was screaming and brought up her hand to grab the blade. I kicked her hand and brought down the blade again, taking her head with a whack that jarred my arm. Her head rolled free; blood gushed. The usual gore, but this time with the odd stink I'd noticed. Spidey-vamp stink.

I raced to the center of the room, hearing Eli shouting, "Lights!" I whirled, seeing nothing, then stopped and closed my eyes. Electric light flooded the place. And the last vamp rammed Eli, taking him to the ground. She was fleshy and powerful, dressed in what might have once been a white dress but was now covered with dried blood and filth. Her dark hair streamed out behind her like a whip as the two impacted.

With my left hand I pulled a silver stake, knowing that the silver wouldn't be deadly even if I hit her heart but all the other weapons might injure Eli. The Ranger rolled, lifting her over his body, ramming her into the wall. I sprinted across the room, bringing my left arm over my head. She rebounded from the wall and landed on Eli before he could find his feet, her momentum bowling them both over. I timed my steps and brought my arm down, piercing her dress, back, and internal organs. Not feeling the heart give, knowing I'd missed. And made her mad.

She raised her head and hissed. I was pulling the M4 around to fire when she leaped. And landed on me.

Her fangs caught my elbow, biting deep, tearing flesh. I didn't feel the pain yet, not with the adrenaline flooding my system. But she was too close to position the shotgun. She growled, and I felt the vibration through the flesh of my arm. She shook me like a wolf shakes prey, to break bones. I felt something inside snap and was instantly nauseous. I fell and rolled with her. Her taloned hands stabbed at me, hitting my jacket and catching on the thin, silvered mesh between the leather and me.

Her jaws ripped out of my arm and I felt it this time. Her fangs tore at my throat, raking at the silver-plated titanium collar, guttural growls coming from her throat. When she couldn't bite through the mesh, she lifted my head and rammed it against the floor, her talons breaking the skin of my scalp. I saw stars for a moment, sparkles of white on a black surface. My vision cleared with a blink to see a metal bar that became the barrel of a shotgun.

The blast shredded the back of her head. She fell away from me. Leaving me gasping on the floor. A second blast took her through the throat, decapitating her. Eli stood over her, making sure she was dead. "Clear," I whispered softly, knowing she was the last one.

He raised the gun and I wasn't surprised to see the M4. I'd dropped it along the way to nearly being vamp bait. He hadn't understood, or maybe hadn't heard, my *clear*, and he walked the perimeter of the entire story, checking for other fangheads while I eased up into a sitting position, fished a tourniquet from a pocket, and clumsily tried to get it around my left arm. The bone was sticking through the leather. "Humerus," I whispered, and laughed, because it wasn't humorous at all. My stomach rebelled. I twisted to the side and threw up my lunch.

I was gasping, the room tilting at a ninety-degree angle. The blood spurting across my arm to the floor seemed important, but I couldn't figure out what to do about it. There was a lot of blood. A lot.

The buzz in my ears went higher pitched, annoying. I shook my head to clear it, but all I did was sling my blood from the talon wounds across my face.

Eli pushed my fingers to the side and secured the tourniquet, his hands feeling hot on my chilled skin. I was going into shock. His lips were moving but I couldn't hear anything except the roar in my head. My vision telescoped down into a single bright light, and then to the blood-spatter stains on the timbers over my head.

CHAPTER 17

I Know I'll Have to Choose

My next coherent moment showed me Eli on the cell, his lips moving. He'd propped me against a center roof support. He closed the phone. I went dark again, and woke to see him taking off my boots. Which was just wrong. His fingers undid the Velcro and the ties beneath, pulling off the boot to expose my white cotton sock. I blinked and my eyes felt dry, like I had ground glass in them. I knew that was a bad sign, but couldn't remember what kind of bad sign it was. "Eli? Whatcha doin'?"

He looked up for a moment and back to my feet. "Good. You're back. Rick's on the way. He says you have to shift to heal the arm."

"You called Rick?" I realized I could hear, the annoying buzz had damped to little more than a high hum. "Why?"

"Boy Toy's the closest thing to furry I know. You took a blow to the head. He says you might have trouble shifting."

"Yeah?" That seemed off. "How's he know that?"

"He's Big Brother PsyLED. He knows his sh— his stuff."

PsyLED knew about skinwalkers? How? Oh yeah. Rick would have told them about me. And they probably had lots of old papers and reports for intel, way more than in the woo-woo room in New Orleans cop central. I worried with that thought while Eli pulled off my other boot. PsyLED knowing all about me was info I didn't know what to do with, so I concentrated on what I did know. Or did want to know. "So, why're you taking off my boots?"

"And your pants."

"You try"—I stopped to breathe and realized I was woozy—"to take off my pants"—more breaths—"and I'll shoot you."

"I disarmed you." I looked down and realized that while I was unconscious, he had unzipped my jacket, pulled my good arm out of my sleeve, and taken every single weapon. They were piled close by, but too far to reach at the moment. I looked back down. I had blood all over my nice, clean silk-knit undershirt. "Well, crap."

"Yeah. Rick said you had to be naked to shift."

"I can get out of my pants and shirt . . . after I shift . . . if you just undo my belt."

Eli gave me that little nonsmile, but I saw the worry in his eyes. "And here I was hoping I'd finally get to see you naked."

"Wish on, Ranger Boy."

He chuckled softly. "I adore you, you know. If you die on me, I'll be seriously pissed."

That idea rested on me for a moment, as heavy as my silver-lined jacket. "Yeah?"

"Yeah. For all you've been in a funk for weeks like some hormonal PMS woman, we're family now. So don't die."

"PMS woman." I giggled. "Puma Monster Skinwalker. Panther Marshmallow Sabertooth."

"Yeah. Funny." He pulled off both socks, leaving my feet pale blue and vulnerable. He stared at them as he said, "You have to shift."

"Okay." Which seemed a totally stupid thing to say after a declaration of familyhood. I should tell him I adored him back. But I didn't. I just blinked at him, puzzled. *I have a family?* "My arm hurts." I looked down and saw a lot of blood. "Oh. Yeah." I looked at Eli. "I have a dangerous job. People keep trying to kill me."

"Yeah. Been there. I took off your vamp collar. Once you shift, Rick says you need to eat, so he's bringing you some raw steaks. But you need to do it fast. I haven't called it in, but the neighbors will have heard the shots fired."

"If I shift," I mumbled, "I can't shift back to human."

"What?" He looked stunned.

"I'll stay a cat until sunset. That's the soonest I can shift back."

He looked at his watch. "It's an hour to sunset. What the hell am I going to do with a mountain lion?"

"Be dinner, if the steaks take too long to get here," I deadpanned. And then giggled.

Eli shook his head, as if shaking away an insect or something he couldn't control. "What do I do to help?"

I raised my good hand and gripped the gold nugget. In the distance I heard sirens. I frowned. "Did you take pics of the dead vamps?"

"You're going into shock and you're worried about pictures?"

"Money." My lips weren't moving right and felt numb. I licked them, and my tongue was dry, sticking to my lips and pulling on the cracked skin. Not good signs. "I have a family to support, you know."

I thought about the snake in the heart of the mountain lion tooth. And dropped into the gray place of the change.

Painpainpain. Like claws of bigger predator, ripping at bones. I saw Eli back away from gray lights and black sparks, moving like prey. Looked down at Jane's body. It was dissolving like snow in summer sun. Becoming Beast. Pelt and claws and killing teeth.

Magics healed and reshaped. Becoming *Beast*.

I panted. Pushed paws against floor, rising to sit. Pushed out of remaining Jane clothes. Drew long, thick tail around paws. I was cold, like winter snow and ice had caught me on hunt far from my den.

"Holy sh—" Eli stopped, his breath like prey breath, fastfastfast. "Jane?"

I hacked. *Not Jane. Beast. Jane sleeps in soul home.* But Eli did not understand. He took another step back, and I chuffed with laughter. Eli was hunter, but showed proper respect to Beast as better hunter. I chuffed again, rotated ears to him, and lay down to show disinterest in prey sport. Did not want to eat Eli.

"Steaks are on the way," Eli said.

I said nothing.

"Pretty pussycat."

I looked at him and he laughed, smelling of nervous sweat and uncertainty. I yawned, showing big killing teeth and boredom all at once. Was good to remind other hunters and prey that Beast had big teeth.

"You really are beautiful." I looked away, indifferent but listening. I liked humans who admired properly. "You're not going to eat me, are you?"

Humans were stupid. I was showing clear disinterest but he did not understand. He was still alive. He should see what I was saying.

I heard a car stop out front. And moments later heard Rick call out. "Eli?"

"Up here, back of the building, up the stairs."

Rick's feet pounded on the steps and he stopped at the top, taking in the room, the dead vampires, and settling on Beast. I panted to show some interest.

Rick said, "Hey, Jane."

I put ears back and hacked. *Not Jane. Am Beast.*

Rick opened bag and tore plastic. Smell of warm cow meat filled room. Last time, Rick had brought dead pig meat, but cow was good too. I stood and padded partway to Rick. When I stopped, he came the rest of the way and set cow meat on floor. I settled beside it and ripped into meat, swallowing fast. Was *hungry*.

Saw movement near stairs and growled low, snapping at meat faster. White wolf stood there, watching. He moved into room and my growl went deeper. *My food.* Wolf stared to growl, but Pea chittered and he stopped. Pea climbed from wolf's back and scampered over to me. She sat on floor and watched, head tilted to side. She did not have big-cat eyes, but she had big-cat teeth. She yawned to show her teeth and smiled, mewling softly, asking nicely. I batted a small piece of cow to her, and she settled to eat. I growled once more to wolf and pulled cow between paws to eat.

Sirens sounded outside. Sound of humans entering house. Rick went downstairs to talk to police. I still ate. Rick was gone long time. Eli stood at top of stairs, guarding.

Belly full, I stretched and yawned. Human males were talking. Not looking at Beast. I nudged Pea with nose. Pea jumped to Beast's back and held on to pelt with sharp claws. Together we walked slowly to stairs, not looking at wolf. Wolf was sitting like dog, back legs spread wide. Wolf looked stupid, like big stupid dog. I stopped close and sat, looking away, so wolf would not think I had plans. Wolf looked at me from sideways eyes and turned head to study me. I did nothing. Wolf slowly reached big head toward me. I did nothing. Wolf sniffed me. I did nothing.

Then I struck. Lifted paw, claws out, and swiped wolf nose. Wolf yelped and I bounded across room, whipped around, and hacked with laughter. Wolf was bleeding on big ugly dog nose. *Fun!*

I sat and lifted paw, licking off wolf blood. Feeling happy. Pea chittered at me, sounding like Jane, scolding, but Beast was smarter than Pea. Pea did not like Beast grooming off were-blood. But were-blood was in belly, not in cut, and I would shift back soon to Jane. Were-taint in belly would not hurt me/us. But was thinking that were-blood in *cut* might not hurt us now.

Beast was always better than Jane and big-cat together. Was even better since we talked with Hayyel-angel. Angel did something to wolf to make him stay wolf. Did something to us I did not understand. Pea did not know this. Jane did not know this. Was mostly sure that Leo's Mercy Blade did not know. Beast was smarter than all of them.

Rick came back upstairs. "We have to get her into the SUV. Jane, will you take a leash?"

I narrowed eyes and snarled. Beast will not walk on leash. Beast is not stupid dog or stupid wolf.

"Guess not," Eli said. "How about I carry you?"

I thought about that. Have not been carried by humans in many years. Would be fun. But not Eli. Wanted mate to carry. I stood and dropped head. Stared at Rick with big-cat eyes, walked slowly to him, shoulder blades rising and falling, stalking him. Rick stared, giving nothing away with human eyes. Were-scent of black leopard was strong on him. Full moon would be soon, and his scent would be strong-strongstrong then. I walked around Rick in circle and stopped to sniff one hand, his fingers curled in fist, as if to hold in something. Huffed and blew warm cat breath on his fist. His fingers uncurled. Was nothing there to hold on to. I breathed on Rick skin. Liked smell of Rick. I stopped in front of him and sat. Lifted one front paw, then the other, and placed both on his knees. Waited.

"If you think I'm carrying you, you got another think coming, Jane," he said.

I stood up on back paws, stretched to full height, and put front paws on Rick shoulders. Put muzzle in his chin and sniffed. Moved nose to his neck and sniffed. I purred.

Eli laughed. I ignored him. "She wants you, man." Eli left, taking stairs, making much noise.

I snuffled Rick, whiskers tickling his neck. Jane said he had taken new mate. I did not smell new mate. Jane was wrong. Rick's hands rose to Beast and he scratched belly. I *whuff*ed and laid head on his shoulder.

"I don't understand you, Jane. And if you think this fixes things between us, it doesn't. But if you want me to carry you, I will." His hands came together and made cradle. I leaped and landed in his hands. "Holy hell, cat. You've put on a few pounds."

I hacked in amusement. *I am bigger. I like bigger. Would like to be a holy hellcat too.* I put chin on his shoulder and breathed his scent. Then I rubbed scent glands over him. *Mine . . .*

Rick carried me downstairs and into street. He opened essuvee of Eli and I jumped inside and lay down on backseat. Had been a good day. I/we had hunted with Eli. I/we had killed vampires. Had eaten dead cow meat. Had swiped wolf nose. Had been carried by Rick. Good day. I closed my eyes and napped.

I came to in the back of the SUV, lying naked under a blanket and feeling great. It was dark out, and the vehicle was parked at Esmee's under the trees, ensuring my privacy. I had no memory of my time as Beast, but the pain in my arm was gone. Clean clothes were folded on the floor in front of me, and I dressed in the dark—panties, jeans, and a thick sweater that smelled of Rick. I held the knit to my face and inhaled. I hated that I didn't have him in my life now. There was so much missing. I closed my eyes and buried my face in the sweater for a moment. Only a moment. I had no intention of grieving for him anymore.

I pulled the sweater over my head and pushed my feet into the oversized flip-flops, which also smelled of Rick. I'd like to think he was scent-marking me, but I knew better. I pulled my hair out of the way and secured it in one fist. That was one thing about shifting: I always came back with clean, smooth hair, no tangles. I opened the door and slid from the vehicle, into the dark of Esmee's backyard. I padded to the back door, pausing when I scented Eli. I stopped, sniffing until I located him sitting still as a statue in the dark. "Thanks for saving my life," I said.

"Turnabout and all that," he said. I joined him on a bench and sat, my mostly bare feet cold. "Jane? You like George. I can tell. There's this . . . energy when you're together." Not knowing where he was going, I didn't answer, just turned to him and drew on Beast's night vision to see his face. He needed a shave, and he looked tired, though he had showered and dressed in fresh clothes. "But your cat, she likes Rick."

"Crap. What did she do?"

"She rubbed herself all over him."

I dropped my head. That was why I was thinking of scent-marking. Beast had scent-marked Rick. And now, whether consciously or not, Rick was scent-marking back. Deep inside, Beast rolled over. *Mine,* she murmured to me. *Both mine.* "That's not good," I said to her, and partly to Eli. "My Beast feels she can have them both, over time. Big-cats don't mate for life."

Eli blew out a breath of derision. "Yeah. Tell that to Rick and George. Two alpha males want the same woman? That's trouble, Janie."

I shrugged. "I know. We're not human. Not any of us. And we're extremely long lived. In the wild, cats each have their own territories. The land overlaps with the territories of other cats, and when a female goes into heat, either she'll go to the male of her choice or they'll come to her. Sometimes the males fight. If the female wants the winner, they mate. If she doesn't like him, then she might run away or she might fight him. But she doesn't keep him forever. Her next heat might take her to another male. But between times, cats are solitary." Which sounded terribly lonely, all of a sudden.

"Your men are acting like cats." He said it as if he were having a revelation. "Circling and waiting."

"Yeah. I guess. I don't want them fighting over me, but when they act like cats, it brings my Beast closer to the surface. It's all so mixed up." My voice was curiously dull, unemotional. And I could feel the familiar depression creeping along the edges of my mind. It was a weird feeling, more a lack of interest than unhappiness. How did people live with it? I shook away the thought and shrugged away the lurking depression, but it didn't go far. It crouched in the corner of my mind like ... like the shadow of Leo that was binding Beast. Was that significant? I couldn't see how, but maybe so. Maybe bindings, when left unattended and unfed, became negativity and eventually depression. I hadn't fed off Leo since the binding of Beast. Maybe—

"Jane?"

I looked up, realizing I'd been silent too long. "Yeah. Sorry. Are we hunting anymore tonight?"

"Rick said you needed to eat and then rest."

"Food, yes. I'm starving. But Rick isn't my mother. Let's work."

"I was hoping you would say that. We need to go to the morgue to make sure Syl took all the vamp heads. And the Kid has one more address we could check out. This one isn't in Under the Hill. It's a house just off High Street."

I smiled at his calling Alex the Kid. The name was catching even for his brother. "High Street is part of the historical district. How far from the last place?"

"Mile or so. Jameson is cleaning your leathers. The sleeve is a goner, though."

"I had the company reserve some leather from that dye batch. I can get it fixed. Let me get dressed again." *And out of this sweater.*

We pulled in to the hospital entrance, my leathers smelling slightly of mink oil. Jameson had tried to care for the leathers with just water, to avoid any chemical stink, but my dried blood was caught in the rough part of the tears. "I'm sorry, Miss Jane," he had said, while I'd stuffed my face with oatmeal and a rare steak. "But I thought the smell of your blood might be worse than the mink oil. For attracting predators." He had a point. But I kinda had that new-car smell now.

Eli spun the wheel and pulled into a space marked for physician parking.

"A forensic autopsy unit in Natchez Regional Medical Center," I said. "Who'da thought?" I hadn't expected to come back to the medical center for any reason, but especially not for this. And if I'd thought about forensic autopsies, I would have thought they would be done in Jackson, Mississippi's state capital.

"Let's chat about taking down revenants," Eli said. "You suggested earlier that the vamps we've been seeing were revenants."

"Assuming that's right, until now I've never seen one," I said. "Never talked to anyone who has. There's no vid on the Net. Only a description by another vamp hunter. He was typing with the three fingers the revenant left him on his right hand. It ate the left hand."

Eli shut off the motor, pulled his phone, and started texting. Ten bucks said it was to Sylvia.

"They can't feel pain," I said. "You know all the zombie movies? Pretty much like that, except they're deadly fast and they'll eat anything, not just brains. You have to take their heads completely, and even then they take a while to die."

"Yeah. Sounds like our critters." Eli grunted, and it sounded like cursing. "Silver?"

"Won't kill them. They—" I stopped and sat up in the seat. "The whole Naturaleza thing has always resulted in stronger, faster, harder-to-kill vamps. Maybe the spidey vamps are Naturaleza *revenants*, are a way to make vamps immune to everything. Silver, stakes in the heart, even partial beheading. Traditionally, less than three percent of staked vamps rise as revenants. Maybe the Naturaleza leader is experimenting on scions, making them into revenants, trying new magics forced from the missing witches to see what works. Some have seemed like rogues, newly risen and unintelligent; others have been in control of their faculties. Maybe the spidey vamps are a stepping stone to vamp perfection, or a mistake along the way."

"I don't really care where they come from or who their mommies are," Eli said. "I just want to kill the suckers."

"Yeah. Okay," I said, thinking. "Me too." But even I could hear the lack of real interest. For once questions about vamps were more interesting than just killing them.

"This might help." He handed me a brown paper bag. It was heavier than I expected, and I nearly dropped it. I looked from the bag to him and back, and reached in. I pulled out a shotgun-shell holder, already loaded with rounds.

I felt my heart lighten. "Swuuueeet." I unsnapped the

strap and drew the Benelli from its spine holster. Eli opened his tool kit, flipped on a tiny tight-beamed light, and quickly mounted the device on the left side of the receiver while I watched. I now had quick access to an additional six shells. "I like. How much do I owe you?"

"Not a dime. Consider it a belated birthday present."

I felt odd and didn't know what to say, like maybe . . . shy. Or something. So I drew on my Christian children's-home manners and said, "Thank you. It's really, really nice." Eli snorted, and I ducked my head, realizing that *nice* was probably not a good description for a weapon accessory, but it was all I had. I turned the holder over, admiring it from every angle, figuring out how the holder would affect the way the gun rested on my body from the strap, and how I'd handle it in the holster, and how the slight change in weight might affect firing. The draw would be different, and I worked through the mechanics of it. "Really nice," I said happily.

I turned as a shadow caught my attention and watched Sylvia Turpin approach the car. "She's pretty," I said.

"She's a knockout. And she likes guns almost as much as you do."

I gave a half smile. *I wish my love life was so uncomplicated.* And then I thought about the two together as a couple. Instead of a white picket fence, these two would have a gun range and a fallout shelter with enough food to hide out for a whole year. Right. There was uncomplicated and then there was Eli and Sylvia. Not uncomplicated; just a different kind of complication.

Eli rolled down his window. Sylvia bent down and rested both arms on the window ledge. She was wearing makeup again, and her hair was pulled back in a ponytail. "Hiya," she said. "The doc's getting ready to start another autopsy. Come on in."

"Coffee anywhere?" Eli asked, opening his door and stepping to the pavement.

"The cafeteria has a coffee bar this month. Something new they're trying to beat back the competition. It's not real coffee—you know. the burnt sludge from the bottom of the pot after it's been sitting all day—but it isn't bad. It's horribly fresh, with all sorts of icky flavorings. And the espresso is made while you wait."

"I'll buy you some of this horrible coffee," Eli said.

Sylvia laughed, and I figured all was okay now with their weird relationship. "The doc's all excited about the vamps' external characteristics. He can't wait to get them open."

"Get them—" Eli grabbed her arm. "You did take their heads already." At her wide eyes he added, "Hell. You didn't get my text. Did you?" Sylvia shook her head. "There's a good chance the new-style vamps will rise as revenants unless you take their heads."

I heard a *beepbeepbeep*. The sheriff went from dead stop to a sprint in a half second, pulling her police radio. She shouted back to us, "That's *man down*! We got trouble in the morgue!" She shouted into the radio as we dashed down the sidewalk, "Take their heads! It's the only way to kill them!" Over the radio, we heard gunshots and screaming.

No one stopped us as we entered a side door that had been propped open with a pencil. Sylvia kicked the pencil out of the way and we raced down a hallway as the door closed behind us, took a right down another hall, and flew down a short flight of stairs. We heard muffled screams and more gunshots. Sylvia rammed open the door at the bottom while drawing her service weapon. I reached up and pulled the M4, adjusted the vamp-killer on my left hip, and let out some of Beast as we ran. Her strength and speed flowed into me like a drug, and I laughed shortly, showing my teeth.

We spun around a corner and stopped. Two cops were lying in a pool of blood, service revolvers out, throats torn away.

And the first *thing* landed on Sylvia.

CHAPTER 18

The Bad Men Are Gone

Eli let out a war scream and jumped in front. Stupid man. I nearly shot him. Instead, I adjusted my aim, braced the M4, and fired point-blank at the next *thing*. They were spidey vamps all right, but next-gen spidey vamps. Faster than lightning and nearly as deadly. The one I shot took the blast midcenter and didn't even pause except to change direction by shoving off Eli's back and leaping at me. I fired two shots in rapid sequence. *Not gonna get chewed on twice.*

The spidey vamp landed on me, gasping, and I let her slide down me to the floor. I put the shotgun to her head and fired. She stopped moving, so I pulled the vamp-killer and took her head. Eli was lifting Sylvia to her feet. She was covered in gore, and my heart fell. "How much of that is yours?" I asked.

"None," she said, and smiled at Eli.

Young love is so cute, I thought. And then realized I'd said it aloud. I shook myself and jogged away from them toward the sound of screams.

Most morgues these days don't use the pull-out, refrigerated, coffin-sized beds, except for new arrivals or bodies still being processed. (That's what they call it. *Processed.* Not *slicing and dicing, measuring and scooping.*) Most modern morgues use a cold room—a walk-in refrigerator where they can store bodies one of two ways: stack them on bunk-style ledges that look like prison beds, but without the charm or the pretense of a mattress, or on roll-in gurneys.

In the autopsy suite, I stepped over the body on the floor. Someone had taken the liberty of beheading a spidey vamp, second gen. He was naked and had a hard carapace, like a spider's, over his chest—or, rather, it was part of his chest. The carapace was brown and covered with coarse hairs, spiked and barbed. If he had ever been human, he'd lost it totally.

Farther in the room was another one, still alive, her head only half removed. She was sitting on top of a human, her face buried in his belly, slurping. For creatures who had a rep for physical speed, their mental abilities were more along the lines of brain-dead. I reared back with the vamp-killer and yelled, "Hey, fanghead!" The vamp looked up and focused on me. Multifaceted eyes bulged from her face. *Fly eyes*. I hurled my arm forward with all my strength behind it.

Though I cut with anger rather than skill, I took her head, the blow sending it spinning, and I could have sworn she stared at me the whole time, until her head whapped into the wall. At my feet, her body was reaching for me. I kicked it away from the human beneath. It was the pathologist, and he was way too dead for any help.

Reaching for the handle of the cold room, I had a moment's memory of the building today with the refrigerator and the white witch circle painted on the floor. This fridge was empty of witch circles, but the moment I opened the door, I was charged by more vamp things. I caught half a breath, pulling the M4 into firing position as they flowed across the space like centipedes, a swirling yet jerky motion. The musk they exuded was dry and ammoniac, and they moved so fast I had only an instant of impression before the first one was on me. Naked, every one, and insectoid. Ick.

The first one latched on to the barrel of the shotgun as if she intended to use it as a straw. Taking her head was easy, and had the added benefit of peppering the vamps behind her with silver fléchettes. It didn't kill them, but it made three of them jump back. I put a hole in the two still moving forward and slammed the door shut. I had counted only four rounds, but the shotgun was empty and I broke open the M4 to reload from my handy-dandy shell holder. I could hear the creatures screaming inside, even over the concussive eardrum damage from the shotgun. They might not look like vamps, but they had the vamp death scream down pat.

To the others, who had gathered close, I said, "I count five," like it was a game we were playing or something.

Eli removed a metal shim from his go-bag and rammed it under the latching mechanism, effectively sealing them in, and the ease of it had me laughing. "That's the easiest vamp trap I ever saw."

He gave me that little no-smile of humor. "After the last time we were in Natchez, I started carrying extra equipment. Let's clear this place and come back," he added to Syl.

"Yeah." I loaded the six additional rounds fast, and moved out behind the happy, courting couple.

There was only one revenant vamp still loose, and he was chewing on a dead security guard. Eli took the vamp's head with his vamp-killer, a silver-plated machete. He used it like he'd had plenty of practice, and made me wonder about the scars on his chest and neck and face. Not that I'd ask. But I did wonder. And I wondered what he'd tell Sylvia, if anything. The cause of his wounds was classified, so it wasn't likely.

The guard was propped against a locked door, an empty can of mace in his lap. "Yeah," I said. "Mace is gonna do a lot of good. It might make the vamp's sense of smell less acute, but it won't stop a brainless killing machine."

We turned away, but I heard a whimper and grabbed Eli's arm. "What?" he asked. I paused, releasing his arm so he would have full range of motion. He stepped behind me, pushing Sylvia nearer me and protecting the womenfolk, the idiot man, but still covering my back, as Sylvia and I studied the hallway. And this time we all heard it: a whimper. Coming from the guard. "No way," Syl said.

I saw a sliver of bloody cloth that had once been white sticking out from under the guard's blood-soaked navy pants. "Crap," I whispered. Silently, I stepped back and bent my knees, wedging my hands under his flaccid arms and standing, pulling him away from the corner. A little girl was curled into a ball behind his body, eyes closed tightly, a thumb in her mouth. Whimpering softly with each breath, a rhythmic moan of fear. I dropped the guard to the side and lifted the girl in my arms. "It's all right, sweetie," I murmured. "The bad men are gone." I stepped over the guard, mentally saluting him, cradling the child. She was dark-haired with death-pale skin and a heartbeat I could hear, racing and bouncing. "It's all right, sweetie," I repeated. "The bad men are gone."

Eli moved in front, guarding our passage out. I handed Sylvia my shotgun and she fell behind, scanning our trail out, walking halfway backward. In the main room, back at the fridge, Eli pulled a flashbang off his vest and nodded at me. "You're faster than Syl. Give her the girl." Understanding what he wanted, I switched the child for the M4. The smaller woman cradled the little girl gently, carrying her out of sight of the bodies. "Stay close," Eli told her. "Just in case."

To me, he said, "Make it fast. On three. One." He activated the stun grenade. "Two. Three."

I pulled out the shim and yanked the door open as he tossed in the grenade. Using Beast's speed, I slammed the door shut, catching the top of a vamp's head and part of a hand before they jumped back again.

The flashbang went off with a massive *thump*, the concussion and intense wattage muted by the thick walls of the cold room, and followed almost instantly by the pealing, nearly ultrasonic screams of vamps in agony. I jerked the door open again and took out three revenants while Eli took three more. I had no idea where the sixth one had come from. Maybe newly risen since the last time I peeked.

Even though I could practically feel Sylvia's disapproval, which I ignored, I took pics of the cold room and each of the vamps—or what was left of them—and then left the gore-spattered place and took more pics of the other true-dead. Proof for payment. When I was done, Sylvia handed me the child and started making calls. Lots of calls. Carrying the little girl, I walked outside and sat in the SUV. I turned on the engine and the heater, wrapped the child in a blanket I took from Eli's emergency supplies, and cradled her on my lap.

Beast sighed at me, murmuring, *Kit. Love kit.* She lay her head on her paws and looked up at me, her eyes lonely. *Want kits. Too long since I suckled kits.* She blew out a breath and twitched her ears, smelling the child. *Want kits.*

Her desire for family stormed up through me, bringing

tears to my eyes, tears that rolled down my face and dripped onto Eli's blanket. I wiped them off, my palm rough on my skin, pulling, hurting, my breathing loud in the SUV. I couldn't give her kits without being in Beast skin for a long, long time. I couldn't have a child without staying in human form for a long, long time. There was no easy answer to her need.

Minutes ticked by as I murmured endearments to the little girl. She fell asleep, her breathing soft and regular. She was so exhausted that she didn't stir when the parking lot filled with emergency vehicles, sirens sounding, lights flashing. Uniformed men and women ran for the building, and most came back out, anger in their postures, faces hard. Their comrades had fallen and there was nothing left to kill. I understood the need for vengeance, and the impotence produced when that was denied.

The SUV was warm by the time Rick drove up, a woman from social services following him. The two stood in the chill night air, talking about the girl, from what I could make out. I turned off the SUV and let the silence cover me as my arms involuntarily tightened on the sleeping bundle in my lap. I was glad I was hidden in the vehicle, so no one could see the anguish I felt over giving her up.

I/we saved her, Beast thought at me, her voice a low growl. *She is ours.*

"She has a family," I whispered. "We have to let her go."

They were not here to protect her.

The security guard protected her, I thought. *That makes him family. And his family her family. She isn't ours.*

Molly's kits are ours. Angie Baby is ours.

"No," I whispered aloud. "Not anymore."

Beast growled and paced away to hide deep in my mind, her eyes slit in displeasure.

The girl was asleep in my arms when the social worker came toward the vehicle. I opened the door and turned in the seat, letting my boots hit the parking lot. The woman was short, stout, and motherly. And took the little girl away. I watched the social worker carry her to her car and drive away, my arms feeling heavy and empty. The darkness I'd been hiding from for days rose in me like a storm cloud, looking for something or someone to take out my fury and despondency on.

Instead of a revenant I could kill, Sylvia spotted me sitting in the dark and walked over, her hand on her gun butt, that angry-cop look lurking in her eyes. She said. "Cops are dead in there, and you were taking *pictures*. So you could get *paid*."

She was right. What could I say? It was a stupid waste of time, but I tried logic. "You take crime-scene pictures. So do I. And, like you, I study them later to see what I missed, what I could have done differently. And, like you, I get paid because of those pictures."

"Don't compare us," she snarled.

And I realized what she really wanted. I smiled, showing teeth, and reared back in the bucket seat, half in and half out of the vehicle, crossing my boots at the ankles. I laced my fingers across my midsection, going for irritating snark in both expression and body language. From the way her mouth tightened, I'd say I'd succeeded.

"Why not? You'd stay on the job if the county said you had to serve for free?" I asked.

"It isn't the same thing."

"No? If our country was attacked and our marines were cut off from supplies and pay, they would keep fighting, no matter what. *They* take an oath. *You* were elected," I goaded. "Pay stops, I bet you'd stop doing the job too."

"You don't know me well enough to insult me."

"Back atcha, Syl."

It took a moment for her eyes to register her understanding, and when they did, her mouth turned down as if she'd sucked on a lemon. Then she sighed and sat down on the curb, almost as if she were showing submission, but I figured it was really just exhaustion. "Guess I deserved that."

"You wanted a fight. I thought about giving it to you. I came close."

"Eli says you'd win." She didn't sound happy about it.

"I'd wipe the floor with you," I said happily.

Sylvia Turpin snorted. "I can't decide if I like you or not."

"Two alphas in the same city. Makes it hard."

"Long as you stay away from Eli," she said, "I guess I can live with it." I started laughing, and Sylvia rolled her eyes. "Okay. That sounded like a high school girl laying claim to the cute boy in class. I'm an idiot. But—" She came to an abrupt stop, clearly floundering with whatever she wanted to communicate.

"But you never met anyone like him, and it worries you that we share a house?"

"Yeah. I guess."

"Friends and family. That's all, Sheriff."

"Yeah?" She thought about that a bit, her eyes on the parking lot at her feet. "Okay. I can live with that." She stood and held out her hand, which trembled slightly. We shook. She didn't release my hand, but held me in place and searched my face. After what felt like way too many seconds, she nodded and stepped back. "Okay. Later, Jane Yellowrock."

"Later, Sylvia Turpin."

It was after two a.m. when Eli and I drove into the historic Top of the Hill district of downtown to check out several addresses the Kid thought looked promising for containing vamp lairs. Some had basements, one had newly installed vamp shutters, and three had belonged to vamps on the kill list.

Like many old Deep South towns, the rich and hoity-toity lived close to the poor and down-and-out, sometimes only one block away or even one yard down. The socioeconomic distribution had been designed in a time when transportation was a major problem and the poor had to walk to work as servants at the rich people's big houses and in town businesses and cotton mills and industry.

High Street was no exception to the rich-house/poor-house rule, and the address we turned in to was way off the street, little more than a shack, maybe six hundred square feet, with a tiny, off-kilter front porch, some kind of brick-printed sheeting hanging loose over rotting boards, and boarded-up windows. Eli put the SUV into neutral and we studied the small place in the headlights. "Looks abandoned," I said.

"Yeah. We can hope." Eli executed a fast three-point turn so were facing the street for a quick getaway. "Let's check it out." He cut the SUV engine, pulled on a baseball hat and a low-light vision scope over it, adjusted the aim of the device, and grunted. "Nothing." Next he tried a handheld passive infrared system and grunted again. "Still nothing."

It started to rain, drops hitting the windshield with heavy splats of sound and tiny little ice crystals in the middle of the dollops of rain. Eli handed me a superbright, 2,200-lumen flashlight and cut the motor. The night descended on us, silent and chill. The cold hit my face as I opened the door, a long-delayed weather front bringing the early stages of sleet with it. A slow, icy wind coursed along the ground, wisps of fog scudding around my legs. Something about the half-melted sleet, slow breeze, and the odd fog made me feel as if I were being watched, so I turned, setting my feet deliberately in a full circle, taking in the dark with Beast senses, breathing with my mouth open, scenting, before turning on the flash. Though I held it carefully before me, it still stole my night vision, so I closed my left eye to preserve what I could.

Leaving his door pushed closed but unlatched, Eli moved out from the SUV and toward the house. Bike riders don't have to think about stuff like getting a car door open for a fast getaway. I copied him and fell in, walking so I could keep an eye behind us, the light illuminating the old street, moss hanging from trees, winter-burned gardens, tilled earth and mulch and lots of brown dead stems, and the shimmer of falling rain. No green plants meant no earth witches, not like Under the Hill, with its lush greenery and tingle of magics.

The dead plants seemed significant somehow, and the feel of emptiness settled on me, featherlight and ominous. The sound of rain intensified and icy drops ran down my face and neck and into my collar. I shivered once, bracing my shoulders against the cold.

Eli stepped onto the front porch, the boards creaking under his weight, and secured his flash to his weapon, so it moved where the gun pointed. With his free hand, he tried the door. It was open. The little hairs lifted on my neck. He glanced at me and I nodded once. He opened the door and moved inside to the left, graceful as a wraith. I followed, moving to the right and setting my back against the interior wall.

The front room was empty except for a bare mattress and drug paraphernalia—needles, syringes, metal spoons, burned matches, stubby candles, a broken glass bong and several that were made out of cola cans, the old scent of marijuana, and the fainter smell of chemical-laced drugs, probably crack and cocaine. The drugs could be cut with so many different products with diverse chemical makeups that they never smelled the same to me. I'd need to be a dog or even in Beast form to detect them well. The dank house smelled of black mold and dead mice and human urine, but it hadn't been used as a drug house recently. And there was no fresh scent of anything, no old-school vamps, no new spidey vamps, no nothing.

We checked the back rooms anyway. Still nothing but broken furniture and food wrappers and used condoms, the stuff of romance for street people.

Eli was silent throughout the search, his face impassive the few times that reflected light bounced onto him. I was just glad to be out of the rain. I wasn't sure that Eli had noticed any discomfort.

When we had determined there was nothing of interest here, I followed him to the SUV, wondering how he got to be point man but not really caring. Macho man protecting the little lady, no matter that I was as tall as he and could kick butt just as well. Better, even.

With rain alternating between sputters and downpours, we inspected six other places, addresses that the Kid had sent us. We found more of the same: empty lots, houses with families sleeping inside, empty houses with FOR SALE signs out front. There were no people on the street, human or otherwise; the city had been deserted, less because of the hour than because of fear of being kidnapped and eaten.

All in all, it was disappointing, and we headed home before dawn with only the kills from the morgue to show for our trouble. But hunting vamps was like that. A lot of records work followed by useless footwork, and then by either blood and gore or disappointment. Tonight we had both, and as we rode home, I e-mailed the kills to the MOC with instructions for electronic deposit into my account. Despite what Sylvia had said, money was money.

When we got home to Esmee's, I sat in the SUV after Eli went inside, feeling at loose ends and not knowing what direction to take this investigation. I hadn't discovered who was in charge of the spidey vamps, and I hadn't found a single insight into where Misha was. I was a failure, and understood that I was creeping up on invisible deadlines that meant I might never find and save Mish, and more humans were dying at the fangs of vamps.

Sleepy, cranky, and angry at myself, I headed inside, not wanting any human interaction. So when Bobby greeted me at the foot of the stairs, sitting on the bottom step with his arms around his knees, I had to smother my irritation. "Bobby? What are you doing up?" I asked, managing to sound unruffled.

He yawned, and that made me more crabby. I wanted my bed. "Jane, I had a dream. It was about a lion."

I had no idea what to do next. How was I supposed to react to *that*? Bobby stood and took my hand, pulling me into the breakfast room, where the lights blazed and Eli sat, his weapons on the table before him, one disassembled. He was fieldstripping and cleaning the guns, a nine-millimeter semi in parts and pieces laid out on a bamboo tray and a layer of old linen napkins probably provided by Jameson. Bobby pushed me into a seat, and I sat. I mean, really. What was I supposed to *do*?

"It was a mountain lion. I think it was you."

Eli snorted softly without looking up.

"Misha says my dreams are symbic. She says that what I see isn't always what the dreams mean."

"Yeah," I said, feeling better now that I had an out. "Most people's dreams are *symbolic*."

"That's the word," he said, pleased.

"What happened in yours?" I asked.

Eli glanced up from his weapons and raised his brows. I grimaced at him and turned my attention back to Bobby.

"You got shot."

I went still, shock sizzling through me. Eli pushed a tray to me that held a universal gun-cleaning kit, and, with nothing else to do after that announcement, I began to disarm, setting my weapons on the table, mags out, chambers open, barrels pointing at an exterior wall and away from people. Like Eli, I kept one close at hand and ready to fire. More than one gunman had been caught with his pants down and all his weapons broken down, and had ended up dead because of it.

"I got shot?" I said. The M4 required no tools to break it

down, and I started fieldstripping the weapon by muscle memory and habit.

"With a dart," Bobby said. "It made you trip over your own feet and fall asleep. And some men came and got you and carried you away."

"Hmmm," I said. Deep inside, Beast crouched and hissed, showing her canines, which was strange. I remembered a few things from the big-cat's memories and I said casually, "Did they put her in a cage? The lion in your dream?"

Eli looked up at that and focused on me, but I was watching my hands while studying Bobby with my peripheral vision. He was upset.

"Yes. And they took your blood," he said. "And then it got nighttime, and you turned into Jane and you opened the cage and ran away. But you were ... you were naked." Bobby was red-faced and watching my hands on the weapons.

"It's okay, Bobby," I said gently. "Thank you. I needed to hear that."

He looked up and then back down. "We aren't supposed to look at porn. It's bad."

"It wasn't porn, Bobby. It was just a dream. We can't control our dreams."

Bobby shrugged, lifting one shoulder, his eyes still on my hands on the weapon. I pulled back the bolt and unscrewed the nut at the top of the barrel on the Benelli, letting my old friend get over the embarrassment. My hands were sure, and the stink of lube formula was strong in the room that usually smelled of bread and bacon and roast. I began to relax at the familiar activity of weapon care and yawned hugely, which made Bobby smile and relax too. "You used to yawn like that at school," he said, "and then you'd growl, low in your throat. Mostly to make people stop picking on me." He looked at Eli. "Jane was my protector. There was this big group of bullies and they were mean all the time when the housemothers and counselors weren't looking. But then Jane saw them being mean one day and she beat them up."

Eli's brows went up. "All of them?"

Bobby nodded, his face lit with some emotion I couldn't name, but might have been perilously close to hero worship.

"All of them at once. And after that, whenever she saw them, she'd yawn and show her teeth and growl and it was so cool. They didn't bother me anymore after that."

I pursed my lips and concentrated on my shotgun. The M4 was good for twenty-five thousand rounds of continuous firing, so it didn't usually need much in the way of maintenance. This time, there was some blood and brain blowback from the spidey vamp who had died while trying to suck the weapon. From the kitchen came the smell of strong coffee—espresso, the way Eli liked it.

I remembered the gang Bobby was talking about, the loosely organized pack that roamed the grounds of Bethel Nondenominational Christian Children's Home and . . . My hands stilled. *Loosely organized.*

Vamps were never loosely organized. They were kept in line by blood sharing and bindings and physical and emotional trauma, and that organization always included the heir and spare. I thought back to the meeting of the clans at the warehouse in Under the Hill. "Eli? Did we ever meet Lotus? The MOC's heir?"

The Ranger was watching me. "Not that I recall. Why?"

"We should have met Lotus." I tried to remember all the faces I'd seen. According to her original dossier, provided by Reach, Lotus was Asian and slight, with long black hair. She should have been introduced to me by now. "She wasn't at the reception when we first got here. I vaguely remember Big H's sons, the Daffodil and the Life."

"Narkis and Zoltar, respectively," Eli said, amusement lurking in his eyes as he reassembled a second handgun, the sounds ringing through the silent house. "Though I'll pay money if you'll call them that to their faces." He reached into the kit and removed a small screwdriver, replacing it with another at the same time. He was neatness personified.

I was betting money that Sylvia was a slob, which would have made me grin had my brain not been otherwise occupied. "Lotus wasn't in Big H's lair when we gave out the doses of antibody, either," I said. "So we haven't met her." I pulled out my phone and scrolled down to Big H's primo blood-servant and hit CALL. When he answered, I said, "Where's Lotus?"

The man didn't answer. I racked my brain and came up with the primo's name. "Clark? Where. Is. Lotus?"

"She has been ... excommunicated," he said slowly. "That is all I may say."

"When was the last time Big H drank from his sons?"

"Four days," he said. "Why—" He stopped quickly. "Narkis and Zoltar have not betrayed their father."

And if he drank from them, he would know. Drinking from a scion or a blood-bonded servant involved a sort of mind reading. I knew that from personal experience. Francis had said the ones closest to Big H had turned on him. Zoltar and Narkis were not the ones closest to Big H. I had assumed, and Francis had let me. I hung up, spun out of my chair, and pounded up the stairs, feeling Bobby's eyes on me as I ran. Behind me, I heard him say, "She can run fast, huh?"

Eli grunted. *Mr. Conversationalist.*

I brought down the papers and the electronic tablet the Kid had given me, both filled with research into the vampire family trees in Natchez, sat at the table, and ran through the list of authorized kills in Natchez. Lotus wasn't there. I wasn't supposed to kill her. So where was she?

I scrolled through the tablet to Lotus' personal info and history, as compiled by Reach, the Kid, and Bodat. Under Lotus' known acquaintances I found Esther McTavish. And Silandre. I sat back with a satisfied smile. Lotus' name wasn't on Hieronymus' kill list, yet she was involved with all this craziness. Either Big H was in love with her or he didn't know how far she had gone to the dark side. So unless she attacked me or a human or I could prove she had drained and killed a human, I couldn't kill her, though she was, maybe, now in charge of the Naturaleza in Natchez.

Like usual, vamp problems and troubles went back decades, sometimes centuries, and untangling the skein of old injury, torment, and conflict was impossible. After a time, old pain became like a living being, with breath and self-determination.

"First we finish the guns," I said. "Then we nap. Then we go back to Silandre's Saloon. Tell your brother to concentrate on relationships between all the vamp females."

Eli shrugged. Bobby smiled happily, his joy like a beacon of contentment in the room, satisfied because I was satisfied. I had forgotten how his inner happiness could radiate and fill up an empty space. Or an empty, lonely heart.

CHAPTER 19

I Look Like a Well-Dressed Street Person

I woke when Charly climbed on the bed with me. "Not now, Charly," I mumbled.

"It's Sunday. We have to go to church."

"Not today, Charly," I mumbled again. I touched my lips. They felt numb.

"Yes. Today."

The covers were yanked off my shoulders and down to my waist. Chilled winter air followed it, covering me, and I was glad I had put on a T-shirt and leggings to sleep in. "No." Blindly, I shoved to push her away, hitting only air while simultaneously grabbing for the covers. And hitting only air again. Cold air. "We'll go to church another day."

"Yes," Bobby said. He grabbed my flailing hand and pulled it. Colder, smaller fingers took my other hand and yanked. Insistent.

"Noooo." I was head and shoulders off the bed when I finally opened my eyes. "I don't want to go to church." It sounded whiny even to my own ears. "I want to sleep."

"And Charly needs to pray." Bobby said.

"I have to pray for my mama and I have to pray to God to make me well. Mama made me promise."

Which went straight through to my heart like a silver-tipped stake and woke me up. "Crap," I mumbled. I wrenched my hands free and braced myself on the mattress, shoving my hair out of the way. "I didn't bring a dress. All I have are my fighting clothes."

"Miss Esmee has a skirt you can use," Bobby said. "She said it's purple. And you can wear a T-shirt. Like you did in Bethel."

Bethel. The children's home. He'd used the Bethel card. I blew out a breath. I knew when I was beaten. "Okay. Get dressed. I'll find a church." The kids left, and I groaned out of bed and to my feet. I braided my hair in the bathroom and smeared on a bit of red lipstick.

Out of curiosity, I peeked into Bruiser's room; it was empty and—by the lack of fresh scent—had been for some time. The chores for his master were time consuming, even though the relationship had undergone a fundamental change. I closed the door and looked over my meager clothing. "Black, black, and more black," I said, putting on a bra and black tee and green Lucchese boots over the leggings. I'd look stupid. But Charly needed to pray. And maybe I did too.

Still, I packed a nine mil in its box, loaded, safety on and no round in the chamber. Locked the box. Carrying it, I stopped and looked at myself in the mirror hanging on the back of the bathroom door. Black hair, amber eyes, copper skin, black circles under my eyes to match the black tee, the black leggings. The only colors were in my irises and the green snakeskin boots. Which clashed. And I didn't have a Bible. I hadn't brought it. I couldn't remember the last time I hadn't brought a Bible out of town. I was going to church, and I packed a gun. How sick was that? I was so going to hell, and not for my sex life or the vamps I killed. But for the slow wandering away from God, from prayer, from any kind of spirituality. I hadn't even remembered it was Sunday. Yeah. Hell.

I went online and found a nondenominational church in town. It was way bigger than any I'd ever attended, and from its Web site, it looked like a male-dominated church, probably one where the little ladies sat with their hands primly clasped and wore little tatted head coverings. But it was the only one close by that looked like something Misha would want her daughter to attend. I saved the directions on my cell phone and left the room, making my way down the stairs.

Esmee met me at the bottom of the stairs, dressed in paisley silk pajamas of a particularly hideous green color and a sunflower-yellow silk robe and matching ballerina bedroom slippers, holding a decidedly plain—for her— purple skirt. It had two layers; the underlayer a heavy, dark purple cotton, and the upper layer a lighter shade of purple, full and gauzy. The waist was elastic, and when I pulled it on, the hem fell to the tops of my boots. On Esmee, it must have dragged the floor.

"It looks lovely on you, dear," she said, patting my hand. "But you'll need some color. This amethyst necklace and the matching bracelet will bring out the darker colors of the underskirt."

I tried to say no, but she drew my head down and snapped the amethyst choker to my throat, and opened the cuff bracelet and slid it onto my wrist. Both were ridiculously heavy and probably cost a fortune. "They go beautifully with your coloring," she said. "You are such a striking girl."

She patted my cheek, her eyes glowing with pleasure at my wearing her baubles. I felt my heart go all mushy.

"And this black shawl will keep you warm in the church." She wrapped me up in the knitted shawl as if I were a little girl, and I let her, feeling all teary-eyed. I am such a dweeb.

I smiled down at her, bent, and kissed her forehead. "Thank you, Miz Esmee. I'll take good care of them.

"I know you will, dear. Here's a Bible." She placed a worn Bible in my hands, her name in gold gilt lettering on the embossed leather cover. I was deeply touched that she would share her own Bible with me. "You are full of woe and darkness and anger," she said, her tone sad. I snapped my eyes to hers. "So go to church and give all that to God. He's big enough to take care of it all."

I shoved down my reaction. I got my best advice from the tribal elders I'd met in my life, and while Esmee appeared to be a dotty old woman, tottering around in a big empty house, hoping for interaction from the outside world, she had seen the darkness inside me as clearly as Aggie One Feather, my Cherokee elder. Esmee wasn't tribal, but she was a woman rich in years and likely rich in wisdom as well, and had insights I hadn't considered. "Ummm," I said.

"It's very simple," she said, reading my thoughts on my face. "It isn't hard or painful or violent or learned or scary. It's just you and the Almighty talking."

Something bright and icy shivered through me. "Yes, ma'am," I said.

"The children are waiting in the car, which that nice young man has turned on and gotten warm for you. Go pray, my dear."

I leaned down and kissed her forehead again before leaving the house, a gun in one hand, a Bible in the other. Charly and Bobby were in the backseat; Eli was sitting behind the wheel in the SUV, drinking from an insulated cup and reading a newspaper—another paper one. It was odd seeing real newspapers twice, like a glimpse back in time. Another cup was in the cup holder in the dash, and when I opened the door, it smelled of tea and spices and milk. I was tired, and more tears pooled in my eyes at his kindness.

Eli took one look at me and his lips quirked up ever so slightly.

"I know," I said. "I look like a well-dressed street person."

"A twelve-year-old playing dress-up. Get in. I'm driving."

I didn't protest. Unexpectedly emotional, I didn't want the responsibility of driving and parking a vehicle larger than a two-wheeler. Balancing three people on Bitsa was out too.

I'm not a big organized-religion person. I was a baptized Christian, dunked in a river one night, and I'm a Cherokee too. I had taken Bible classes all through my time at the children's home, and a comparative-religion course in high school. I'd learned a bit about Buddhism and Taoism and Islam and several other major religions. I'd even taken a course about the Greek and Roman gods. But I was raised to put all that comparative stuff aside and just read the Bible, and if something differed from the Bible to not let it offend me and just to walk away from it. Nothing in that philosophy was offended by my Cherokee spirituality, which was something other than and different from organized religion. It was about the health of the spirit, the body, the home, the clan, and the tribe, more so than about God. So I

can be Cherokee and a Christian and go to church anywhere, at least for a while. Or almost anywhere.

But . . . this church was huge. Not huge like some Roman
Catholic places of worship. Not huge and painted and
gilded like Saint Louis Cathedral in Jackson Square, but
way bigger than any church I attended when I was a kid. Or
since, for that matter. The building was brick, the windows
and the doors were pointed arches—Gothic, I think they're
called—and though the windows weren't stained glass, they
were etched glass and made the interior look removed, isolated, and sequestered. We arrived just in time for the early
service, and the man at the front door didn't look askance
at my odd clothing or at my companions, but instead guided
us to an empty pew and gave me a paper with the scriptures
and the music and the theme of the day's sermon photo-
copied on it. The preacher's name was on the bottom.
Preacher Herman Hosenfeld, which made me smile for no
reason that made sense.

We sat midway back, and I studied the cross that hung
high on the wall at the front. In this church, two smaller
crosses hung, one to each side, to represent the thief and the
murderer who died with Christ. Ever since I had learned
the origination story of the vamps—how they were created
with the wood of the three crosses—it had struck me as
strange that Christians would hang three crosses, of which
only one was holy, in their churches. Somehow now three
crosses felt wrong, as if vamps should worship the three and
Christians only the one. It also felt strange that vampires
and Christians shared the same origination event, the yin
and the yang of sacrifice and deceit, of hope and death and
life eternal.

The service started off simply with a call to prayer, and I
lowered my head. Beside me, Charly took my hand and
bowed her head and closed her eyes. I watched her through
the prayer, and she listened to the preacher with a focus
that was unusual in one so young, her lips moving with his
words, her head nodding in agreement.

After the prayer, the Lord's Supper was given, and we
took the unleavened cracker and the grape juice, even
though I wasn't sure I should. I'd been taught I should be
right with God to take it, and . . . I wasn't. Not at all. Uncer-

tainty crawled through me on slimy little feet. *I shouldn't be here. I don't deserve to be here.*

After the ritual, I relaxed back against the wooden bench and let my thoughts meander, not listening. Until I realized that Charly was up and moving to the front of the church, Bobby trailing behind. "Charly!" I hissed. But she was already at the front of the church, and I shuffled around in my brain for the last thing I'd heard before the kids moved. Preacher Hosenfeld had called for prayer needs. "Crap," I muttered under my breath, frozen in my seat.

The congregation shifted and strained to see. This was something out of order and unexpected, and they were intrigued. Many of the curious looks fell on me and I lowered my head, keeping an eye on my charges. What was I supposed to do? Having no idea, I stayed put, my eyes on the children as Charly pulled the preacher down and whispered into his ear.

Hosenfeld's face changed, and he nodded, dropped to one knee, listened, spoke, and listened again. Then he raised his eyes to the congregation and said into the mic, "This little girl is a visitor in God's house today, and she has a need. I'd like her to say it to us all."

"Crap," I muttered again. I put one hand on the pew in front of me, ready to pull myself to my feet and grab Charly back to her seat.

"My mama is missing," Charly said, holding the mic like a pro. "We think she's been kidnapped by vampires. And I have leukemia and my hair is falling out, and I need to be healed. So you got to pray. Thank you." She handed the mic back to the preacher and pulled Bobby back down the aisle by the hand.

Preacher Hosenfeld blinked back tears. "Let us pray," he said. Charly and Bobby retook their seats and Charly took my hand, her other one still holding Bobby's. Her fingers were icy and ashen and a tremble quivered through her like a cutting pain, her pearl ring sliding around her slender finger. Getting up in front of the church had taken too much out of her. I removed my shawl and wrapped her up in it. Then pulled her on my lap and dropped my head into her hair. No more was loose. No more clumps. But I could see patches of her scalp through what was left.

The preacher's prayer was heartfelt as he addressed his god for the sick and needy in his church. When he reached Charly's requests, his voice lowered, softened. "Almighty God."

And I remembered Miz Esmee's words at the front door earlier.

"Heal this little girl," he said. "And bring her mother home safe from the clutches of the blood-drinking evil in our town. In his holy name. Amen."

I was glad it wasn't one of those long, flowery prayers full of *thee*s and *thou*s and names of God. This one felt real and somehow potent. It was how I prayed—just talking. And I realized I had been praying with him, for the first time in a long while. I took a ragged breath.

Charly was exhausted, fighting to stay awake, and I shifted her on my lap to cradle her better, and stood. As I walked out of the church, the preacher told the congregation that there was to be a baptism in the font at the front of the church immediately after the service. I smelled water, then, and knew it was to be an old-time dunking.

My eyelids were glued together when I woke in the afternoon, and I knew someone was in the room with me. I sniffed and smelled . . . Rick. And he smelled like cat. Too much like cat. I mentally reviewed the time until the three days of the full moon and realized we had only a little more than twenty-four hours. Inside me, Beast woke and stretched, yawning and showing me her teeth.

Black leopard big-cat. Want as mate, she thought.

You said you wanted Bruiser, I thought back, still smelling him on my sheets where he'd sat as we chatted.

Want more. Want both. She parted her lips and panted at me. *Want Ricky-Bo.*

And the full moon was nearly here, a time when Beast was more in control than I wanted. *Not good.* Rubbing my eyes, I managed to open them, pushed up in the bed against the pillows and headboard, and found him sitting in the corner, in a beam of slanted sunlight that had made its way between the blinds. He had been there a while.

Feeling no overt threat, my eyes traveled over him, my mouth opened to take in his scent. Beast leaned close and studied her former and prospective mate. One knee was up,

Rick's jeans as black as the coat of his were-animal, his feet bare in the shadows. His eyes were glowing softly greenish gold, his black hair falling over his forehead, far longer than when I'd first met him, and forming ringlets at the ends that nearly brushed his shoulders. He was shirtless, his chest that wonderful olive shade from his French and Cherokee heritage, marked with a perfect triangle of fine black chest hair trailing down into the low-riding waist of his jeans. His mangled tats no longer looked like a mountain lion, a bobcat, and mountains, the scarring of his torture by werewolves twisting them into shapeless masses and white scars, all except the four glowing gold spots of cat eyes. I knew if I touched the eyes, the golden tats would be hot beneath my fingers, part of the spell that was still working in his body, the spell that kept him from changing into his were-cat form, and might keep him forever in cat form if he did ever shift. My fingers curled into the covers to keep from reaching for him.

Rick closed his eyes, taking in my scent. Minutes trickled by like sand through a glass. He didn't attack. He didn't do anything except breathe, until he said, "I see the way he looks at you. I smell his scent in this room. Have you taken him as mate?"

I flinched. "What do you care? You have Monica." My tone was childish and laced with hurt, and I wanted to cringe. It also sounded as if I'd slept with Bruiser, which I hadn't.

He opened his eyes and a smile pulled at his lips, a real smile, not a heated or resentful one, as I'd expected. "Monica? You mean Monkey?"

I looked away, trying to place the name. And then I remembered. Monkey was one of Rick's sisters, the only name I'd ever heard him call her. "Monica is *Monkey*? Oh, crap," I breathed.

Rick's smile spread. "Yeah. You are jealous of my baby sister," he said, sounding pleased. I wanted to crawl under the covers and hide. "Do you remember a talk we had about boyfriends, the morning after the first night we were together at my place?" he asked.

Instantly, I did. It had seemed important even then. And might be vastly important now. Bruiser had called, we had chatted, and I had hung up on him, rudely.

"That your other boyfriend?" Rick had asked.

Shock had zinged through me and I rolled back on the bed on top of him. I remembered the swish as I slung my hair out of the way. "Other *boyfriend?*"

"If you want to call me that."

"I'll think about it. But if I had a boyfriend, there'd be only the one."

"Hmmm," Rick had murmured. The vibration had rumbled through him like a big purr. *"Wonder if he knows that."*

"I remember," I said now, hearing the insecurity in my voice. Which I hated. "I haven't slept with Bruiser."

Rick looked down, his lips going soft. "Good. Selfish of me, under the circumstances, but good." He looked back up, meeting my eyes, his with the golden-greenish glow of his cat. "We can't be together right now. Not like you and Bruiser can. But eventually I'll find a way out of this were problem. And then . . ." He let the words trail off.

I swallowed, my throat dry. Beast peered out of my eyes, purring deep in my mind. "Then what?" I managed.

"Then if you're sleeping with him, I'll kill him and take you."

Electric shock blasted through me and I caught my breath. Rick just smiled, showing his teeth, and made a huff of amusement, all cat. He stood with the grace of his leopard and strolled to the door. He opened it and left the room, the low light playing across his skin. The door closed silently, and I felt more than heard him stalk away. "Holy crap," I whispered.

A knock came on my door and I called, "Just a minute." I rose, pulled on jeans and a T-shirt and my sweater, and opened the door. My knees were still knocking.

The Kid stood there, his multitudinous electronic gizmos in hand. "I think I found something," he said, "about Silandre and Hieronymus' heir, Lotus, and—" He stopped and waved his hand as if wiping away everything he'd just said. "Eli's in the breakfast room. Come on."

I went. My personal life could wait. Like, for years.

"Esther and Silandre were pals back in the eighteen hundreds," the Kid said. "Bodat found out about this photographer dude, and he got a pic of the women together in front of a whorehouse that catered to Union soldiers and sympathizers both during and after the War between the States. And to me it looks like the front of Silandre's Saloon."

"Dude. We did it together," Bodat said from the kitchen door, where he stood, a chicken leg in one hand. The unmistakable scent of Popeye's fried chicken filled the air.

"Yeah. We did," the Kid said. "And the best part? Lotus is in one of the photos."

Something warm and anticipatory danced along under my skin. Eli and I bent over the back of the Kid's chair. The sepia-tint photocopy was faded, with a slightly fuzzed focus, but it was clearly of three women, two Caucasian, and the third Asian. The house in the background might indeed have been Silandre's Saloon. "Lotus, Esther, and Silandre. They look mighty chummy," I said. "Wonder if one of Esther's pals turned on her and beheaded her."

"Backstabbing vamps?" the Kid asked. "Say it isn't so. I also found these."

He handed me a stack of old photocopies. The top one was a deed to a four-hundred-acre piece of property just outside Natchez proper. It was owned by Lotus in the year 1801. The page beneath was a copy of a page from a legal ledger, a list of signatures for marriage licenses. Circled in red were the names *H. E. Hieronymus* and *Lotus Song Hieronymus* in the year 1802. The names were close; they belonged to the same people of today.

The Kid pointed. "Next in the stack is a death certificate for H. E. Hieronymus and wife, lost at sea in 1820, followed by the posthumous sale of the original property to a couple named *D. L.* Hieronymus and his *sister,* Lotus Hieronymus. And then here"—he pointed to another page—"they died again and the property was inherited by them later, with different names. This was one way vamps got around the inheritance laws and kept their property through the ages. You know, from before they were out of the closet and could just keep their real holdings in perpetuity if they wanted. It was old-fashioned real property and wealth management."

"Up until the nineteen forties," Bodat said, "when Hieronymus didn't let Lotus have the property back. He kept it all in his name."

"He cheated her," Eli said. My head was spinning with all the names and times, but I agreed.

"Right," the Kid said. "Instead of the property going back to them both, Big H bought it and kept it. The next page is a court ledger, listing legal claims. One is a claim of misappropriation of inheritance filed by Luminous Song, claiming to be the daughter of Big H and Lotus. She tried to get it back. She wasn't successful."

"It's convoluted," I said, "but it's motive."

The Kid leaned over me and flipped pages. "I marked the pages for the good stuff." There were properties all over the state listed in versions of the names Silandre, Lotus, and Esther.

"They were business partners?" I asked. The Kid nodded.

Bodat wiggled his eyebrows in what I took to be an affirmative. "They formed a corporation called Lotus Blossoms, which ran brothels Under the Hill."

"And then Big H cheated them out of about half their ill-gotten gains," the Kid said.

"So why didn't they just offer a Blood Challenge and get it back the vamp way?" Eli asked.

"Those are mano a mano, which any of them would have lost, not three on one, which they might have won," I said, thinking. "They took the long view and waited until a stronger vamp came along and showed them a better way. Maybe when they heard about Lucas Vazquez de Allyon, Esther left Natchez and swore to him. When Death's Rival made his move on other cities, Esther probably worked a deal with him and her old business partners to take over Natchez territory."

"And then you cut off de Allyon's head," the Kid said. "Kinda spoiled their big plans."

"Yeah." I breathed out, putting the stack of papers on the table. "But knowing all this really doesn't help us find the missing humans, witches, or the BBV."

"It narrows the focus," Bodat said, "which means we can create an algorithm to find—"

I held up a hand, stopping him. "You guys did good work. Really good. Narrow down the list of properties we need to search to ones with basements only. We're spinning our wheels right now." I held up the poor-quality photo of three bawdy women, corseted, wearing large hats and stacked heels, with their skirts thrown up to reveal a lot of stockinged legs. Photos of vamps were nearly impossible to make until the era of digital photography. The original might be worth a small fortune.

"Okay," I said. "Eli, let's weapon up and check out Silandre's Saloon again by daylight. Maybe we missed something."

CHAPTER 20

I'll Get Well Later

We were back at Silandre's, the place looking more garish by daylight than it had by night, and that was saying an awful lot. Buddy and Bubba's ATV was still there, parked near the kitschy plastic flamingoes. I stepped from the SUV, feeling again that strange tingle of magic I had noticed Under the Hill, but it passed over and was gone. It left me feeling unsettled, but I had no idea why. Shrugging to relieve unexpected tension, I turned my attention to the saloon.

The white-painted board siding had so many coats of paint on it that it looked nearly flat, rippled instead of stacked. The windows were mostly old blown-glass panes, the few replaced panes having a different refractivity and clarity than the older ones. It hadn't shown in the dark, but the gaudy pink paint on the woodwork was two-toned. Bleagh. But, then, I'm not a girly kinda gal and don't care for pink, especially the bright, brassy shades Silandre had chosen.

The front door was unlocked, and when we entered, a brass bell over the door rang with a tinkling sound. It hadn't been there the last time we were here. Someone had been moving things around; the front room was no longer overcrowded with kitsch and there were no fanged dolls at all. However, the place was so filled with commercial scents that I couldn't smell anything but the floral-fruity-lavender-cherry-spice combo. I holstered the nine mils I hadn't even known I'd drawn and pulled the M4, cradling it in my arms.

A young woman stuck her head out of the middle room and called a cheery, "Hello. I'll be with—" Her accented words came to a complete stop as she focused on the weapons. She had sounded vaguely Russian as she spoke, and now her eyes went wide with fear.

I held up a hand, fingers spread. "It's okay. We're here with Big H's permission."

"Hieronymus," Eli corrected.

"Yeah. Him. We're not here to hurt you or anything."

Moving slowly, the girl came out from the wall, revealing a slight frame, long, straight hair, and dark eyes. She looked like a child, willowy but tall for her age, the way girls look when they have grown a foot in a year, all knobby knees and elbows below a pink shirt and plaid skirt. Much like I had looked during my first year in the children's home.

I had no idea what she was doing here or if Big H's people had cleaned up our mess in the back. We had left an awful lot of blood in the back room. "What's your name?" I asked.

"Nostrana," she said. Yeah. Middle or Eastern European.

"Have you seen Silandre?" I asked.

"No. She has not been here."

"How about the back room?" Which was a coward's way of asking if Big H's cleanup crew had gotten all the blood out.

Nostrana shrugged. "Someone purchased the entire set, I think. The room was empty when I arrived two days ago. I have been rearranging everything, making it into a doll room." She stopped, biting her lip, as if she had said too much.

"Nostrana," I tried to pronounce it like she had, all liquid sounds and sophistication, but it came out sounding flat and Southern. "You work for Silandre?"

"Three days a week, and during the three days of the full moon and the one night of the new moon. It is odd schedule, but I am exchange student in university, so I can make it do."

"There's no university anywhere near," Eli said, sounding cold and hard and managing to call her a liar.

Nostrana's head came up and she firmed her lips. "I take classes on Internet. And I take bus to campus three days a week."

"Long trip," Eli said, still disbelieving, this time almost snide.

"Is not your concern. What do you want?"

I smiled. Nostrana was no pushover. "To look around," I said, sliding the shotgun into the spine sheath and showing both hands open and empty. Reluctantly, Eli holstered his weapons, but he kept a hand on one. When Nostrana didn't object, I walked through the disordered room toward her. And felt the tingles on my skin. I stopped. This didn't make sense. "You're a witch."

Her eyes narrowed and she reached into a pocket. "Also not your concern."

"Witches are disappearing in Natchez. Have you been approached by anyone? Been followed?" I asked.

"No." Her left hand clutched something in the pocket.

"No need to use magical defense on us," I said. "We're going."

"Please. Quickly. And not to come back unless Silandre is here."

I jerked my head at Eli and backed away, stepping carefully to the front of the saloon/store and out into the meager sunshine without turning my back on her. I didn't speak again until we were back at the SUV. "Witches are missing. Vamps are turning into cockroaches, and Nostrana is a witch working for a vamp."

"If she was telling us the truth," Eli said.

"She smelled of the truth." Eli gave me an odd look, one I've come to associate with me admitting to being anything nonhuman. Like most of the other times, I ignored it. "I need to talk to Francis."

Without commenting, Eli started up the SUV and we rode along the Under the Hill streets and passed by the old warehouse/bar where we had fought and survived. Once again, a surge of magic hit me, a sharp, bitter tang in the air. "Stop the car." Before Eli had come to a complete stop, I was out of the SUV and moving between buildings, following the scent. Within three steps, Eli was behind me. In my pocket, I felt something hot and I dug a hand in, pulling out the coin the tribal elder had given me in the church-that-wasn't. The silver coin was hot to the touch, the temperature variant a sure sign of witch magics. I reached into another pocket and touched the pocket watch. It too was heated. And stank of old blood.

"Here. It's here." I turned in a slow circle, holding the coin out before me, feeling the coin heat and cool, like a childhood game—"You're getting hot! Cooler. Cooler. COLD! Hot again!" Leading me toward the middle street . . . and as suddenly as it had appeared, it was gone.

The coin was now neither warm nor cold and the watch was my body temperature. Maybe the change in temp had been my imagination. Maybe I'd been palling around with supernats for so long that I was starting to scent magics everywhere. I dropped my arm. Stuck the coin in my pocket. The old blood smell of the watch clung to my fingers. "Crap. Okay. Let's go home, Eli."

He raised his brows. "You'll tell me what this little jaunt was about later." It wasn't a request. More a command.

"Yeah, yeah, yeah. Whatever. Let's go." While he drove, I texted. A lot.

There wasn't much left of the winter afternoon when we got back to Esmee's. "I have some dirty work in the garage," I said.

"We killing the vamp?"

"Francis? I hope not. But we may have to cut off his clothes."

Eli's forehead wrinkled. "Say what?"

"Francis is one of the new spidey vamps. I've been smelling old blood on Francis, stinky stuff." Stinky stuff like the pocket-watch amulets, but I didn't share that with Eli, not yet. "Francis is healing even without blood meals. I think our boy may have something on him that's helping him heal and transform, maybe even controlling him somehow. It might be what allowed de Allyon to do what he did and control the vamps under him so well, and take over other cities, and be a Naturaleza in a world where all the other vamps were Fame Vexatum."

Eli shook his head, but I thought it was in surprise, not negation. I pulled out the pocket-watch amulet.

"Didn't you ever wonder why the priestesses and the European council allowed de Allyon to keep his own territory, operating as a Naturaleza in open violation of the Vampira Carta? And no one tried to stop him?"

"So far as we know," he hedged.

"So far as we know," I agreed, as Eli pulled the SUV to the garage. "He had to have something on the other vamps, some kind of weapon or way to protect himself until he discovered the vamp plague."

"A witch circle," Eli said, surprised.

"Exactly. Powering some kind of amulet or *objet d'foci*," I said, playing on *objet d'art*, "that allowed him to do all kinds of stuff. Then he discovered the vamp plague and he decided it was the perfect weapon to expand his power base." I flipped open the pocket watch, catching a whiff of that almost-familiar stink. Remembering where I'd first gotten the amulets—off Naturaleza vamps and humans sworn to de Allyon. "This isn't powerful enough to be the amulet or focal object. But I think it's tied in somehow."

We left the vehicle, walking into the daylight. It wasn't bright and the sun was hidden behind layers of clouds, but it was daylight. It would do. Inside the garage, the shadows enfolding us, we stood, letting our eyes adjust.

Eli said softly. "Francis is one of the revenants. He's faster and stronger than anything I've ever seen."

"Yeah. And what I'm thinking is that some of the revenants have been killed true-dead more than once and brought back. And that every time they get brought back, there are more changes."

Eli let that sink in a bit, staring off at the horizon. "What's your strategy?"

"I'm gonna tell him to strip. Then when he doesn't, I'm gonna pull his cage into the yard, out back where the kids can't see it happening, and let him burn for a while. Then if he doesn't give me what I'm looking for, I'll kill him and cut his clothes until I find it."

"You sound mighty cheerful about it."

"I am."

Eli shrugged with his eyebrows, which was really cool, and followed me into the dark.

The interrogation didn't take long. Even with his accelerated healing powers, Francis Adrundel was no match for the sun. After two minutes outside, smoking and blistering and screaming, he emptied his pockets. I picked up the pocket watch and tucked it into my other pocket. I didn't know what the watches did, but I had an idea that getting them together could eventually be a problem.

Once I was done, I called Clark, Big H's primo, and asked him to send some blood meals by to feed Francis. The *thing* he was becoming had to die true-death eventually, but so far, he'd been useful. I wanted him kept undead.

I had timed it well. An hour before sunset, I called my escorts into the dining room. Bruiser was back, with no explanation of where he had gone, Soul was dressed in silver-colored gauzy clothing that reminded me of moonlight, and Rick was glowering, wearing earpieces with his magic-spelled music coming from them. Brute and Pea looked beautiful and cute and deadly. Part of me wanted them on my team, and the other part of me knew that would be a mistake. I'd eventually have to kill the wolf and I really didn't want to kill anything that an angel had cursed.

"Soul, can you do another magical scan for Misha? Or maybe a scan for a full witch circle?"

"I have tried questing," she said softly, "and found nothing because of the interference. All I could detect was the massive magical energies in Natchez and Under the Hill."

"Okay. Bobby and I are going for a ride," I told them.

"You think he can dowse for you while he's awake?" Eli asked.

"Only one way to find out."

"I'll come along."

"Whatever," I said. "Soul, will you look after Charly?"

"Certainly."

"The rest of you eat, hydrate, and gear up like you're going to war."

Rick and Bruiser looked each other over and didn't move. Rick's glower heated up, his eyes starting to glow that weird shade they did when his cat was scratching on his spirit. He was looking at Bruiser when he growled, "Why?"

I wanted to say, *Because I said so,* but that might not be effective on my crew. "Because things might get hairy."

"Are you going to tell us your plans?" Soul asked.

"Sure. Right now, I'm trying to narrow down the locations where Misha might be prisoner. As soon as we get back, we're going to rattle some cages until a pretty flower falls out."

"Lotus," Soul said, sounding pleased.

"Bingo. And I'm not picky how we get our info, begging PsyLED's pardon," I added. I stood and checked my pocket watches. Each was in a separate pocket, so they couldn't touch. Just in case.

The sun was setting, a red blaze on the western horizon, amazing from where Bobby and I stood dead center of Under the Hill. The Mississippi was a mighty, roiling monster, currents twisting and diving, carrying debris beneath the surface to reappear farther on. The river air was heavy with moisture and chilled with winter.

Two barges moved upstream and one down, all heavily laden. The long call of the barges sounded and were answered, like the mating calls of water birds. A riverboat casino docked near shore advertised in neon, a startling purple scene of palm trees and three round circles above them that looked like something on a slot-machine screen or gambling chips, or maybe three full moons.

As we watched, the river changed color, tinted bloody by the falling sun. Behind us, to the east, clouds still massed on the horizon, as thick and roiling as the river, blackened by the coming night. The first stars of night were out, brilliant in the icy air. A police car rolled by, its engine noise muted by the wet night.

High on the hill behind us, the night lights of the city of Natchez burned bright. On the streets around us, a few tourists were wandering, taking in the sights—not nearly as many as usual, thanks to the deaths that were making the news. Eli was patrolling the streets and yards, unseen somewhere nearby.

It was the first night of January's full moon—the full moon known by many American Indian tribes as the Full Wolf Moon. The silvered orb was still below the horizon, but soon it would rise slowly behind a final thin layer of clouds, like a virgin bride dressed in lace veils.

Which was pure poetic crap. It was an icy ball of rock trapped by the gravity of the Earth. I knew that. But every ancient culture on Earth had revered the moon, had planted by its cycle, married and buried by its cycle, traveled by it, harvested by it, sailed by it. Animals mated by it, especially cats of all kinds. And Beast thought it was beautiful. For that matter, so did I. Just not poetic. No way.

It was . . . useful. Yeah. To ancient peoples. And to Beast when she hunted antlered bucks in harvest time, and skinny, cold deer of any gender in snow time. Useful. That was the moon.

Beside me, Bobby laughed, the sound familiar and comforting somehow. He put his cold hand into mine and I clasped it. Without looking away from the sunset, I said, "You should have brought gloves."

"But I need to feel the watch. Bare skin is best for that," he said, sounding like the grown man he was, sounding sure and certain and in control. This was a new Bobby, not the child of my youth, despite the remembered, childlike laughter.

"Are you sure of this?" I asked for the umpteenth time.

"No. But trying is the only way. And Misha is dying."

I blinked back tears at the misery in his voice. Misha was his family. Misha had taken him in when his own family failed him or died out. Would I have done the same? I wanted to think that I would have taken Bobby in, but I had to doubt it.

"You always doubt yourself," Bobby said.

I started. "You a mind reader now too?" I asked harshly.

Bobby shook his head, and I saw it in my peripheral vision. "No. But your magics change color when you don't believe in yourself. They go all green and muddy, like the river down there."

I held in my sigh. I had forgotten how much Bobby saw of the physical world when he was a child. It had translated into the metaphysical world as an adult. He'd grown into his magic in a totally natural, perfectly fitting way.

I managed a smile. "So I'm muddy?"

"Kinda muddy," he agreed, nodding, not hiding his smile.

As he spoke, the last red sliver of the sun vanished below the horizon. The far shoreline was lit by Vidalia, Louisiana. Here on the Natchez side of Under the Hill, the lights were fewer and glowed less brightly, the moon witches in Under the Hill having made certain to leave off porch lights, to work by candlelight while inside, hurrying to gather supplies until the moon was ready to rise. Then the witches would be outside, in gardens and yards, in copses between trees in the woods, in well-marked circles, absorbing the moon's power, working their craft.

"The moon will be up in ten minutes or so," I said. I took his elbow and pulled Bobby off the sidewalk onto a patch of grass at the curb.

Bobby breathed out and let go of my hand. He closed his eyes and dropped back his head, as if he were falling asleep on his feet. But his hands rose, fingers splayed, as if searching in the darkness, waiting for a gift to be placed in them. "Magic is everywhere here," he said, his tone a thing of wonder and delight. "So much magic."

He threw out his arm in a slow, broad sweep, to include all of Under the Hill. "There's small circles everywhere tonight. I never felt so many witches before." He pointed upstream. "There's a small coven there, all from the same family. Misha would say it was nicely balanced."

I tilted my head, studying him. That was an odd thing to say. For a human.

But . . . not for a witch.

Misha? I sucked in a breath, grabbing a puzzle piece that might not fit anywhere. It might not belong in the image I had been constructing at all. Or it might be the one missing piece. *Misha was a witch?* The evidence said no. I remembered the smell of the three in the closed hotel room the day I got to town. Human—all of them smelled human—and I had a sense of smell Beast-acute. Even Bobby smelled human. Bobby, who had magic and shouldn't smell human.

This was crazy. Misha had *never* smelled witchy, not ever. But witches don't come into their power until they hit puberty. I had no idea how old Misha had been when she became a woman grown, as the old saying went.

But . . . Charly's illness—witch children were prone to childhood illnesses and cancers.

Charly was wearing an adult-styled pearl ring that was too big for her finger. Misha had worn a pearl necklace that first meeting. Had the scent of magic been spelled away? Was their jewelry spelled to shield them from discovery?

Softly, I asked, "What kind of witch is Misha?"

Bobby laughed, the sort of laugh he might have had had

he been born differently. "Mish thought you would figure it out. Charly wanted to tell you right away, but Misha said to wait. She never let us tell anyone, to protect Charly. She said her being a witch didn't matter because she had the spell to hide what she was."

"The spells are in the pearls?"

"Anti-witch-detection spells," he said with a quiet laugh. *So much for my sense of smell.* "But then she came here to write the book," I said.

"But it still didn't matter," he said, "because she wasn't going to see witches. She was going to see vampires." He dropped his hands and lifted his head, surprise on his face when he looked up at me. "Are you mad, Jane?"

I had never been good at hiding things from Bobby Bates, and he could read my reaction on my face. As honestly as I could, I said, "No. I'm not mad." But Misha had been wrong about her being a witch not mattering, because any vampire would have known Misha was witchy the instant the vamp bit her, and no Naturaleza would have turned down a free meal. Misha had gone for a story and research and to find a vamp willing to donate some blood to her daughter. And now she was most likely part of the witch circle I was looking for, being used for God knew what.

But Bobby had no way of knowing that, and I wasn't going to tell him. The poor decision and the possible catastrophic results weren't his fault. It was Misha's for making the decision, and maybe a little bit my fault for not figuring it out already. I was too dependent on my nose, and maybe always had been.

"Moon's up," Bobby said, holding out his hand. An instant later, I felt it too, and the magic in Under the Hill increased dramatically as witches everywhere settled into circles, bathed in moon power.

I pulled the pocket watch from my pocket, and Bobby stepped back fast. "That is ugly and it stinks, Jane."

I turned it over. It was just a cheap pocket watch, base metal with a flying duck in bas-relief on its cover. As far as I knew, no human had noticed the spell smell. "Ugly how?"

"Bloody magics, like rotten meat. Like dead things dug out of the ground."

Which was an apt description for a vamp, in many ways. "Do you still want to do this?"

Bobby scowled and jerked his left hand at me, demanding.

The plan was to test the waters by letting Bobby hold one pocket-watch amulet and see if he could pinpoint the witch circle that powered it. Then, if nothing happened, we'd try it with two pocket watches, then with three. Of course, there was no safe way to test my method, but I had been holding the watches and they hadn't hurt me.

I settled the watch into Bobby's palm and he drew in a hissing breath, as if the thing burned him, but he wrapped his fingers around it tightly and closed his eyes. Instantly his hand lifted and he pointed, one finger rising from the watch. "There. I think—"

Bobby fell, midword, midgesture. Only my Beast reflexes let me catch him before his head hit the ground. I grunted as I let him down gently. Eli rushed up, a vamp-killer in one hand, his small sub gun in the other, his eyes covering the street and houses and even up in the air. As if maybe vamps could now fly. Which gave me pause.

I checked for a pulse and an airway. Bobby was breathing and his heart was steady and strong. I peeled back his fingers to reveal the pocket witch—and the blistered flesh beneath. I swore softly, and Bobby coughed out a laugh. "You gonna get in trouble, Jane."

Relief swept through me. "Yeah. Mouth washed out with slimy soap. Then put on toilet detail for a month."

"Crapper detail," he said, laughing. "Owww. My hand." He looked at it and his eyes went wide. "I'm hurt, Jane."

Eli knelt, opened a small med kit, and squeezed a packet of gel on the blisters. He popped a second packet and placed it over the gel, and closed Bobby's hand gently around it. "Those are second-degree burns. We need to get him to a hospital, but this is a coolant. It'll take out the sting for now."

I couldn't see the writing on the packet, but I figured it was some high-tech military dealio. I had more immediate worries. As I helped him to sit up, I asked, "Bobby, has this ever happened before? Passing out? Getting burned?"

He strained up and balanced on his unhurt arm. "No. But it doesn't matter. Give me another watch."

"No way, Bobby boy. I'm not letting you get hurt again."

"Misha needs me. Charly needs me. I'll get well later."

"When you two finish arguing," Eli said, "I texted Soul. She said to put Bobby in a circle with the amulets and see what happens. It won't hurt him that way."

"How do we make a circle?"

"Do I look like a witch? Security expert here. You're the magic-using part of the triumvirate."

"Bobby?" I asked. "Have you ever been put in a circle? Do you know how?"

"Misha just draws a ring in the dirt."

"How about drawing one with a piece of chalk on the sidewalk?" Eli asked.

"Nope," Bobby said. "Those TV shows and books are wrong. It has to be a complete circle. Breaks in the circle let the power out or in, and the rough sand on the surface make it not complete. Chalk can be used on a clean floor, though, if there are no cracks in it."

Which was way more than I knew. As I watched, Eli started kicking a circle into the soil with his combat boot. I stayed kneeling and scooped the loosened soil out of the narrow trench. We quickly had a circle around Bobby, with a small area still open. He looked so alone sitting on the ground, his face pale in the moonlight, his freckles like dappled shadows.

"I'll take the amulets now," Bobby said. "And will you open them so I can see the faces? Please," he added, politely, the years of children's home manners showing.

Curious, I put the three pocket watches in the circle with him, opened the amulets, and turned the faces so they were easy to read.

"Thank you. May I please borrow an ash stake, Jane?"

I handed him two ash stakes. "The stakes are for what? Killing vamps while you're . . . You can't stake vamps while you're in a circle."

Bobby grinned and folded his legs, guru fashion, and put his injured hand in his lap. "If I have to move the watches, now I don't have to touch them, so I won't get burned. And I'm a dowser, remember? Wood might help."

I felt like an idiot. Dowsers sometimes used wood to find . . . whatever they were dowsing for. "Oh. Yeah. Right."

With his right hand, Bobby took up an ash stake and

positioned the watches in a line in front of his knees, each about an inch apart. He looked up at the moon, now partially visible between brightly lit, scudding clouds. "Okay. Close the circle, Jane."

"Then what? Without a witch to power the closing, nothing will happen," I said, knowing I was procrastinating, worried that Bobby would be hurt worse.

"I think I can do it. I've watched Misha do it." He nodded once emphatically. "I can do it. I know I can."

I pulled a vamp-killer. "If something goes wrong, I can cut the circle with iron and silver and pull you out."

"It might burn you."

"To quote a friend of mine, 'I'll get well later,'" I said. Bobby gave me a thumbs-up. I closed the circle.

He dropped his head back again, like he had done earlier. One minute went by. Then two. With Beast vision, I saw the circle in the torn soil begin to glow softly. Unbelievable. Bobby had activated the circle. He wasn't a witch, but the little guy had more magic than I had thought.

At Bobby's knees, the pocket watches began to glow as well. I smelled the faint stink of blistering flesh, and Bobby hissed with pain. Bobby was being injured. I raised the knife, ready to bring it down on the circle, severing its ties to the Earth.

"No, Jane," Bobby said. He took a sharp breath of pain and raised his head to normal. "Not yet. I'm not finished." As he spoke, the three pocket watches before him shifted slightly. My fist tightened on the knife handle but I held off the blow to the circle as the amulets aligned toward some point that I couldn't name. It wasn't the North Star, sunrise, or sunset, which meant—

A hard smile thinned my mouth. The three watches were aligned with the source of their power. The number twelve on all three watches pointed toward the witch circle that might hold Misha. That meant searching as many as twenty buildings and grounds or maybe as few as five, which was way better odds than before. It meant we might find her tonight or tomorrow night. The smell of burning flesh rose on the air. *Bobby was in trouble.* I raised the knife to cut the circle.

"No!" he said. "Not yet!" Bobby was breathing fast, the smell of burned flesh growing stronger. He lifted the ash

ness in him. "Bobby," Eli said, "can you wait in the SUV while Jane and I check out the house?"

"No." Bobby shook his head hard. "I'll go with you. I want to help save Misha."

"You don't have body armor, so I can't let you go in with us, man. I need you for a different job. Jane and I need you to sit in the SUV with a cell phone and call the sheriff if things go bad. We won't have time if fighting starts. I'll set the phone to a one touch and put it on speaker."

"I'll have your backs? That's what they say on TV."

"Exactly. And, hey. We couldn't do it without you."

Bobby grinned, and I had to look away or get all teary eyed. Eli helped him to his feet and got my old friend settled in the SUV. I used the time to text the Kid to get our team down to Under the Hill to help rescue the witches. I also put away the amulets, careful to not let them touch one another. I still didn't know what they would do, but I wasn't going to chance anything.

When he got back to me, Eli said, "Not many people would have been able to sit there and get burned in order to do their job. He's a good man."

"So are you, Eli." My cell vibrated and I checked the screen. "Our team is on the way. ETA fifteen. Let's go reconnoiter. And then let's go rescue some witches."

"And kick some vamp butt. And then I'm thinking pizza tonight."

My mouth fell open. "You? *You* are going to eat *pizza*?"

"With sausage and pepperoni, double cheese, mushrooms, and heavy on the onions. I can taste it now. With a pitcher of beer. Close your mouth, girl. Mosquitoes will fly in."

The house Bobby had picked out was freshly painted, white with purple gingerbread trim, one of many that had been recently restored. It had a new cement block-foundation, making it sit high off the ground, a four-room square house on a tiny lot with a picket fence. And not a hint of magics about the place. Until I stood back and viewed the house with Beast vision. Then the blackish-purplish, bloody-broken magics stormed up from the house in a writhing, heated swarm, like frilled snakes or flaming worms, magic so strong it was nearly sentient, yet broken like a battlefield still full of the dead.

"Holy crap on a cracker," I whispered.

And Eli laughed. "That swear, I like."

We took a circuitous route to the house, and the closer I got, the stronger the witch stink got. This was the smell I'd found on the wind several times over the past few days, but couldn't place. And it was no wonder. The spell covering and warding the house was strong magic, highly contained. It was based on a *hedge-of-thorns* spell, but a hundred times stronger; part of its makeup was a keep-away spell and another part was a containment spell to hide the magics. To get a more complete view, we circumnavigated the house, but made a point to stay far back, as the magics were hard and strong and burned when we got too close. The ward was a sphere buried below the surface of the ground that rose to cover the entire lot and nudge up against the taller buildings to either side. The structures on either side were each three stories tall, though the one on the left had a raised false front to look like a fourth story. Both were empty, with flat roofs and arched windows, and looked as if they were in original condition, unrestored.

The house they dwarfed was in far better condition, but the only way in was a small opening at the top where the magics met. I had only one idea how we might get inside. And it wasn't something I wanted to do.

It was closer to half an hour by the time the two cars arrived, Rick and his team in one, Bruiser driving solo. Soul hopped out of the car before it came to a complete halt, her gauzy clothes swirling around her like waves of water. She stood in the middle of the street, her eyes wide. Brute leaped to her side, snarling at her.

Rick parked and got out of the vehicle more slowly. He was dressed in jeans and a button-front shirt and a windbreaker with the word PSYLED on front and back. And he wore a Kevlar vest under his shirt. Even money it was one of the new ones just hitting the market—Kevlar to stop bullets, a layer of some new plastic to slow even the sharpest knife blade, and a spell woven in to protect the wearer from attack spells. His earpieces were in his ears, music pouring out of them to hold the need to shift at bay.

His eyes were glowing softly, his cat peering out at the world, and he looked tightly wound but in control. I'd sat through his first full moon with him, before he had the music spell, and it hadn't been pretty. Rick didn't acknowledge me at all but walked up close to the house, holding a device, a small black box. A psy-meter, or psychometer, that measured the strength and quality of magics. He walked back and forth in front of the house, holding the meter over his head.

Bruiser stood at his car, studying the entire block, while Eli stood off to one side, his subgun at the ready, his mission look on his face, his body angled so he could see the house, the street, and the SUV with Bobby in it.

"I walked these streets," Soul said, frustration in her voice, "looking for magic. This was *not* here."

"It's got a powerful ward," I said. "Only when the moon came up did it become visible."

Rick swore softly and put his device away. "Too much ambient magic to get a reading. All I could get was a redline."

Soul nodded, blinking as if her eyes had dried out from staring so long. "Yes. It would show a redline. The ambient magics here are . . ." She shook her head, unable to find a word to express it. She settled on "astounding. We can't get inside, not from here. It would take the magical equivalent of a nuclear bomb to get through that."

I sighed, hating what I was about to say. "I can get in."

They all turned to me, and an acute discomfort sank its claws into me. Beast snarled. *No. Will not let you.*

You don't have a choice. Not if you want a chance to save the kit's mother, I thought back. "I can shift into a bird and fly over it, and dive through the hole at the top and land inside." I thought Soul's eyes were gonna pop out of her head, and I tilted my head in a wry shrug. "Only problem is that the magics I'll be flying through might actually kill me. Or might force me to shift back while I'm in bird form, and I'll lose too much mass and die. Either way—"

"Mass transference is difficult?" Soul asked.

"Yeah. Dangerous at every step along the way." Which was all I was going to tell them about me, and way more than I wanted to tell them at all. If not for Misha maybe being trapped inside, I'd have never said anything.

Bruiser, looking like a million dollars, rounded the car he'd driven and said, "I can see the shadows of the spell, but not how high it rises. Is it higher than the buildings to either side?"

I pulled on Beast sight, and Soul stepped back to study the top of the spell. "No," I said. "It reaches just above the top of the house's roof, maybe three feet above the central roof beam. And as the spell curls down, the same distance above the chimneys." The house was old enough to have been heated by wood or coal, and two brick chimneys were balanced at the front and back.

Bruiser picked up some stones from the street, small rocks used in the paving, and tossed one at the front of the house. It bounced back with a sizzle of sound and a shower of crimson energies. The second stone went higher, and would have landed on the roof had the *hedge* not been in the way. He studied the entire structure and pulled back his throwing arm. With a careful release of strength and precision, he tossed the stone up. It arched over before dropping, and passed through the energies escaping out the top. A shower of blue sparks rained down as the rock fell through, into the center of the sphere, and hit the roof before bouncing slowly down the incline and off the eave to the ground.

"Yeah. That's the hole I could get through," I said. I hadn't known until now that Bruiser could see magics. Most humans couldn't. But, then, Bruiser wasn't human. Not anymore.

"If we could span a line over the house," Eli said, "from the buildings at either side, we could reach the spell's center opening and drop through, crawl to a chimney, and shimmy down it."

"We would still have to pass through the energies that are escaping from the opening," Soul said, "and to me, it looks like enough magic to fry a human body."

"I'm not human," Bruiser said, shocking me that he would admit it aloud. But, then, with humans and witches missing, a lot of things that were better left in the dark were being exposed to the light. "And neither is Jane. Soul, can you make an amulet of death strong enough to fool the sphere for perhaps twenty seconds?"

I raised my brows. "Death? Oh. The sphere thinks we're stones or bones or something and doesn't react to us? Much?"

"Precisely," Bruiser said, his eyes on Soul.

Soul went still, her body seeming to hunch in on itself before she straightened, looking poised for flight or fight. A silence stretched between them as they measured each other, Soul not at all happy that Bruiser seemed to know something about her nature that she hadn't told him, Bruiser looking unmoved. He had access to the database of the biggest, baddest Master of the City there is. Heck, he had probably compiled most of it. Did she think he wouldn't know something about her? But he hadn't known about Leo's own son or about me either, so he wasn't omniscient. Finally she spoke. "And if I can do this?"

"Then Rick and I will run a line from the roofs of the buildings to the side, and Jane and I will drop through."

Beast pressed down on my mind, her claws out and piercing me with a headache. She peered out through my eyes. *Fun!*

I just shook my head in disgust at the plan. "I always hated gymnastics in school."

"Why not Jane and me?" Rick asked.

"Because the magics might short out your electronics," I said, pointing at his earpieces. "I'd rather not be trapped on the roof of a spelled, warded house with a screaming, half-insane black panther in a human body."

"She has a point," Eli said, trying to be helpful.

Rick snarled, turned, and walked away, around the building and to the left of the house we were trying to enter. So much for teamwork and effort.

"How long to make a death charm?" I asked.

"Before dawn," Soul said.

"Eli, nothing we can do here. Let's get some shut-eye. And hey, Soul?" She looked up at me, her platinum ponytail falling over one shoulder. "Before we head out, would you take a look at Bobby's hands? They got burned when he was dowsing for the magics."

Bobby—healed and out of pain—was asleep in his bed when we again slipped quietly out of Esmee's and into the SUV, to meander our way back to the warded house. Rick was still there, and so were Bruiser and Soul, and none of them looked very happy. I got out of the vehicle and looked over the house. Nothing was different except for the thin line that ran from the front of one roof to the back of the other roof of the three-story buildings standing on either side of the warded structure. Someone had found mountain-climbing devices and lots of rope. On the highest point hung woven mesh straps and buckles and more metal, like a zip-line trolley and harness. With Beast vision, I could see that the rope passed directly over the opening of the *hedge* ward.

Eli followed me from the SUV, our feet silent on the sidewalk, our shadows long and diffuse in the light of the moon that appeared to be falling off the edge of the world. The magics of the first full-moon night were more muted now, many witch circles closed after the witching hour, others just closing down as dawn approached. There was a strange smell on the air, like burned hair and hide and odd chemicals, but it was old and faint, and I couldn't place it. When we were close enough to be heard without raising our voices, I said, "Hey, Eli. How come I think our little experiment is gonna be way more dangerous than they expected?"

"Maybe because they look like death warmed over themselves," he said. "What's up, guys?"

Soul examined me. It was a way more intense examination than I'd ever gotten from her before, and it made me feel the way I used to when a schoolteacher suspected that I had done something wrong in class behind her back. I'd learned to stare back, mostly expressionless, a little curious and a lot bored—a look teenagers master early—and I used it on her now. She gave me a small, unamused smile. "Are you willing to risk death to possibly help your friend, who may not be inside?"

I thought about that, tucking my thumbs into my leathers, fingers hanging down as I came to a stop at the small group. "No. But I'm willing to risk it for her daughter. I promised Charly I'd get her mother back."

Rick growled at that stupidity. Bruiser chuckled. Soul's expression didn't change, but I felt the tingle of magics as something happened to her or in the air around her. Her dress wafted and swirled before settling again. "I can't make a magic that will survive a fall through a *hedge* that strong. I tried. The charm failed." More softly, Soul said, "But I *am* a magic that will survive it."

I looked over the guys, estimating their weight and Soul's,

and put two and two together, hoping I wasn't coming up with four. "Sooo, I'm guessing that you want me to carry you on a zip line to the middle of the house, hoping that your magics will protect us from the magical seepage at the top of the *hedge*, and then drop us both through. And I'm guessing that it's got to be us, because the boys weigh too much."

"Yes," she said, watching me like I was an interesting experiment.

"The pitch of the roof is steep," Bruiser said. "When you land, you risk tumbling off the house. Once you are stabilized, you have to catch Soul. Then shift into your cat, or, even better, a big snake, slither down a chimney, and figure out how to turn off the ward so we can come inside. All without disturbing whatever biological deterrents are waiting inside."

"Biological deterrents?" Eli asked. "Like the spidey vamps we've been killing?"

"Soul says there are at least four undead guardians inside," Rick said, his voice less growly now that the night was nearly gone. "One in every room. The witch magics are so strong, she can't pinpoint the location of any of them. If you shift on your fall through the opening to the *hedge*, you might die. If you slide off the roof when you land, you *will* die. If you can't get inside through the chimneys and get stuck up there, you might die. And if you can't fight off the things inside, you might die."

"We don't want you dead," Bruiser said.

"And yet you've strung the line," I mused.

"Because we had hoped that Soul and I could do the job. Or Soul and Rick."

I placed the odd smell and started laughing. I couldn't help it. And it only got worse when I saw the sour look on Rick's and Bruiser's faces and the confusion on Eli's. Soul didn't react, but her very nonreaction was funny. "How bad did you get burned when you tried it?" I asked them.

"I was unharmed," Soul said, "and was able to heal the wounds of the others."

"But I bet it hurt. Didn't it? Still trying to protect the little woman?" I said, less kindly, shooting my anger at the two men.

"I refuse to apologize," Bruiser said.

"We were afraid you'd shift when you hit the ward's energies," Rick said. "We're still afraid you'll shift. And if you do, you'll probably die."

It was interesting to see the two men on the same side of an argument for once. Even more interesting to see Rick siding with any male this close to the full moon. "Only one way to find out," I said.

I began to divest myself of weapons and put them into a go-bag I had brought for that very purpose. I hadn't been able to sleep back at the house, but had spent the time sitting with Eli in the breakfast room, him binging on coffee, me binging on strong tea, brainstorming, coming up with a plan, talking through the equipment we might need and gathering it all up. I'd have felt better if Eli had brought a shoulder-held rocket launcher, but he didn't have one handy. That was his reply when I mentioned it. I was relatively certain that meant he had one somewhere. My partner was scary. In a totally cool, macho, U.S. Ranger kinda way.

"Eli, you want to tell them what we have planned?" I asked.

"I'll plant explosive devices at every corner of the building, right up against the ward. Jane and Soul will move over the opening, shielded by the dead-thing charm on Soul. If Jane shifts, Soul will open the harness and let Jane's cat fall through the opening. Then drop her clothes. Then drop her weapons. The cat will snag everything with her claws, prop them in the cleft of the roof and chimney, jump up on the chimney, and look down to see if the chimneys are open passageways or sealed, which they could be. If they are open, Jane will gauge the size, shift back to human, and eat to restore her energies, and catch you as you drop."

He looked at Soul. "If she doesn't shift, she'll catch her equipment and you, when you fall through the ward opening."

"And then?" Bruiser asked.

"Then I'll drop an explosive device or three into the chimney," I said, "and Soul and I will hide on the far side of the roof. Eli will set off the devices at the corners of the building to attract the attention of the guardians, and three seconds later, I'll set off the ones in the chimney. Hopefully it will blow a hole in the roof big enough for me to get through, and disrupt the ward long enough for Soul to get you guys through the opening and onto the roof. While she's doing that, I'll drop inside, and you guys will follow as fast as you can. If we time it right, the sun will be rising and will scorch some bad guys. We'll kill us some guardians and save the witches. And hopefully find out where the leaders of the Naturaleza are."

Bruiser smiled that quirky smile I liked so much. Rick snarled. Soul tilted her head, considering. "It might work," she said. "I can make my clothing part of my death charm and extend a scarf, so that as you fall, the charm will extend with you. However, I put the chances of us all surviving at forty percent. The chances of us escaping unscathed at less than twenty percent. Are these acceptable to you all?"

"I put them much higher," Eli said. We shared a smile. Eli was really, *really* good at setting explosives. And he'd brought enough to do the job.

I just hoped he had calculated the necessary explosives with the age and construction condition of the old building and didn't blow it up around me. "Yeah. I think we're looking at a seventy percent chance of survival." To Bruiser, I said, "I saw a fire escape on the back of that building," I pointed to the one on the right. "That the best way up?" At his nod, I said, "Meet you on the roof, Soul."

With Beast vision, the *hedge* ward was fiery in the early dawn light. I tried to measure the size of the hole I needed to fall through while I pulled off my boots and stored them in the second go-bag. If I shifted in the harness, I needed to be mostly clothes free to allow me to fall and catch myself with my claws. Beast thought it looked like fun. I thought it looked risky and potentially deadly, no matter my seventy percent claim.

I had brought shoes with a grabby sole, loose pants, and an oversized tee, and I quickly stripped, putting my leathers into the bag with the boots.

While I changed, I also checked the stability of the zip line, which was attached to the highest point on the roof—the fake fourth-story wall. I had taken a mountain-climbing class a year or so after high school, and the line was wrapped around the entire wall instead of attached with gear into the mortar, which was smart. The height on this side allowed the line a slight angle across the chasm of the *hedge* to the building on the other side, where it was secured, out of sight.

I didn't think I would have done anything different had I set it all up myself, and I wondered who had arranged the gear, Rick or Bruiser. I was betting on Bruiser, not the boy from the Deep South.

By the time I could hear the others climbing to the roof, I was shivering in the cold, dressed and wearing sneakers, all my gear stored in three different bags, watching the sky brighten prior to sunrise.

Bruiser appeared first, Soul right behind him, and I looked over the MOC's primo. He was dressed all in leather in his Enforcer clothes, but unlike mine, his duds had been custom made and fit him like a glove. Leather pants, leather boots, and a leather coat over what had to be a silk shirt. Bristling with weapons. His dark hair slicked back.

"Nice gear," I said grudgingly, as he looked me over.

The morning breeze spun by, blowing my clothes against my limbs. His smile widened, making him look lean, mean, and dangerous. "Beautiful woman," he said.

I didn't know what to say to that, but felt a flush spread through me, just as Rick stepped from the fire escape. He was carrying standard cop weapons, except for the earpieces and the small wire trailing to his jacket pocket, the sound of tinny music coming from it, a pair of nice vamp-killers strapped to his thighs, and the feral greenish glow of his eyes. All that was nonstandard issue. He had pulled his hair back in a queue, and I was reminded of the way Leo Pellissier wore his hair. Rick stalked across the flat roof, moving like a cat, his eyes on Bruiser.

I stepped between them. "If you can't keep it together, you can go back to the street," I said to Rick.

"I'll keep it together. As long as he keeps his hands off you."

Anger pumped through me, part embarrassment, part something else that I didn't take the time to identify. "Just so you know. Jealousy is not a turn-on." I swiveled on a heel and stepped into the zip-line harness, ignoring the two men.

From behind me, Brute snarled as if he were an attack dog defending his master. He was showing his teeth, which left me confused until Beast pressed in on my brain again and sent me a mental picture of her scratching the wolf's nose. I/we snarled back, and I growled, "Nice *doggie*."

His growl deepened at the insult and his ruff stood up. And while I was itching for a fight, it wasn't with a wolf. I'd rather hit Rick. Or Bruiser. Or both. But Beast didn't want to let it go and sent her claws deeper into my brain. "So far I/we have broken your nose two times, little doggie," she said through me, her voice low. "Scratched you. Are you *stupid*, dog?"

Brute tensed, but quieted when Soul put a hand into his fur and scratched. Pea scolded the wolf with a burst of chitter. Rick stepped between us. Bruiser chuckled, the sound goading. The wolf turned angry eyes to the primo. For a moment more we tottered on the edge of violence. I pushed back on Beast, knowing this wasn't helping to create a team. I took a calming breath. "Sorry. It's the full moon. My Beast is . . . difficult. Come on, Soul. I'll get you into the harness."

"I have never done this before," she said, leaving her team. As she walked, a sense of peace spread outward, and I knew we were being manipulated by her personal magics, but I let it happen anyway. We needed to be calm. We needed a sense of coherence. Or her percentages might become real and half of us could die.

Wolf should die, Beast thought at me. *Thief of meat. Stupid pack hunter.*

"No problem," I said to Soul. But it was. Her dress made it difficult to get her into the harness in such a way that she could release the harness and fall without catching the clothing on the gear and maybe hanging her.

Finally we were in position, me in front with a zip-line steering trolley, her behind me in an abbreviated mountain-climbing harness, attached to the line with sturdy carabiners. I showed her how to release it so she could fall. Her scent changed as I spoke, and she tied the end of a scarf to a loop on my pants. Her magics began to rise.

When we were ready, I leaned down to see Eli staring up at me. He raised a thumb and melted into the shadows. The explosive devices were in place.

"Okay," I said. "Let's do this. Soul, let the harness take your weight, and put your feet against the roof wall to hold you still." When she was secure, I pulled on gloves, eased down on the line, and hooked my carabiner to the zip-line trolley.

"We have to be close," she said, her voice shaky, "for the death spell to start. I need to put my legs around you and hold you to me."

I nodded, and Soul wrapped her legs around my waist, pulling me in close. It was a lot closer than my Beast liked. Her idea of personal space was something like miles away, unless it was a kit or a mate.

She said, "Are you ready? This may feel . . . odd."

I nodded, and Soul took a deep breath and said, "The die is cast."

Which made no sense at all. For a moment.

CHAPTER 22

"Thank You," the Corpse Croaked

The scent of the grave surrounded me first, followed almost instantly by the visual transformation. Soul rotted before my eyes. Her body fluids melted into my clothes, her face sagged, the fluids and blood pooling with gravity while her eyes dried out. I looked at my hand and saw the same level of decomp. *Ick. Eww*. I was gross.

"Hurry," she said, the croak sounding like the dead. The stench of her breath made my eyes water, and I pushed off the false wall with a thrust of my legs, out into the air and over the buzzing magics of the augmented *hedge of thorns*.

While the purpose of zip-lining is to gain speed on a downward-sloped line, one can adjust speed with the gloved hand behind the trolley and one's body position. In our case, the line was too gently sloped and I expected that I'd have to pull us along with my hands. That was before my body reacted to being embraced by a ten-day-old corpse. My shove off the wall was too hard, and I had to brake, one gloved hand on the line, dragging behind the corpse's carabiner, my other hand atop the trolley, holding us stable. I was so busy working on the braking that I almost missed the energies passing over us as we reached the small hole over the top of the *hedge*.

When I felt the faint burst of magics, I adjusted our position carefully. The opening was only five feet below us, but the distance to the house roof was three feet more, making it a difficult leap and landing. Ankle breaking. And nowhere to roll afterward, just drop, hit, and stop. Hard.

I set one of Soul's hands behind her carabiner to hold her steady, and she made sure her scarf was still attached. I said, "I'm ready to go. And just for the record, no offense intended, as I am very grateful that you got us here safely, but we really stink."

"Thank you," the corpse croaked, unwrapping her legs from me.

"Yeah. Dropping now." I unhooked myself, held still until my body stopped rocking, bent my knees slightly to take the landing, and fell. Adrenaline spurted through me. My stomach followed a split-second later. Vertigo hit as I passed through the *hedge* opening. The scarf spiraled down with me.

The roof slammed me like . . . well, like falling off a zip line onto a roof. The jar whipped up from my toes, through my body, and out the top of my head. My teeth clacked together. I dropped to my knees, one foot on either side of the ridgeline, feeling the strain in my ankles and knees. My feet slid in opposite directions. I caught myself with my gloved hands, the rough roof beneath them grating. I stank of the grave, the stench so strong I wanted to gag. Beast, who had helped with the landing, withdrew.

The first thing I did was untie the scarf and set it to the side. When I was sure I could stand, I inspected myself. I was whole again, albeit still a bit stinky. I held up my hands for my gear, and the corpse above me dropped them one at a time. I positioned each bag on the roof and let them slide into the crevice of the rear chimney.

When they were secure, I held up my arms for Soul, having no idea if I would be able to catch her as she fell, even with Beast helping, or if I would drop her to the ridge, injuring her badly. I braced myself and nodded to her.

I wasn't sure what I was seeing as she fell. Her body blurred, elongated, stretched, and narrowed. And she landed on her own two feet. Or maybe her own four feet. The most I did was steady her balance as she reformed into her usual gorgeous self, the corpse gone. Even the awful smell was gone. So was the scarf I had put aside.

She smoothed down her dress and looked up at me, her face innocent. "What?"

I felt something push at the boundaries of my mind, and Beast rushed against it, slamming both front paws down on the mental intrusion. The compulsion fell away, and Soul opened her eyes wide. "What was that?"

"You tell me your secrets, and I'll tell you mine," I grated out. I was usually lying when I said that, but this time I was actually willing to trade. I had known she wasn't human, but I had no idea what Soul was.

"I—" she stopped. I waited. "Perhaps we'll talk sometime."

"Yeah. *Perhaps*." I dropped my arms and she wavered on the roof, but now that I knew that looking human was all for show, I didn't help to balance her. "Let me get changed, and we'll set the charges."

Drawing on Beast again, I half walked, half slid down the roof to the chimney, opened the bag holding my clothes, and stripped off the outer clothes I'd worn when I'd been afraid I'd become Beast in midair. I knew I was in plain sight of the men and wolf on the roof, and I had planned for this, so I wasn't naked but in boy shorts and sports bra. I didn't look up. And I didn't let myself blush. This was a rescue job, not a pole dance.

I dressed in my leathers, which wasn't easy, having to work stooped so my head didn't get taken off by the softly sizzling ward just above me. I sat in the crevice of the chimney to pull on my boots and strap the Velcro over the ties. Still sitting, I opened the second go-bag and worked my way into the weapon harness. Nothing was going to be a smooth draw, not with the shirt bunched up where I couldn't reach it without falling or getting scalped, but I felt immeasurably better once I was armed.

From the last bag, I pulled three explosive devices—each of them composed of C4 and det cord wrapped with tape, and the three ends sealed together with a long-delay detonator. C4, also called plastic-bonded explosives or PBX, was a malleable explosive that required a strong charge to set it off. I unspooled the detonator cord from around the block of explosive material and stood to peek over the edge of the chimney into the dark center. I half expected a huge, hairy spidey vamp to leap out at me, but the opening was clear all the way down. I nodded to the guys on the roof and lowered the chunk of C4. Eli had told me more than I ever wanted to know about the explosives, but the only thing I *needed* to know to make this work was how many of the devices to put down the chimney and how low to drop it. And he couldn't tell me any of that. It was either do the math or eyeball it based on experience, neither which I had. But I had flown by the seat of my pants all my life, so why stop now?

I studied the mortar holding the bricks of the chimney flue together and decided that this was the original brick, which meant it was old, porous, and unstable, so it should come down easily. Not that I was taking a chance. I dropped the first block of C4 all the way down to just above where a faint light could be seen from the open fireplace. If there was an old-fashioned vent, it was long gone. I secured the cord to the top of the chimney cap by taping it with long lengths of duct tape. I unspooled another block of C4, let it down the chimney, and secured it about where I assumed the ceiling below me was. I wrapped it into the same tape as the first det cord and cut off the last device. One might work. Two surely would. Three would be overkill and might kill the witches below me.

Regular detonation cord is really just a long, thin explosive. When set off, it detonates—explodes—at a rate of about twenty-four thousand feet per second, so Soul and I were using a long-period-delay detonator, or LPD. Even so, we needed to be on the other side of the roof long before it went off. I pointed to the far chimney, and Soul scampered across to it. I put the go-bags around my neck and moved more slowly, unwrapping det cord as I went. Once over the ridgeline, I slid down the roof to the chimney and wedged myself in with Soul.

"They'll be waiting for us. We've made enough noise to wake the dead," Soul murmured.

"The undead, you mean," I said dryly. Soul tinkled with laughter and I laughed with her, pulling hard hats from the explosives go-bag. I handed Soul hers and shoved my own on. I stuck my fingers in my ears, opened my mouth, and nodded to the guys on the roof at the same time.

Four seconds later, Eli's C4 at ground level went off. I felt the concussions through my teeth. Above us, the *hedge* ward wavered and rippled, its energies interrupted by the explosions. I ducked my head and pressed my detonator, then re-covered my ears. Three long seconds went by, and the LPD det cord activated.

The blast took off the chimney. And the entire front of the old house. Debris shot into the air and fell, showering us. Bricks fell, some still intact. It was a miracle we weren't brained by the falling debris. As it was, stuff peppered our hard hats.

Above us, one man zipped in and dropped, unburned by the wavering ward. Bruiser whipped past me and rammed an ax head into the roof. Using the handle, he swung over the roof edge and into the attic. Rick followed him and used a rope that was tied to the zip line to do the same thing. Brute landed, having leaped the whole distance. Beast was impressed and, not to be outdone, shoved me after him.

I pulled on my gloves and said, "Let's move."

I clattered over the ridgeline and skidded toward the hole in the roof, my boots sliding on the old roof tiles. The hole came at me fast. It was big enough for me to swing through. Big enough for me to fall through. If I misjudged, I'd be chopped up by the *hedge* and hit ground far below on what had to be a pile of rubble. I twisted fast in a one-eighty turn and dropped toward the attic. Grabbed a roof joist. It gave. *I'm falling.* My stomach slapped against my throat. The joist caught, yanking at my shoulder as I swung into the attic and landed.

The floor of the attic—loosened by the C4—fell through into the room below. I barely caught myself on my hands and hauled myself up, my breath fast, a heated sweat starting. Below, in the house, I could hear the sounds of fighting.

Soul landed beside me with that flowing, blurring motion that was in no way human. She didn't bother with the innocent look this time, no longer caring that she had proven herself some kind of shape-shifting supernat. She gestured for me to lead the way. I didn't argue, but this time I tested the joist before dropping my weight on it.

I landed on the floor just as the first rays of the sun burst across the horizon. Pinkish light filled the sky, brightening everything. Including the fight in the center of the house. In a single eye blink and inhalation, I took in the scene and found pattern in the madness. The stench was awful—death and a miasma of dust and rot. And two monstrous *things* were fighting Bruiser. One looked like a wasp with human legs and arms; the other like a spider. *Spidey vamp, for real.* And Bruiser was standing over Rick, who wasn't moving at all. *Crap.*

Bruiser's swords moved so fast I couldn't follow, cutting, cutting, a whirlwind of steel, the center of the double-edged blades silver plated and catching the pink glow. It seemed important for half a second until one *thing* whirled and lashed out at me.

I leaped to the side, into a ray of light. The spidey-revenant-vamp-thing didn't follow. I drew my M4 and braced it against my shoulder. Aimed at what looked like a stinger, two-pronged and wicked sharp. I fired. And fired again. The stinger was gone, leaving a drooling stump and a wash of greenish goo. All I could think of was the old movie *Ghost Busters* until, off balance, the thing reeled to me and I got my first good look. This was no Casper.

The carapace that seemed to grow out of its back looked like a huge hornet—not human at all, though it had only vestigial wings. It had a human jaw and vamp canines. Its eyes were multifaceted. Its shoulders, torso, and legs were human, though furred and striped like a hornet. And on its chest hung a pocket watch. I didn't bother aiming for anything that might kill it. I aimed at the amulet and fired. The vamp jerked to the side as if it knew what I aimed at. I fired. And fired. Hitting the creature, knocking off chunks, but seemingly doing little damage. It came at me. Rushing on its human legs.

Backpedaling fast, I fired again. This time I hit the amulet. The spidey vamp stumbled. I had one shell left and braced my feet. Took careful aim at the amulet hanging on the *thing*. Fired my last shot.

The silver fléchettes smashed the amulet. The creature fell. But it was still twitching. I pulled my vamp-killer and started hacking at the neck. Its flesh was hard, with a carapace just under skin. But I kept at it until the head separated from the rest of the misshapen thing, and rolled a short distance, hit a brick from the fireplace, and stopped in a ray of pinkish light. An eye seemed to be looking up to me, as the head started to sizzle and burn. The stink of rotten, burning meat filled the air.

The body was still in shadow. I leaned down and gathered up the remains of the amulet. Stuffed it into a pocket. And pulled the spidey vamp across a black arc painted on the floor and into the sunlight. It weighed a ton. The body started to smoke. Good riddance.

Reloading from my handy-dandy belated birthday present was a whiz. It was only six rounds, but it was a lot faster than pulling them from an ammo bag. I was breathing hard as I readied the weapon and took in the room.

Bruiser was still fighting, but now Soul stood over Rick, her arms doing something witchy with blue sparks flying. It looked like a ward, but it didn't seem to be doing much. "Go for the amulets!" I shouted, pressing the stock against my shoulder. "Bruiser! Drop and roll!"

As if he understood perfectly, Bruiser folded his blades and threw himself into a somersault, over the blades and behind me. The spider he was fighting spun to follow and saw me. I didn't waste time evaluating it; I just spotted the amulet in a patch of spiky hair, aimed, and started firing. I must have hit it, because the spidey thing fell. I had no idea where its head was located. Bruiser pulled a shotgun and fired four rounds, two into each eye. It went still. He reloaded and started firing again. Soul raced into the back of the house, into the shadows.

I bent over Rick. He was bleeding from the mouth but was breathing, and I could see his pulse in his throat. I checked his pupils, which were equal and reactive. But his earpieces were gone. Not good. Even though the moon was over the horizon, it was still full—even more than last night. As I released his eyelid, his hand slammed into my side with all the power a were-animal can muster. Knocking me to the side.

I rolled with the force of the blow and ended up with Rick on top of me, his eyes a brilliant golden green. He growled and hissed and showed me his teeth. Soul appeared behind him and placed her hands on his head. Rick went still as a block of ice. His partner was holding the earpieces. The glow of his eyes faded, and he took the earbuds and inserted them. He drew a deep breath and stood, pulling me to my feet.

My ears were mostly gone from the concussion of the explosives and shotguns, but the shadows on the walls told

me we weren't finished. The wolf was in the back of the
house, fighting for his life. I pointed and Rick sped past me
into the back room, Soul on his heels.

Eli had made it inside at last, and he and Bruiser raced
through another doorway on the right. That is when I realized. There were no witches here. Not one.

"Son of a freaking gun," I muttered. "We've been
conned." On the run, I picked up the parts of the amulet
that I could find and stuck them into another pocket.

The front part of the house had been a kitchen, dining,
and living room. Now the roof and ceiling sagged, and the
space was full of brick and debris from the exploded chimney, green goo, and smoking and burning bodies like aliens
out of a horror movie. No furniture. No nothing except a
weird black painted arc on each of the floors.

The back of the house was much darker, divided into
two bedrooms and a bath, all damp, with wallpaper hanging
off the walls and furniture debris scattered everywhere—
parts of a bed and mattress, parts of tables and chairs, a
busted bathroom sink and toilet, and human bodies, clearly
drained and left to rot or rise as vamps, as nature and the
intent of the master intended.

Two of them were children.

My Beast couldn't take the sight of more dead children.
She roared inside me, screaming, *Kits!* I dropped the empty
shotgun as power struck through me like a battering ram
and I/we leaped for the back of the *thing* in the room. In
midair I drew a nine-mil. The *thing* was seven feet tall and
had pinchers, which I ignored. I landed on his back, reached
around, grabbed the chain holding the amulet, and fired re-
peatedly into the pocket watch, the bullets and ricochets
hitting the creature or bouncing off.

It roared and I/we pushed off with back legs. Sprang to
the floor. As I fell, I ripped the busted amulet from his neck.
Dropped and rolled. Eli emptied his sub gun into the thing's
head. I put the busted amulet into a pocket. I was gonna run
out of pockets soon. Which made me laugh. Eli looked at
me like I was crazy, and then he laughed with me.

He pointed to the front of the house and grabbed a
pincher. I looked at the iron-covered windows and understood. I grabbed a human-shaped foot, and together we
dragged the *thing* into the sunlight. When we trotted into

the last room, we found Rick and Bruiser hitting the last creature with swords, trying to decapitate it.

I bent over and braced my hands on my knees, cussing under my breath. It was over. And all for nothing. No witches. Not one.

No one spoke as we tugged the last spidey vamp into the sun and walked out through what was left of the front door. We were met with cops and guns, all pointed at us. I held up my hands and dropped to the porch floor, glad to see I was sitting in a spot clear of smoking bodies and goo.

These were city cops and they were strangers, men and women I might have seen after the debacle in the three-story building de Allyon had rented and refurbished. But I didn't really know any of them. And they were yelling at us.

I was deaf from the fighting. We all were, so whatever they were ordering us to do, none of us could hear. I pointed to my ear and shook my head. "We're deaf!" I shouted to them. I pointed to the house. "We killed the *things* inside. The *things* inside killed the people in back." I figured that would buy us some time until someone who knew us got here.

Even as I had the thought, Sylvia arrived, no lights, no siren, because it wasn't her jurisdiction. She wasn't on duty, but whatever Syl said caused the cops to lower their weapons. They didn't put them away, not then, but at least they weren't pointed at us.

With Soul's help, the cops found a torn place in the ward and entered. Three of them checked out the house, and two of them came out gagging. The other one was stone-faced, evaluating us in light of the death inside.

I looked at Soul and shouted, "Better than seventy percent." She laughed and dropped down beside me, shaking her head, her platinum hair falling around her face. Her clothes were dirty and she had green goo drying on her face, but otherwise she looked as beautiful as ever.

Soul sobered. "The witches are not here."

My own mirth dimmed. "No. And the ward is still going. I don't understand it."

"Me neither," she said. And Soul looked worried. I didn't think I'd ever seen her worried.

While the cops did the cop thing, I emptied my pockets of the three busted amulets and spilled the parts onto the

porch in front of me. I had never taken a pocket watch
apart, but figured the wheels and gears were part of it. Also
the spring and the little button screw. But the discs were
sort of a surprise. They looked like iron with a coating of
bright copper. I turned one over and over, seeing nothing
special about it, but nothing useful either. Until I pushed
one close to another one. They ratcheted together like mag-
nets, becoming one thing.

I blinked, not sure what I had seen, but absolutely certain that it wasn't good. I put the one free iron piece into a
pocket that had a zipper to keep it closed; I didn't want
them getting anywhere near each other. Sitting there as the
day brightened around me, I tried to fit the pieces together,
and I remembered a tiny bit of info that had never fit anywhere.

"Long years past," Kathyayini had said, "was cold iron,
blood, three cursed trees, and lightning. Red iron will set
you free." Which had made no freaking sense then and
made none now. Except that now I had some red iron. She
had also said, "Shadow and blood are a dark light, buried
beneath the ground."

Shadow and blood. Shadows like the shadow land of the
old church. *Blood* like in *blood magic*—black magic. I had
done black magic once, as a child. It was how I'd gotten
Beast. *Buried beneath the ground.* Like my soul home? The
cavern I always saw when I was doing spirit work with Aggie One Feather?

"If the cops will let me go," I said, "I have a woman to
see. She might have answers."

"I'll see to it," Soul said, "I'd have done it sooner, but I
couldn't hear until now." She took a cleansing breath and
pulled a black case out of a pocket and flipped it open. Inside was a gold badge with the letters HS in gold relief, and
below them, in smaller lettering, PSYLED. Soul, a VIP in
Homeland Security, was about to pull rank.

Eli gave me the keys to the SUV, but I was too tired to
drive, so the Kid drove. Which was scary on a whole different level. I didn't even know the Kid had a license. If he did.
I had also forgotten he was here, but he'd been monitoring
the action from the street with his brother's military obser-
vational toys and filming the action—I guessed in case we

all died and he had to report it to the police and PsyLED. As we pulled into the early traffic, I eased the small silver coin from my pocket, the one with the sea serpent on one side and the square on the other.

Fingering the small silver coin, I gave him directions, and wondered if Kathyayini would come to me in the daytime.

CHAPTER 23

Vampire Blood. Mixed with Something.

The lot was vacant, lit by bright morning sun. But no church. Just an empty space. I recognized trees I had seen the night I came here, and when I looked hard, I could see the outlines of an old foundation, mostly gone, marked more by the way the grass grew than by any rise in the ground or scattered stone or brick.

"Wait here," I said to the Kid. "If I disappear, don't freak. But if I'm not back in an hour, tell Eli to bring Soul here. She might be able to find me."

The Kid looked at the lot, at me, and back at the lot, his brows creased together. "Disappear? Like into some kinda interdimensional space-time fold?"

I huffed a laugh. "Been there, done that once, a long time ago." The Kid's eyes bugged out. "Long story. This didn't feel like that. Not exactly. But maybe there were similarities. Last time I was on the outside of the bubble. This time maybe I was on the inside."

"Can I film it?"

I started stripping off the weapons and the weapon harness, because one should never take weapons into a consecrated place or into the presence of an elder. "Go for it," I said. "But I'm guessing you won't see a thing." I thought a minute. "Maybe a lot of fog."

Weapon free, with nothing on me except the silver coin, pocket watches, and the discs, I got out of the SUV. Took a slow breath and blew it out. Another. And wished I'd taken the time to get a shower. I was rank with the sweat of battle. I squared my shoulders, gripped the coin between the index finger and thumb of my right hand, and walked between the trees. Nothing happened.

I sat on the ground in front of where I thought the front doors of the church had once been and crossed my knees — which was not a comfortable position in the leathers and boots. The sun was warm on my shoulders, the fickle winds of the Mississippi chasing away the night's chill. I pulled off my leather jacket and set it behind me. Finally got my shirt straight, now that the weapon harness was off.

My socks were still twisted. I wanted tea. Breakfast. My stomach growled. Nothing else happened. I studied the amulets and the iron discs. And realized that the stuff I thought was copper was actually something far darker. *It was blood.* I lifted one and sniffed it, pulling on Beast's senses. Vampire blood mixed with the iron itself. And with . . .

I dropped the disc, staring at it on the grass. *Skinwalker blood.* It all came together.

Lucas Vazquez de Allyon had killed off my kind everywhere he could. But one miniature painting I had seen in an old book had depicted him holding a bowl of blood, with dead and drained skinwalkers from the Panther Clan everywhere around him on the ground. Skinwalkers like me.

I looked at the silver coin in my hand. Kathyayini had known what I was. Somehow she had known. As I fingered the coin, I found a sharp edge, just a spot where the coin had ground against something sharper or harder once. I spat on my thumb and rubbed it on my jeans, cleaning it, and pressed the pad of my thumb on the coin. Nothing happened. I gripped it in my left hand and cut into my right thumb with a hard, fast motion. My flesh tore. A shock of pain flashed through me.

Blood welled and dripped into my palm. I put the coin into the pooling blood. In the distance, from a clear sky, thunder rumbled. In the echo of the rumble, the sky darkened and a low fog appeared. Lightning flashed, a spreading fan of power that reflected off the clouds boiling up in the sky in this place that wasn't. I remembered the whole quote.

"Long years past was cold iron, blood, three cursed trees, and lightning. Red iron will set you free." Then: *"Shadow and blood are a dark light, buried beneath the ground."*

Lightning, like now, in a mystical place full of storms.

Dream-walkers were mystics. Mystics opened themselves to spiritual possibility, and being mystical meant that they seldom communicated logically. They left spiritual hints and clues ... and the most mystical aspect of vamps was their creation story, an act of black magic that had unintended consequences. And beings who did good magic and black magic were ... most often witches.

Red iron and trees, I thought, trying to find sense in the dribs and drabs of knowledge I had. The Sons of Darkness, the witch sons of Judas Iscariot, had used the three cursed trees of Calvary to bring their father back to life. The wood from the three crosses had been mixed with blood and black magic to create the first immortal, and when they ate his flesh, they became the first two vampires and fathers of all the vampires who followed.

My breath released in a slow exhalation. I was close to something. Very close.

Night had fallen around me. The SUV was gone; so was everything else. *Shadow and blood are a dark light.* There were shadow and my blood in this place.

There had been shadow and blood on Golgotha the evening the Christ died. There had been his blood on the tree. And on the cold iron that pierced his flesh, holding him there.

I took a slow breath, not moving, not fighting for it—whatever it was that my hindbrain was putting together. The words rolled through my mind again, low and sonorous, potent as the lightning: *Long years past was cold iron, blood, three cursed trees, and lightning. Red iron will set you free.* Then: *Shadow and blood are a dark light, buried beneath the ground.*

Some outclan priestesses had a sliver of the wood of the crosses that had been used to make the vampires. *But what had happened to the iron?* Had it been melted down and used for more black magic? Like the transformative magic that was turning Naturaleza into spidey vamps?

Lightning cracked again, slamming into the ground only yards away. The power of it sent electric shivers through me. My loose hair stood on end, and my skin crackled with the pain of electric shock. On the ground in front of me, the last red iron disc slid across the grass and snapped into place atop the other two. The pocket watches that were still whole glowed with a greenish light in the gloom of wherever or whenever this was.

Red iron and three cursed trees. Is it possible?

I closed my eyes and took a cleansing breath. When I opened my eyes, the church was before me. I started, even though I'd been expecting it. Overhead, thunder rumbled, close and ominous. Rain pattered down, just as the last time I was here. I gathered up my jacket, the amulets, and the thick iron disc, putting them into pockets where they couldn't touch one another. I held the silver coin in my bloody fist as I walked up the short steps and into the church. The doors crashed shut behind me, an angry *boom* that reverberated through the church.

I walked down the aisle, but Kathyayini wasn't there. The church was empty. Which sent willies down my back. My heart sped, an irregular pain, and I massaged my chest with my fist as I walked, not thinking about the blood until the air chilled it on my skin. Rain pounded down outside and on the roof over me. The din of the storm was incredible. I could feel the power through the soles of my boots. Wind hit the side of the church, and the old building groaned.

I reached the front, the church dark, lit only by lightning strikes outside. Each strike was intense, showing me the pews, the cross over the entry door that I hadn't noticed last time. It was painted red. I eased my backside onto the dais and sat, feet dangling. And waited.

"You don't got no match? It's dark in here." *Kathyayini.*

I sighed out a breath, relief so strong it hurt as the air left my lungs. "I don't carry matches," I said.

I heard the scratch of a match striking right beside me and I flinched at the sound, the smell, and the flickering light, after the long minutes of darkness and lightning. Kathyayini lit a candle and then another, and a third. "You don't listen too good. Do you? This a lot harder in daytime." Kathyayini hopped up on the dais beside me and sat. She was wearing a different dress this time, with a biblike front over her chest and a red T-shirt underneath. The fabric of the dress had huge red flowers on a pink background. It wasn't flattering, but it did look comfortable.

I said, "I was busy getting inside a witch-warded house

during the night. At dawn, I was busy killing vamp things, spidey vamps, inside the house."

"Sounds messy. That why you stink?"

I chuckled and my shoulders slumped. "Yes, ma'am."

"You save everybody?"

"We didn't save anyone. There was nothing in the house except bodies several days old."

"Huh." Kathyayini pursed her lips, her mouth wrinkling up like a dried plum. "There shoulda been a witch circle there."

"There was nothing."

"You sure? No circle painted on the floor?"

My head came up. "*Crap!* There were black arcs painted on the floor in each room. Not a circle, but something."

"Quarter circle? Like the whole house was the circle? You not very bright if you don't see that."

"Couldn't be a witch circle. It was broken by the walls of the house."

Kathyayini pursed her lips, the wrinkled skin drawing up like a dried apple. "Some circles are symbolic, proof of power used somewhere else."

I hadn't known that. Once again others might pay because I didn't know enough of the arcane. I pushed off the dais and landed on the floor below the podium. "I have to get back there. Now!"

"No." She waved a hand at me as if my intention was of no interest to her. "You got to sit down and listen. We got things to talk about." When I took a step away, she narrowed her eyes at me and said, "*Sit!*" There was power in her command, so strong my knees buckled. I grabbed the dais to keep from falling and I sat. She pulled a strip of cloth from a pocket of her bib and pointed at my thumb. It was still bleeding, which was odd. My skinwalker metabolism would usually stop the bleeding of a scratch quickly. I wrapped my small wound and gripped the cloth over it, applying pressure.

"What have you learned so far?" she asked, though it was more command than request.

"That an old Spaniard, a conquistador, was a vamp. He drank down the power of the best warriors of the Tsalagi and then used some of their blood to make amulets, maybe using the iron from the spikes of the crosses to give his magic power."

"Hah. You not so stupid as I think."

"At some point," I went on, "he figured out how to use the amulets to focus enough power to keep the rest of the vamps in the U.S. and Europe at bay, so he could practice Naturaleza, free from interference, for centuries in Atlanta. That was enough for him until he discovered a way to make vampires sick. And then he concocted a plan using the vamp plague to take over the entire U.S. But Leo Pellissier stood in his way. Leo and me.

"I killed Lucas and his heir took over the amulets and added a full witch circle to the mix. The added power created transformational magic. I think the purpose of the magic was to make a super vamp able to be truly immortal, withstand the sun, silver, crosses—every weakness that vamps have. And the magic was tested by creating revenants to see what came back. And what has come back so far is monsters."

"Not bad." She patted my knee. "But let's talk about the Tsalagi warriors from long ago. They not all dead. Are they?"

She means skinwalkers. "Uh, no, ma'am."

"You killed the other one."

My eyes whipped to hers, and she smiled in the light of the three candles. "You been here many moon cycles, setting things in motion. Stopped other things. Maybe that other Tsalagi like you was supposed to do something important for this old Spaniard, and you killed him instead. What you think that might be?"

I shook my head in confusion, trying to rearrange my thoughts and the things I thought I had figured out into some new semblance of order. "Maybe Immanuel was supposed to kill Leo, so de Allyon could take over?"

"And so, maybe *you* the catalyst for his plan, not the plague. Or maybe both together. You showing up in New Orleans caused him a headache, I betcha." She cackled with laughter. "And he tried to kill you, yes?"

I remembered the attack in a hotel in Asheville. "That was to kill Leo."

"You not so smart now. Old blood drinkers got plans on top of plans, everything tied together like a big knot"—she held her hands out as if gripping a soccer ball—"like a clock, around and around. He was doing bunch of things at once and you stopped all of them. He had to rethink his plans."

I felt a chill, like a winter wind over a graveyard. "Everything I've done since I got to New Orleans has brought me here, to this moment."

"Now you see? You getting smart now."

"If you knew all this, why didn't you tell me last time?" I ground out, my frustration making my voice loud enough to echo through the old building. Outside, lightning hit the earth close by, lighting the inside of the church in a flickering burst of power. "You gave me a riddle that made no sense."

"Eh. You figured it out." She flapped a hand at the unimportance of it all. "Musta made some sense, it did. Besides, what make you think I knew everything last time? What make you think I know them this time? What make you think any of this is real?" She swept an arm around the old church, to include herself. "If none a this is real," she said, "where it all come from?" She tapped my head with a bony finger. "You knew lots of it already. I just gave you a nudge with my riddle."

I pushed her finger away and passed my hands over my face, pressing in on my eyeballs. I could smell my own blood soaking into the cloth. My bleeding still hadn't stopped. "Okay. What do I do next?"

"What you think you do next?"

"I think I have to figure out how to use the quarter witch circles in the old house"—I stopped, remembering another circle, the one in the refrigerator of the other house—"because the witch circles will take me somewhere else. Where the witches are."

"Now you talking like a smart girl. Get. I got stuff to do."

"But—"

"Don't forget to save us. The Acheé witches, we in big trouble."

Lightning hit the top of the church with a sound like doom. The candles went out. And I was sitting on the ground, in the grass, in the middle of a downpour. My jacket was behind me, the three pocket watches were on the ground in front of me, and I was holding the red iron disc in one hand

and a bloody silver coin in the other. I put the watches in separate pockets and the iron coin in the zippered one. And trudged back the way I came. Between one step and the next, I was in the daylight, staring at a shocked Alex. He was only a foot away, his eyes wide and his mouth open.

"You disappeared. And then you came back. Like ... like magic or something. And why are you all wet?"

I grunted sourly, striding to the truck. "Get in and drive."

We went back to the old saloon and bar where Eli and I had rescued the three girls chained in a bathroom, where I had shifted into Beast to save my life. As he drove, I loaded my shotgun and the nine millimeter I had emptied into a spidey vamp and weaponed up over the soaked clothing. When the Kid braked at the curb, I found one of Eli's huge flashlights, got out, and went to the bar. I yelled over my shoulder, "If I'm not out in fifteen minutes, call Eli!"

The door was covered with a piece of plywood and taped over with crime scene tape. There was a gap at the bottom, and I wriggled my fingers under the wood and got a good grip, braced one foot on the doorjamb, and yanked.

The door groaned up and out at an angle, nails pulling out of the wood. When it was high enough to get through, I ducked and went inside, drawing a nine-mil and turning on the flash. My sense of smell told me the place was empty, but I scanned the front room and behind the bar to make sure before I took the long hallway to the back.

The women's restroom was empty but still smelled of pain and fear. The door in the back of the building was missing, allowing in a lot of light. The refrigerator stood open once again, either because the cops left it that way or because vamps had used it since then. I was betting on vamps. I stood in the doorway, studying the white-painted circle in the center of the fridge. "Flying by the seat of my pants could get me killed this time," I said to myself.

Beast answered, *We are Beast. We are more than Jane and big-cat.*

"Yeah, yeah, yeah." I pulled the three watch amulets out of my pockets and laid them on the floor of the fridge, inside the white circle. Then I stepped over and into the center of the circle, unzipped the pocket, and took out the thrice-made red iron disc. It was clumsy, but I held the weapon and the flash in one hand, and bent my knees, spread my feet into a modified shooting stance, and with my other hand pressed the disc into the bloody cloth.

The floor fell out from under my feet. My stomach lurched. Vomit rose in my throat.

I landed hard in the dark, dislodging the flashlight. Dropping it. It landed with a hollow *thud* and rolled, illuminating a place I had never seen before. It was a tiny square room, maybe three feet on a side. It stank of old earth and blood and the dusty reek of spidey vamps.

I'd just been transported through space by a witch spell. Nausea danced a tango up my esophagus again, but I swallowed it down. *Kirk and Spock never spewed after a transporter trip,* I thought, panicky giggles close on the heels of the thought. *That would be totally uncool.* I managed a shuddery breath and locked the giggles and the nausea away.

Just beyond the walls, I heard a voice. Eli. *Eli?*

I put it together fast. I had to be in a hidden room in the house we had raided at dawn. Back where I started from. Well, that was ducky. But it explained the quarter arcs in each room—symbolic of a place to land. Picking up the flash, I inspected the small space. The walls were painted black, with strange symbols all over them in a reddish-brown color. The symbols meant nothing to me, except I thought they were runes, stuff I had seen at Molly's. I had a feeling these were painted with blood mixed with other stuff. What else would a psycho vamp paint witch symbols with but blood? My breath came faster and I breathed through my mouth and nose to take in the scent/taste/texture of the air in the coffin-sized place. As there was nothing to shoot, I holstered my weapon. I had no idea why a witch circle would deposit me here, but there had to be a reason.

On the other side of the walls, Bruiser said something and Rick laughed. The two of them being jovial together. It was creepy. Worse, the flashlight showed me that there was no way out except through the walls, which were surely spelled. No door or latch or catch, no window, hidden panel, or bookcase to search for the book that would release the wall. Zip. Nada.

I took a step to pound on the wall and my boot hit something solid. I aimed the flash down. It illuminated a handle in the floor. A trapdoor.

"The one you seek," Kathyayini had said, *"she is bound to the Earth. She didn't mean to be bound, but she cannot get away now."* The three pocket watches had been transported with me, and were aligned in a semicircle around the handle, all open, all set for twelve noon. Or midnight.

I opened my mouth to call out to the guys, and snapped it closed with a *clack* of teeth. If I called to the men on the other side of the walls and they broke them down, would that dislodge whatever magics had brought me here? I'd hate to go boom when I'd finally found something that might be useful. I tucked the fatter disc into my pocket, zipped it closed, and gathered up the pocket watches. The minute this thing was over, I was busting the watches and dropping the discs into a bucket of sulfuric acid.

I reached down, grabbing the handle in the trapdoor. And pulled.

CHAPTER 24

That Was Before I Killed Her Sister

It opened silently, not with the hair-raising *creak* I expected. Nothing jumped out at me. Nothing moved. Nothing made a single sound.

The smell from the crawl space was the fetid stench of a mass grave. I aimed the flash down to see bare, sandy ground and what might have been ankle bones with two leg bones sticking out of it. The angle wasn't good enough to see anything more, but I was just happy not to see hundreds of rats squealing away. Dead bodies, I was getting used to.

Seven small steps led down, like a ladder, open and rickety. I got a firm grip on the weapon and the flash and paced carefully down them. I stepped onto the ground, finding it firm and dry and sandy. The floor above me was not insulated, just bare boards, and I could hear people up there walking around, muffled voices through the wood and sheets of old linoleum.

I flashed the light around the crawl space. I didn't know what I was seeing at first. Then I realized it was a head. Human. Witch. Sticking out of the sandy earth. It was also alive. The head was female, upright, and I could see a slow pulse in the neck, maybe forty beats a minute.

I scanned my light to the right and saw another head, this one less buried, with a neck and shoulders and one arm free from the ground. Female. She was wearing clothes over her thin skeleton, skin and bones showing at wrist and collar, and her hair was matted into a slimy mess. She had a chain around her neck and an amulet hung from it, open, set to three o'clock even. A little farther to the right was another woman. Only her face was visible, the rest of her buried, her head tilted back, her mouth open like a drowning victim gasping for a last breath. Witches, all. All glowing with witchy power in swirling, oily, foul shades of energy, like the death energies of everything that had ever been alive.

I moved the light again. And again. The seventh woman was Misha. She was sitting up, her legs partially buried in the sandy soil, her hands free. She still wore traces of lipstick, mascara smeared below her eyes in the bruised hollows. She had put up a fight. She had a black eye and a puffy lip. That was not like the passive Misha I had known as a child. "Good for you," I whispered.

The light caught the gleam of metal. A cell phone rested on her lap. The amulet on her chest was open, the clock set at ten even. I wanted to rush to her, but I had no idea what to do for her and no idea if I would kill her if I tried to pull her from the dirt. I moved the flash around the rest of the circle. All of the women were buried to some extent or another. None of them were the Acheé women.

The floor was low and I bent, studying the witches. All of them were alive except the ones at my feet. I shone the light down and saw a skull with some connective tissue left, some hair, her teeth showing the black of old fillings and metal dental work.

Beside her was another skull, less preserved. They appeared to be laid out in the beginnings of some pattern I didn't yet understand.

I moved the light around the witch circle and realized that the witches and dirt they were buried in looked ... wrong. As I watched, something moved over Misha's knee. And I realized that the women hadn't been deliberately buried. The earth of the circle was instead swallowing them. I picked out the women who had been buried the least amount of time. And I studied the witch who was the most buried. She didn't have long. The dead witches at my feet were probably the ones who had died in service and been replaced, though I didn't know if someone had dug up the dead and dragged them here or if the earth spit them out when it was done with them. I figured the Acheé witches were hidden elsewhere, intended as replacements for the ones nearly buried.

I had no idea how to get the witches out of the ground. No idea how to stop the spell they were powering. No idea what would happen if I interrupted a working full circle and pulled a witch to safety. But I knew who might know.

I nearly jumped out of my skin when my private cell buzzed in my pocket. I flipped it open to see Eli's icon. "Jane," I said.

"Where are you? Alex said you disappeared inside the vamp bar."

I looked at the low boards over my head. I could almost make out his words through the floor as well as through the cell. "Would you believe about twenty feet from you? And down a level?"

"How?"

"The black arcs painted on the floor in each room are a witch circle. Don't ask me how they go through the walls. I don't know. But in the center of the house is a small square place without a door, like a tiny hidden room. I think the walls are spelled, so don't try to break in when you find it. Whoever is accessing the witches belowground is using the circles to zip from other places to this tiny space."

"So no one sees them coming or going," he said. "And you, being so smart and all, stepped into the witch circle in the refrigerator in the bar. Just to test it out, right? Without a witch with you to tell you where you might end up."

"Pretty much."

"You're an idiot."

I felt the tension ease away from my shoulder and spine. "I love you too. Our witches are sitting down here, under the house, directly under the circle on the floor, half-buried in the ground. Misha's here too. They're locked into whatever working they're being forced to do. I have no idea how to stop the working or save them, and one witch looks like she may be near death."

"So, how do we get *you* out of there?"

"I don't know that either. If you break through the walls, you may trigger a latent defensive spell and blow yourselves up. If you come through the floor, you may trigger a spell. I don't know how we blew up the roof without blowing up all the witches."

"What *do* you know?"

"You can try to send Soul through the witch circle at the bar. Maybe she can figure out something. Meanwhile tell Rick to call Evan Trueblood and tell him to take my call."

"Okay. Done. Five on the call to Trueblood, ten on getting Soul to the bar."

I hung up and checked the time. I had a few minutes, so I climbed the steps and pulled the trapdoor closed, sealing me in with Misha and her new pals. I didn't want to be stuck down here with the stink and the decomposing bodies and the silent, half-buried witches, but I didn't want Soul to materialize halfway inside me either. I also didn't want Soul coming through the witch circle and falling through to the ground.

I walked around the circle again as I waited for time to go by, my light settling on each witch as I passed. The pocket watches were all open, each set at an even hour. I realized that each witch was buried at a point on a clock, and the position of the witch was the time on the clock. So far so good. The dead bodies in the center, near the stairs, were also laid out in a pattern, like spokes on a wheel. I had a feeling that the patterns made by living and dead witches were intended to increase the magical working, adding a layer of complication, another part of the outcome, whatever that outcome might be intended to accomplish.

I found the woman who had the magical number 12 on her amulet. She was elderly, with sagging skin and gaunt features. She had been here long enough to be sitting up to her waist in the soil. I wondered if the parts of her that were hidden belowground were dead already.

Misha hadn't been here for long. I held the light over her legs, watching for a hint of human movement—a skin twitch, anything—but I could detect nothing. I wanted to feel for a pulse on the top of her foot, but touching her seemed dangerous for us both.

Dissatisfied, I returned to the steps and sat. When my five minutes were up, I hit speed dial for Evan Trueblood, husband to Molly Everhart Trueblood, once my best friend. Of course, that was before I killed her sister.

"This better be good," Evan growled into my ear.

I almost smiled. "I'm in Natchez, Mississippi, standing below a witch circle painted in black on the floor of a single-story home. On my level are twelve witches, all buried to some extent in the earth, involved in a working that is sucking them down into the ground and killing them. Is that good enough?"

"If you stayed away from bloodsuckers, everybody would be safer."

Which was mostly what I had been thinking not that long ago, but I was feeling obstinate. "Yeah, because you witches take such good care of your own problems. Like a dead body rolled in a carpet, and a witch using the death magics of dozens of dead witch children to get revenge and make herself beautiful and young again," I accused, speaking of secrets the Everharts and Truebloods once kept. "So, yeah, go ahead. Blame me. It's so much easier than taking responsibility for your own problems."

I could almost feel the fury vibrating through Evan, but I wasn't going to say anything nice to make it better. This had been a long time brewing. "Now," I said, making it clear I was changing the subject back to relevant topics. "Do you want to bitch about it, or do you want to save some witches? Because if you don't help, I'm going to try to free them, and we might all blow up." The silence after my tirade was almost palpable.

"Tell me everything you know about the spell," he snarled.

And so I did, starting with de Allyon, adding in Kathyayini's riddle, the bloody iron discs, the crosses and spikes, and ending with witches on the points of the clock. Evan asked succinct questions and listened without further comment. When I was done, he went silent. After a long moment, I heard him take a breath. "Why do you always end up with death magics to undo?"

"Just lucky?" But that wasn't what Kathyayini had said. She had told me that I was the root cause of everything. Just like Evan had said. Which could be casual cruelty, or a way to teach me something about myself or make me face some hidden flaw. Or it could be the simple, unvarnished truth. Either way sucked.

"At least now I know why Leo hired me," he said.

"Hired—?"

"I got a gig at the Darkness Is Forever Bar in Mobile, Alabama," Evan interrupted, "paying me a small fortune to do an update on the lighting and sound systems. I had no idea Leo owned the joint until yesterday. He knew I wouldn't hang around to help *you*, so he kept me close in case you needed my help. And because the MOC is paying me so much money, I did what he said." Evan snorted softly. "I'm a bigger whore than you are, taking money from the chief fanghead of the U.S. *Arguably*," he added. "I guess it's possible that the MOC of New York has more scions, but not as much territory." He fell silent, seeming to have run out of things to say on that odd note and leaving me to understand that the *arguably* did not refer to whether I was a whore. But I held in the snarky comeback.

"I have to study on this," Evan said, "and make some calls. Don't discuss us with PsyLED officials." He disconnected.

I closed the phone when I heard something bump overhead. "There's a handle in the floor. Pull it up," I shouted. And only then remembered that someone other than Soul might arrive. Adrenaline rushed through me, and I shivered with reaction. I can be so stupid sometimes. I pulled a vamp-killer and a handgun, then put away the gun. I might hit one of the witches.

But when the trapdoor opened, it was Soul's hand I saw and Soul's feet. She had tiny feet in tiny little black boots. I put away the blade, shone the flash onto the stairs, and waited as Soul slowly descended the steps.

"Oh," she breathed softly as she turned in a slow circle, taking it all in. "Are they wearing iron?"

"The clocks on their chests each contain an iron disc coated with blood. I'm guessing it's de Allyon's blood," I said, not adding the part about skinwalker blood being in the mix. I wasn't going to share unless I had to. "The blood-donor vamp is very, very dead. Does that make a difference in breaking the spell?"

"Even if he were here, I have no idea how to break such a powerful spell. But without his blood, I fear we are hamstrung."

"Maybe this will help. 'Long years past,'" I quoted Kathyayini, "'was cold iron, blood, three cursed trees, and lightning. Red iron will set you free. Shadow and blood are a dark light, buried beneath the ground.'"

Soul's eyes went round. "Where did you hear this?"

"An old tribal woman said it to me. She also said, 'The one you seek is bound to the Earth. She didn't mean to be bound, but she cannot get away now.' Neither riddle made sense at the time. But now we have the blood-iron discs, possibly made from the iron spikes of Golgotha, and the buried witches." I stopped, remembering the scene in Big H's house, all that white and fancy furniture and silk and satins and one butt-ugly necklace around the neck of the blood-master. He had dangled it outside his clothes, as if proud of it, though it didn't mesh with anything around him. He wore it as if he wanted it to be seen. By me. As if drawing attention to it.

"And the Master of the City of Natchez wears a copper chain on his neck with something made of corroded metal, wrapped in copper wire, hanging from it. I thought it was just ugly jewelry, but why would he display jewelry so different from anything else in his taste? What if it's the same iron?" I tried to find sense in it all, but it was like trying to untangle a snarl of copper wire or a skein of yarn after a cat had played with it. And so much for Evan's order to say nothing to PsyLED.

"I don't know if he's bound like the witches or took it as a trophy or using it now himself. But—I know you said it had to be something big, like a boulder or a tree—but what if the necklace is the focus we're looking for? The amulet."

"It should be something large," she started. "But this is something I've never heard of before. I shouldn't base my conclusions on old experience," Soul said.

"I think the thing Big H is wearing is something from de Allyon, the maker of this circle, and Kathyayini's riddles were meant to light a path into a possible future. I think he's wearing blood iron."

"It is still daylight. You can find Hieronymus' lair and take the necklace. Find a way to undo the working. But you don't have much time if we are to save that one," she pointed at the woman whose face was nearly under the sand.

"Yeah, sure," I said, baiting her, herding her where I needed her to go. "All we need is the location of his lair. Easy-peasy. We'll torture his primo, Clark, for the location. And then I'll break and enter and steal the necklace."

Soul's face underwent a change as she got what I was

saying. "I will not give up the lives here," she said fiercely. "And, yes, I'm willing to turn a blind eye to stop them from dying."

Soul's eyes latched onto me with claws, the feeling of being under her regard much like the feeling of Beast's claws in my brain. "You have a plan." Again it was more an accusation than a statement.

"Maybe I do," I said. "But to make it work and not go to jail, I need PsyLED to stay out of my way for a while. Maybe keep the local cops away."

"Are you going to kill anyone?" she hedged.

"Not if I can help it. At least no one human. And I'll have the Master of the City of New Orleans' approval for it."

"Legal papers signed with Leo Pellissier's official seal?"

"Eventually."

Soul looked at the woman whose head was nearly buried by the sand. As if memorizing the witch's features and her expression of total horror, Soul said, "I can do what you are asking. I can look the other way. But I do not think that Rick LaFleur will allow you to go without him."

"We're not gonna tell Ricky-Bo."

"I think that is wise. His attachment to you is deep. As is his pain."

"Ummm . . ." I stopped. That was all I had. And I had no idea what kind of pain Soul was talking about. Rick had a lot of pain every day of the full moon, but I didn't think that was what she meant.

"Do you love the primo?" she asked.

Shock zinged through me at the question. "Bruiser held me down while I was forcibly bound to Leo Pellissier." My words hung on the air like a bell rung in an empty tower. Soul's eyes were appalled at the violation. I sucked in a painful breath. "We done here?"

"Yes. Go break the law, Jane Yellowrock. But be careful. If you kill humans, all bets are off."

"I plan to kill only the ones trying to kill me."

"That is difficult and will result in far too much paperwork, but it is acceptable."

"Are we bonding here?" I asked.

"I would love to have tea with you sometime, when lives are not in danger and when I am not doing something that goes against all the rules of law that I hold dear."

"Ditto. Café au lait and beignets at Café du Monde. Except that we'll have tea."

Soul's eyes traveled around the witch circle, her body flowing in a balanced pirouette. "Excellent. I'll follow you out soon."

I pulled my weapon and, hoping I wouldn't be transported to some distant place, I bounded up the steps and closed the trapdoor. My stomach wrenched at the transition. Happily, I landed back where I started.

I called Eli from the refrigerator in the old bar. "We're gonna deplete your store of sleepy-time bombs. And we need some antiriot rubber bullets and a riot gun." I told him what else I needed, and Eli Younger started chuckling.

"It might work," he said. "What are you going to be doing?"

"I'm going to put on dry clothes, run by Walmart for supplies, and then go talk to a preacher."

CHAPTER 25

Cat Reflexes, One;
Blood-Servant Reflexes, Zero

I buzzed the secretary from the security door, staring into the security camera and asking to speak to the preacher. She didn't want to let me in, this motorcycle mama in leather, with dark circles under her eyes and a look of death and danger about her, but I told her to tell Preacher Hosenfeld that the little girl with leukemia needed his help. Moments later, I saw the older guy coming down the hall to the door. He was wearing a cheap suit, white shirt, and tie, even on a weekday, his gray hair combed back with some kinda goop like they wore in the fifties, though he couldn't be old enough for that style to have been around in his formative years. He studied me through the windows before I heard several locks click and the door opened. "I hope I'm not being foolish opening the door to you, young lady."

"I kill vamps for a living, including the one who has Charly's mom. I intend to get her back."

"Charly. That is the little girl from Sunday," he said, hesitant.

"Yeah. A vamp put her mother, Misha, into a charmed circle and it's killing her."

Hosenfeld looked confused. It cleared up fast. "A circle. She's a witch, then, this woman you want to save."

I felt my heart shrivel. A lot of Christians felt witches were of the devil. "Yes," I said tersely.

"Are you a Christian?"

"Baptized in a river when I was a teenager. I go to church most Sundays. My favorite Bible verse is 'Jesus wept.'"

"Because it's the shortest?" He almost smiled.

"No. Because it says that Jesus knew what it meant to grieve. He'd just let his best friend in the world die of illness when he could have gotten there in time to save him. I'm thinking he was between a rock and hard place, and the hard place let his friend die. He grieved. Then, when he could, he went and raised his friend from the grave, and he knew that if he did that, he'd die himself."

"That is a very complicated scenario." His smile was wider now, and his shoulders had relaxed. "And do you pray?"

This man was an elder. He was asking me questions, and one did not lie to an elder. I blew out a breath and tried to find an answer to his question. "I think about God. I confess. A lot. But at the same time, it's been a while since I . . ." I shrugged, uncomfortable, "since I got on my knees."

"I have never met a Christian warrior such as yourself."

I opened my mouth and closed it. I had no idea what to say about that and no desire to debate it either. "Here's the deal," I said. "I want to use the church's baptismal water to flush out the vamps," I held up the empty vials I had bought from Walmart. "and I don't have time to play word games. But it isn't like I can steal the water."

"And you want me to help a witch," he clarified.

I shrugged and settled on, "People of all faiths are responsible to help the weak, the downtrodden, the sick, and the helpless, especially children. And of all the religions in the world, Christians are the only ones that are commanded not to judge, yet we do every day—gay people, ethnicities different from our own, people in mixed relationships, people with gifts they were born with, power they were born with, genetic mutations they were born with, illnesses of the brain and body. I've got a little girl's mother to save, and, yes, she's a witch. Are you gonna make it possible for me to save her?"

Herman Hosenfeld's face wrinkled up in a smile. "Of course. How do we do it?"

"*We?*" My voice squeaked just a tad on the word.

"Of course. I'll be there for prayer support, and"—he

held up a hand to stop my reply—"I promise to stay out of your way. There are no other options, young lady. I have a daughter who is a lesbian and married to her witch partner for the past fifteen years. My wife and I lost her years ago through misunderstanding and judgmental attitudes and sheer, blind stupidity. I am no longer so foolish to think God sees her lifestyle with greater ire than he does my judgments."

"The name is Jane Yellowrock, I am not young, and I am not a lady. And you are *not* what I was expecting."

"You are a surprise in my day too."

We had a small parade of vehicles all idling in front of an empty lot, wasting gas. It had started to rain again, spats of sprinkles hitting the windshield, making the cars behind us waver through the Earth's tears. Eli opened the driver's door and climbed in. He was slightly damp, and his hands were empty. He turned on the wipers and said, "Canisters discharged. But without a better idea of the cubic feet of space—"

"I know," I interrupted. "I understand." There hadn't been time to do the necessary research, even for whizzes like the Kid and Bodat. We had no floor plans or maps of the lair under the house. Most important, we were even guessing that Big H was still in his Clan home, having based that assumption on the fact that I had given him the plague vaccine at dawn and he would have been too tired the following night to move to another location. Guesswork and assumptions. *Crap.* Eli tilted his neck to the side and his cervical spine made a rapid series of cracks. "How's it going?" I asked over my shoulder.

The Kid and Bodat were in the backseat of the SUV, computers in hand, monitoring everything from police and emergency responsiveness to the weather, and keeping eyes on the inside of the house we were about to attack. "Piece of cake once we drilled into Big H's security system," Bodat said. "The vamp has cameras all over the place."

Excitement sparked down my nerves and worry pulled at my mind. This could go wrong in so many ways—not least that my theory about the copper necklace was wrong and the pendant was something else.

Or that the holy water wouldn't work. I rearranged the

vials of holy water attached to my jacket. I had it in plasti-
cized glass, so I didn't risk them cracking or shattering. But
it still sloshed. I had never carried so many vials before.

I checked the gun in my lap again. It was a U.S. model
M32, a lightweight, six-shot, 40-millimeter launcher that
could be a grenade launcher or a riot gun. It was loaded
with six rounds of rubber bullets and, while it was a pain in
the butt to reload, it gave me a chance of keeping my promise to Soul to not kill humans. I adjusted the military combat helmet with ear protectors and the built-in com unit. It
felt weird on my head.

"We are live," the Kid said into the headset he wore.
"Flash headlights if you can hear me." Lights flashed behind us. Eli and I raised our hands, thumbs up.

"The security system is in my hands," the Kid said, his
voice all business.

"Alarm system is off," Bodat said. "Elevator is shut
down."

"Feed is now being sent to your cell phones," the Kid
said into the headset, "so use them if you get separated.
Doors to the basement stairs are unlocked and will not
alarm." His fingers clacked on the keys of his tablet, and he
took a breath that hissed into my earpieces. "Totally cool
underground escape passageway is sealed. No one can get
in or out through it."

"Eli, time?" he asked his brother.

Eli, his eyes on his chrono watch said, "Now. Air should
be clear."

Alex shouted into his mic, "Go, go, go, go, go, go, go!"

Eli rammed the transmission into drive and took off with
tires spitting debris, even with the extra load and the rain.

We pulled up to Big H's fancy-schmancy house outside
of town, but we didn't stop at the curb. We squealed into the
drive and then straight up to the front door, ruining the
vamp's perfect green lawn and squashing a patch of azaleas.

Moving fast, Eli and Bruiser met at the back of the SUV
while I pounded up the steps and into the house. I paused
in the middle of the ornate foyer and took a quick, explor-
atory breath. I could smell fumes, but nothing we couldn't
handle.

A man in a gas mask raced through the dining room
opening, a shotgun in one hand. But he experienced a mo-

ment of indecision. Was I there to save his master? Or was I there to do him harm? In that single heartbeat of indecisiveness, I coldcocked him. He fell like a sack of potatoes, and I dodged the gas mask as it flew off but caught the human.

Deep inside me, Beast huffed with laughter and milked my brain with her claws. *Fun,* she murmured.

"Sorry, Clark," I said, as I eased him down to the floor. "I promised Rick's Soul not to kill humans. I didn't promise not to hurt a few." I picked up his shotgun and broke it open, tossing the rounds and laying the gun on the nearest white couch.

I raced for the stairs and paused in the entrance, looking back. Behind me, Bruiser secured Clark with heavy-duty zip strips, pushing the body out of the way. Behind him came Eli. Framed in the doorway, back at the street, a figure stood in the rain. It was Herman Hosenfeld, his eyes closed, his hands half-raised in prayer. He was shivering in his cheap suit, a cold wind blowing and icy rain pelting him. Beside him stepped a woman wearing gauzy greens, her clothes whipping around her, looking already drenched. *Soul.* She spread her fingers, her lips moving. She was speaking a warding of some kind. Hosenfeld paused, looked at her, and smiled before going back to his praying.

A dark form sped in through the door. Faster than any human. *Rick,* his eyes glowing greenish. I cursed into my mic and the Kid said, "Sorry," into my earpiece. Rick was beside me in an instant, his cat musk strong in the air. There wasn't time to argue, and arguing with a big-cat is a waste of time anyway.

Eli looked up from the equipment he was readying. "I called him. We needed manpower."

I snarled and told Rick, "Put in your music spell."

Rick snarled back but put the earpieces in. He didn't have a helmet and wouldn't be able to hear the com channel, but if I kept him close, it shouldn't matter. I dropped the CNB—the communications nexus box—at the top of the stairs and aligned it, pointing it down. The tactical radio system being run by the Kid was designed to work in places where physical or electromechanical interference was high. When we went through the doors and lost direct radio signal, the Kid would switch to the UCU—underground com units. It wasn't the way I had envisioned using the set, but it was a handy thing to own when fighting vamps.

"Ready?" I asked Eli and the Kid.

"On your mark," Eli said.

"We are in the house's intercom," Alex said.

I nodded to Bruiser. He pushed a button on his mic mouthpiece and said, "Attention, all Mithrans." The sound of his voice rang through the house, echoing through the intercom and sound system. "I am the Enforcer of the Master of the City of New Orleans, here for the Naturaleza, the breakers of law, the drainers of blood, the takers of lives. Leo Pellissier has the pledge of Hieronymus. Leo Pellissier has the right of might and of law and of the Vampira Carta. We have your lair. Give us your hands, and no one will die. Fight us, and all will suffer. I have spoken." He switched off the mic and nodded to me.

I handed the M32 to Rick and said, "Rubber bullets." It took a moment for understanding to enter his eyes, but he nodded once, a downward jut of his chin, his eyes going darker and more human. He took the weapon and checked it for firing. Braced it against his shoulder. I pushed open the door to the stairs leading down to the lairs. Rick fired three shots, hitting three humans, one with each shot. Cat reflexes, one; blood-servant reflexes, zero.

The gas-masked blood-servants fell. Semiautomatic weapon fire chattered off the stairway walls, a ricochet going wild. Rick caught a servant who fell forward and over the railing, hauling the man up by an arm. We raced down the stairs, Rick at my side, the M32 at the ready, followed by Bruiser and Eli, working together on our weapon. I just hoped that Big H hadn't equipped *all* his blood-servants with masks.

The hallway branched at the bottom of the stairs. "Which way?" I asked into my mic.

"Left," Bodat said. Behind us came the sound of running feet, the squeak of rubber, and the sliding of heavy synthetic fibers. I looked back and nodded to Eli.

There were three rooms. Bruiser held a PIR device to the door and said, "No vamps. Passive infrared shows humans. Two, both prone."

I opened the door to show the expected humans, asleep. "I love technology," I said.

Using the PIR device, we cleared each room. All were full of sleeping humans, zonked in the middle of daytime activities by the sleepy-time gas. "Hallway is clear," I said.

"Go to your right now," Bodat said. "After that we are blind. There are no more security cameras, and we have no idea of the layout."

More humans slept in the rooms on the right. "Floor is clear," I said. "Heading down one flight." I dropped a second CNB and angled it down. It was the last one we had. Fortunately, the stairway ended in a foyer with three more closed doors.

Bruiser held the PIR up to each door and motioned at each one. There were two vamps in one room, four in another, and more than six in the last one. That made my stomach clench. If this didn't work, we were in trouble. We had no backup.

Scenting my reaction to that thought, Rick snarled. He pulled two handguns, semiautomatics. "Silver," he growled, his voice low, speaking of the ammo he carried. "Purest ever refined."

I pointed to the room with two vamps in it and Bruiser nodded. I snapped two vials of holy water off my weapon harness, unscrewed the tops, and nodded to him. He stood to the side, out of my way, and met my eyes in warning. "We have no firsthand confirmation that holy water works on vamps," he whispered, his words no more than breaths, "and our best experts say it's unreliable." He was talking about the Kid and Reach, who hadn't been able to offer proof positive that holy water worked against vamps. The historical record was iffy at best, perhaps being a matter of the quality of the water itself, as if maybe it went bad after a time, like sour tea or old eggs. But this stuff was fresh, the preacher was outside praying over it, and I was willing to try it.

I said loudly, "So let's try out our new secret weapon." Sometimes fear is better than a blade, and the idea of a secret weapon might give us the advantage. Especially if it worked, and the vamps in the other rooms had no idea what was happening until it had already happened to these two.

He nodded once and pointed to the direction of the cool bodies in the room. I would have a single instant to decide if the vamps were surrendering, shooting, or fighting. And then react accordingly. That put me on defense. In a fight, the one on offense always has the advantage.

Beast leaped into the forefront of my mind. *Hunt!* She thought at me. Her power flooded into me, and the world went sharp and stark. Energy so intense it heated my skin and each breath felt as if it contained the power of the universe, a black star of might at my core. I knew my eyes were glowing gold.

I nodded at Bruiser. He tried the knob, expecting the door to be locked. It opened.

I had a single glimpse. Two vamps, both male, vamped out, were in midair. Leaping at me. I tossed the opened vials of baptismal water, and Bruiser slammed the door. On the other side, heavy *thump*s sounded—vamps hitting the door. And then the horrible screams that vamps make when they are dying. Or think they are. Beast hacked with delight. By the screams, they were heading away, probably to the nearest showers.

Bruiser caught my gaze, taking in the gold glow. He looked at Rick and the greenish-glow of the cop's eyes. Whatever was in the men's eyes, I ignored.

Preacher Hosenfeld would be pleased that the baptismal water from his church worked against vamps as well as some old myths suggested that water blessed by a priest would.

Bruiser held up the PIR and smiled grimly. Loudly enough to be heard clearly through the other two doors, he said, "That heated them up a bit."

Rick chuckled, the chuffs of a cat. Beast turned to him and hacked with delight.

Bruiser looked at neither of us and moved to the next room, holding up four fingers to remind us of the numbers of vamps inside. I nodded and stepped back. Four was too many for me to handle alone. Eli dragged the heavy nozzle behind him. I had no idea where he'd gotten the fire hose, but this particular one would allow us to pump up to 210 gallons per minute through a special nozzle he'd gotten from a plant nursery—one that allowed a wide spray rather than the usual concentrated, unidirectional spray used for fighting fires. The tank it was attached to held a thousand gallons of baptismal water. And now we knew it would work against vamps.

I pulled two more vials, just in case. Eli braced himself, met Bruiser's eyes, and nodded. Bruiser tried the door. This one was locked, which was going to make our job harder, but we had planned for vamps with brains and good security personnel.

The former Ranger quickly placed charges of plastic explosives at the sites of the hinges and the lock. While he worked, we all backed into the relative safety of the stairwell. I had to hand it to him: the guy was fast, unwinding the det cord behind himself as fast as he could shuffle. I didn't know what we would be facing, so I screwed the tops back on the vial and pulled a blade and an ash stake. The last two vamps had been normal vamps. The old methods of vamp fighting should work.

Protected by the wall, he looked at us until he had our attention and counted down silently, mouth moving: *One, two, three.* He hit a switch. The door blew. The world went into slow motion, the kind where I could see everything in harsh layers of action, overlapping and intense.

Bruiser hit the holy water switch. I could see his fingers move. He was too late. A fraction of a fraction of a second too late.

Two vamps moved at us so fast, there would have been a pop of air had any of us been able to hear it. *Vamped out. Deadly,* I thought, even as their bodies catapulted over the spray of water. One landed on me. Her claws dug into my shoulder, catching on the plastic armor. The claws of her other hand swiped at my face. *Normal vamps.* Her legs swept up to wrap around me.

In my peripheral vision, I saw holy water shooting out of the nozzle like a hundred tiny jets. And Rick, with his mouth on a vamp's neck. A spray of blood flew into the air from his jaws.

Beast-fast, I stabbed up with an ash stake, hitting my attacker in the abdomen. She fell, the wood taking her in the central artery leading down to her legs. Immobilizing her. Her blood cascaded over my right leg. I dropped her, holding the stake in place as she fell.

The holy water hit the next two vamps in midair. They screamed and did ninety-degree turns, bouncing off the walls. They raced away, screaming in agony. I looked at Rick. He was rising from under the vamp that landed on him. The vamp had an ash stake in his heart and only half of his throat left, the bones of the spinal column visible. But he was still alive, gasping. I figured he'd heal. Sooner or later.

Rick's eyes were glowing green. He had fangs on his upper and lower jaw. Eli and Bruiser were backing slowly away from him. Rick spat and snarled, his human skin and flesh stretching like a cat's. Gently, slowly, I lifted my arm and my hand to him. And took up an earpiece. My ears were covered by the helmet, but I could hear tinny sounds of music from it. I lifted the piece toward Rick.

He jerked his head away but kept his eyes on me. I stopped all movement and waited, barely daring to breathe. Rick's face relaxed just a hair as the music became audible to him too. Then his mouth closed. I placed the earpiece in his ear. His eyes lost some of the glow and darkened toward his usually Frenchy-black eyes. He took the other earpiece and put it in. He chuffed out a breath. "Thanks," he said. The word was slurred as his mouth tried to return to human. "Don' wanna get stuck partway." Which might happen if Rick ever changed to his big-cat, thanks to the tattoos on his shoulder.

"Pain bad?" I asked.

"Yeah. I'll stay back here for the other door," he said, "and cover my ears. Don't get yourself killed."

"Not my plan," I said.

"You two finished playing nice-nice? Good." Eli said, his own words a snarl, nearly as good as a big-cat's. "Six vamps inside," he said, "clustered at the back of the room, probably trying to get out the locked escape hatch. They're gonna be pissed when they realize the hatch won't open and they're trapped. And it won't be long before we have wet, pissed vamps, fresh outta the shower and wanting revenge. On three, people."

In the moments we had been standing there, Eli had used the last of his C4 on the third door. He didn't bother to count silently, and I drew a silver stake and my fourteen-inch-long vamp-killer as he counted down. "One, two, three."

The door blew. And nothing happened. No vamps flew at us. Nothing happened. At all.

I raced past Eli and Bruiser, passing through the baptismal water, feeling it splatter on my hair and across my neck and back. Leaped through the splintered door, into the room. Landed, weapons out to either side, my body bladed, left foot forward, balanced. Ready for anything. I stopped. Water swirled into the room and around my feet.

Clustered in the back of the room were six vamps. Big H was in the middle, standing with his arms out at the sides, his fingers seeming to claw at the wall. Two vamps were on either side; one was crouched at his feet. All of them were vamped out, snarling, their bodies oddly twisted, but not like the spidey vamps. Like regular old vamps. None of them moved.

And I had no idea what to do.

I just stood there. Weapons ready. Breathing like a bellows. Inside me, Beast snarled, puzzled. Behind me, Eli turned off the water. Silence fell.

The guys moved into the room, forming a semicircle behind me.

Like the upstairs, this suite was done in white and scarlet, with a bed big enough to play touch football on, white-painted columns for bedposts, a seating area big enough to seat both teams on, tables and chairs at one end of the room, an en suite bath visible through an open door. And a pile of vamps so still they looked like statuary.

Hieronymus took a faint breath and said something I couldn't hear. I pulled off my helmet and he repeated, "I cannot."

I stepped closer, feeling the guys behind me keeping pace. "What can't you do?"

His face warped, as if his skin had been pulled to the side only to resettle like soft clay or putty that, left alone, returned to its original form. Something was hinky here, not what I had expected, not even subconsciously.

I took another step and sniffed, my mouth open to take in the scent of the room, which I hadn't done since I started down the stairs to Big H's lair. The smell of vamp was strong and herbal: the floral of funeral flowers, the dry scent of sage. But the smell of sickness was missing, as was the acrid, dusty scent of the spidey vamps.

I walked slowly toward them, the guys on my trail, spreading out and around furniture, keeping the vamps covered. I was close enough that in Beast's vision, I could see the necklace around Big H's neck. And I realized that his neck was burned beneath it. It hadn't been that way before; I was sure of that.

To the female vamp at his feet, I said, "Unbutton H's shirt."

An expression of utter relief crossed her face and vanished. She stood gracefully, reaching long, delicate fingers to her master. They unbuttoned Big H's white shirt, exposing his chest. Which was blistered and pitted and blackened around a shard of iron wrapped in corroded, ancient copper.

"Tag. You're it," I said. When the vamps didn't react, I said, "The Naturaleza tagged you. They put that on you sometime after you hired me to come kill them off and before I got here. It's controlling you. Isn't it?"

The female vamp nodded once, then froze.

"If I take it off, will you die?"

Hieronymus' face twisted again, and I realized it was with the effort to speak. Nothing came out, but his lips moved. He said, "Take it."

Keeping the vamp-killer to the side, I sheathed the stake, dropped the helmet, and reached up a hand. I touched the copper necklace. Lifted it slowly. The iron wrapped in copper tore H's skin as I lifted it away. Blood trickled down his chest. There was no clasp, and I wasn't going to get close enough to lift it over his head. "This is gonna hurt," I said.

With a single massive jerk, I broke the chain and leaped back.

The vamps collapsed to the floor in a tangle of arms and legs. The iron swung on the chain, back and forth, dangling in my fist. Power surged up from it, snaring me in its might. The entire room went black.

And I was falling.

CHAPTER 26

Mr. Prepared for Anything

I was in a dark place, empty and cool. It smelled of wet and age and eons of time. It pressed down on me, heavy and dense and dangerous. It was so dark I couldn't tell when I closed my eyes. I reached out and the vamp-killer clanged against stone. The fist holding the necklace touched stone on the other side. My heart leaped into my throat. I was underground. I was buried.

But the stone fell away as I continued my turn. A light, faint and dim, appeared to my right. I took a step, another, moving slow and easy. Moving through the underground dark, a tunnel, cold and wet and chill, its dimensions somehow organic, widening and narrowing. *A cave.* I sheathed the blade and placed my feet carefully, redistributed my weight warily, expecting to find no ground beneath me at every step.

As I moved, I heard the slow *plink* of water. Smelled water and smoke, heard the crackle of fire licking at cold, dry wood. The passage opened up to reveal a large cavern in the rock, domed, with stalactites hanging down from the roof and stalagmites rising up from the floor, the walls smooth and pearlescent like a shell.

The fire burned near the back wall, its light flickering. I recognized my spirit home, the cavern of my youth, the place where I first learned to shift when I was a child of five. The place I went to in my mind when I was in danger or when I had something I needed to learn. It was a hard place, but it was mine. A place of strength and a place of dreams.

Near the fire sat an old woman, her gray hair in braids hanging down to her lap on either side. Her head was down, staring into the fire, the light showing me only the top of her head and her wrinkled forehead. I thought it was Kathyayini, but the clothes were all wrong. This woman wore no flower-sack clothing, but a cotton shirt in a vibrant yellow, a pullover shirt intended to tie at her throat. It hung open, revealing a necklace of carved and dyed bone and porcupine quills and glass beads. Her skirt was canvas, dyed blue, worn at the hem and belted with worked hide in beads to match the necklace. Tied to the belt was a series of small leather bags, pouches for herbs and minerals.

I paced slowly to the fire. When I stood there, my shadow elongated behind me, I had no idea what to say. This was a Tsalagi elder. A shaman. I should have taken off my weapons. One didn't wear weapons into the presence of an elder of The People.

"Tsilugi, Dalonige i Digadoli, aquetsi ageyutsa." Welcome, Golden Eyes, Golden Stone, my daughter.

My legs folded, and I sank to the ground. *"Elisi?"* She raised her head and the firelight moved over her wrinkled face. Her eyes were amber, like mine. "Elisi," I whispered. *My grandmother.*

"Forgive me for coming into the presence of an elder with weapons."

"You are warrior woman." She waved away my apology, her hand gnarled and ribboned with veins. "Weapons are part of you. You *are* a weapon." She shrugged. "I made you to be so."

I thought about that, about the memories I had recently gained and refused to look at again, memories of this woman putting a blade into my hand. I had been a child, maybe five years old, the year that everything changed. The hairs rose on the back of my neck, and when I breathed, I tasted sweetgrass and burning oak on the back of my tongue. "When you put the knife into my hand," I whispered. "That's when you made me a warrior?"

"Together, we killed a man. Slowly. For killing your father. You remember?"

I nodded.

"You remember the first cut?"

I closed my eyes, sucking in a breath. Remembering.

The blade was too large for my fist. The bone handle was cold, but warmed quickly. I raised the knife to the white thing hanging over the pit, tied with rope. It was a leg. It bucked, trying to get away. Above it came strangled sounds, like a pig full of fear. The leg in front of me was hairy with light brown hairs, and white-skinned, like a dog. It stank of fear, this yunega who had killed my father.

I cut it, the blade opening up a line of red. The thing hanging above squealed again, and piss ran down his leg. I reached up and cut him again.

I jerked back from the memory, back from the fire. I landed on my open hands, my palms on the cold stone floor. Staring at my grandmother.

"To kill a human when so young may change a child," Elisi said. "May make her a man killer. Sometimes a killer only. You have done well to learn to love. You have done well to bring family into your heart, even though they are family not of your blood or your clan or your tribe. This will keep the darkness away for many years."

"Did ... Did you become *U'tlun'ta?* Did you become stone finger, the liver eater?"

Elisi's eyes flew from amber to gold, two glowing orbs. Her face melted and folded, bristling with pelt. Two sets of fangs grew, distorting her jaw. She growled the word, *"Tsisdu!"* And leaped at me.

I landed hard, my body hitting as if boneless, my jaw impacting the floor. My teeth clacked together, the sound strange and clicking. *Tsisdu.* Elisi had called me *rabbit. Prey.*

I rolled to my feet in Hieronymus' room, the necklace in my fist. "Why did you let me take this?" I growled at the vampire on the floor. My voice was on a lower register, my words distorted. I touched my teeth with my tongue and felt fangs. *Oh, crap.*

Hieronymus pushed to his feet, one hand going to his throat, touching it gently. The blisters weren't healing, and I knew he needed blood, but he seemed to gather himself. He placed his other hand on his scion, as if to soothe her. "All is well," he said to her.

His eyes studied me, taking in my features. "I had heard of this, of Leo's Enforcer, the one who takes the form of a puma." He dipped his head as if in recognition of something important, something I didn't understand. I'd have to think about that later.

"This has been foretold," he said. "This is a time of change, when the old ways return, when old darkness fights for supremacy against that which is new, against the light of the world."

I had heard those exact words at some point in the last year, but I couldn't place them. Before I could ask, he went on.

"My heir, Lotus, my *erede*, she fed from another, pledged allegiance to another, unbeknownst to me." Hieronymus stroked the hair of the female vampire who had knelt at his feet, his hand soothing her. "When Lotus came to me to offer her blood and her devotion, she reached around to embrace me. And she placed the cursed thing"—he pointed to my fist—"over my head. There is a spell of binding within it."

"Binding?" I looked at the necklace in my hand.

"The binding of Santa Croce," he whispered. At my confused look he said, "*Il sangue . . .*" He struggled for words and said, "The blood on the crosses and the sacrifice of blood, this created the Mithran, the immortal drinker of blood."

"Master, no!" The female scion raised her fingers to his mouth.

He smiled and caught her hand, twining his fingers into hers. "We have lived with secrets for too many years, my daughter. These secrets have now appeared, as if from the grave, and they bit us. They drained us. Leo sent this creature to right the wrongs."

Not exactly, I thought, but I didn't say it. "I know about the creation story," I said, my mouth moving almost normally now.

"The priestess of the sepulcher—she told you this hidden story?" Big H asked.

I figured he meant Sabina Delgado y Aguilar, the oldest Mithran I knew. She had told me a lot of stuff that vamps usually keep secret, including the origin of vampires via the crosses of Calvary and Golgotha. I nodded.

He sighed, a sound almost human; he moved slowly to a chair and sat. "Forgive me. I am fatigued from the healing of the medicine. It has been many centuries since I felt thus. I find I do not miss it at all." He stretched out his legs. "I will tell you the rest of the story, of the iron that bound flesh to tree. *Ferro chiodo*. The others, however, must leave. This is for your ears only."

"I'm not going anywhere, fanghead," Rick growled.

"Yes. You will," I said, studying the vampire Master of the City of Natchez. His bald head was paler than it had been, but his motions were more human than before, something that took control and practice. He was in control of himself and of his people. "Go on. I'm okay. Please," I added, without looking away from the MOC.

I heard Rick growl, and the hiss of whispered words, and then the sound of people and equipment moving away into the stairwell. Big H smiled grimly. "I never heard of such an attack, of using holy water by the gallons against a Mithran's lair. How did you get a priest to bless such a volume of water?"

"Baptismal water," I said, figuring it would get out anyway.

Big H made a *hmmm* sound, as if rethinking his security arrangements. I had a feeling that drains would be installed in all his lairs soon.

"They're gone." I said. You were speaking of the *ferro chiodo*. Whatever that is."

"I speak of the iron spikes that bound Christ to the cross," the older man said, his voice reverential, his eyes on the thing in my hand. "But do not think that there is something holy in this tale." His voice took on the pitch of a story told often, and when he spoke, he quoted the same words I had heard spoken by Sabina. "When the sons of Ioudas heard that the master had risen, they went to the mount of the skull to find the cross where he died, to steal the wood bathed in his blood, to work arcane magics with the blood and the cross. But the crosses of the thief, the murderer, and the rabbi had been pulled down, broken up, and piled together, the wood confused and mixed."

Around him, the vamps settled to the floor, watching the Master of the City. Others entered through the broken door and sat there as well. Some small, irreverent part of me saw it as a bunch of preschoolers sitting around at story time, and I had to swallow down my laughter. I figured that if I giggled at the creation story of the curse of the Mithrans, I might get drained in retaliation.

"They took it all, all the wood of the crosses. By dark of night they pulled their father's body from the grave, and with their witch power and arcane rites they laid his body upon the pile of bloody, broken wood. My own histories say they sacrificed the life of their small sister on the wooden pile. Others say not. But with arcane rites, they sought to raise their father from the dead. And he rose, though he was yet dead, his soul given over to the night and the dark. Soulless, he walked for two nights, a ravening beast. And he could not be killed, though he rotted and the flesh fell from his bones to writhe upon the ground. And thinking that some benefit might yet be gleaned from their sin, his sons drank the blood and ate the flesh of their father. And they were *changed*."

I nodded. I had heard the story, almost word for word.

"But what is not spoken of is the iron," he said to me, his cadence changing back to his usual accented English. "Forged metal was rare in ancient times and of great value. For death on a tree, most were hung with ropes made of plants or the ligaments of animals, easy to make and to replace. For iron to be used, the punishment required a swift death. With the holy day of the subjugated people upon them, the Romans who crucified the three required such speed."

Big H's voice took on the storytelling tempo again. "When the Sons of Darkness gathered the wood, they found, piled nearby, the iron that had bound the three, and they gathered it and the wood from all three trees. When their father could not be killed and yet walked the Earth, a rotting corpse, they melted the iron spikes down into one great spike with which to kill their father."

I looked at the necklace in my hand, the sliver of iron wrapped in copper. I opened my mouth to say something, but I had no words. None at all.

"When the Mithrans were forced into the diaspora, the outclan priestesses took the *wood* of the crosses and created weapons to be used against our kind. The Naturaleza took the *iron*, and created weapons of binding and control.

Two great tribes arose, the Fame Vexatum and the Naturaleza. A war was fought for many years and across many countries, until the Naturaleza heard of the New World. And they came here. Lucas Vazquez de Allyon was one such."

"And with the weapon of the iron spike, or a part of one, and the magics of the witch circle and the sickness that the vamp . . . ires"—I finished the word as an afterthought—"he hoped to take over the New World now, in the twenty-first century, after the first vampires walked the earth."

"Yes. And more." Big H looked up from the necklace I still clutched. "The *ferro chiodo* creates. With its binding powers it takes that which is and makes that which is darker, stronger. The *spirito malign*, the immortal that cannot be killed, the thing of legend and nightmare."

"Like the father of the Sons of Darkness."

"When they have the methodology and spell for the transformation, the Naturaleza will stake themselves and rise on the third day. Invincible. No weapon, not even sunlight, will kill them. The only way to defeat them will be to take their heads and it would become a bloody, difficult venture."

That sounded pretty sucky. I had a moment to wonder if a bomb might work, and realized that if it blew them apart, it would also take their heads, so yeah. I pulled the fused iron discs out of my pocket. "These are being used for binding witches into a circle."

Real fear crossed Big H's face, wrinkling his forehead up into his bald pate. "How many of those things do you have? And how many witches in the circle?"

"This one was three. The discs got close to one another and they fused. Twelve witches make up the circle, each with her own disc. At midnight tonight, it will be the true full moon. It's likely that the working will be complete then."

"You must find Lotus and take her head before that," Big H said. "I will give you the location of her lair." He smiled slowly, all pretense of humanity peeling away, all fang and vamped-out eyes, the huge black pupils in scarlet sclera like dark pits falling straight into hell. "You will destroy my enemy and bring me the blood-iron of the crosses."

*   *   *

The SUV's heater was on full blast. The sun was setting, the evening growing colder and wetter. Ice was starting to build up on the trees and shrubs, and icicles were starting to form on the eaves of houses. We sat in the dark, staring at the house, silent. We'd been here for an hour, waiting. It should have been tense or uncomfortable or something. It should have felt weird. But it didn't. It felt like coming full circle somehow.

We had done this job by the book, researching like crazy, gathering all the records, following all the paper trails. We had then done all the footwork, checking out the properties owned by Lotus, by Silandre, even those owned by Big H. We had checked out so many other places, but they were empty; no lairs or only vacant ones. And all that basic research had been a waste of time. All I had needed was a scrap of paper given to me by the MOC of Natchez. He had known where she was all along, but until I ripped away the binding, he hadn't been able to tell me, and none of his people had been able to speak of it either.

Lesson learned—save the MOC first. Then go after his enemy.

Now Bruiser and I were back at the house with the turret, the one where we had found Esther McTavish beheaded, and a charnel room in the basement.

I hadn't gone down to the basement then, hadn't inspected the place. I should have. I had screwed up, thinking that no one was left there.

Now it was just Bruiser and me, waiting in the icy rain for our backup. There would be no debate now, no unexpected visitors, no preacher standing in the rain, praying for us to succeed. No Rick to tear out the throat of a vamp. No Soul to ward us.

We would go in without the Kid or Rick. . . . My hands clenched in the dark. It was just the two of us, because we had snuck out of Esmee's and taken off like bats on fire, leaving behind anything electronic that the Kid could use to track us. We would go in alone because we were the only ones who stood a snowball's chance in hell of surviving. And everyone knew what happened to a snowball in hell. I smiled grimly at the thought.

We had found what we were looking for, and Bruiser had called Leo, who had authorized the funds. And then

Leo had called in the backup we needed. Leo. Not me. Because he wouldn't have come for me.

A pickup truck pulled in behind us; a bear of a man climbed out of the truck, the whole thing rocking like a toy.

Without speaking, we unbuckled and left the SUV, not locking the doors, and walked around to the back of the vehicle to meet Evan Trueblood, Molly's husband. He stood in the rain like a mountain in the fall, topped by red hair and beard, a man so big he made two of Bruiser, and without an ounce of fat on him.

"How many people now know what I am, what my daughter must be, because of you?"

"Too many," I said. Justified guilt swarmed through me, earned because Big Evan's being a sorcerer had been a secret until I came along. And because his secret was out, Angie Baby and Little Evan, his children, faced future danger. "Leo's vamps know. Rick. But not Rick's partner. Soul. She knows there's a witch because of Rick's spell music, and she might have figured it out, but she hasn't been told, and therefore, PsyLED doesn't know. But when they find out—and they will eventually; that is always a given—we'll be there to protect you and yours."

I could hear his molars grinding. "You know how much I hate you?" he ground out.

"Yeah. I also know that what happened to your wife and to your kids when they were attacked by witch vamps was not the fault of my being evil. Just me being in the wrong place at the wrong time. I also know that the real reason you hate me is that you feel like you didn't do a good enough job of protecting your family. And because you can't stand that thought, you hate me instead."

Evan growled, so much like a bear that I chuckled. "You through being a pop psychologist?" he asked. "Because I'm here to a job and get back home. To my family."

"No," I said. "I'm not done. You need to forgive yourself. I understand misplaced guilt. I totally understand it." Before he could raise one of his massive fists and knock me into the next state, I held out the discs from the pocketwatch amulets. As per Evan's instruction, the discs had been removed from the amulets and were now all fused into one circular lump. "Now I'm through."

Evan growled again but extended his hand. I dropped

it—them—into his left paw. I placed the iron sliver in its copper wiring in his right hand, just like he had texted me. The moment his hand closed on the small spike-shaped sliver, Evan started to glow a weird yellowish color in the grim gray light.

I looked at Bruiser and said, "Let's do this."

Bruiser was heavily armed, as befitted a true Enforcer, and I was carrying everything I owned that had a point, a sharp edge, or would fire ammo, plus the bag full of stuff Evan had required, under my arm. I drew the shotgun, checked the load, and headed inside, following Bruiser, who broke through the crime scene tape and busted open the door with a well-placed kick. He-man stuff. Which would have made me smile if my face still remembered how.

Inside, the house was cold but dry, the heat off. The electric company hadn't turned off the power, however, and the house had little lights along the walls, like Christmas lights, to show the way. I took the lead and found the hidden door to the basement. Opened it, as I had the first time I was here.

The smell ballooned out, as if it had been under pressure and opening the door released the effluvia. It was horrible. It would never go away, no matter how many cleansers they used, no matter how many coats of paint, how many gallons of chemicals. This smell of the grave never, ever, went away. They would have to burn the place. But now, nearly hidden below the stink of the grave, the place smelled of spidey vamp.

I stepped down the stairs. The men followed, and I turned on lights as I came to the switches, illuminating the room below. The cement floor was a reddish brown—the color of the blood that had seeped into the porous surface. There was no furniture, only bookcases on all four walls, the shelves bare. The place had been cleaned out by the cops searching for an entrance, a vamp lair. They hadn't found one. But I had a new secret weapon, even better than holy water. I had Molly's husband.

I set the shotgun nearby, where I could grab it up in an instant—not that having it handy was gonna help me against the things we had come to kill. The best it would do was slow them down. I opened the bag and took out the full-sized white bedsheet. It was brand new and I ripped the plastic wrap, stuffing the trash into the bag, and spread open the sheet. On it I drew a circle with black marker, the chemical stink vanishing beneath the smell of rot, and left a small opening. Evan, still glowing pale yellow, walked through the opening, and I closed the circle behind him, drawing the black marker onto the sheet, and capped the marker.

Evan sat, his legs bending into the small space with difficulty. He laid the fused disc on the sheet between his knees, keeping the copper-wrapped iron in one fist. With the other hand, he pulled a small wooden flute.

"Are you sure?" I asked. It was an awfully weak circle.

Big Evan glared at me. "I do this my way. This is witch business."

I shrugged, and Evan placed the flute between his lips. He started to play. It was a simple melody, only four notes, something he could play with the fingers of one hand, four notes in a dirge of song, primitive and plaintive.

He had played for less than five minutes when the disc between his knees moved slightly, angling to the right only a few millimeters. It paused, then traveled over the sheet the way iron moves toward a magnet, and stopped at the edge of the black circle I had drawn and Evan had powered. The witch stopped playing, the sad notes hanging on the air for a moment. "The lair is there. Behind that wall and down."

Bruiser pulled a crowbar out of his belt, and I smiled. "Mr. Prepared for Anything," I said. He flashed me a smile before he wrenched back and stabbed forward, wedging the sharp end of the crowbar into the wood of the shelves. Within minutes, the back of the bookcase was in splinters, revealing only brick, until he splintered a long board off the wall and a small aluminum handle appeared down near the floor. I took up the shotgun and braced it against my shoulder. Set my feet and bent my knees slightly. Bruiser looked at me, and I nodded. He bent forward and gripped the wood. With a single savage jerk, the damaged shelves squeaked open on hinges. A black maw appeared.

Something white smudged across the darkness. Time slowed into the consistency of glue, each moment clear and concise, as if trapped in amber. All I could think in that long, stretched-out moment was that Molly would never survive the loss of her husband. My godchildren, whom I hadn't seen in months, would grow up without their father. If this didn't work.

Silandre waved through the opening, as if pulled along by more than four limbs. Big Evan stood, as if safe in his weak circle. I fired once, twice, three times as Silandre raced up the hidden stairs. Missing her each time as she wove side to side. The vampire launched herself at Evan, the witch in her lair.

I pivoted, following Silandre's wavelike charge.

Bruiser fired at the form that followed Silandre. Fired again, at Lotus, her black hair flowing like a skein of silk. The rounds hit. But the silver fléchettes didn't slow the vamp.

Silandre seemed to fly through the air. And across the circle. Around Evan, the witch circle imploded. *It's not going to work.*

Faster than I ever expected, faster than any creature should be able to move, Evan reached out and scratched Silandre. Her blood shot into the air.

Big Evan adjusted the angle of his hand and reached for the witch still moving toward him. He scratched Lotus. And both vampires fell.

It was anticlimactic after all the killing and all the blood. With the iron spike wielded by a witch, the vampires were bound. Not dead, but in a form of stasis.

"Huh," Big Evan said. "Would you look at that? It worked." The sound of surprise in his voice made me shudder.

From the black hole leading down to the lair came a moan of pain.

CHAPTER 27

While There Is Breath, There Is Hope

I flipped on the switch and looked down the stairs. At the bottom was a tiny room, barely big enough to hold the oversized bed. The walls were unadorned; the mattress had no sheets. The room smelled of damp and mold and human blood and human waste.

Curled up on the floor, wedged between the wall and the floor, were four forms. Three women and a child. "Evan!" I said. I leaped the distance down, landing in a small, clear spot of floor, and touched the woman nearest. She flinched. "It's okay," I said, "You're safe now."

The woman turned her head to me and blinked. She was pale as death, and her throat was bloody from forced feeding. It was an Acheé witch. I looked at the others, trying to see beneath the blood loss and bruises, and I realized that we had all of them and all were still alive. Including the old woman who had walked my dreams, Kathyayini, who slept, scarcely breathing, in a corner of the small room.

I blinked back tears, thinking of the time they had spent here in this lair, tortured and tormented, all because I hadn't come down to search. I ignored the small voice that whispered I wouldn't have found the witches, not without Big Evan and the spell he used on the discs. Like the accusation I had made to Big Evan, I wasn't ready to forgive myself yet. Not about everything. Not about this.

I said again, "It's okay. You're safe now. Let me hand you up the stairs."

The witch started to cry. Above me, Big Evan bent over the hole to the lair. He started to curse softly beneath his breath.

We were standing in front of the refrigerator in the old bar, waiting to step into the witch circle. Just Big Evan, Bruiser, and me. And two unconscious vamps. Evan hadn't been gentle with them, not since treating the Acheé witches. His eyes had filled with tears over the girl, not yet an adult, abused and nearly catatonic with fear. Kathyayini was in a coma, still dream-walking when the ambulances came.

And he had been taking his anger out on the vamps ever since. Yet I knew that Evan would have a problem taking a life, even a vamp's undead life, even with justice so long overdue. He had already refused to kill, saying that no witch would use blood magic to break black magic. And I wasn't sure if he could break the spell of the full witch circle without taking their blood and their heads.

"Time?" I asked.

"Eleven twenty-four," Bruiser said.

"Close enough," Evan said, urging us on.

I didn't have to have my cell phone handy to know that the others were looking for us, worried sick. I could actually feel Rick's panic, like a burr stuck in my paw. He had nearly changed already once, and the pain had been unendurable. Now the moon was at her fullest, almost midnight of the full moon, the witching hour. We had been waiting for hours, Big Evan setting the timetable and outlining the plan.

And now, at last, it was time to save Misha.

"I'll go through first," I said, "and open the trapdoor. Then you send the vamps through. They'll fall through the opening into the circle below. Then I'll close the door and you two come through, one at a time."

I had wanted to do it all by myself and not risk Big Evan again, but breaking a working this strong took a witch and the blood of the vamp who set it into motion. Since he was dead, I was hoping that the blood of his killer and the blood of his heirs would do. I stepped into the fridge and fell.

Even though I was expecting it, I nearly lost my supper. I caught myself only by the most delicate line of luck. I landed hard, stumbled, and ended up on one knee and both hands. Moving fast, I turned on the flashlight and opened the trapdoor. The reek that flowed up through it was so close to the stench of the charnel lair that my stomach roiled again. I dropped through and stood to the side, the trapdoor open. I didn't look around with light. I couldn't make myself. I was such a coward sometimes.

Moments later, the two vamps fell through to bounce at my feet. They were bound with silver and steel and a spell. And a full roll of duct tape, Big Evan's last-ditch protections against vamp strength. I closed the door, and when it opened, Bruiser walked down, followed moments later by Big Evan, whose bulk barely fit through the opening.

The big man swore at the sight of the twelve witches, taking the flashlight from my hand without asking and studying them. He spent the longest on the witch who was nearly buried. Now only her mouth and nose were above the ground, but even he was afraid to brush away the sand, for fear the spell would activate and kill her instantly. "While there is breath, there is hope," he whispered.

His face was grim as death when he came back to me, harsh lines and angles in the sharp light of the flash, his body bent to protect his head from the floor system above. He nodded at me, and I opened another new sheet, this one already partially marked with a circle, part of the preparations we had made in the hours while we waited for midnight.

I spread the sheet over the uneven floor, in a place between the bones that littered the surface. Normally Evan would have used a spade to dig a circle in the earth, but the bones and the absolute concentration of power made that unpractical.

He picked up Lotus and tossed her into the circle. Bruiser tossed Silandre. Both vamps were rounded, sensual, and warm to the touch, full of witch blood. Neither showed signs of the transformative process of the witch working and the binding of the red iron. And neither had spoken since they were captured, maybe silent in the presence of lesser creatures. Maybe waiting out the clock for the few minutes left until midnight.

Evan stepped into the circle and sat, rolling the vamps close and digging in the bag I had carried for his supplies. This would be Big Evan's show, not mine. I was just the helper. Bruiser was the muscle, standing guard at the bottom of the steps below the closed trapdoor. He was silent, watching us, his face impassive, his body loose and ready for anything that might land in the circle above us and come through the door.

Walking sunwise—or, in this case, literally clockwise—I walked the witch circle, setting out twelve candles, one beside each buried witch. I lit them according to my instructions, beginning with the witch wearing the pocket watch set at the number one. When I was done, Evan asked, "Anything else you need to tell me?" When I shook my head, he said, "Say it again."

I restrained a sigh and a retort. I wasn't a witch, I wasn't used to memorizing spells, and I had never crafted one. He wanted to make sure I hadn't left anything out that would help him with the spell and had made me repeat Kathyayini's words over and over. "Long years past was cold iron, blood, three cursed trees, and lightning. Red iron will set you free." I opened my hands as if holding a tea tray flat on my palms, as if saying, *See? Just like last time,* and telling him with my eyes, as I had told him with words, that all this part had been figured out.

He nodded for me to continue.

"Shadow and blood are a dark light, buried beneath the ground." I pointed to the witch nearest. "The one you seek," I said, pointing to Misha, "she is bound to the Earth. She didn't mean to be bound, but she cannot get away now."

"We still don't know what is being used as a focus for the spell?" Evan asked. I shook my head. "Time?"

"Eleven fifty-two," Bruiser said.

"Good." Evan drew a knife, an athame. The whole thing, handle and blade, was purest sterling silver. He pointed the tip at the circle, and I closed it with the black marker. I drew a blade. Mine was steel with silver plating, but, really, even plastic would have done. I went to kneel near the witch who was almost buried. It was my job to scrape away the sand the moment the working was broken.

Big Evan Trueblood was an air witch, meaning he worked with air currents, sometimes with weather, with wind, with storms. But most often Evan worked with sound. He pulled a box from the bag he had brought and opened it with quick metallic-sounding snaps of the latches. Within was a flute. The witch placed it to his mouth and blew a long, slow note. This wasn't a wooden flute, with a hollow sound and a limited range, but a large, silver flute, larger than any flute I remember seeing used in the high school band. The tone was haunting and low as single notes became a melody.

Beneath my feet and knees, I felt the sand shiver with the deep vibration of the music. It was sweet one moment, discordant the next, melancholy and joyful by turns. Moment by moment, the sand beneath me grew more and more disturbed, until I could hear its disquiet over the music, a scratching, dry abrasion, the surface sand worrying across the deeper-packed earth.

It moved as if alive, shook as if frightened, slid as if sentient. And as I watched, a bead of sand crept closer to the mouth of the buried witch. I looked to Evan, sitting in the center of the circle, playing his flute, his form placid, his melody serene.

Another bead of sand slid within her mouth. She didn't move. Didn't react. But my heart rate spiked. The music sped, its tempo rising, the notes climbing high, only to fall into the deeps. I glanced at Misha and started to rise. She was sinking, sinking fast, into the sandy earth. As if she were in quicksand, her body sank, note by note.

The two female vamps in the center of the circle with Big Evan sat up. Lotus shook, her body moving with a tremor like a seizure. My hand holding the vamp-killer started to sweat. I changed my grip, and changed it again. Something was wrong. I looked to Bruiser, and he shook his head. He didn't understand what was happening either. But what wasn't happening was an ending to the spell.

Which meant something else was happening. The spell was speeding up. Whatever was supposed to happen slowly was suddenly happening faster.

Silandre lifted her head, her mouth open, and she took a breath so deep it made the candle flames waver. She sang a note. Only in that moment, with the single, strident note vibrating against my eardrums, did I recall Bodat's comment back when we first started researching Silandre. She had been into opera. She and Lotus had sung opera. And the note she sang was interfering with both the spell and Evan's attempt to break it.

The woman beside me shuddered and slid beneath the

earth. All around the circle, the witches were sliding deeper, their faces stoic and unyielding as the dead.

Lotus took a breath, as long and slow as Silandre's, about to join in the singing. I was out of time.

And that was the spell. *Time.* Immortality. Not the enhanced life span of the vampire, tied to the night and to the taking of blood, but true immortality—dependent on nothing, with the speed and power and physical perfection of the flawless predator. I raced forward, my arm swinging back, my grip changing with my purpose. Settling and firming. From the corner of my eye, I saw Bruiser draw his own blade, following my lead.

Lotus' note sounded, a clarion call to eternity. And I stepped over the circle. The ground shook. Lightning danced over my skin. Striking deep as my foot landed on the inner side of the circle. Pain shot through me, but my foot landed true. My body pivoted, all my weight behind my arm. My blade followed, sweeping ahead of me. Taking off Lotus' head. The note stopped the instant her head left her neck. There was little blood. A drop that flew upward, a trickle that followed gravity. Her head spun, her silken hair flying in an arc, obscuring eyes that looked, for a moment, startled.

Silandre's head left her body an instant later, falling toward the sheet. Evan pulled the flute from his lips, stopping his melody. The silence was awful for three rapid heartbeats that fluttered against my eardrums. The heads landed, soft *thud*s. The bodies slid down.

The earth moved. The clock-working fell in a shower of sparks. With a roar of sound, like a sandstorm, the earth disgorged the witches. Bodies erupted from the grave.

I fell. Bruiser's feet slid, his balance gone. Evan caught himself on one hand.

On hands and knees, feeling my way in every respect, I crawled across the moving earth to Misha. When I reached her side, I grabbed the amulet on her chest. Gave it a mighty jerk. Misha's eyes opened. She gasped.

"The amulets," I shouted. "Rip them away!"

The next moments were never clear in my mind, seen in snapshot instants of memories, as Big Evan raced widdershins and Bruiser raced sunwise, ripping the amulets from the witches, including the one who had been swallowed alive by the earth and regurgitated, gasping and vomiting sand.

Then the house above us began to groan and shudder, dust and debris raining from the old floor. There wasn't time to get us all up through the trapdoor. Evan Trueblood took up his flute and, with a working he had ready, stored for use, he blew a hole through the foundation wall.

We grabbed every live being and threw them out the hole into the icy, wet night. I had a feeling that Evan held the house up through force of will and every spell he had stored, because it fell just as Bruiser and I dragged the last witch to the curb.

Two days later, Big Evan sat in his pickup truck, his head bowed, his hands draped over the steering wheel, fingers dangling. He had been avoiding me, so I had ambushed him in his truck. I waited till he had the key in the ignition, opened the passenger's door, and leaped in. "Not before we chat," I said.

He heaved a sigh that moved the air through the cab—or maybe that was just his magics settling. "First," I said, "You worked with me when you might have sent me packing and tried to do this job on your own. Thank you."

When Evan didn't look up from his hands and only pursed his lips, I went on, realizing later that he might have been pursing his lips to kill me with a whistle. "Second, I tried, I really tried, to do it the witch way. And I'm sorry I interfered with your spell—"

"It wasn't working."

I closed my mouth. I wasn't sure what wasn't working, but these were the first words Evan Trueblood had spoken in my presence in two days and I wasn't going to get in the way.

"I thought I had all the math in my head. I can do math around ten other witches, I can see it in the air around a working. I thought I had it. But I messed up."

I was staring at his hands now too, not sure where this was going, but it sounded perilously close to an apology.

"If you hadn't been there, the fangheads would have gotten totally free of the temporary binding and attacked me, and I'd have been part of the circle. And they would have finished the working. All of the witches would have died. Molly would have killed me."

I smiled at that, but Big Evan wasn't watching me. He turned his hands over and stared at the empty palms. "In the past hundred years, the witch population in the Southeast dropped by seventy percent." He turned his head to take me in. I was sitting there in my jeans and sweater, my hands pale from the cold, attempting to keep my face unemotional, nonreactive. "Vamps are responsible. We knew it, but we couldn't prove it. The European council of Mithrans wasn't interested in anything we said, though we petitioned them for decades at every convocation, or whatever the fangheads call their gathering of the chief bloodsuckers.

"Because of *you*," he nearly snarled the word, "because of the investigation you did into the Damours, the holder of the blood diamond, Leo Pellissier had to admit there was a problem, had to admit to the kidnappings, the murders, the whole nine yards. He had to report it to the European vamps."

Evan shook his head and, frowning sourly, looked out into the day. "The Witch Council had been trying to get the MOC involved in the investigation for decades and he wasn't interested. Not till you got involved and discovered the answer to something that we had been investigating for more than twenty years. And you did it all in a matter of weeks, without getting my children killed."

"Nearly."

"Shut up. I'm not done."

I sat back and shut up.

"You saved my wife. You saved my kids. Admittedly, you put them in danger in the first place, but I know my wife, and she was right in the middle of the trouble anyway. Then you killed one of us who had been caught up in the darkness of demon calling. You saw it and you dealt with it, and I didn't see it and I did nothing. You saved us all. And I have treated you like shit. And, yeah, I know how you feel about that word, but that's what I treated you like."

Evan laughed again, this one through his nose and almost real. "You can talk now."

"Wow. That's a lot of self-flagellating hooey."

"I am— It is not— You are so fuc—"—he paused, fisting his hands—"dang polite, it's sometimes hard to remember

you carry an arsenal and have a posse to do your bidding."
He looked from his fists to me and said, "Stop grinning and
go ahead. *Talk*. I'm listening."

"Okay. Thank you."

Evan glared at me, and I shrugged. "Seriously. Thank you.
I love Molly. I love your children. I even love you, though
that shocks the heck outta me. And I have missed you all so
much. I want back the family we once had, but I know that
Molly may never again let me. It makes a huge difference to
know that you aren't sabotaging that in any way."

"I know it wasn't sensible to have been so angry at you
for everything that happened," he said. "Evangelina was
out of control, so steeped in demon magic and blood magic
that the entire Witch Council working together might not
have been able to bring her down. You did us all a huge
favor taking her on. You put your life on the line."

I shuddered, remembering the way her flesh gave to the
pointed blade. The feel of her blood, hot and thick, as it
erupted over my hand. "I would take it back, if I could," I
whispered.

Evan sighed. "I knew all along that my feelings weren't
logical and that I should just *deal* and get over it. I knew
that. But . . . there's stuff you don't know. About me and my
history. And it makes it hard to let people in, close to my
family."

He took a breath that sounded relieved and shaky and
determined all at once, which was a lot for most people, but
probably not for an air witch like Evan Trueblood. "I'll let
you talk to Angelina. And I won't say anything when Molly
is finally ready to call you. She forgives you, by the way. For
killing her sister."

Joy swept through me at the words. I nodded and wiped
away a stray tear that had escaped down my cheek.

"It's just hard yet. I think she'll come around soon and—
Are you *crying*?"

I nodded, miserable. "I'm not sure, because I'm not good
at this stuff, but I think it's supposed to be happy tears,
though that always sounded stupid to me. Why cry when
you're happy. You know?"

Evan said nothing to that, but I could smell his scent
change. He was horrified. Which made me laugh and cry at
the same time. "Okay. We need to talk business," I said.

"Good. This was a little touchy-feely for me." I could hear the relief in his tone.

"Three things. One: I'd like for you to listen to Rick's spell. He nearly turned on the first night of the full moon. He was hurting and worried that he'd get stuck in his cat form. Can you tweak his spells?" Evan nodded, and I went on. "Two: The vamp in the garage that Soul told you about? It admitted to being present when Bryson Ryder and his family were killed. And though I can't prove it, I'm betting he was the vamp who talked to Misha, claiming to be Ryder, a primo of a nonexistent vamp clan. He liked playing games with females, and when Misha described the voice, it fit — old, elegant, Southern. If so, then he was the one who gave Misha to Lotus, Silandre, and Esther."

"So you killed him," Evan said flatly.

"No. I turned the thing he'd become over to Big H, carapace, tiny little wings, bug-ugly face, and all."

Evan's beard curled into a smile. "Losing that much money musta hurt."

I smiled back. "The MOC paid me part of my fee even though his head was still attached. And it was worth the loss of the rest to keep you magic-using types happy.

"And three: I know you and Molly offered to show your healing spells to Misha for Charly. I know you're going to work with her as soon as she's able to travel. But I want you to consider what might happen to your spells if you added a vamp's blood in."

Evan went still as a vamp. For a long time he didn't seem to breathe. Slowly he turned his head to me. "No witch has acquired access to a vampire's blood in my lifetime. Use of it is nearly mythical." He studied my face for proof that I was jerking his chain. "There are spells and workings from hundreds of years ago that show the efficacy of vampire blood in healing witches. How are you gonna get Leo to order a scion to donate?"

"Leo owes me one. A boon, sorta."

"A vampire owes you a boon?"

I was getting pretty good. I had astounded Evan several times today and it wasn't even lunchtime yet. I quoted, "'In recompense of your debt and in honor of your service, you may choose a gift from among mine. Choose wisely.' Sounds like a boon to me."

"Yeah. That is . . . stellar." Then his face twisted into a frown so dark it looked like a storm was raging inside him. "Let the other shoe drop."

"Well, there's just one problem. Somewhere around here is the spike from Calvary, used to make amulets. It was probably the focus for all the power from the circle of witches, and with it, it's possible to do transformational magic. And Hieronymus, Master of the City of Natchez, wants it for his very own."

Big Evan groaned. "It just never ends with you. Does it?"

EPILOGUE

Bobby stood straight and tall, his red hair brushed and shining in the noonday sun, his new suit sharp and neat. Misha and Charly stood to his sides, dressed to the nines. Misha still looked drained, pale, and wan, but she was alive and writing and working on her book's deadline. Charly looked better than I had ever seen her, her hair growing back out and her skin pink and healthy. I knew the impression of good health was only skin deep. She still had leukemia, but the combo of vamp blood, Evan Trueblood's magic, and chemo seemed to be working, at least for now. I stood at a right angle to the three, wearing my full vamp-fighting gear, at Bobby's request. He wanted me to look like a vamp killer on his special day.

Eli, wearing full-dress military uniform, stepped slowly, formally, to Bobby, his eyes staring straight ahead, his every movement ceremonial. When he reached Bobby, he stopped, put his feet together, and slowly, so slowly, saluted Bobby. My old friend's blue eyes followed every motion, every movement, full of wonder.

The Ranger slid a box from the crook of his left arm and opened it. Inside was a Purple Heart. I had argued against Eli giving Bobby his own medal, but Eli had laughed and said, "I won't miss it. I've got two more." Which was a story for another day. I hoped.

Tears gathered in my eyes as Eli lifted the medal from the box and carefully pinned it over the left side of Bobby's chest.

Bobby's eyes swelled with pride. He stood straight and tall, his eyes never leaving Eli's. The Ranger stepped back and saluted Bobby again. Bobby raised his hand and touched the medal, and then sought me out. "I'm a hero too now, Jane."

"Yes, Bobby Bates. You really are. You always have been."

Love Jane Yellowrock? Then meet Thorn St. Croix.
Read on for the opening chapter of *Bloodring*,
the first novel in Faith Hunter's Rogue Mage series.
Available from Roc.

*No one thought the apocalypse would be like this.
The world didn't end. And the appearance of seraphs
heralded three plagues and a devastating war between
the forces of good and evil. Over a hundred years later,
the earth has plunged into an ice age, and seraphs and
demons fight a never-ending battle while religious
strife rages among the surviving humans.*

*Thorn St. Croix is no ordinary neomage. All the oth-
ers of her kind, mages who can twist leftover creation
energy to their will, were gathered together into enclaves long ago; and there they live in luxurious con-
finement, isolated from other humans and exploited for
their magic. When her powers nearly drive her insane,
she escapes—and now she lives as a fugitive, disguised
as a human, channeling her gifts of stone-magery into
jewelry making. But when Thaddeus Bartholomew, a
dangerously attractive policeman, shows up on her door-
step and accuses her of kidnapping her ex-husband, she
retrieves her weapons and risks revealing her identity to
find him. And for Thorn, the punishment for revelation
is death. . . .*

I stared into the hills as my mount clomped below me, his massive hooves digging into snow and ice. Above us a fighter jet streaked across the sky, leaving a trail that glowed bright against the fiery sunset. A faint sense of alarm raced across my skin, and I gathered up the reins, tightening my knees against Homer's sides, pressing my walking stick against the huge horse.

A sonic boom exploded across the peaks, shaking through snow-laden trees. Ice and snow pitched down in heavy sheets and lumps. A dog yelped. The Friesian set his hooves, dropped his head, and kicked. "Stones and blood," I hissed as I rammed into the saddle horn. The boom echoed like rifle shot. Homer's back arched. If he bucked, I was a goner.

I concentrated on the bloodstone handle of my walking stick and pulled the horse to me, reins firm as I whispered soothing, seemingly nonsense words no one would interpret as a chant. The bloodstone pulsed as it projected a sense of calm into him, a use of stored power that didn't affect my own drained resources. The sonic boom came back from the nearby mountains, a ricochet of man-made thunder.

The mule in front of us hee-hawed and kicked out, white rimming his eyes, lips wide, and teeth showing as the boom reverberated through the farther peaks. Down the length of the mule train, other animals reacted as the fear spread, some bucking in a frenzy, throwing packs into drifts, squealing as lead ropes tangled, trumpeting fear.

Homer relaxed his back, sidestepped, and danced like a young colt before planting his hooves again. He blew out a rib-racking sigh and shook himself, ears twitching as he settled. Deftly, I repositioned the supplies and packs he'd dislodged, rubbing a bruised thigh that had taken a wallop from a twenty-pound pack of stone.

Hoop Marks and his assistant guides swung down from their own mounts and steadied the more fractious stock. All along the short train, the startled horses and mules settled as riders worked to control them. Homer looked on, ears twitching.

Behind me, a big Clydesdale relaxed, shuddering with a ripple of muscle and thick winter coat, his rider following the wave of motion with practiced ease. Audric was a salvage miner, and he knew his horses. I nodded to my old friend, and he tipped his hat to me before repositioning his stock on Clyde's back.

A final echo rumbled from the mountains. Almost as one, we turned to the peaks above us, listening fearfully for the telltale roar of an avalanche.

Sonic booms were rare in the Appalachians these days, and I wondered what had caused the military overflight. I slid the walking stick into its leather loop. It was useful for balance while taking a stroll in snow, but its real purpose was as a weapon. Its concealed blade was deadly, as was its talisman hilt, hiding in plain sight. However, the bloodstone handle-hilt was now almost drained of power, and when we stopped for the night, I'd have to find a safe, secluded place to draw power for it and for the amulets I carried, or my neomage attributes would begin to display themselves.

I'm a neomage, a witchy-woman. Though contrary rumors persist, claiming mages still roam the world free, I'm the only one of my kind not a prisoner, the only one in the entire world of humans who is unregulated, unlicensed. The only one uncontrolled.

All the others of my race are restricted to Enclaves, protected in enforced captivity. Enclaves are gilded cages, prisons of privilege and power, but cages nonetheless. Neomages are allowed out only with seraph permission, and then we have to wear a sigil of office and bracelets with satellite GPS locator chips in them. We're followed by the humans, watched, and sent back fast when our services are no longer needed or when our visas expire. As if we're contagious. Or dangerous.

Enclave was both prison and haven for mages, keeping us safe from the politically powerful, conservative, religious orthodox humans who hated us, and giving us a place to live as our natures and gifts demanded. It was a great place for a mage-child to grow up, but when my gift blossomed at age fourteen, my mind opened in a unique way. The thoughts of all twelve hundred mages captive in the New Orleans Enclave opened to me at once. I nearly went mad. If I went back, I'd go quietly—or loudly screaming—insane.

In the woods around us, shadows lengthened and darkened. Mule handlers looked around, jittery. I sent out a quick mind-skim. There were no supernats present, no demons, no mages, no seraphs, no *others*. Well, except for me. But I couldn't exactly tell them that. I chuckled under my breath as Homer snorted and slapped me with his tail. That would be dandy. Survive for a decade in the human world only to be exposed by something so simple as a sonic boom and a case of trail exhaustion. I'd be tortured, slowly, over a period of days, tarred and feathered, chopped into pieces, and dumped in the snow to rot.

If the seraphs located me first, I'd be sent back to Enclave and I'd still die. I'm allergic to others of my kind— really allergic—fatally so. The Enclave death would be a little slower, a little less bloody than the human version. Humans kill with steel, a public beheading, but only after I was disemboweled, eviscerated, and flayed alive. And all that after I *entertained* the guards for a few days. As ways to go, the execution of an unlicensed witchy-woman rates up there with the top ten gruesome methods of capital punishment. With my energies nearly gone, a conjure to calm the horses could give me away.

"Light's goin,'" Hoop called out. "We'll stop here for the night. Everyone takes care of his own mount before anything else. Then circle and gather deadwood. Last, we cook. Anyone who don't work, don't eat."

Behind me, a man grumbled beneath his breath about the unfairness of paying good money for a spot on the mule train and then having to work. I grinned at him and he shrugged when he realized he'd been heard. "Can't blame a man for griping. Besides, I haven't ridden a horse since I was a kid. I have blisters on my blisters."

I eased my right leg over Homer's back and slid the long distance to the ground. My knees protested, aching after the day in the saddle. "I have a few blisters this trip myself. Good boy," I said to the big horse, and dropped the reins, running a hand along his side. He stomped his satisfaction and I felt his deep sense of comfort at the end of the day's travel.

We could have stopped sooner, but Hoop had hoped to make the campsite where the trail rejoined the old Blue Ridge Parkway. Now we were forced to camp in a ring of trees instead of the easily fortified site ahead. If the denizens of Darkness came out to hunt, we'd be sitting ducks.

Unstrapping the heavy pack containing my most valuable finds from the Salvage and Mineral Swap Meet in Boone, I dropped it to the earth and covered it with the saddle. My luggage and pack went to the side. I removed all the tools I needed to groom the horse and clean his feet, and added the bag of oats and grain. A pale dusk closed in around us before I got the horse brushed down and draped in a blanket, a pile of food and a half bale of hay at his feet.

The professional guides were faster and had taken care of their own mounts and the pack animals and dug a firepit in the time it took the paying customers to get our mounts groomed. The equines were edgy, picking up anxiety from their humans, making the job slower for us amateurs. Hoop's dogs trotted back and forth among us, tails tight to their bodies, ruffs raised, sniffing for danger. As we worked, both clients and handlers glanced fearfully into the night. Demons and their spawn often hid in the dark, watching humans like predators watched tasty herd animals. So far as my weakened senses could detect, there was nothing out there. But there was a lot I couldn't say and still keep my head.

"Gather wood!" I didn't notice who called the command, but we all moved into the forest, me using my walking stick for balance. There was no talking. The sense of trepidation was palpable, though the night was friendly, the moon rising, no snow or ice in the forecast. Above, early stars twinkled, cold and bright at this altitude. I moved away from the others, deep into the tall trees: oak, hickory, fir, cedar. At a distance, I found a huge boulder rounded up from the snow.

Checking to see that I was alone, I lay flat on the boulder, my cheek against frozen granite, the walking stick between my torso and the rock. And I called up power. Not a raging roar of mage-might, but a slow, steady trickle. Without words, without a chant that might give me away, I channeled energy into the bloodstone handle between my breasts, into the amulets hidden beneath my clothes, and pulled a measure into my own flesh, needing the succor. It took long minutes, and I sighed with relief as my body soaked up strength.

Satisfied, as refreshed as if I had taken a nap, I stood, stretched, bent, and picked up deadwood, traipsing through the trees and boulders for firewood—wood that was a lot more abundant this far away from the trail. My night vision is better than most humans', and though I'm small for an adult and was the only female on the train, I gathered an armload in record time. Working far off the beaten path has its rewards.

I smelled it when the wind changed. Old blood. A lot of old blood. I dropped the firewood, drew the blade from the walking-stick sheath, and opened my mage-sight to survey the surrounding territory. The world of snow and ice glimmered with a sour-lemon glow, as if it were ailing, sickly.

Mage-sight is more than human sight in that it sees energy as well as matter. The retinas of human eyes pick up little energy, seeing light only after it's absorbed or reflected. But mages see the world of matter with an overlay of energy, picked up by the extra lenses that surround our retinas. We see power and life, the leftover workings of creation. When we use the sight, the energies are sometimes real, sometimes representational, experience teaching us to identify and translate the visions, sort of like picking out images from a three-dimensional pattern.

I'm a stone mage, a worker of rocks and gems, and the energy of creation; hence, only stone looks powerful and healthy to me when I'm using mage-sight. Rain, ice, sleet or snow, each of which is water that has passed through air, always looks unhealthy, as does moonlight, sunlight, the movement of the wind, or currents of surface water—anything except stone. This high in the mountains, snow lay thick and crusted everywhere, weak, pale, a part of nature that leached power from me—except for a dull gray area to the east, beyond the stone where I had recharged my energies.

Moving with the speed of my race, sword in one hand, walking-stick sheath, a weapon in itself, in the other, I rushed toward the site.

I tripped over a boot. It was sticking from the snow, bootlaces crusted with blood and ice. Human blood had been spilled here, a lot of it, and the snow was saturated. The earth reeked of fear and pain and horror, and to my mage-sight, it glowed with the blackened energy of death. I caught a whiff of Darkness.

Adrenaline coursed through my veins, and I stepped into the cat stance, blade and walking stick held low as I circled the site. Bones poked up from the ice, and I identified a femur, the fragile bones of a hand, tendons still holding fingers together. A jawbone thrust toward the sky. Placing my feet carefully, I eased in. Teeth marks, long and deep, scored an arm bone. Predator teeth, unlike any beast known to nature. Supernat teeth. The teeth of Darkness.

Devil-spawn travel in packs, drink blood and eat human flesh. While it's still alive. A really bad way to go. And spawn would know what I was in an instant if they were downwind of me. As a mage, I'd be worth more to a spawn than a fresh meal. I'd be prime breeding material for their masters.

I'd rather be eaten.

A skull stared at me from an outcropping of rock. A tree close by had been raked with talons, or with desperate human fingers trying to get away, trying to climb. As my sight adjusted to the falling light, a rock shelf protruding from the earth took on a glow displaying pick marks. A strip mine. Now that I knew what to look for, I saw a pick, the blackened metal pitted by ichor, a lantern, bags of supplies hanging from trees, other gear stacked near the rock with their ore. One tent pole still stood. On it was what I assumed to be a hat, until my eyes adjusted and it resolved into a second skull. Old death. Weeks, perhaps months, old.

A stench of sulfur reached me. Dropping the sight, I skimmed until I found the source: a tiny hole in the earth near the rock they had been working. I understood what had happened. The miners had been working a claim on the surface—because no one in his right mind went underground, not anymore—and they had accidentally broken through to a cavern or an old, abandoned underground mine. Darkness had scented them. Supper . . .

I moved to the hole in the earth. It was leaking only a hint of sulfur and brimstone, and the soil around was smooth, trackless. Spawn hadn't used this entrance in a long time. I glanced up at the sky. Still bright enough that the nocturnal devil-spawn were sleeping. If I could cover the entrance, they wouldn't smell us. Probably. Maybe.

Sheathing the blade, I went to the cases the miners had piled against the rocks, and pulled a likely one off the top. It hit the ground with a whump but was light enough for me to drag it over the snow, leaving a trail through the carnage. The bag fit over the entrance, and the reek of Darkness was instantly choked off. My life had been too peaceful. I'd gotten lazy. I should have smelled it the moment I entered the woods. Now it was gone.

Satisfied I had done all I could, I tramped to my pile of deadwood and back to camp, glad of the nearness of so many humans, horses, and dogs that trotted about. I dumped the wood beside the fire pit at the center of the small clearing. Hoop Marks and his second in command, Hoop Jr., tossed in broken limbs and lit the fire with a small can of kerosene and a pack of matches. Flames roared and danced, sending shadows capering into the surrounding forest. The presence of fire sent a welcome feeling of safety through the group, though only earthly predators would fear the flame. No supernat of Darkness would care about a little fire if it was hungry. Fire made them feel right at home.

I caught Hoop's eye and gestured to the edge of the woods. The taciturn man followed when I walked away, and listened with growing concern to my tale of the miners. I thought he might curse when I told him of the teeth marks on the bones, but he stopped himself in time. Cursing aloud near a hellhole was a sure way of inviting Darkness to you. In other locales it might attract seraphic punishment or draw the ire of the church. Thoughtless language could result in death-by-dinner, seraphic vengeance, or priestly branding. Instead, he ground out, "I'll radio it in. You don't tell nobody, you hear? I got something that'll keep us safe." And without asking me why I had wandered so far from camp, alone, he walked away.

Smoke and supper cooking wafted through camp as I rolled out my sleeping bag and pumped up the air mattress. Even with the smell of old death still in my nostrils, my mouth watered. I wanted nothing more than to curl up, eat and sleep, but I needed to move through the horses and mules first. Trying to be inconspicuous, touching each one as surreptitiously as possible, I let the walking stick's amulet-handle brush each animal with calm.

It was a risk, if anyone recognized a mage-conjure, but there was no way I was letting the stock bolt and stampede away if startled in the night. I had no desire to walk miles through several feet of hard-packed snow to reach the nearest train tracks, then wait days in the cold, without a bath or adequate supplies, for a train that might get stranded in a blizzard and not come until snowmelt in spring. No way. Living in perpetual winter was bad enough, and though the ubiquitous *they* said it was only a *mini*–ice age, it was still pretty dang cold.

So I walked along the picket line and murmured soothing words, touching the stock one by one. I loved horses. I hated that they were the only dependable method of transport through the mountains ten months out of the year, but I loved the beasts themselves. They didn't care that I was an unlicensed neomage hiding among the humans. With them I could be myself, if only for a moment or two. I lay my cheek against the shoulder of a particularly worried mare. She exhaled as serenity seeped into her and turned liquid brown eyes to me in appreciation, blowing warm horse breath in my face. "You're welcome," I whispered.

Just before I got to the end of the string, Hoop sang out, "Charmed circle. Charmed circle for the night."

I looked up in surprise, my movements as frozen as the night air. Hoop Jr. was walking bent over, a fifty-pound bag of salt in his arms, his steps moving clockwise. Though human, he was making a conjure circle. Instinctively, I cast out with a mind-skim, though I knew I was the only mage here. But now I scented a charmed *something*. From a leather case, Hoop Sr. pulled out a branch that glowed softly to my mage-sight. Hoop's "something to keep us safe." The tag on the tip of the branch proclaimed it a legally purchased charm, unlike my unlicensed amulets. It would be empowered by the salt in the ring, offering us protection. I hurried down the line of horses and mules, trusting that my movements were hidden by the night, and made it to the circle before it was closed.

Stepping through the opening in the salt, I nodded

again as I passed Audric. The big black man shouldered his packs and carried them toward the fire pit. He didn't talk much, but he and Thorn's Gems had done a lot of business since he discovered and claimed a previously untouched city site for salvage. Because he had a tendresse for one of my business partners, he brought his findings to us first and stayed with us while in town. The arrangement worked out well, and when his claim petered out, we all hoped he'd put down roots and stay, maybe buy in as the fourth partner.

"All's coming in, get in," Hoop Sr. sang out. "All's staying out'll be shot if trouble hits and you try to cross the salt ring." There was a cold finality to his tone. "Devil-spawn been spotted round here. I take no chances with my life or yours 'less you choose to act stupid and get yourself shot."

"Devil-spawn? Here?" The speaker was the man who had griped about the workload.

"Yeah. Drained a woman and three kids at a cabin up near Linville." He didn't mention the carnage within shooting distance of us. Smart man.

I spared a quick glance for my horse, who was already snoozing. A faint pop sizzled along my nerve endings as the circle closed and the energy of the spell from the mage-branch snapped in place. I wasn't an earth mage, but I appreciated the conjure's simple elegance. A strong shield-protection-invisibility incantation had been stored in the cells of the branch. The stock were in danger from passing predators, but the rest of us were effectively invisible to anyone, human or supernat.

Night enveloped us in its black mantle as we gathered for a supper of venison stew. Someone passed around a flask of moonshine. No one said anything against it. Most took a swallow or two against the cold. I drank water and ate only stewed vegetables. Meat disagrees with me. Liquor on a mule train at night just seems stupid.

Tired to the bone, I rolled into my heated, down-filled sleeping bag and looked up at the cold, clear sky. The moon was nearly full, its rays shining on seven inches of fresh snow. It was a good night for a moon mage, a water mage, even a weather mage, but not a night to induce a feeling of vitality or well-being in a bone-tired stone mage. The entire world glowed with moon power, brilliant and beautiful, but draining to my own strength. I rolled in my bedding and stopped, caught by a tint of color in the velvet black sky. A thick ring of bloody red circled the pure white orb, far out in the night. *A bloodring.* I almost swore under my breath but choked it back, a painful sound, close to a sob.

The last time there was a bloodring on the moon, my twin sister died. Rose had been a licensed mage, living in Atlanta, supposedly safe, yet she had vanished, leaving a wide, freezing pool of blood and signs of a struggle, within minutes after Lolo, the priestess of Enclave, phoned us both with warnings. The prophecy hadn't helped then and it wouldn't help now. Portents never helped. They offered only a single moment to catch a breath before I was trounced by whatever they foretold.

If Lolo had called with a warning tonight, it was on my answering machine. Even for me, the distance to Enclave was too great to hear the mind-voice of the priestess.

I shivered, looking up from my sleeping bag. A feasting site, now a bloodring. It was a hazy, frothing circle, swirling like the breath of the Dragon in the Revelation, holy words taught to every mage from the womb up. "And there appeared another wonder in heaven; and behold a great red dragon. . . . And his tail drew the third part of the stars of heaven, and did cast them to the earth: and the dragon stood before the woman. . . . And there was war in heaven: Michael and his seraphim fought against the dragon; and the dragon fought, and his seraphim." The tale of the Last War.

Shivering, I gripped the amulets tied around my waist and my walking stick, the blade loosed in the sheath, the prime amulet of its hilt tight in my palm. Much later, exhausted, I slept.

Lucas checked his watch as he slipped out of the office and moved into the alley, ice crunching beneath his boots, breath a half-seen fog in the night. He was still on schedule, though pushing the boundaries. Cold froze his ears and nose, numbed his fingers and feet, congealed his blood, seeped into his bones, even through the layers of clothes, down-filled vest, and hood. He slipped, barely catching himself before hitting the icy ground. He cursed beneath his breath as he steadied himself on the alley wall. *Seraph stones, it's cold.*

But he was almost done. The last of the amethyst would soon be in Thorn's hands, just as the Mistress Amethyst had demanded. In another hour he would be free of his burden. He'd be out of danger. He felt for the ring on his finger, turning it so the sharp edge was against his flesh. He hitched the heavy backpack higher, its nylon straps cutting into his palm and across his shoulder.

The dark above was absolute, moon and stars hidden by the tall buildings at his sides. Ahead, there was only the distant security light at the intersection of the alley, where it joined the larger delivery lane and emptied into the street. Into safety.

A rustle startled him. A flash of movement. A dog burst from the burned-out hulk of an old Volkswagen and bolted back the way he had come. A second followed. Two small pups huddled in the warm nest they deserted, yellow coats barely visible. Lucas blew out a gust of irritation and worthless fear and hoped the larger mutts made it back to the makeshift den before the weather took them all down. It was so cold, the puppies wouldn't survive long. Even the smells of dog, urine, old beer, and garbage were frozen.

He moved into the deeper dark, toward the distant light, but slowed. The alley narrowed, the walls at his sides invisible in the night; his billowing breath vanished. He glanced up, his eyes drawn to the relative brightness of the sky. A chill that had nothing to do with the temperature chased down his spine. The rooftops were bare, the gutters and eaves festooned with icicles, moon and clouds beyond. One of the puppies mewled behind him.

Lucas stepped through the dark, his pace increasing as panic coiled itself around him. He was nearly running by the time he reached the pool of light marking the alleys' junction. Slowing, he passed two scooters and a tangle of bicycles leaning against a wall, all secured with steel chains, tires frozen in the ice. He stepped into the light and the safety it offered.

Above, there was a crackle, a sharp snap of metal. His head lifted, but his eyes were drawn ahead to a stack of boxes and firewood. To the man standing there. *Sweet*

Mother of God . . . not a man. A shadow. "No!" Lucas tried to whirl, skidding on icy pavement before he could complete the move. Two others ran toward him, human movements, human slow.

"Get him!"

The first man collided with him, followed instantly by the other, their bodies twin blows. His boots gave on the slippery surface. He went to one knee, breath a pained grunt.

A fist pounded across the back of his neck. A leg reared back. Screaming, he covered his head with an arm. A rain of blows and kicks landed. The backpack was jerked away, opening and spilling.

As he fell, he tightened a fist around the ring, its sharp edge slicing into his flesh. He groaned out the words she had given him to use, but only in extremis. The sound of the syllables was lost beneath the rain of blows. "Zadkiel, hear me. Holy Amethyst—" A boot took him in the jaw, knocking back his head. He saw the wings unfurl on the roof above him. Darkness closed in. Teeth sank deep in his throat. Cold took him. The final words of the chant went unspoken.

ABOUT THE AUTHOR

Faith Hunter was born in Louisiana and raised all over the South. She writes full-time and works full-time in a hospital lab (for the benefits), tries to keep house, and is a workaholic with a passion for travel, jewelry making, orchids, skulls, Class III white-water kayaking, and writing. Many of the orchid pics on her Facebook fan page show skulls juxtaposed with orchid blooms; the bones are from roadkill prepared by taxidermists or a pal named Mud. In her collection are a fox skull, a cat skull, a dog skull, a goat skull (that is, unfortunately, falling apart), a cow skull, the jawbone of an ass, and a wild boar skull, complete with tusks. She would love to have the thighbone and skull of an African lion (one that died of old age, of course) and a mountain lion skull (ditto on the old-age death).

She and her husband own thirteen kayaks at last count, and love to RV, as they travel with their dogs to white-water rivers all over the Southeast.

CONNECT ONLINE

www.faithhunter.net
facebook.com/official.faith.hunter

R0150

Also available from

Faith Hunter

HAVE STAKES WILL TRAVEL

Stories From the World of Jane Yellowrock

AVAILABLE ONLY AS A DOWNLOADABLE PENGUIN SPECIAL

In *Have Stakes Will Travel,* readers get a chance to go deeper into the thrilling world of skinwalker and vampire hunter Jane Yellowrock. In "WeSa," the Beast who lives inside Jane watches as her hunting grounds become prey. In "Haints," Jane and her best friend, witch Molly Trueblood, are hired to investigate mysterious paranormal phenomena—and the evil they find brings a new meaning to the words "haunted house." "Signature of the Dead" tells the story of the vampire massacre that made Jane Yellowrock a household name. And in "Cajun with Fangs," Jane makes a new friend who turns out to have old enemies, and finds herself drawn into a vicious blood feud, fueled by dark magic and ancient grudges.

Available wherever e-books are sold or at
penguin.com

facebook.com/AceRocBooks